Pr...
Christina Kingsto...
Ride f...

"A wonderful read with warm, complex characters, a page-turning plot and a delightful ending. . . . *Ride for the Roses* is a delectable plunge into Regency times."
—Patricia Potter

"This is a delightful Regency tale of mistakes and match-making following a traditional plotline that is enhanced by a cast of endearing characters. *Ride for the Roses* is a debut that heralds a new talent." —*Romantic Times*

"A wonderful not-to-be-put-down read." —*Rendezvous*

"A pleasant Regency romance that includes a number of charming characters. . . . Christina Kingston shows she is a talent worth reading, for her audience will find much entertainment value in her debut novel."
—Harriet Klausner

"A wonderful, exciting tale that takes the reader on a pleasant ride. The enjoyable story line entertains the audience with warmth and humanization of the entire ensemble. . . . A first-place winner that deserves several sequels." —*Affaire de Coeur*

"Pick this book up—it's exciting to see such a strong debut romance. If you enjoy a well-written historical with a smart heroine and an engaging hero with a good sense of humor, this is one ride you'll be glad you took."
—*All About Romance*

"A most enjoyable Regency historical. This is an impressive debut and I look forward to many more fine books from Christina Kingston." —*The Romance Reader*

The
Night the
Stars Fell

Christina Kingston

JOVE BOOKS, NEW YORK

This is a work of fiction. Names, characters, places, and incidents are either the product of the author's imagination or are used fictitiously, and any resemblance to actual persons, living or dead, business establishments, events, or locales is entirely coincidental.

THE NIGHT THE STARS FELL

A Jove Book / published by arrangement with
the author

PRINTING HISTORY
Jove edition / April 2001

All rights reserved.
Copyright © 2001 by Christina Strong.
This book, or parts thereof, may not be reproduced in any form
without permission.
For information address: The Berkley Publishing Group,
a division of Penguin Putnam Inc.,
375 Hudson Street, New York, New York 10014.

The Penguin Putnam Inc. World Wide Web site address is
http://www.penguinputnam.com

ISBN: 0-515-13041-9

A JOVE BOOK®
Jove Books are published by The Berkley Publishing Group,
a division of Penguin Putnam Inc.,
375 Hudson Street, New York, New York 10014.
JOVE and the "J" design
are trademarks belonging to Penguin Putnam Inc.

PRINTED IN THE UNITED STATES OF AMERICA

10 9 8 7 6 5 4 3 2 1

To the many readers who have made the ride so successful,
especially to Yetta who has always believed

Prologue

On a black, moonless night, a lone rider reined a restive stallion to a halt. The wind moaned eerily around them as they stood, tense and listening, in the heavy darkness under the twisted trees beside the high road. Finally, their vigil was rewarded as the thud of hooves and the jingle of harness came from the distance.

The rider's hand unconsciously tightened on the reins, and the huge stallion snorted and threw his head up in protest.

"Quiet!" It was a stern command, and the horse obeyed instantly.

The same wind from the sea that had shaped and bent the trees now sent their leaves flying. Gusts carried the sharp tang of salt from the Channel, strong on its turbulent air. The night was wild, and growing wilder, and rain wasn't far away.

It was no fit night for man or beast, but they had no choice. Desperation held them here where danger rode the wind, for the approaching coach had to be stopped and searched. It was unfortunate that Hal couldn't be here to do it himself, for this was his responsibility, but with his broken leg it was impossible. Even if he could manage to ride, he'd be too easy to identify.

Someone had to be here to do the job of holding up and searching the coach—and there was no one else to do it. They'd had a great piece of good fortune in learning that the jewels stolen by the Mayfair Bandit always took this route to the Continent. Now they desperately needed to be lucky enough to stop the very coach that carried some of them!

Doing that was their only chance of discovering the man behind the jewel thefts—the self-styled "Mayfair Bandit." That discovery was the only thing that would prove Hal innocent, and Hal's name must be cleared.

Muffled in a long black cloak, the rider cursed it as it ballooned and whipped in the wind. The horse remained immobile as a statue now that he'd been ordered to stand. Only the increase of white showing around his eyes gave away his nervousness.

As the minutes crawled by and the wind rose, the quality of the big stallion's stillness developed a hint of panic. Every now and again, his owner could feel him quiver, as if he sensed and shared his rider's high state of anxiety. And the rider, in that overwhelming anxiety, prayed hard that God would grant that rapidly fraying nerves wouldn't sap the courage needed to clear a brother's name!

Suddenly, the wind dropped for an instant, and they could more clearly hear the sound of hoofbeats and the jingle and clink of harness fittings. The coach they were lying in wait for was coming around the last bend.

The cloak was quickly tucked under the rider's thighs so that it couldn't flap loose. The last thing they needed while committing highway robbery was a distraction.

The black stallion, considerably relieved by the absence of the cloak's wild gyrations, responded to the light touch of his rider's heels and walked forward. As one, they left the shelter of the young trees in which they'd been hidden, and moved up onto the road.

"Steady, boy. Easy." His rider, dressed completely in black

from cloak to riding jacket to breeches, kept the great horse standing quietly. There in the pool of deeper darkness under the tall trees that overhung the road they were almost invisible.

A few moments later, their quarry, a handsome traveling coach drawn by a lathered team of four perfectly matched horses, rounded a curve and thundered down on them, the dust of the road a roiling cloud behind it. It was still far enough away to make a panicked stop when the lone rider breathed a hasty prayer and shouted, "Stand and deliver!" while reaching under the voluminous cloak to draw out her pistols.

Chapter One

In spite of the urgent reason for his journey, Chalfont Blysdale, Sixth Earl of Blythingdale, was bored. Forced inactivity had always bored him, and right now he had nothing to do but sit in this blasted carriage. He yawned. Out of habit, he put a long-fingered hand up in front of his mouth to conceal his yawn even though he was alone. Then he grinned and yawned again without that automatic gesture of a well-bred, well-reared gentleman. His strong white teeth glinted in the dim light from the interior carriage lamps.

With a deep sigh, he lifted his long, doeskin-clad legs and rested his boots on the velvet-covered seat of the wide bench opposite him. He should have ridden his stallion. From the sound of the wind, whistling over the noise made by the jingling harness and pounding hooves of his horses, this journey would have been considerably more exciting astride a highly strung bit of blood. Unfortunately, his favorite mount was miles behind him, tied to the rear of the carriage bringing his luggage.

Griswold, formerly his batman, now his valet and right-hand man, was in charge of that carriage, as it held, in addition to Blysdale's clothing, a small armory. When Bly found

the men he sought, he intended to be ready to defend or
avenge them, whichever the situation called for.

For just a minute, he considered riding one of his carriage horses. Every horse in all of his stables was trained to
ride as well as drive, even his racehorses, who hated to pull
anything. Of course, it would hardly put him in good standing with his coachman if he were to decide to ride one of
the team at this point.

So Blysdale tried to make himself content to be inside
the carriage and safely out of the worsening weather, but it
wasn't easy. Bly was by nature a restless man. Leisure seemed
to avoid him like the plague, and that was a circumstance
that he'd never regretted. He much preferred an active life.

Until a month ago, his life had run smoothly—for *his* life
at least. He'd gone to London for a card party with friends
and attended the races at Newmarket with them. Together
the six of them had foiled a kidnapping and apprehended a
murderer, and he'd capped the adventure by being best man
at his friend Taskford's rather unusual wedding.

It had been a full and pleasant enough schedule, but when
it was over, disaster had struck. Now, two of the men who'd
shared that adventure had disappeared. Two good friends,
and there weren't many men Blysdale would call friends.

Mathers and Smythe had last been seen in this very neighborhood. Their coachman had been found murdered near
here. Blysdale was here to set the score straight—one way
or the other. Until he reached the coast there was nothing
he could do about it, no matter how infuriated he might be
by the situation, so he sought refuge for his temporarily im-
potent rage in boredom.

Bly knew himself well enough to be aware that inactivity always put in him the foulest of moods. He also knew
that it wasn't a good thing for anyone to encounter him when
he was feeling this way. He recognized that something lived
just under the surface in him—something savage that
crouched and waited with sharpened claws. Something that
was always alert . . . and certainly never bored. Right now it
waited impatiently to be loosed against the men who'd cap-

tured his friends and killed their coachman. It was to be in
position to let loose that beast that, last week, he'd written
and forced an invitation to stay at the home of one of his
junior officers, Josh Clifton—an annoyingly dashing out-and-
outer who'd lately become a marquess.

According to his spies, young Clifton was even trying his
hand at smuggling now, rather than attending to the business of running his sprawling estate here on the coast. Blysdale smiled mirthlessly. He'd be willing to bet that his letter
had scared the young pup blue. So what. He couldn't care
less whether or not Josh Clifton was smuggling wines and
laces over from France. The war was over, and the money
France made selling contraband to English smugglers no
longer bought guns to kill English soldiers, so it was no
longer his concern. He wasn't a blasted revenue officer. In
fact, if he thought about Clifton's smuggling at all, it was
merely to remind himself that the brandy at Cliffside was
likely to be Napoleon's best.

Suddenly, there was a cry in the night. "Stand and deliver!" rang out above the howling of the wind.

"Whoa! Whoa, boys!" His coachman threw on the brake.
The vehicle rocked violently to a halt. The horses stood trembling in their traces. Bly, who'd braced himself the instant
he heard the shout, was not moved.

A holdup? Surely this was an odd place for one. Blysdale checked the small pistol strapped to his right forearm.
Could this be what had happened to his comrades, Mathers
and Smythe? Was he about to lay his hands on the man or
men who could tell him their fate? His eyes hardened as he
waited for the next development.

It wasn't long in coming. The door of the carriage was
yanked open, and he saw a slender figure framed against the
blustery night. The spymaster in him leapt to the fore. By
the dim lights of the carriage lamps, he studied the highwayman. Unfortunately, there was nothing to see but a pair
of fine eyes. Greenish, he thought—it was damned hard to
tell in the dim light—and the skin around them was smooth.

A youth, obviously. Sizing the lad up, he decided that, robber or no robber, he wasn't vicious. His eyes were too clear.

Those eyes, calm and watchful, regarded him alertly. There was intelligence in them.

Bly smiled. Above all things, he prized intelligence. Prized it even more than courage. Brutes could act courageously by reflex. He'd seen that time and again on the battlefield. Intelligent men overcame fear by an act of will, and that he could admire.

He felt his curiosity building. All pretense of boredom retreated into the cave where it belonged in the back of his mind. Blysdale was interested to see just what this young man was up to.

No highwayman in his right mind would choose to ply his trade on this lightly trafficked road. So . . . what was the boy after?

Gesturing him out of the coach, the muffled youth pointed to the side of the road. Obligingly, Blysdale followed the unspoken order because it amused him. Trained as he was, he could easily overcome his erstwhile robber if necessary. Chalfont Blysdale possessed abilities lesser men could only wonder about, and the highwayman had already let him get too close. Far too close.

To vanquish the youth, Blysdale would need neither the small pistol in his right sleeve nor the slender blade that lay snug against his forearm in his left. Even without these traditional articles of mayhem, Blysdale was a dangerous man.

He'd passed the robber meekly because he wanted to know what the devil the young highwayman was after. With a subtle gesture he kept his coachman from interfering.

The youth proceeded to enter and search the confines of the coach with a single gloved hand, holding his pistol firmly in the other and still keeping his eyes fixed on Blysdale. Bly, in turn, kept his gaze on the searcher. There was not a great deal for him to see. Therefore, he particularly noted the excellent quality of the young man's boots. They were of the finest, most supple leather, and they fitted the slender calves they adorned snugly from knee to toe. They were boots made by a master, without a doubt. From them, it would seem that highway robbery paid this gentleman very well despite the lack of regular road traffic in this particular area.

Frustratingly, there was nothing else for Bly to learn about his assailant, thanks to the black cloak that fell from shoulder to heel. That made Blysdale even more curious.

Finally, the highwayman signaled to him with a slight movement of his pistol that he was to reenter the traveling coach. Keeping his weapon trained on his victim, the youth backed away and remounted his handsome all-black stallion with remarkable grace.

Blysdale watched the horseman intently. Too bad the hands were covered, gloved in rich, supple leather, for a great deal could be learned about a man by studying his hands. Bly's disappointment at not being able to see more was acute. He decided he'd just have to content himself with the fact that the hand that held the cocked pistol pointing at his heart was steady.

Nevertheless, he *was* disappointed by this lack of clues. He kept his gaze fixed on the highwayman's face. It irritated Bly that the narrow strip of smooth, fair skin with its pair of intriguing eyes was all that he could see of the well-muffled would-be robber.

The highwayman's eyes widened slightly at the intensity of his victim's gaze. His hand tightened on his reins. A brief hesitation, then he spun his horse on its haunches and was away. He'd disappeared into the night before the smile that came to Chalfont Blysdale's firm lips had finished curving them. Lord Blysdale was no longer bored.

Deep in the woods only half a mile away, Lady Katherine drew rein. Here in the shelter of the majestic oaks of the home woods, the sea winds were kept at bay and it was almost silent in the clearing. Only the very tops of the trees sighed in the wind that came in from the sea.

She sat very straight and very still for a long moment. Then she pulled the silk scarf down from covering the lower half of her face and sighed. Sliding from the saddle, she spoke fondly to her mount, "Thank you again, Star. You were wonderful to be so steady in all this wind."

The great horse nickered softly.

She slipped her arms around his neck and laid her cheek against its satin warmth. "There was nothing to find in that coach, either, and I had such high hopes. That gentleman was the first person we've held up who even came close to looking as if he might be a clever jewel thief."

She pulled away and stroked the horse's neck. She put her disappointment in the form of a question to her horse. "Do you think we will *ever* come up with proof of Hal's innocence?"

Star blew gently down his nostrils, then gave her shoulder a light shove.

His mistress smiled. "Was that to offer me comfort, or to tell me you're anxious to get back to your stall?"

An eager whicker sounded at the mention of his *stall.*

Kate gave him a gentle shove and chided, "All right, I get the point. You want that boot blacking washed off your forehead so you can be left in peace with your hay, don't you?" She swung easily back into the saddle, catching the off stirrup on the toe of her right boot and thrusting her foot home even as the huge stallion started off. "I suppose all you can think of now is that you want what's left of the night to sleep."

Star flicked an ear back at her to signify that he heard, then turned it forward again as he concentrated on where he was going.

Bent low on his neck to avoid the low-hanging branches she knew were over the path, Kate sent him trotting down a dim trail toward home. There was nothing she didn't know about these woods. As a little girl she'd run wild in them, playing with imaginary friends and trying to tame the forest creatures. Back then, she had claimed the woods as her very own, and now, only Lady Katherine of Cliffside had the courage to enter them at night. They were, thanks to her efforts, rumored to be haunted.

Even Josh and Hal, her two usually intrepid older brothers, gave the forest a wide berth after the sun had set. To her utter delight, they said they felt as if they were being watched by hostile eyes when they ventured into the deep shadows of the ancient trees.

Kate chuckled. She'd "haunted" these woods with wild cries and gruesome moans for years. What had started as a child's petty revenge for her older brothers' indifference had turned into an adult woman's cheerful joke. The happy result was that now she had her beloved forest all to herself.

She was careful to maintain the illusion, too. If ever one of the family remarked on her seeming lack of sleep, Kate was quick to use the forest to explain it away. Her reply—"I couldn't sleep because of all the awful cries coming from the home wood. Didn't any of you hear them?"—served to keep the dark reputation of the wooded area intact.

Lately that had become a matter of grave importance. Twice she'd been pursued after stopping a coach. Once she would have been caught if she hadn't had the woods to hide in.

Thinking of that, Kate was glad that the man she'd just held up hadn't had a riding horse with him. Somehow she knew he'd have used it to pursue her. Those piercing eyes of his told her he'd not have given up easily, either. She felt certain he wasn't the sort of man to be put off by stories of ghosts and demons, even if he'd chanced to hear them, and she had no doubt that he'd have chased her into the woods. Yes, and if she didn't know the forest paths better than anyone alive, he might have caught her, too!

A little shiver passed through her. A premonition? She wondered at it. She wondered, too, what was it about *that* particular man that caused such an odd reaction in her.

He wore arrogance like a cloak, and Kate detested any arrogance but her own. And he wasn't handsome. He was too dangerous looking to be. His aquiline nose and lean features gave his face an ever-watchful expression, like that of a hawk. The black of his hair and his swarthy complexion might emphasize the bright blue of his eyes to a startling degree, but they made him appear sinister, as well. She was at a loss to explain why she felt a strange . . . she couldn't put a word to it, because she refused to call it attraction. . . .

She gave herself a mental shake. "Call it uneasiness, then, and be glad that you'll never have to face him again." She said that aloud, then wondered if unease were indeed what she had felt—all that she had felt.

It wasn't, but she shrugged off that admission. After all, what did it matter if the man fascinated her? She'd never see him again. Like the proverbial ships in the night, they had passed, caught a glimpse of each other, then gone on. The man was just another traveler on his way to one of the ports farther down the coast—and that was certainly fine with her.

The blazing intelligence she'd seen in those piercing blue eyes would have made her afraid of discovery if she thought she might ever encounter him again. Since discovery could lead to a hangman's noose, it was certainly better that she *not* see him again. Far better.

Resolutely putting the elegant man out of her mind, Kate rode on. After all, she had more than enough to handle when it came to men just now.

With two brothers who were determined to get themselves hanged and an ever-present and very insistent suitor whom she absolutely detested, Kate didn't need any additional problems!

Chapter Two

The next morning, lost in thought, Kate wandered down to breakfast. She was annoyed because she couldn't get the man from the coach she'd held up last evening out of her mind. Certainly, right now she didn't need anything more to think about. Juggling the running of the family estate for her oldest brother, Josh, with her attempts to prove her next eldest brother, Hal, innocent of jewel theft made for a thoroughly busy schedule. She was getting tired and distinctly irritable about it, too. The last thing she needed was to lose sleep thinking of the dark-browed stranger!

Kate had hoped for a rest last fall when she'd returned home to her three brothers here at Cliffside after the unexpected death of her husband. Instead, she'd been shocked to find the family's ancestral estate in sad condition. The cottages on the farms were all in need of repair. Some of the tenants, most of whom had been there for generations, had been ready to leave.

The comfortable mansion her grandfather had built inside the walls of the ruined castle on the cliff top had developed leaks around several of the windows that faced the sea, and a number of the great chimneys had ceased to draw properly for want of regular sweeping. There'd been smoke damage in several of the bedchambers, and the servants, faced with this subtle deterioration of the stately mansion in which they'd always served so willingly, had become less diligent as their pride in Cliffside waned. Kate had been appalled.

She'd approached her oldest brother as soon as she'd looked over the situation. Josh, for all that he was now the head of the family, hadn't shown the faintest inclination to take care of matters, and they had quarreled.

Kate had faced him and told him in no uncertain terms, "You have to take up your responsibilities, Josh. Things are falling apart here at Cliffside." She'd placed a hand on her older brother's arm and said, "Please listen to me, Josh. I know what I'm talking about. My husband was a perfectly charming man who had a lackadaisical attitude just like yours. And believe me, I learned to recognize the signs when things on Lionel's estate needed attention."

"Such as?"

"Well, besides the repair of buildings, I had to learn all about crops and sheep and cattle. About the best times for mowing hay and the safest ways to store it. I learned how grain is harvested and how to keep it from damp." Seeking to be convincing, she made an earnest effort to tell him all that she had been forced to see to. "I had to acquire a working knowledge of weaving hedges and building unmortared stone walls and about thatching the roofs on tenant cottages." Then she'd given him the coup de grace. "Josh! I even had to learn about fertilizing!"

Far from sympathizing with her, Josh had thrown back his head and shouted with delighted laughter. "Why, Kate! This is incredible. Better than anything! Who'd have thought that my beautiful sister would have gotten herself qualified to be Cliffside's very own bailiff!" He gave her a brief bear hug. "What an excellent idea, Kate! If you did all that at Rushmore Hall, there's no reason you can't do it here." He was grinning at her like an idiot. "And since I'm a mere soldier, you'll be able to take much better care of the estate than I ever could." He'd given her another big hug and said,

"So to tell you the truth, I'm greatly relieved. Better you than me, Katherine Elizabeth. Better you than me!"

Then he'd picked her up, whirled her around, kissed her resoundingly on the cheek, and set her back on her feet. "And Kate, I do hereby give you my permission to make all repairs, changes, and decisions and to spend me dry if need be. Even if you clean out the family coffers and send me to debtor's prison, I'll still continue to thank you from the bottom of my heart for taking the burdens of Cliffside from my unwilling and ignorant shoulders." With that, he'd all but run to the door, where he'd turned as he reached it and thrown her a kiss. "Bless you, dear sister Kate, bless you!"

That had been the first of several extremely disappointing conversations Kate had had with her brother, and Kate, fervently wishing she'd known how to curse fluently, had run Cliffside ever since. Cliffside. It was certainly not turning out to be Kate's sanctuary, that was obvious! Here, instead of finding the rest she'd sought after nursing her young husband through his lengthy final illness, she'd fallen prey to her present inescapable web of duties to home and family.

In a later conversation with Josh, Kate had met with further frustration when she'd tried to talk him out of his new "adventure" of smuggling. No one was going to convince *him* that he'd find better satisfaction and more of a challenge in striving to put his neglected lands back in order. Josh just wasn't interested. After years in Wellington's army, Joshua Nathan Merryman Clifton, Sixth Marquess of Cliffside, found civilian life just too *dull*.

Kate told herself aloud, scowling, "I should have run off to London when I saw how matters stood here at Cliffside."

That would have been the easiest course, but she hadn't been able to take it. Cliffside had been her family's home for over two centuries, and there was no way she could turn her back on it. The farms and the tenants on them were already suffering because of the neglect occasioned by her father's long illness and the years Josh had spent in Wellington's army. There was no excuse for them having to suffer any longer. Not if she could do anything about it. So Kate had taken over the problem of the tenants' welfare. And indeed all other matters pertaining to Cliffside, more fool she.

Now, in her role—her proper role—of chatelaine, she inspected the hall as she walked along it. Everything was in perfect order. The brocade-covered walls and the carpet were freshly brushed. The wall sconces at intervals along the passage were gleaming, and fresh candles had replaced those from the night before, with the wicks of the new ones properly blackened. Every doorknob and key plate to the bedchambers and suites opening off this hallway gleamed. There was no speck of dust, no cobweb, to mar the perfection of the halls through which Kate passed.

From the top of the grand stairway, she looked down into the great hall that her grandfather had had saved, repaired, and incorporated into the mansion he'd built for his comfort inside what remained of the ancient castle walls. This and the east wing, which stood on the edge of the cliffs, were the only original parts that he'd preserved of the ancient castle.

With a tiny thrill of pride, Kate looked down into the great hall. Every suit of armor shone. Ancient banners hung, clean and in perfect repair, from iron rods that spanned the thirty-foot-high vaulted ceiling. Every pane in every one of the multitude of tall leaded windows set into the massive stone walls was spotless, and the morning sunlight flowed through them like a spill of yellow diamonds. Here in Cliffside Manor all was once again in order. The servants, at least, had come through for her.

Still, Kate was frowning again as she started down the encircling stairway. Thank Heaven there was order somewhere. God knew that everything else pertaining to her life seemed to be unraveling.

As if having the manor house and farms to run weren't enough, just last week, when her next oldest brother, Hal, had come home on crutches, white-faced and tight-lipped, Kate had willingly added impersonating a highwayman to the rest of her load! And the load was getting heavy.

She looked around her at the splendid luxury that was

her home. Loving every inch of Cliffside had been bred into her. But she wondered, and not for the first time, whether she'd made a big mistake in answering its siren call.

Sometimes she regretted leaving Town, for even if she was in mourning there were things she could have done to amuse herself in London, things that would have kept her quite busy without the bone-grinding exhaustion that frequently accompanied her endeavors here. *And,* she thought as she reached the ground floor, in London she would have been safe from Gordon Mallory, too.

How she loathed that man. She always had. Now the despicable rogue had not only resumed his pursuit of her—an unwelcome pursuit that had been blessedly interrupted when she'd married Lionel Halsted and become Countess of Rushmore—he'd also persuaded her brother Josh to join with him in a smuggling venture!

"Just brandy and laces from France, Josh," he'd cajoled like some evil demon at her brother's shoulder. "A lark. Something to help you keep your edge now that you're out of the army and stuck at home," Mallory had said. And her reckless—impatiently she corrected that thought to *stupid*—brother had joined him without a moment's hesitation.

"Devil take you, Gordon Mallory!" Kate muttered. Then she quickened her pace to reach the family breakfast room.

Kate had a lot to do today, and she was coming down to breakfast later than usual. She'd overslept because, despite her late arrival home from her "adventure" last night, sleep had not come quickly. Instead of claiming her as it usually did before she'd even finished her prayers, sleep had eluded her for more than an hour. And it was all because of the man in the carriage she'd held up.

Try as she might, she hadn't been able to get him out of her mind then, and she still couldn't. His attitude both disturbed and puzzled her. What had he found so amusing about looking down the barrel of a pistol? And *how,* she demanded not for the first time, could he smile about having his life threatened?

True, his smile had barely lifted the corners of his thin-lipped mouth, but she was willing to wager that genuine smiles weren't something that *that* particular man ever dispensed freely. Yet, he *had* smiled.

Kate frowned. It was true, of course, that highwaymen seldom shot their victims, but sometimes they did. So, what sort of a man smiled at a potential killer? And why had there been a glint of amusement in those hooded eyes?

She shook her head impatiently. And most of all, *why* couldn't she get him out of her mind!

Perhaps it was because, though he was far from the handsomest man she'd ever seen, he was certainly the coolest she'd ever encountered! He had—

Mercifully, Kate's thoughts broke off as she entered the high-ceilinged breakfast room. One glance told her that she wasn't the only one who'd slept late. Josh had apparently been out last night, too. He was standing at the buffet loading a plate to dangerous heights while attempting to swallow a yawn.

Kate's heart sank. *He's been out smuggling again. Thank God he wasn't caught!*

She walked over to the buffet, smiled a good-morning at the butler, and accepted the warmed plate he handed her. "Thank you, Jennings. Tea, please."

"Oh, Kate," her brother called as if he were surprised to meet her here in the breakfast room. "Just the person I wanted to see. I have something to tell you." Josh turned away from the buffet, his plate heaped high with scrambled eggs, kippers, rashers of bacon, and slices of toast. "My old colonel, Chalfont Blysdale, is coming for a visit. Should be along any day now."

"What?" Kate was anything but pleased. She scowled. She seemed to be doing that a lot lately. She hoped it wouldn't make a permanent wrinkle between her eyes. She made no effort to hide her displeasure as she asked, "Why in the world would he do that? You've never mentioned that you and your colonel were such friends."

Jennings pulled out her chair for her then poured tea into her cup. Steam rose gently into the air.

Steam should have been rising out of Kate's ears. This was the outside of enough as far as she was concerned. "Without so much as a by-your-leave, Josh?"

"What?" Josh turned to her, astonished. "Dammit, Kate what's a single guest to you? You invite better than fifty to our house parties. Besides, the servants do all the work. And besides that," he added petulantly, "I *am* the Marquess of Cliffside."

Kate made an unladylike sound and, suppressing the urge to kill the head of her family for his last remark, fought against the irritation that rose in her at the thought of having to entertain any guest at this time. She was pulled seven ways to Sunday already, what with the running of the manor house and the estate, seeing to the tenants and farms, and managing her clandestine new pastime of holding up coaches for Hal.

She didn't want to have to be polite to some ruddy-faced, pot-bellied old warrior who prosed on and on about the War with Napoleon and his admittedly heroic part in it. There simply wasn't enough of her left for that.

Striving not to feel completely inhospitable, she offered, "As I just said, you never told me when you and the colonel became such good friends." She touched the side of her tea cup. Through the translucent china she could tell the liquid was still too hot to drink. *Blast!* She needed her tea. Now.

"We aren't," Josh said. "Nobody dares to call Lord Blysdale friend except the rest of the group of men he belongs to that Wellington seemed to think most highly of—the group the rest of us called the 'Lucky Seven.' Only one of them got killed. All the others seemed to have charmed lives. They got slashed and shot occasionally, but they came through it all in the end."

Kate shuddered at the casual way her brother talked of personal injury to his comrades-in-arms. Men! It was no wonder she was annoyed with them.

Josh cocked his head. "Come to think of it, I don't remember that Blysdale's very cordial even to *all* of them that are left. When it comes right down to it, I guess Mathers

and Taskford are the only two men old Bly really cries friends
with, though he's kind enough to old Smythe." He grinned
fondly. "Everybody's nice to Smythe, of course. He's so
damned decent it positively gets on a fellow's nerves." The
grin faded. "But Blysdale's a cold man." He pretended a
shiver. "Got eyes that could pierce a steel breastplate."

Kate knew an instant's uneasiness as a memory of the
eyes of the man she'd held up last night flashed through her
mind. No. Surely not. It couldn't be. Besides, Josh had just
called his colonel "old" and said that he would be here any
day now, not that he was already here. The disturbing man
in the dark-lacquered traveling coach was most definitely
here, and he certainly hadn't been anywhere near old, either.

She rallied and asked, "Well, if he isn't your friend, what
on earth is he doing coming here to visit?" In her mind, she
grumbled, *And why the devil does he have to do it now!* Just
what she needed. Another man underfoot. Another person
from whom to hide her nightly forays.

What had she done to deserve this added aggravation? After
all, she'd never actually *robbed* anybody. And she certainly
hadn't done anyone bodily harm. Surely, God couldn't be *this*
cross with her.

"He's coming to look into the disappearance of two of
the 'Lucky Seven,' I'd wager. Mathers's coach was found
near here with the coachman murdered and Mathers and
Smythe—that's the Duke of Smythington—have gone missing."

Kate shot bolt upright in her chair. "Why, that's dreadful, Josh! I'd heard about the coachman, of course, and that
was bad enough. I'd no idea there'd been any disappearances."

"I think it's been kept quiet. Waiting to hear from whoever's got them. Ransom and all that, you know." He wolfed
down several forkful and sloshed coffee down after them
in his haste to continue. "Now that nobody's heard anything,
Blysdale's coming here to look for the men that did it. And
he'll track 'em down. Count on it."

"Why does he have to stay here to do that?"

"Yes, well," Josh sat back, patted his lips with his napkin, and picked up his coffee cup again. His hunger temporarily appeased, he wanted to placate his sister. "Blysdale wrote a nice letter and explained that he'd try not to be any trouble, but that if he stayed at an inn instead of bothering us—that's the way he put it, Kate, 'bothering us'—it wouldn't give him an in with the people hereabouts like staying with us would." He looked at his sister. "He put it better than that, of course."

"Of course," Kate said in a dry tone. When that had no effect, she gave up subtlety and accused, "I suppose it would have been too much trouble for you to have shown me his letter?"

"Aw, Kate. It slipped my mind." He smiled winningly at her. "Just believe me when I tell you that Blysdale was really apologetic about putting us to any trouble, and he said he hoped we wouldn't mind having him. And he *is* a hero and all that. And he's looking for two more heroes who've gone missing. It really is the least we can do."

Kate refrained from commenting. She sipped her tea instead. There was evidently no trouble Josh wouldn't take to make his colonel welcome—as long as Kate was the one taking it.

Obliviously, Josh reapplied himself to his breakfast, content, now, that his sister would take care of the matter.

"How very nice of your colonel to tell us he won't be any trouble." Even though Kate knew her sarcasm was wasted on her brother, she couldn't refrain from it. True to form, Josh didn't pay any more attention to her now than he had when she'd been a child. It had been frustrating when she was a little girl and aggravating when she was a young lady. Now, since she was the one who kept his farms and manor running smoothly, she found Josh's offhand attitude nothing short of infuriating.

All that aside, though, she realized that she was behaving badly by being inhospitable about having his colonel. And the colonel wasn't to blame. It was Josh's attitude that made her so negative. Feeling guilty about her own poor attitude, she scolded herself.

After all, it wasn't this Lord Blysdale's fault that her nerves were stretched to the breaking point, and it was, after all, very good of him to come searching for word of his friends. One had to admire that in the man. She'd just be sure to concentrate on that, and doing so would get her through this unexpected visit.

Kate watched her brother drink his coffee and tried not to feel irritation. She'd never understood before how Josh could leave the management of his estate completely in the hands of a younger sister, and she certainly didn't understand it now. For some reason, that aggravated her more today than usual.

Of course, her nerves had been on edge since her encounter with the man whose piercing eyes had held that strange hint of amusement last night. That was probably why she wanted to snap at her irresponsible sibling.

Knowing that snapping at Josh would do no good, and worse, that she would just regret it later, Kate bit her tongue. There was no way she nor anybody else was going to change Josh if becoming Sixth Marquess of Cliffside hadn't done the trick.

Kate sipped her tea and hoped the day would improve. Instead, things got distinctly worse. Firm footsteps sounded in the hall and Josh's friend Gordon Mallory strode in. "Hallo, you two! Hope I'm not intruding."

Kate turned in her chair to scowl at the big man who stood just inside the dining room archway. "Good morning, Gordon," she said in her frostiest tone.

"Good morning, my love." He was a large man, well built and handsome, with roguish brown eyes and hair of a deep auburn that caught the light from the windows and flamed. Radiating self-assurance, he smiled at Kate, letting his gaze roam slowly over her.

"I am *not* your love!" she snapped at him. He gave her the feeling that she might as well be sitting there unclothed.

"Ah, but love will come, Kate. I won't rest until it does."

He smiled at her possessively, his even teeth white in his tanned, handsome face. "Mind if I join you for breakfast?" Without even waiting for her reply, he picked up a plate and perused the buffet.

"Not at all," Kate's voice dripped sarcasm as she tried deliberately to insult him. When the effort failed, she said, "I have just finished mine, however." With that, she rose and left the room, leaving her untouched breakfast in full view of her most definitely unwelcome guest.

Chapter Three

Once out in the fresh air, Kate gulped great breaths of it. She wanted to clear the imagined stench of Gordon Mallory from her nostrils. How she detested that man! She always had. She hesitated a moment on the broad steps leading down from the side terrace, then headed straight for Star's paddock.

If things had been normal, she'd chide herself for behaving like a troubled young girl running out to talk to a horse, of all things! But nothing *was* normal. Nothing had been normal since she'd gotten here.

Her aging abigail was, as she had always been, the perfect confidant, but there was only so much that Kate was willing to tell her, no matter how badly she needed to talk. Dresden, bless her heart, was worried sick already.

Her brothers were clearly no help. *They* were, by and large, the problem. Josh was impossible, he was so self-centered. Hal was the person she was trying to prove innocent of jewel theft, so she could hardly complain of it to him, and Jamie, at ten, was far too young to confide in.

Now, complicating everything further, Gordon was back.

Blast Gordon Mallory. Yes, and blast Josh for taking up with him!

Right now, her stallion was the only male with whom Kate was in complete charity. Crossing the deep, wind-rippled grass, she called out, "Star! Come!"

The big black stallion lifted his head and looked in her direction. Whinnying a greeting, he cantered toward her, sliding to a stop with his great iron-shod hooves scant inches from her toes.

Her heart lifted, as it always did at the sight of him, and she could feel her peevish mood begin to evaporate. "Hallo, boy." She ran her hand down the satin hide of his neck, then scratched him behind the ears and said very softly, "Hallo, Star."

He nickered and pushed his head against her in response. She stepped back to inspect the star in the center of his broad forehead. She had to be sure she'd gotten all the boot blacking off from the night before. Things would get touchy indeed if one of the grooms wondered why there was black stain coming off the great horse's face. Kate had to be careful that nothing gave her game away. Satisfied that the star on his forehead was clean, she leaned against his shoulder, drawing comfort and strength from the huge bulk of him.

Star nuzzled her, his velvet lips toying with the lace on the bodice of her dress.

Calmer now, Kate threw a glare back toward the castle. "How the blazes can Gordon Mallory believe I might someday come to love him, Star? I detest the man. If I thought I could get him to do it, I'd ask Josh to order him to leave me alone." As she turned back to her horse, she caught a movement from the manor. The terrace door opened, and her brother Hal came swinging on his crutches down toward her.

"Kate! I've been looking for you."

"Good morning. I was late coming down for breakfast. I overslept."

"So that was it." He stopped to catch his breath. "I thought you'd left early for some farm chore."

"You should have asked Jennings where I was."

"Yes. He keeps good track of you. I suppose I'm just so used to you being off overseeing something or other around the estate that I assumed you'd gone again."

"Fortunately, I wasn't needed today. Tomorrow we drain that pasture I want to try to convert to a hay field."

"Oh, Lord, Kate. That's no job for a lady. Now that I'm at home, you must teach me how to see to some of this. I can at least try to help you."

Kate took one look at the lines the pain of his broken leg had etched into her brother's handsome face and said, "Hal, the important thing right now is for you to let that leg heal. You need to keep it still, not bump it about the farms on horseback."

"So you say." His voice was bitter. "Then perhaps you'll permit me to participate in your endeavor to capture one of the jewel thief's gang?"

"Hal! You know you can't ride with that leg."

"I'd find a way."

Kate lost patience with him. "And I suppose you'd find a way to blind everyone in the coaches you stopped so that they didn't notice your splints?"

"Kate, I—"

"And, of course, you'd cause everyone in the neighborhood to forget that Hal Clifton had come home from London with his leg broken, so that no one could identify you as the highwayman."

Hal blushed furiously. "There's no need to be sarcastic, Kate."

"I think there's every need, Hal. You aren't thinking clearly. I have to jolt you into doing so. You broke your leg jumping out of Lord Kenderly's window in pursuit of a burglar and—"

"And got accused of being that burglar, myself." Hal's self-scorn was loaded with bitterness.

"Actually, I thought you'd been accused of being a jewel thief." Her lips twitched as she tried not to smile at him.

"Don't provoke me, Kate. You can't laugh this off. Smiling won't change things, and I'm not going to be distracted into forgetting that I want you to give up this dangerous idea of stopping and searching coaches."

Kate leaned back into Star and took a deep breath. Her brother was upset. He was frustrated at his own helplessness, and he wanted to keep her safe. She understood all that, and she was sorry for him, but none of that mattered. She couldn't let it matter. Finally she said, "Hal, we must be reasonable."

"I am being reasonable!"

"No, dear, you're not. We have no choice but to do as we are doing." With an upraised hand, she silenced him. "All our hired investigators have been able to discover is that the Mayfair Bandit sends the stolen jewels to France to be re-mounted, and that he sends them there from Clifton-on-Tides."

"I *know* that! But . . ."

"There are no buts, Hal. The only chance we have to clear your name is to catch someone carrying the stolen jewelry to the port. That's the only clue with which we can find the real Mayfair Bandit and prove your innocence."

He was silent for a long moment.

"Please, Hal. Try not to mind it so much. I'm being very careful. Nothing will happen to me."

He reached for her, crutches and all, and enfolded her in his arms. "Oh, God, Kate. I can't believe this is happening to us. I can't believe I'm letting you expose yourself to such danger for my sake."

Kate searched her mind frantically for something to put his mind at rest and came up with, "But, Hal, you just said it. This is happening to *us*. To all of us. It's our good name as well as yours, you know. We're a family."

Hal grunted and released her but he didn't comment.

"It'll be all right." She put her hand on his cheek. "You'll see."

"Damn this leg," he muttered and swung away. Kate had already seen the tears of frustration and gratitude in his eyes, though, and the sight of them brought tears of quick sympathy to her own.

She watched him drag himself along through the thick,

high grass until he reached the terrace. He looked back at her for a long moment before he disappeared into the great house.

Kate wiped her eyes with the back of her hand, then turned back to her horse and pulled at Star's mane, combing wind-whipped tangles out with her fingers. As she did, she could feel the sea wind teasing her own heavy hair loose from its confining braid.

Star nickered softly and curved his head over her shoulder. Was it possible he could understand her concerns?

Her heart twisted. Hal. Charming Hal, the darling of London society. Of all of them who might be maligned, it was worst for her favorite brother. He was the only one of them who truly cared for the good opinion of the members of their class. Josh was too devil-may-care, Jamie too young, and Kate, after years at the center of London's frivolous society, was quite frankly indifferent. But Hal cared. Hal cared a great deal, and Kate was deeply troubled for him.

She could hardly believe that Hal had been accused of being the infamous thief who'd been stealing jewelry from the richest members of the *ton*. There was no proof of it, of course. There couldn't be, because Hal was innocent. But when had society needed proof to blacken a man's character?

There'd been no formal charges made because no jewels had been found in her brother's possession. Hal had merely been accused by Baron Runcason—an old enemy of the family. The only support behind the accusation was the fact that Hal had been present at the scene of all the robberies. But that hadn't stopped Runcason, and once the rumor had been started, the rest of the houseguests had been swift to believe the worst. No one had bothered to point out that they had almost all been present at the scene of all the robberies!

Kate told Star, "Of course Hal had been at all the houses at which robberies had taken place. Hal goes to *everybody's* house parties." She stroked Star's nose. "Everyone invites him so that they'll get an invitation to come here when we give ours."

Star began to lip the end of her braid.

"No, that's not true. I'm being spiteful because I'm so angry. They invite Hal because he's the most pleasant of us all and everyone loves him. Or did. Loyalty doesn't seem to be one of the strongest character traits of the *ton*, unfortunately." She gave a mighty sigh. "I know the charge is ridiculous, but I'm worried. You just don't realize how easily a reputation is destroyed in Town." She smiled at her horse, finding her statement ridiculous. "Well, actually, you couldn't, of course." She laughed aloud, but still said, "Believe me when I tell you that it's quite a simple thing to malign a person in London society. So many of the people there enjoy malice.

"And Hal is so miserable if he isn't in the middle of *ton* activities. It'll kill him to be shunned." Her jaw tensed. "But why didn't Hal stay there in London and fight till everyone had to believe in his innocence, Star? I would have. You can just bet I wouldn't let some brandy-guzzling old peer make false accusations against me and force me out of any place I cared to be a guest!"

She snatched her braid away from Star as he began to chew the end of it. "Stop that! You know that isn't hay!" She inspected the slightly damp, curled ends of her hair. "Besides, it's straw colored, and horses don't eat straw. They *sleep* on it." She pushed him away as he stretched his neck out, mouth open, for the braid. "Stop it."

Star lifted his upper lip like a foal begging kindness from a threatening larger horse.

Kate laughed. "You big clown."

Star reared and raced away, bucking.

"Silly horse!" Kate called after him. "What are you so pleased about?" Then she knew. He'd made her laugh. Quick tears misted the sight of the horse bucking and cavorting across the meadow. "Oh, Star," she whispered. "Why don't people realize how special horses are?"

When he turned to look her way, she opened her arms, and the great beast thundered back to her, stopped, and lowered his head to press it gently against her. Kate wrapped her arms around it and rested there. Finally, peace crept over her.

After a long moment, she began working at the wind-twisted sections of Star's mane again. She gave a yank to one of the more difficult ones. It came undone, but Star grunted his displeasure at her harsh treatment.

She dropped her forehead against the great horse's face. "Oh, Star." She fingered another elflock halfheartedly. "Your mane is a simple matter, my love, but look at what a tangle *I* am in!"

From the tall windows of the Cliffside breakfast room, Gordon Mallory watched the slender woman and the massive stallion. Seeing the obvious affection between then, he decided to get rid of the horse once the woman was his. She'd be easier to bend to his will if she lacked all emotional support. Josh didn't give a damn about her feelings, Jennings and Dresden he could pension off, and Runcason had already taken care of Hal for him.

That had been a stroke of genius—accusing Hal of being the Mayfair Bandit. Of course, it had only been Runcason's vicious striking out at an old enemy, but the blow had been perfect. Hal was disgraced, and if he, Gordon Mallory, had anything to do with it, Hal Clifton would soon be transported from the shores of England as a thief.

Then, at long last, he'd take Kate for his own. Josh would agree, and there'd be no one else to stop him. With no one to champion her, it wouldn't take long for him to bring Kate to her knees and extract payment for all the slights she'd dealt him.

His smile was slow to spread, his expression gloating. Gordon Mallory was more than satisfied with himself. He had every right to be. In less than a year, he'd recouped the fortune his old fool of a father had gambled away, and he'd done it without anyone being the wiser. He was again—though all the world thought "still"—a force to be reckoned with.

The Mallorys' position in life had always been secured by his great-grandfather's fabulous wealth. Now it was again, by his own. No one need know that there had been that brief period of panic. Panic that had resolved itself when he'd ended his father's tenure of the Mallory fortune—and his pitiful life.

Now the family fortune was repaired. His ventures in the Middle East were proving even more lucrative than his sale of the jewels that Hal Clifton was accused of stealing.

The gods were smiling on him. Everything seemed to fall easily into place for him, and nothing was going to stop him from achieving his heart's desire. Soon he would add the exalted Clifton name to his family tree, just as his grandfather had always wanted him to—whether or not it suited Lady Katherine Clifton.

Below him in the pasture, he saw Kate turn away from the huge black beast she loved so well and start back toward the house. Time for him to get away from the window. It was no hardship. He'd looked his fill and could be patient. After all, it wouldn't be long now before the last few pieces of his plan were in place and Kate would be his.

Kate, back in her luxurious green and gold bedchamber, had just dunked the end of her braid in the bowl of warm water her abigail had brought her and was swishing it to be sure that the last traces of Star's interest were removed when a knock sounded on her door.

Dresden went to see who it was, murmured, "All right, I'll tell her," and hurried back to Kate. Her professional gaze swept over Kate's dress. "You'll need a fresh gown. That one has a black smudge on the bodice."

Blast! Kate looked down. There it was, a black mark just where Star's face had pressed when she'd hugged him. She hadn't got all the boot blacking off last night, after all. Now she was wearing some of it.

"What is it you have to tell me?"

"The gatekeeper has sounded the horn. Jennings says that a guest, or guests, will be arriving shortly."

"Oh, dear." Kate ran to the window in the deep alcove formed by the thickness of the ancient castle wall here in the

east wing. Looking out, she saw two carriages approaching
from far down the drive. Obviously the legendary Colonel
Blysdale had arrived. "We must hurry, Dresden. I must get
downstairs as quickly as I can." She turned to let her abigail
help her into a fresh gown. With approval, she saw the soft
green wool day dress Dresden was holding, and held up her
arms to be helped to change.

As the soft wool fell clinging around her, she thought that
she really must find something more efficacious with which
to remove the boot blacking from Star's forehead in the future.

Outside on the graveled drive, a tall slender man dressed all
in black stepped out of a handsome black-lacquered coach.
Only a moment before it had been drawn by its four perfectly matched black geldings up the manor drive, equipage
and horses gleaming in the sunlight.

Perfectly trained, the horses stood statue still; the only
movement among the four of them was in their wind-tossed
manes. The carriage, too, was perfection. The coat-of-arms
of the Earl of Blythingdale was painted on the door in dark
colors subtly rendered to blend with the black of the coach.
They could easily be overlooked by the unobservant.

The elegant equipage was followed by another only slightly
more utilitarian vehicle carrying Blysdale's man and luggage.
Two very handsome saddle horses were tied behind it. Cliffside's butler was there on the lower terrace to meet them. At
Jennings's signal, the baggage was removed by footmen and
grooms hurried forward, ready to escort the impressive ve-
hicles to the stables.

The first carriage door was closed by a liveried footman,
and the vehicle moved smartly off. Chalfont Blysdale stood
where he had gotten down. His gaze raked the facade of the
impressive pile before him. He'd been very interested in seeing how a comfortable mansion had been built that still incorporated sections of an ancient castle on the cliffs.

It had been done well. The great hall remained the front
entrance, and it looked as if the wing nearest the sea had
been cleverly preserved, as well. The view from its windows

would be magnificent. Blysdale imagined that it contained bedchambers.

His curiosity about the manor satisfied, he turned and looked out to the bright sea beside it. His eyes held a quiet, speculative expression.

"Your lordship. Welcome to Cliffside Manor." The tall, silver-haired butler escorted Lord Blysdale up across the terraces on which the manor house stood, to its imposing entrance. As Blysdale sauntered up to the front door, Josh Clifton hurtled out of it. "Welcome to Cliffside, Colonel." He grinned. "That is, your lordship."

Blysdale smiled. "Thank you, your lordship. It is kind of you to permit me to come."

"It's an honor to have you. My pledge on it." Josh stepped aside to allow Blysdale to precede him into the great hall. "Come and meet m' sister, Kate. She runs things here."

Blysdale looked around with interest. Ever since he'd heard about the extensive renovations that had been made at Cliffside Castle to change it from a fortress to comfortable manor, he'd been curious. Knowing that this part of it had only been carefully repaired, not changed, Blysdale was interested in how this great hall compared with that in his own half-ruined castle on the shores of Normandy.

As he looked around the sunlit space, there was a flurry of skirts at the top of a magnificent sweep of stairs that curved around three walls of the huge room. He directed his gaze there.

A woman's light step sounded as she hurried down the ancient stone stairs. Blysdale stood and watched her come, only half-listening to his host. His breath caught for an instant as she passed through a beam of sunlight from one of the multitude of windows that made up three walls of the great hall. She was tall and slender, her magnificent figure clearly revealed by the molding of the soft, fine wool of her gown.

Blysdale was impressed. Knowing his host so well, he'd expected his sister to be a feminine version of the Marquess's sturdy good looks. Nothing could be further from the truth.

Josh Clifton's willowy sister made the young Marquess look
like a poorly bred musk ox.

Blysdale watched as she passed through the sunlight from
another window. She had glorious hair, golden and dark with
streaks of almost white blond. It was loosely caught at the
nape of her neck by a ribbon that matched the pale green of
her dress.

Bly had a sudden absurd desire to untie that ribbon.

She reached the foot of the stairs and hurried gracefully
toward them. The sun was full on her. In the strong light of
it, Bly saw that her complexion was perfect. In defiance of
fashion, her face was lightly sun-kissed, but neither tanned
nor freckled. Obviously this lady was not so careful of her
fair skin as to avoid the pleasures to be found outdoors. He
liked that, he found.

His eyes narrowed as he studied her. High color stained
her cheeks, her lips were nicely shaped and slightly parted.
Unbidden, the thought came, *as if they are waiting for my
kiss.*

Calling himself sharply to order, he continued his study
of his hostess as she stopped before she was quite in front
of him. Her bright green eyes were brimful of intelligence—
and something else. He smiled then, recognizing the look.
The lady was less than glad to have him in her home. That
was interesting.

Kate felt as if she'd just run into a stone wall. Her heart
beat fast and hard. It was *him!* It was the man from the coach
she had stopped last night.

Dear Lord! Josh had called his colonel "old." This man
could not possibly be forty yet, and "old" was not a word
that fit him in any way. Lithe and alert, he made her think
of a rapier in an unseen swordsman's hand—poised to attack
instantly in any direction. Kate just hoped it wouldn't be hers.

"Fustian," she told herself inaudibly. It must be the black
clothing he wore that made him appear so sinister. She forced
herself to move toward him again, and the sun was shining in her eyes, making him no more than a slender, broad-
shouldered silhouette, light-limned.

Surely the feeling she had of impending danger was a reasonable one. She *had* held up his coach, after all.

She lifted her chin and smiled at their guest. "Welcome to Cliffside Manor, your lordship." She extended her hand in greeting.

Blysdale took it in his, bowed over it, and, watching her from beneath his dark brows, kissed it.

An electric current passed up Kate's arm. She stiffened and tried to withdraw her hand. Her own brows rose, the eyes under them wide and startled.

Bly noted the strength in her slender arm and in her long-fingered hand. Here was no drawing room miss. His eyes smiled at the discovery, but the smile never reached his lips. Colonel Chalfont Blysdale was not a man who gave anything away.

"This is my colonel from the Peninsular War, Kate, I've told you all about him. Lord Blysdale, Earl of Blythingdale." Josh turned to Blysdale. "And this is my sister, Kate. Lady Katherine." He hastened to add, "Uh, Countess of Rushmore."

He looked from one to the other, waiting for some response. When they stood simply looking at each other as if they had met many times before, Josh was at a loss. Finally, he said, "Ah, yes. Well. Er, shall we go into the drawing room?"

Kate broke off staring at Blysdale with a visible effort. The man was mesmerizing.

With another effort, she transferred her regard to her brother. Her eyes lost their slightly dazed expression and she gave him an icy look that told him she'd have something to say to him later about his inexcusable lack of social skills. Then she turned on her heel and led the way to the drawing room.

Chapter Four

"Well, I'll tell you this, Colonel," Blysdale's man told him the instant the door closed behind Josh Clifton and his butler, "Lady Katherine did very well by you in giving you this grand bedchamber, whether or not she wants you here." He looked around the sumptuous cavern of a bedchamber and shook his head. "We could have stabled the whole regiment in here, had we been fightin' in England."

"True, Gris. And been a hell of a lot more comfortable than we ever were on the Peninsula." Bly looked around the room. He always studied his quarters carefully, as if he were planning an escape. It was a habit of long standing, and one he had no intention of breaking. A quick look out the nearest window showed him a balcony and an ancient oak. He gauged the distance to the closest bough and decided he could make the leap if the need arose.

Behind him, Griswold laughed. "Aye. Take every precaution, Colonel. You never know when your reluctant hostess, yon Lady Katherine, might make a real effort to be rid of your unwanted presence."

"She won't get rid of me until I've found Mathers and Smythe, no matter what she does, Gris," his former commanding officer answered grimly. Then he turned with a smile and asked, "Was it that obvious she was resistant to the idea of having us, then, old friend? I'd hoped I'd been the only one who perceived the lady's reluctance."

"Well, I was right behind you, guarding your back as ever. And the sun was shining full on the lovely lady's face when she greeted you." He cocked his head, considering the memory. "Of course, her peevishness could have been for the young lord, her brother."

"Yes, I suppose it could have been. Certainly he inspires a certain . . . irritation." Bly smiled. "Heaven knows he's done it frequently enough in me."

"Clifton always seemed a good enough officer."

"His impetuosity had a tendency to put his men in danger too often to suit me." Blysdale's eyes narrowed as he looked into the past. "However, he always managed to get them out again. Still, I found it . . . annoying."

Griswold stopped in the act of folding Blysdale's cravats into a drawer. Straightening, he turned toward his friend and employer. "Not every man has ice water in his veins, Bly."

"Is that supposed to tell me that I have?"

"'Tis generally allowed that you are an exceeding cool man under fire."

"Really." Blysdale's voice was a bored drawl. It wasn't pretense, Griswold knew. Blysdale just didn't give a damn what other men thought. Except for three. He cared about the opinions of Taskford, Mathers, and Smythe. Not overly, but at least he cared somewhat. On very rare occasions, Blysdale tolerated Griswold's opinions, as well.

Bly's friend Taskford was safely wed and at home with his beautiful Countess, Regina, awaiting a summons from Blysdale, his former colonel, to help in this present matter. Mathers and Smythe, of course, were missing, and that was why they were here. Blysdale was going to find them—or ascertain what had become of them and avenge them. More than once when he'd considered that possible vengeance, Griswold had muttered, "God help the poor sods if they've harmed them."

Griswold had thought that his colonel would go mad waiting to gather all the information—scant as it had proven—that he could obtain about this area before he left London. Finally, when he'd garnered it all, he'd sent for his two best men, had Griswold pack a small arsenal, and come to Cliffside himself.

Gris decided to treat Blysdale's "Really" as a question. "Aye," he answered it. "The whole army thought you hadn't a nerve in your body." He closed the drawer on his lordship's cravats and went back to unpacking the trunk. "Some of the young recruits even had another name for you."

Bly looked up inquiringly from checking the pair of dueling pistols in the case Griswold had just lifted from the trunk. "Another name?"

"Piqued your curiosity, did I?"

"Yes, you did." Blysdale chuckled. "Touched my vanity, too. I thought I knew all the names men called me. All the specific ones, that is."

"Aye, there was them that called you the unrepeatable sort, too."

"Rarely within my hearing, however."

"That's true. They had an aversion to being skewered, I expect."

At that, Blysdale laughed aloud. "Come now, Gris. I fought no more duels than any other bored officer in Spain. Not as many as some."

"You didn't have much opportunity to. Not after what you did to Treckler."

Bly looked at his friend, his face stern. "Treckler was a rapist."

"Not anymore he isn't."

Blysdale picked up the coat he'd chosen to wear to dinner. "He's lucky I let him live."

Griswold said very softly, "Some might not think so." Then went to where Blysdale stood in his shirtsleeves waiting to be helped into his coat.

Blysdale shot his cuffs and glanced into the pier mirror. "Damn thing's too tight."

"They always are. That's the fashion."

Blysdale crossed the vast room and hesitated at the door. "You haven't told me what the young recruits called me."

"You've room enough in that coat to eat and to do the pretty. You'll just have to doff it if anybody challenges you to a duel."

Griswold's evasion didn't work. Bly demanded, "You *still* haven't told me what the young recruits called me. I'm waiting."

"So you are. And if you're not careful you'll be late."

"Gris." The nickname had an ominous sound.

Griswold knew when to surrender. "Beelzebub. Beelzebub Blysdale. That's what they called you."

Blysdale released a shout of laughter. He was still laughing as he walked down the hall.

Griswold shook his head at the unaccustomed sound as he closed the bedchamber door.

In the drawing room, Blysdale was welcomed by his host.

"Ah, there you are, sir." Josh hurried to meet and escort his ex–commanding officer into the room, falling to the left and slightly behind his former colonel. Old military habits died hard.

Bly wondered if it looked as if he were being herded to meet the group gathered around the fireplace. His eyes held a glint of amusement at the thought. Looking at Lady Katherine, he saw an answering sparkle in hers. The sight warmed him.

"Permit me to introduce my brothers." Josh indicated a tall, blond man probably a year younger than himself, who was on crutches, and a boy of about ten with the same blond hair and blue eyes. Josh gestured the older brother forward. "This is my brother Hal. He's just come down from London to rusticate for a while."

The young man started forward, but Blysdale closed the distance between them in one long, fluid stride, stopping the man before his crutches thumped the carpet a second time. The younger man smiled his gratitude for Blysdale's thoughtfulness, hesitated an instant, then firmly clasped the hand that Blysdale offered. "Your servant, Lord Blysdale."

Blysdale wondered at the hesitation in Hal Clifton's manner. At his close inspection, Hal colored slightly. As soon as Bly released his hand, he turned away as if embarrassed.

Blysdale's curiosity rose. What had this younger Clifton to be embarrassed about?

Immediately Josh brought the youngest member of the family forward. "And this is James Everett Clifton. Our Jamie, Colonel."

The boy stood ramrod straight and waited for Blysdale to acknowledge him, his eyes wide. Bly shook the boy's hand, his face solemn. "Your servant, Master Clifton."

When Bly bowed slightly as well, Jamie's excitement overflowed. "You're *Colonel* Blysdale."

"Guilty as charged."

"Josh has told me all about you. How you saved his life and everything. All the fabulous things you've done! How you're one of the 'Lucky Seven.' They were Wellington's favorites!" He didn't notice Josh's efforts to silence him but went on, "Everything about them is wonderful!" His eyes clouded for an instant as he said, "Except that one of them got murdered so the murderer could steal his horse." Jamie's face became grave. "That must have been awful for you when you found that out, sir."

"Yes, Jamie." Bly's voice dropped a note. "It rather was."

"But you caught him, and he paid the price. Kate told me."

Bly shot a look at Lady Katherine. The amusement they had shared as he was herded into the room by her brother was gone from her eyes now. Bly saw compassion there instead. One of his eyebrows rose, querying.

"Did she?" Blysdale wasn't really talking to Jamie.

Katherine felt her face flame. "Lord and Lady Taskford are friends of mine," she offered by way of explanation.

Blysdale leveled an unreadable look at her. Immediately, Katherine felt as if she had been caught in an indiscretion. How dare he make her feel guilty of a *faux pas*? She was sorry she'd offered this overbearing man any sort of explanation!

This is absurd! I've a perfect right to discuss whatever I wish to discuss with my friends. None of us knew you were going to come charging down here into our neighborhood! Why in the world should she feel this way? Why was she letting Blysdale give her this feeling that she'd been guilty of some trespass? And why the blazes did she give a tinker's dam *what* he tried to make her feel like?

Her lips tightened and she frowned at her newly arrived houseguest. He'd been here only a few hours and already he was making her uncomfortable. Wasn't it bad enough that she was already worried that he might recognize her eyes, or her way of moving? Did she have to watch every word she uttered in front of *him,* now, too? And why was *she,* who had always thought in declarative sentences, suddenly ending her every mental comment with a blasted *question mark?*

Had this man been born just especially to tear up her peace? And if so, what the blazes was the matter with *her* that she was letting him do it?

Finally, in a superhuman effort to be fair, Kate decided that the feelings she was experiencing came from the fact that she was living on her nerve ends just now, not from anything the enigmatic Blysdale had done. She resolved to try harder to be less prickly.

At that moment, Jennings came to the door of the drawing room and announced in ringing tones, "Dinner is served."

As guest of honor, Blysdale had the privilege of escorting Kate into the dining room, where he was seated next to her at the long, gleaming mahogany table. This made conversation with him inescapable, and, prickly or not, Kate wasn't sure she liked the idea of conversing at any length with Lord Blysdale.

The dratted man had the reputation of being far too observant. Too aware. She'd seen proof of that for herself when he'd looked so hard at Hal. He was obviously curious as to why Hal had been reluctant to shake his offered hand. Though he'd no way of knowing that Hal felt he was unworthy while he was under a cloud of suspicion, Blysdale had sensed something in Hal's hesitation to take his hand. His considering regard had told Kate plainly that he wanted to know what it was that had embarrassed her brother.

Lord! Suppose something about her reminded him of her? Of her as the highwayman, she meant, of course. Some inflection in her voice? The way she held her head? Some gesture?

When she held up coaches, she always tried to disguise her voice, and to move in a masculine manner, but she'd been told—a thousand times—by Josh, that Blysdale wasn't an easy man to deceive. And he was, by her own observation, so . . . intense.

When the usual platitudes and the requisite discussion of the weather were over, Blysdale asked, "Have you had much trouble with highwaymen here so near the coast, Lady Katherine?"

Kate nearly choked on her wine. Carefully, she forced herself to swallow, thinking Lord Blysdale was lucky she hadn't sputtered wine all over him. Fighting to sound nonchalant, she responded, "There have been a few instances of coaches being stopped, but nothing much has come of it."

From under her lashes, she was regarding him sharply. Did he suspect that it had been she who'd held up his coach? Her fingers went cold around the stem of her wineglass. She thanked her Maker that they didn't visibly tremble, as well. "Why do you ask?" She managed a casual tone. "Were you accosted?"

Blysdale was watching her closely. "As a matter of fact, my coach was stopped the evening before we arrived here."

"Ah." Knowing full well where he'd been stopped and ordered to stand and deliver, she said, "Then it couldn't have been our highwayman. He seems to operate only nearby." She put her wineglass down and forced her fingers to uncurl from the death grip she had on its fragile stem.

"Actually," Blysdale leaned back in his chair and said

softly, "it *was* very near here. Just before we would have turned into the Cliffside Manor road, in fact."

Kate took a deep breath to steady herself and turned a cool, politely interested gaze on him. She would have smiled but she was afraid that if she did her lips might quiver and give her away. So she raised her eyebrows at him and trusted herself to say no more than, "Oh?"

"Yes." His gaze rose from where it had rested on her bosom when she'd taken her steadying breath. Languidly it caressed her full lower lip, still damp from her having caught it with her teeth, then went on to her eyes. Now his eyes held her gaze like a fox would hold a rabbit's as he told her, "A cocky youth on a great black horse stopped my coach and searched it."

Kate felt as if her heart had stopped beating. She felt her nostrils flare as she sought her next breath.

From his place at the opposite end of the table, Josh cried, "Oh, I say! That was the devil of an impertinence, Colonel. Bad enough to offer to rob a fellow without invading his privacy like that, what?"

"What, indeed?" Blysdale was steadily regarding Kate's mouth.

She caught her lower lip with her teeth again to be sure it didn't quiver.

"Am I upsetting you, Lady Katherine?" He was purring.

"No, not at all." This man missed nothing, and she suspected he knew very well he was upsetting her. She shook that off before fear of discovery could overwhelm her and concentrated instead on the fact that he'd been helpful, too. His statement that he'd been accosted almost at the turnoff to Cliffside alerted her to the fact that she must range farther from home for future holdups.

The fact that she should have thought of that herself pricked her. She was beginning to be annoyed. To Blysdale she said, "I was wondering why, though, when you had been held up at the very turnoff to Cliffside, you did not come here to the manor."

"It was late in the evening, Lady Katherine. I could hardly

disturb you at that hour. I went on to the inn, so that I might present myself at a more conventional time today."

"But didn't you want to report the robbery?"

"My dear lady," he said, still watching her closely, "it was hardly a robbery since nothing was taken."

Kate could feel a muscle tighten in her jaw. "Weren't you even alarmed?"

"Actually," he drawled, "I was rather intrigued."

"Intrigued?" she asked coolly. *Well, that was certainly not what I intended!* Kate felt challenged.

"Yes." Blysdale's voice was a lazy caress; his gaze roamed her features as if memorizing them, lingering again on her lips. "I had been bored, you see, and the youth alleviated that boredom. I not only appreciated that, but I found myself quite fascinated."

Kate pressed her hand to her stomach to help her breathe. What had he found so fascinating? Had he . . . ?

"Oh! Ho, ho!" Josh cried from his end of the table. "I know that tone of voice, sister mine." He looked from Kate to Lord Blysdale. "You just watch. The Colonel will be turning the whole neighborhood upside down searching for the identity of that highwayman!"

And suddenly, even pressing her hands to her stomach as hard as she could wasn't helping Kate to breathe.

Chapter Five

Blysdale's attitude at the dinner table about the young highwayman put an end to any hope Kate might have had of a peaceful night's sleep!

The moment she could do so, she excused herself from the men, ostensibly to go up to her suite. She made one stop on the way to scrawl a hasty note. Jennings, with a query in his eyes that Kate did not answer, did as he was requested and dispatched a groom to ride with the message to the village inn.

Though Kate then walked to her chambers with perfect dignity, the instant the door closed behind her, she abandoned all pretense. She tore off her gown, rushed to the huge armoire that held her riding things, and pulled out a habit.

"Calm down, Kate! He's only a man. You're acting as if he were the devil himself!" She turned and regarded herself in the dressing room's free-standing pier mirror. The young woman staring back at her looked anything but calm. Blond hair torn free of its chignon by the haste with which she'd removed her dinner gown rioted about her shoulders, and the reflected green eyes had a wildness Kate had never seen in them before.

This would never do. If she couldn't keep a cool head, she'd be good for nothing. "Dammit! You've never had this problem before," she told the woman in the mirror. Then added, "You've never had a man like Blysdale under your roof before, either.

"Blast it! Damn and blast!" Kate seized her hair and began braiding it into submission. It was the truth. That man was the cause of this. His knowing eyes seemed to pierce beyond her defenses and to announce that he was aware of her secret—even though she knew that was impossible. His intent regard was unnerving. And if there was one thing Lady Katherine Elizabeth Clifton Halsted, Countess of Rushmore, did not need, it was to be unnerved!

Nor, she admitted in the secret recesses of her mind, did she need to be so aware of Blysdale. As a man. As more man than she had ever encountered. She thrust that little collection of thoughts back into the hidden place where it belonged. She'd no time—nor any inclination—to find herself attracted to a man right now. One danger at a time was quite enough, thank you.

Kate twisted her hastily braided hair into some semblance of order, pinning it so that it would stay until she crammed her hat on to hold it and went looking for her gloves and riding crop. A last glance in the mirror to be sure she looked presentable and she was ready to go.

Thank God her great-grandfather had kept this east wing of the castle for bedchambers! Thanks to some long-forgotten ancestor, there was a secret stairway in the thick outer wall of her rooms that led down to a concealed exit. She had once seen her grandfather open it, and had never forgotten its location. Without this secret escape, Kate would have found it impossible to play highwayman.

Snatching up a candlestick, she lit its candle from one of the dozens that lighted the room and touched the same carved wooden fleur-de-lis as before. The section of wall slid back and she entered the dark passage beyond.

Hurrying down the winding, time-worn steps, Kate paused at the bottom to place her candle carefully on a ledge there, moved the resident flint and steel to rest close beside it, and paused again before blowing out the candle.

Darkness enveloped her. Complete and utter, it seemed to stop her breath and mute all her senses. She breathed deeply, demanding calm in spite of her involuntary fear at having lost her ability to see.

Taking one last deep breath, she told herself, "You're being foolish, Katherine Elizabeth." She spoke aloud, steadying herself with the soothing sound of her own voice.

Her softly spoken words calmed her, leaving only annoyance. This foolish fear she had of dark places was something that always had to be conquered. She knew very well that it came from her childhood—from the time Josh had locked her in the closet she'd chosen as a hiding place in one of their games and left her there. She'd been a prisoner in the dark until Hal had threatened to tell their father if Josh didn't tell him where to find Kate in time to keep her from getting in trouble by being late for dinner.

The experience, nothing more than the casual cruelty of a teasing older brother, had nevertheless left an indelible mark on Kate when it came to small dark places. Every time she stood here at the foot of the secret stairs, she had to reconquer the unreasoning fear her brother had caused in her. It wouldn't do, however, to leave a candle lit to let light escape her secret exit when she opened and left it.

It was especially chancy with Chalfont Blysdale about, she thought sourly. The Colonel was definitely proving himself to be a complication she could well do without. She would have to find a way to solve that dilemma later, though. Kate ran her hand down the wall next to the ledge that held her candlestick and the flint and steel. Finding the lever was quickly done, and the massive mechanism that moved aside a section of heavy castle wall rumbled to life. As soon as the space was wide enough, Kate slipped through and pressed hard against the stone that reversed the machinery and put the wall back in place. With the skirt of her habit draped over her arm, she hurried away from the lichen-covered castle wall toward the stables.

Half an hour later she had reached the village, hidden her horse, and was safely in the basement of the inn. Seth Linden, the inn's proprietor, was Kate's right-hand man. Without the information he gathered and passed on to her, Kate would have been helpless in her quest to absolve Hal.

The door at the top of the basement stairs opened and Linden called down softly, "May I bring you a glass of wine, your ladyship?"

"Tea would be nice, Mr. Linden. Thank you." Their meetings always began with them each being properly formal, but Kate and Seth Linden had known each other all their lives, and the stilted conventions never lasted long with them. She seated herself in one of the chairs around the table the innkeeper had recently put in the basement for her use. Two weeks ago, when Kate had received the first report from the men she'd hired to investigate the activities of the jewel thief her brother Hal had been accused of being, she'd called on the innkeeper. On that visit, she had easily won Linden to her cause and sworn him to silence. Of all her acquaintances and friends, she had taken only Linden into her confidence. As children, he and Hal had been best friends.

Kate was truly grateful to him, and she wanted to warn him about Blysdale.

Linden returned with her tea, and ale for himself. He set the tray down on the table. "Lady Kate! Is it true that *you* hold up the coaches?" It was a demand more than a question. Linden had known her since she was a grubby little girl trailing around after her two older brothers. As a result, proper respect for her station in life was often lacking in their relationship. It was in short supply right now. "Damnation, girl. If I'd known that, I'd never have taken part in this mad scheme!"

"Now, Seth. Who did you think was to do it?" Kate's gaze was as cool as his was frantic.

He raked a hand through his hair and plopped in the chair across the table from her. He was a big man and the chair creaked under his weight. "Glory to God. I suppose I didn't think at all. Josh! Hal! Me, maybe. I don't know. But not you!"

Kate sat quietly, waiting for her childhood friend to calm down and realize she was right. That there was no one else. Kate wished that there were.When Linden had taken a long pull at his ale and wiped his mouth on the back of his hand, she spoke. "There is no way I could trust Josh to be discreet and careful enough, Seth. As you know, he has always been reckless." She waited until she saw him reluctantly acknowledge the truth of her remark, then went on. "Nor, obviously, could Hal hold up coaches just now. Not with his broken leg. And he's far too angry about these false accusations to look sharply to his own safety even if he could ride a horse. Not to mention that a highwayman with a leg in splints would be pretty easy to trace!"

Seth blinked at that. Then he frowned and, again reluctantly, admitted that she was right.

"So, that leaves me."

"I could go."

"No," she said quietly. "Hal is my brother. This is *my* responsibility." She paused and pretended to seem hesitant. "I probably have asked you to risk too much already."

Her statement had the desired effect.

Seth rushed to reassure her. "Nonsense, Kate. I grew up with you lot from the castle. Hal is my best friend. I'll do all that I can to help."

"Believe me, Seth, you already are. Without the information you get on coach activities from your brother and the boys you send to me with your messages, I'd be useless." She added softly, "And Hal would be lost." She reached out and put her hand on his arm. "You're doing all that I could wish for now, Seth. Keeping watch, and sending word when a coach is on its way to Clifton-on-Tides is all that I need. That's an indispensable service."

It was true. How else would she know when someone was heading for the seaside cluster of fishermen's cottages from which she'd been informed the real jewel thief sent his ill-gotten gains to the Continent to be sold? "Without your doing that," she told him earnestly, "how could we ever hope to intercept a shipment of stolen jewels and use it to trap the real culprit?"

"And I suppose you have a plan for a trap?"

Kate stifled a sigh and forced her voice to a firmness she was far from feeling. "Not just yet. Unfortunately, we shall have to wait for further developments to make those plans."

"Kate, have you ever thought . . . ?" Seth stopped, unable to go on.

"Yes. Yes, I have." She shook her head in utter misery. "I have thought of that. I've thought that the very boat Josh goes playing smuggler on could be the one taking the jewels to the Continent."

Linden exploded, "Josh is a great fool to go smuggling with that rogue Mallory and worry you so!"

"I know, Seth. But he won't listen. He thinks Gordon Mallory is his good friend."

Seth snorted. "Ha! Mallory's never been anybody's friend but his own."

"Yes, I know. When we were children I mistrusted him, and growing up hasn't changed my feelings."

"You're wise there, Kate. The man isn't to be trusted, though I've never known anybody to catch him at anything. He's too clever by half."

Kate sighed. Unfortunately, Josh's smuggling with Mallory was something she could do nothing about—short of breaking her oldest brother's leg to match Hal's. For an instant she wished she could. Kate hated being frustrated.

Linden saw her distress and changed the subject. "I've got a feeling you've called this urgent meeting for another reason, Kate." He leaned forward, his elbows on the table.

"Yes." Kate wasn't certain how best to broach the subject of Blysdale.

"Well? Don't keep me in suspense, Kate."

"Very well. The problem is that Josh has invited his Colonel to visit." No need to tell him how Blysdale had commanded the invitation. If Seth ever met him, he'd recognize Blysdale as a force to be reckoned with easily enough.

"Well?" Seth looked puzzled. "What's so bad about that?"

"You'd have to see him. To spend a few minutes with him. There's an intensity about him that . . . frightens me."

For a moment it looked as if Seth were going to make a joke. He'd always found Kate fearless. The idea that any man—short of a murdering lunatic—frightened her was ludicrous to him. Instead, he took a slow breath and asked, "How long is he going to stay?"

"I haven't any idea."

"Do you know why he's here? I mean, Josh isn't the most stimulating host on earth, nor Cliffside anything like as exciting as London." Linden's voice dropped to a low rumble. "Maybe he's here for reasons of his own." His worried glance touched the brandy kegs stacked in the dimness against the back wall of the basement.

Quick concern for her older brother caused Kate to gasp, "Oh, no! I've no doubt that he has come here with a purpose—that of finding his missing friends. But I never thought that perhaps he *might have* an additional reason—a dual purpose." How strange that she'd never thought of that before.

Of course Blysdale could be here to investigate smuggling in the area as well as to discover what happened to his friends. He could very well think the two were tied together.

Dear God! That was all she needed. Now, on top of her determination to get the evidence she needed to clear Hal, she'd have to strive to protect her reckless brother Josh from his former commanding officer as well!

For just an instant, Kate felt fear run along her nerves. What if she wasn't equal to all these tasks? What if she failed to protect her family? There was no one else to do it.

Even if her late husband, the Earl of Rushmore, were yet alive, there'd still be no one else. Lionel Halsted had never been a forceful person—and he'd been a totally self-absorbed one as well. Lionel Alphonse Halsted, Earl of Rushmore, had definitely not been the sort of man she needed now.

Suddenly, an image of the sardonic face of her unwelcome houseguest flashed through Kate's mind. Yes, she admitted grimly, Blysdale was exactly the sort of man she needed now. Strong, intelligent, and . . . deadly. And quite possibly on the other side of this matter from her.

She found herself taking a deep breath at that admission. But why not admit it? It was the truth. The man certainly exuded an aura of danger at present, but then Blysdale had always been thought a dangerous man. The reputation for being so that he'd brought home from the Peninsular War approached the point of legend. Official dispatches had constantly sent proof of it, reporting one daring deed after another. It was too bad that instead of a possible solution, he was an additional problem.

"Kate!"

"Oh, sorry. I was thinking." She turned to the innkeeper. "You could be right, Seth. Lord Blysdale just might be here because of the smuggling in the area. Partly, anyway."

"That could make things difficult."

Kate knew that was an understatement. Linden owed the fine quality of his cellar to smuggling runs. If Blysdale *had* come to spy out the area's "gentlemen," as smugglers were called, he would find more than a little opposition to his investigations.

Kate sighed. "Do you know if he has brought additional men here to help him?" she asked. "At Cliffside, there are only he, his manservant, his coachman, and two grooms."

"There are two more of his men here," Linden offered. "They came with his baggage coach."

"What are they like?"

Linden considered, stroking his chin for a long moment. Kate needed to be given accurate impressions in this endeavor. "They look like soldiers turned clerks."

"Why do you think that?"

"They have something of the military about them. The way they stand. The way they walk. Ask for things."

"That would make sense," Kate mused aloud. "Soldiers home now that the war is over are having a hard time finding work. It stands to reason that any who applied to their former commanding officer might very well end up in his employ."

"Aye," Seth admitted. "But what do they *do* for Blysdale? Ask a lot of questions is all, as far as I can tell."

Kate let go a sigh. "Yes. This isn't a place that can do with a great deal of questioning just now, either. Not with me holding up coaches, and Josh"—she grinned—"and *others* of us smuggling."

"So what are we to do?" Seth sounded frustrated.

Kate's face was serious in the golden light of the candles. "I think we shall have to find out what questions the two men here at the inn are asking, for a start."

"Aye," Seth agreed, "I think you can leave that to me, your ladyship."

Kate smiled at her friend and affection welled up in her. What had she ever done to be so blessed? Never could she have accomplished any of this alone.

"You know, Kate, I hear a bit while tending to the men who come to the bar here. Suppose I just make it a point to spend more time serving there. A little replenishing of drinks that I seem to forget to charge for, and tongues should loosen up a bit." He smiled a tight smile. "Remember too, there are only so many of us living hereabouts. Only so many men to ask questions of, don't you know? If I keep my ears open, we should soon know what the ex-soldiers are after."

"That would be wonderful, Seth." Kate rose and offered him her hand, shaking his like a man when he took it. "Thank you. I truly don't know what I would do without you." Tears glittered in her eyes for an instant.

Seth saw them and crushed her in a quick hug. "Knowing you, Kate, you'd have found a way. You always do." Quickly he stepped back and ran up the stairs to the outside door, opened it, and looked out. "All clear. Time for you to go." He ducked out to get her horse for her.

Kate ran lightly up the steps after the innkeeper. Outside, she took her reins from him and waited for him to help her mount.

"Kate,"—Seth grabbed her hand to stay her—"be careful."

"There's nothing to harm me on the way back to the manor."

"That's not what I meant, Kate."

She regarded him steadily. There was so much she had to be careful about, but she knew exactly what he meant. Seth would never forgive himself if she came to grief because he had let her know a coach was on its way from London and she was caught holding it up. "I'll be careful, Seth. I promise."

He was still worried, but he had to be content with that. Tossing her into the saddle, he watched as she rode away. "God keep you, Kate," he murmured.

Then he made it a prayer.

Chapter Six

Kate thought she'd arrived home safely and without being noticed. She'd just begun to release the breath she was holding when the slender shadow in the darkness beside the door reached out and took her arm.

"Careful, Lady Katherine," Blysdale's low voice cautioned. "Someone has left their basket of gardening tools just here on the step."

Kate stifled the cry that had welled up in her throat and managed instead a choked, "Thank you. You have saved me a possible fall."

Blast the man! Did he have to be everywhere? Stepping around the basket of gardening tools, she tried to pull away from him.

His grip on her arm tightened a little. He drew her to him.

His head bent to hers. His lips inches from her own, he demanded, "Just where have you been, Lady Katherine?"

She pulled her head back so their faces were not so close and said, "I fail to see that that is any of your business, sir." To her chagrin, the breathlessness he was causing was evident in her voice.

"I fear that, since your brother seems to be absent, I must make it my business."

Kate controlled herself to keep from appearing startled at the news that Josh wasn't at home. The idiot could only have gone smuggling! How dare he take that chance with Blysdale in the house? Making her voice calm she asked, "Surely you aren't under the impression that Josh would care that I have gone for a ride and am coming in late?"

"As you are his sister, and *supposed* to be a lady in more than just your title, I would naturally assume he would be concerned, yes."

Her breath caught in a sharp, angry gasp. "You are insulting, sir."

"So I've been told."

"My whereabouts are none of your affair, Lord Blysdale. I am quite able to look after myself, and feel no need of your interest!"

"Interest." His gaze traveled her face with slow deliberation, studying every detail—the winged brows, the perfect skin—and lingered on her soft, red lips. "Hmmm. Yes. The word is appropriate, Katherine. You do interest me. You most definitely do interest me."

Kate brushed past him and entered the house. She was careful to maintain the cool dignity with which she had passed him for as long as she thought he could see her. As soon as she was certain that she was out of his sight and that he hadn't followed her, she broke into a run.

When she reached her rooms, she slammed the door and shot the bolt as if locking him out of her room could keep him out of her mind. Not that he'd physically followed her, of course. It was simply that the man haunted her mind.

Throwing herself down on the bench in front of her powder table, she yanked off the stylish shako that was her riding hat and began pulling the pins out of her hair, muttering, "Of all the insufferable things he might have said! *Interest* him. Interest him, indeed. And I suppose that I'm to be pleased that I 'interest' him?"

Kate stared at her reflection. Big green eyes stared back,

and she could see her irritation in them . . . and something more. Behind the irritation there was still that breathless anticipation there, too, as if she'd been waiting for . . . "For what?" she demanded angrily. "Surely you didn't think he was going to kiss you when he lowered his head to yours? Surely you didn't *want* him to!"

She looked away from her reflected accusing eyes. A kiss. Had she thought he was going to kiss her? Or had she, just for an instant, *hoped* he might?

She made a rude sound of denial and carefully avoided looking into her mirror. Finally, her sense of fair play got the best of her and she turned back to it. She regarded her reflection for a long minute. Then her eyes narrowed as she considered the question with her habitual honesty. Reluctantly she admitted, "Yes. Perhaps you did want him to kiss you. He's arrogant and annoying, but when he locks his gaze on your mouth, Kate Clifton Halsted, you feel a tingle all the way down to your toes."

She saw herself blush and laughed. "Yes. And you're eaten out with curiosity about it, too. Wouldn't you just love to see how it feels to be kissed by the notorious Beelzebub Blysdale!"

Again she felt that strange electric current run through her from her lips down to her toes, and she shivered. It had been stronger this time. Much stronger.

"Oh, my," she told her reflection, softly. "Oh, my."

Then she laughed again, picked up her silver-backed hairbrush, and began to draw it through her hair. After a while, the slow strokes calmed her. She held firmly to the calm and strove to think rationally. Rational thought was a must in her present position.

Blysdale was definitely a different sort of man than those she was accustomed to, and he was definitely proving to be a problem. The very fact that he'd told her he was looking out for her in her brother's absence meant that Blysdale was aware that Josh was gone. And *she* knew that if Josh were gone, then he and Gordon Mallory were making a smuggling run to France. Blysdale mustn't be allowed to discover that. "Dear Lord, no," she was startled into exclaiming. Her head snapped up as she realized her brother's danger.

There was nothing else to do, and no one else to do it. She must take action. In spite of the late hour, she must go back downstairs and do her very best to try to distract Blysdale.

Quickly changing out of her riding habit, Kate chose a dress she could don without assistance. She didn't want to summon her abigail; it was late and Dresden needed her rest.

The simple blue silk dress she'd picked had a drawstring that tied under the bust to adjust it to fit, and she could manage that without help. Her only concern was that it was light and had a tendency to cling to her figure as she walked. Perhaps it was a little provocative?

For just a minute, she wondered if she wanted to entertain a strange man in quite such a gown when her eldest brother was not in the house. Then suddenly she laughed and said aloud, "Perhaps, idiot Kate, it is exactly the thing you *should* wear to distract Colonel Blysdale. If he's distracted enough by your running around in this revealing gown, then he won't be overly curious about where Josh has gone! Besides," she added more practically, "it's the only suitable thing you can get into without help from Dresden."

When she found that she couldn't wear a chemise under the silk gown, she almost gave up her plan to go downstairs. Then she thought of Josh coming in smelling of salt air and seawater and being accosted by the ever-watchful Blysdale. She couldn't let that happen.

She pulled the gown on, then hurried back to the dressing table to search through her ribbons for one to match it. She'd never be able to do anything more than tie her hair back at the nape of her neck, not without Dresden's expert assistance. So, finding a blue ribbon only slightly darker than the dress, she hastily tied it, found and put on a pair of matching satin slippers, and rushed from her room.

Her only purpose now was to locate and detain Blysdale to keep him from spying on Josh. And she must do it quickly; it was getting very late.

The dimly lit hall seemed to go on forever, but finally she was speeding silently down the wide stairs. Even with all the wall sconces lit with pairs of candles, it was not possible to dispel the gloom of the baronial hall at the foot of the grand staircase. The great hall was a chamber designed to be lit by the flare of large torches and the light of huge fires in the two cavernous fireplaces.

Kate felt a thrill of pride at the thought of the mighty warriors, her ancestors, who had caroused here. Lost momentarily in the memory of tales of them that had been told to her as a child, she nearly tripped when a voice spoke out of the shadows that haunted the great hall.

"You look lovely, Lady Katherine. Are you on your way somewhere . . . else?"

Drat the man! Her heart threatened to hammer itself out of her chest. He'd startled her half out of her skin, and insulted her in addition. He was obviously insinuating that she was on her way to an assignation. Well, this time, she wasn't going to let him annoy her. Much.

Blysdale stepped into the pool of light from one of the wall sconces. Kate could see him now. He was dressed in a looser, more comfortable coat than she'd seen him wear before. It was still the dark fabric she'd already learned that he preferred, though. She stood stock-still, staring at him. Was he dressed more comfortably so that he could go spying? Spying on the smugglers—and on Josh?

Blysdale stared back at the woman in front of him. What was there about this woman that so fascinated him? She was not a breathtaking beauty, yet when his gaze happened to touch her mouth, he was suddenly aware of a need to think about his breathing to accomplish it. It was as if just the sight of her rosy lips took his breath away.

Which was nonsense, of course. Blysdale had kept as his mistresses some of the most seductive and gloriously beautiful women in the world. Not one of them had ever caused this reaction in him.

No doubt this unaccustomed fascination he felt for Kate Halsted was because he had always been granted ready access to the perfumed and willing bodies of the women he kept, but dared not touch Lady Katherine. One could hardly seduce one's hostess, after all. That sort of thing was against the rules.

And why should he want to? She was far too tall. She could almost look him straight in the eye. Through narrowed eyes, he stared harder. Her hair was glorious, of course, spilling down her back to her hips in a thick cloud of deep gold that gleamed here and there with bright highlights at every change in the light around her.

Her eyes were lovely, too. Emerald green now in the dim light from the candles in the wall sconce, though they'd been brighter green in the sunlight in which he'd first seen them. But it wasn't the color of her eyes that held him, it was the intelligence he saw in them.

Bright and eager, the spirit of an extraordinary woman lurked in their depths. Rarely had he seen such intelligence in a woman's eyes. And he was more than a little intrigued, too, by the wariness he saw in hers.

What was the blasted wench afraid of? No. That wasn't the right question. What was she *guarding*? He decided it was high time he found out.

Blysdale put out his hand, politely offering to help her down the last two steps of the grand staircase. His eyes smiled. He didn't know of a woman who needed the courtly gesture less than Kate Halsted did. Nevertheless, as etiquette demanded, she accepted it.

Kate braced herself for the electricity she knew would leap between them when they touched. As a result, she had the perverse satisfaction of seeing Chalfont Blysdale give a slight start when they did. It gave her even greater pleasure to hear his sharp intake of breath. It was worth the bother of changing into proper—well, almost proper—clothes and coming down to entertain him.

She was smiling as she glided down the two steps to stand beside him. She pretended she had felt nothing. Her eyes mocked him as she invited, "I couldn't sleep and came down for a book. Would you care to accompany me to the library, my lord?"

Blysdale offered his arm and they strolled toward the east wing. In the three-story-tall library that was a large part of Cliffside's fame, three of the night-duty footmen scurried around the vast room lighting scores of candles for them. Tables of fine, well-polished mahogany, their surfaces covered with stacks of books and open maps, stood scattered here and there in the huge room, and the footmen hastened to light all the many-branched candelabra that sat on them, too. Even so, minutes passed before there was sufficient illumination to appreciate the collection of books amassed by generations of Kate's family. A king's ransom stood on those shelves.

"Magnificent."

Kate smiled at him then, a genuine smile. The first he had had from her. "It is, rather, isn't it? I missed it dreadfully while I was married and away."

"Of course you did." Blysdale was looking around at the shelves and shelves of leather-bound volumes that soared from floor to lofty ceiling. He smiled at Kate. "I don't think this would be an easy place to leave."

Kate looked at him quickly. His smile was a real one, too. He was younger when he smiled, and this smile went to his eyes. Could it be that Blysdale shared her love of books? She found that strange in a man who was so renowned as a warrior. Strange, and somehow . . . endearing. She was surprised to find herself offering, "It's best in the daytime." She walked over to the wall and touched a tall window's closed velvet drapery. "With these opened, the room is full of light and you can actually see all the books."

Blysdale looked around at the six windows spaced at regular intervals between the shelves. Their tops were lost in the gloom near the vaulted ceiling. "It's a room to envy."

"Yes." Her glance shot his way. "Yes, it is, isn't it?" She cocked her head, suddenly wanting to know, and asked him, "Do you like to read?"

Blysdale's response was immediate. He said simply, "Very

much." Then he looked back at Kate and added truthfully, "More than almost anything."

Kate forgot her weighty responsibilities and the danger he was to them. Instantly, she was lost in the pleasure of finding someone with whom she could talk books.

Blysdale was as delighted as she was. He had always read, but seldom found anyone with whom he could talk over what he had enjoyed. He gave one last, long, lingering look at the way the soft blue silk of her gown clung to Kate's firm, high breasts, and surrendered instead to the pleasure of the written word.

They spent most of the rest of the night sharing remembrances from their favorite books with each other.

As dawn neared, an exhausted Josh came home from his smuggling run and was told where they were. He looked into the candle-lit library and found his Colonel and his sister seated next to each other on a settee in one of the groups of comfortable furniture spaced throughout the huge chamber.

The bright and the dark head were bent close together over a large book. Shaking his own head at the thought that anything that interesting could be found on the pages of a musty old tome, Josh yawned mightily and took himself off to bed.

Chapter Seven

"Sweet Heaven!" Kate flung the covers off and leapt out of bed. One glance at the sunlit window and she knew she had badly overslept. "I'm late." And today was the day she was to supervise the draining of that large pasture!

She ran to her dressing room barefoot, thankful for the thick Oriental carpet covering the cold stone of the old castle floors. She'd flung open the door of one of her wardrobes and was tearing out and pulling on one of her older riding habits when Dresden walked in smiling.

"Here's your chocolate, dear."

Kate spun to look at her. "Oh, Dresden. Why did you let me oversleep? It must be almost nine o'clock!"

"It's only eight, dear. The maid came in to open your draperies, and said you slept right through her doing it." Dresden went to the bed and piled the pillows against the headboard, then the abigail smiled and held the chocolate out to Kate. "When she told me that, I hadn't the heart to wake you. You needed sleep and I wanted you to have it. Now come put those bare feet back under the covers and drink your chocolate while I get your clothes for you."

Dresden's mothering concern kept Kate from showing her

she was upset. Kate was aware that Dresden knew she had to get her mistress up and dressed in time to oversee the workings of the estate, and most mornings she did. She was also well aware that Dresden disapproved of Kate working so hard. Dresden felt that the master of Cliffside should do those tasks—or hire a competent steward to do so. The old abigail didn't feel it was suitable for a lady to engage in such endeavors, especially Kate, whom she had raised and loved as if she were her own.

Well, neither did Kate feel it was suitable! But that didn't provide an able steward, poof, like a genie out of a bottle. And with the estate in the condition it had fallen into with her father dead and Josh away fighting Napoleon, a more than able steward was needed to put things to rights.

With all her heart, Kate wished it could be as Dresden wanted it. Some days, she'd like nothing better than to be the pampered, spoiled, well-loved ornament that Dresden wished she could be, but it just wasn't in the cards. Somebody had to bring the estate back to its former glory, and unfortunately, that task had fallen to her.

Right now, pressured by the thought of her work crew waiting for her since seven, she wanted to rail at somebody because she couldn't be a languid lady, but that was simply not done. So she held her tongue and instead she told her abigail patiently, "Dresden, I *must* oversee things around the estate, you know that. And you must be responsible for letting me do so. I need your help in this." She put a gentle hand on Dresden's arm. "Is that clear, my dearest friend?"

Dresden sighed. "Yes, my lady." She sighed again. "It's clear."

"Good," Kate said, "Because I need, really need for you to understand." Then she hugged her aging abigail and requested, "Tell them to saddle my mare, please, Dresden."

Blysdale had been searching the area around and including Cliffside since before dawn. He'd finished making a rough map of it, searching as he did so, and found nothing to arouse his suspicions. Not that he needed anything. He was already suspicious as hell. The thing that was frustrating him was that he'd found no place in which a large number of prisoners could be held undetected, and there had to be one. And it had to be nearby.

His suspicions that there was a slaving operation were based more on rumors, hints, and fragments of strange stories than on solid facts. His investigators had run into them in their search for clues that would lead Blysdale to Mathers and Smythe. Even though they hadn't been certain the slavers had anything to do with the disappearance of his two good friends, they had reported everything they heard to his lordship. Even when pressed, they'd been unable to pin anything down enough to make it fact, but Blysdale's instincts had kicked in. Too many disappearances were linked to the tiny seaport of Clifton-on-Tides. And it was in this area that Mathers and Smythe had gone missing.

When he thought of his two absent comrades, Blysdale didn't get that awful hollow feeling he'd gotten when Ashley Stoddard, Mathers's cousin and one of the "Lucky Seven," had been murdered. Because of that, he was certain they were still alive somewhere.

Blysdale knew he had instincts that surpassed those of other men, and he knew why. It was because of his strange, reclusive childhood.

Whenever Bly thought of his childhood, his stomach tightened into a hard knot and his teeth set themselves on edge. And he'd been thinking about it lately. The thoughts had been brought on by the sight of Katherine and the obvious love she had for her three brothers. Even the wry tolerance she had for the recalcitrant Josh was full of deep affection. Just by being, Lady Katherine was bringing much to the fore that Bly habitually kept imprisoned in the darker recesses of his mind. He didn't think he'd thank her for it.

Born to parents who hated each other, he'd been raised in a remote mansion on a bleak moor by servants who'd been forbidden to coddle him. Playmates, even if they'd been available, would have been denied him. Growing up totally alone, to all intents and purposes, the boy Blysdale had turned in on himself at an early age. As a result, his intuition had become more finely honed than that attributed to many women. It had stood him in good stead on many an occasion.

No one, therefore, was going to convince Chalfont Blysdale that Mathers and Smythe were dead. Furthermore, if more proof were needed, alive, they would never let their families and friends suffer the grief that was so much a part of their lives, now, if they could prevent it.

Blysdale had always known that he himself might step off the end of the earth and no one but the scant handful of men he called friends would give a damn, but Smythe, particularly, had a family who were grieving deeply. So, by God, if man could help them, Blysdale vowed to be that man!

Frustration was rising to an unacceptable level now, and Blysdale was not a man who tolerated frustration. It always made him feel as if he were choking to death. Therefore, his temper was rising to the same unacceptable level.

He was on his way back to the manor for a fresh horse and something to eat. His stomach was empty, and hunger had never improved his mood.

Topping a rise as he neared the manor house, he saw a group of workmen in a wide pasture not far from the Channel. Surprised, he saw that the person overseeing the work wasn't his host, as he'd have expected, but Lady Katherine. The sight annoyed him. Where was the oaf that should have been seeing to the business of his estate? What did Josh Clifton mean by letting his sister sit out in the sun doing his bailiff's job—or his *own* job in a bailiff's absence? Bly was finding his host more lacking in merit every day.

Lady Katherine was sitting on a chestnut mare watching a group of men digging drainage trenches. In spite of his disapproval of her being there, Bly had to admit he enjoyed the picture she made—and the way the sight of her seemed to loosen the knot in his stomach.

Something about this woman gave him peace.

Her hair was loose, not even tied back, under a broad-brimmed hat with green ribbons. The ribbons were tied firmly in a businesslike knot under her chin to keep the steady wind off the Channel from sending it flying. Her hair stirred and lifted like something alive in that breeze from the sea, while the sun shot golden glints from the depths of it.

Suddenly, Blysdale wanted to run his fingers through that deep golden wealth to see if he could actually feel the life he saw in it. He wanted to comb through it with his bare hands to count the various colors he knew he'd find in the strands of it.

Hell, he wanted to see it spread out like spun gold across a pillow. His pillow.

Kate gestured, probably explaining what she wanted the men to do next, and the men moved in another direction. Blysdale was too far away to hear what she told them, but he was interested to see that the workers moved speedily to do her bidding. Not having seen many women that men would take orders from, he was impressed.

Blysdale sat his horse in the shadow of a mammoth oak and watched his hostess direct her workers. Little by little he began to relax. The woman fascinated him. When her mount fidgeted, Kate calmed it with a word, and the mare settled down as commanded. Obviously, even her horse was used to work.

Finally, one of her men glanced his way, noticed Bly, and pointed him out to Katherine.

Kate looked over and saw him. With a welcoming wave, she turned her mare and rode toward him.

Blysdale tightened his calves against his horse's sides, and the big black gelding cantered to meet her.

"Good morning, Lady Katherine."

"More like 'good afternoon,'" she answered with droll humor. "I'm afraid our mutual appreciation of the printed word caused me to oversleep."

"Shall I apologize?"

"Please don't." Her smile was open. "I can't remember when I've enjoyed an evening so much."

Her comment startled him. A woman who found the library more enjoyable than the ballroom? The idea surprised him. Her free admission that she had taken pleasure in his company surprised him, too. It was a far cry from the coyness he was accustomed to, and it pleased him immensely. "I'm glad you enjoyed it."

Kate looked as if she felt a sharp disappointment. Had she hoped for more? And if so, what more?

Blysdale saw the disappointment in her eyes and it pricked him. Lady Kate had truly enjoyed their time together in the library and hadn't been afraid to admit it.

It had been a very special evening to him, too. Why, then, was he so damned incapable of telling her so? This further evidence of his inability to admit he enjoyed the company of another human being underscored his conviction that he had none of the graces a woman needed from a male companion. Finally, with a self-deprecating smile, he said, "To be honest, I enjoyed it uncommonly well, too." He smiled with his eyes, as well, this time, and everything was made right. Gesturing toward the workmen he said, "Tell me what you're doing here."

"I'm trying to establish a drainage system for this piece of land." A sweep of her arm defined the area in question. "I think it will make a good hay field if I can get it to drain properly. The soil is good. As it is now, however, it's little more than a bog, and just as useless." She was all business, and Blysdale was intrigued. "I can't even put sheep in here as it stands. They churn it to mud in no time. They destroy every drainage trench simply by grazing. You can imagine what cows would do."

"Actually, I almost can. Must be like moving artillery in the rain." His eyes held mirth.

"You're laughing at me!"

"Yes. I am a little," he admitted. "It just struck me as amusing that you'd think I might know anything about such matters. And it both amazes and amuses me that you *do* know."

"Oh." It was Kate's turn to be surprised. "I expect you to know because you must have estates somewhere."

"True, I seem to have more than my share of them, actually. I have estates both here from my father's family and across the Channel in France from my mother's. But I've been fighting wars for years, and know nothing about running them." He quirked an eyebrow at her, then gave a very Gallic shrug. "It's of no matter. I have stewards to look after my properties for me."

"Huh!"

The unladylike sound endeared her to Blysdale. A bolt of genuine affection for her shot through him. He didn't know how to handle it.

Kate went on, "Josh had a steward while he was away, and look what a mess the man made of Cliffside."

While he wrestled with the unfamiliar emotion, Blysdale said quietly, "Fortunately, my stewards know better than to neglect my interests."

Kate felt like she was going to shiver in spite of the warmth of the sun. Rather at a loss, she chose to turn her feeling into a joke. "Ooooh," she teased, "you make it sound as if it would be dangerous for them to neglect any duties they were performing for you."

Blysdale regarded her levelly. After a long moment he answered quietly, "It would be."

Kate took a long, audible breath and let it out softly. It was definitely time to change the subject. "Well, at least your wife doesn't have to spend her time in the fields supervising, as I do."

"Wife!" Blysdale gave a sharp crack of a laugh. "My God, woman, you think I'd have a wife, do you?"

His attitude startled her. She answered defensively. "The idea is hardly ridiculous, my lord. Most men your age do have them, you know."

"Ah, yes. To assure the title, of course. Well, I fear that my title will just have to revert to the Crown."

Kate was shocked. She opened her mouth to say something, then closed it. Lord Blysdale's marital state was none of her business, after all.

"I've shocked you. My apologies."

Kate offered the hint of a smile to accept.

A heartbeat later, he said, "I am a harsh man, Lady Kate. A difficult man. Gentleness. Compassion. Kindness. Patience. I lack them all. I have been a soldier too long."

She sat her mare and looked at him solemnly. "And yet you are a brave and honorable man. And a loyal friend."

"Those are not the things women need." Blysdale had had enough. His smile was twisted. "Suffice it to say that the stars will fall from the sky before I decide to marry."

Kate could only stare at him. It was sad that such a magnificent man should feel that way. But she didn't speak. There seemed to be nothing else to say.

Silence lengthened between them. This one was not a comfortable silence.

A moment later, he sent his gaze beyond her. "It looks as if your men are ready to begin work again."

Kate smiled sadly as she turned away. "And it seems that it's my turn to ask *you* to forgive *me* for making *you* uncomfortable."

She cantered off before he could reply.

That evening as everyone dressed for dinner, Jennings brought Kate a sealed note. "This just came for you, my lady. It was delivered by a rather grubby urchin from the village. One of Linden's nephews, I believe."

Kate turned from her mirror. "You sent him to the kitchen for something to eat, of course."

He smiled at her. "Of course, my lady. Though he appeared well enough fed, I imagine Cook's apple tarts will meet with his approval."

"I'm sure they will. They always meet with mine. Have him wait until I see if I want to send a reply, please."

"As you wish, Countess."

"Thank you, Jennings."

The butler bowed and left the room.

Dresden finished Kate's hair and went to the wardrobes in the next room to select a dress for her. Stopping just out of sight, she watched to see what her young mistress was up to. Dresden had become very concerned about Kate lately.

Quickly Kate opened and perused the note. Scanning it in an instant, she nodded grimly, rose, and went to her writing desk. Scrawling only, "I'll come at ten," she refolded the note as it had been and sealed it with sealing wax into which she pressed a seal bearing her husband's crest.

She was reseated at her dressing table when Dresden, with a little frown on her forehead, came back in carrying a pale green satin slip of a gown with a diaphanous overskirt embroidered with pearls. Kate smiled at her reflection, understanding, now, why her abigail had insisted on twining pearls through her hair. As she pulled on her long white gloves, she said, "Lovely, Dresden. I shall look especially nice tonight, thanks to you."

That was the least she could do for having been cross this morning, and she was happy to see pleasure chase the worry from the older woman's face. Seeing the worry there had made Kate feel like a worm. Dresden didn't deserve to be upset just because Kate was tired and out of sorts. She'd only been trying to get Kate some much-needed rest, after all.

"Thank you, Dresden." Kate rose, hugged her abigail, and scooped her fan and the note off her dressing table.

Dresden rushed forward to open the door for her, and Kate almost ran into her brother as he lurched toward her door on his crutches.

"Hal! What on earth are you doing here? You should be in the drawing room entertaining our guest."

"Don't try to fob me off, Kate. I have a hard enough time catching you alone as it is." He scowled at her. "I saw Linden's messenger. What are you up to now?"

"Why, what do you mean, Hal?"

"Don't play innocent with me, Kate. I mean that I want you to stop putting yourself at risk for my sake." He ran a hand roughly through his thick blond hair. "I won't have it!"

"Keep your voice down!" Kate hissed at him, "Do you want the whole house to hear you?" Then very calmly, she told him, "It really doesn't matter what you would prefer, Hal. I've set out to find proof of your innocence, and I intend to find it. I'm truly sorry that it upsets you, but your name is my family name, too. A woman's sense of honor can be every bit as strong as a man's, and mine is, I promise you, every bit as strong as yours!"

"Kate!" He grabbed for her arm, but she slipped out of his reach and Hal lost his balance and fell into the wall.

"We'll be late for dinner if you don't hurry, Hal," Kate threw back over her shoulder as she rushed away down the candlelit hallway. She could almost hear Hal grit his teeth, but she had more pressing concerns than her injured brother's state of mind. She thanked heaven he was too incapacitated by his splints to do anything foolishly heroic and hurried on her way.

Her diaphanous overskirt flowed behind her on the breeze caused by her hurried steps. Not only was she anxious to avoid further words with her favorite brother, but she had to find Jennings. Before she ran into Blysdale she had to give the butler the note she'd scrawled for the boy to take back to the village.

Repeatedly running into Blysdale had become a real consideration for Kate. The man not only seemed to be everywhere, he also seemed truly to deserve his dreaded reputation of possessing an uncanny ability to know everything that happened around him, no matter where he was.

At the moment, Blysdale was at the end of the hall Kate was walking down. Strangely, even though she was thinking about Blysdale, Kate didn't see him slip out of sight.

Blysdale had seen Kate quarrel with her brother, but hadn't been able to hear their words. As Kate came his way, he turned and ran lightly down the steps, determined to reach the drawing room before his hostess.

Kate was still concerned about her saturnine guest and his seemingly acute power of deduction as she approached the stairway. She certainly didn't want him to use his amazing powers to discover what was happening with her.

The idea of being dragged before a magistrate and sentenced to be hanged for highway robbery held no appeal for her. And she especially abhorred the idea of being dragged there by Lord Blysdale. Obviously, she was finding the man strangely attractive—and she was doing that at a time that couldn't be less convenient!

Once again, in spite of the fact that he shared her appreciation of the works of Shakespeare, Kate most heartily wished Lord Blysdale gone from Cliffside.

Behind her, Dresden drew her head back in the door and closed it softly. The sound of something hitting against the wall had been her dear boy, Hal, and obviously, from the way he was thumping down the hall with his lovely curls falling into his eyes with every firm placement of his crutches, something upsetting had transpired between him and her darling Kate.

Dresden stood wringing her hands in anxiety. Both of them were so dear to her. She'd devoted her whole life to them, starting at thirteen as a junior nursemaid to Kate's mamma so very long ago. She couldn't just stand by and see them in trouble. She knew that that worthless boy Josh wouldn't do anything to make matters improve. So, what could *she* do?

After a few minutes, she gave a decisive nod of her head and walked out of the room. By the time she reached the stairs, she was sure she'd made the right decision. As she walked down them, her steps were firm. So was her resolution. She was going to find Jennings and make him her ally. She desperately needed his help in forming a plan to protect Kate from whatever odd, clandestine affair her precious darling had become embroiled in!

Chapter Eight

Kate had been unable to locate Jennings to give him the note for Linden. She'd had to take it to the boy in the kitchen herself. As a result, when she rushed into the drawing room even Hal had beat her there. She was late, late, late to await the call to dinner and Blysdale was, of course, present. Which proved conclusively that wishing did *not* make it so! For Kate wished with all her heart that the man who was such a distraction to her would go away.

Blysdale was attired in black from head to toe, his long, muscular legs encased in the Beau Brummell–set fashion called trousers. The effect was to make him seem even taller . . . and more sinister than ever. Kate's breath caught when she saw him, and he smiled a crooked smile when he saw her rush into the room with her sea-mist green skirts swirling around her from her haste. In a quiet, drawling voice he said, "Ah. The Botticelli Venus, arriving in a froth of sea foam."

Kate realized then that Dresden had styled her hair, hanging almost free and entwined with pearls, in a manner slightly reminiscent of that famous painting, and smiled at Blysdale's reference. The froth that she felt she was in had nothing to do with the sea, however. She was anxious to get to the village to learn what it was that Linden wanted.

First, though, she had to play gracious hostess at Josh's dinner table. She mentally reiterated her displeasure at having had Blysdale foisted on her as a houseguest, in spite of the attraction she felt to the saturnine man. If *he* hadn't been here at Cliffside, she would have been able to forgo her duties tonight as hostess and get on the road!

Her thoughts were shattered by a bray of laughter. Unfortunately her brother had overheard Blysdale's quiet comment about Botticelli's masterpiece. From across the room in his position in front of the fireplace, Josh said, "Don't remember that the Venus on the Half Shell had any clothes on, Colonel."

Blysdale went rigid with displeasure. He silenced his host's merriment with a glance and a cold, "I'm surprised that you remember Botticelli at all, Clifton."

At the same time, Hal protested, "For God's sake! Don't embarrass our sister, Josh."

Blysdale bowed to the quiet brother before he turned back to his former subordinate. In a bored drawl he asked politely, "I suppose, your lordship, that it would be quite pointless to inquire if you were, perhaps, adopted?"

Josh was struck dumb. He couldn't even think of a reply. Everybody knew he couldn't have inherited his father's title if he were adopted!

Hal laughed behind his hand. Jamie giggled.

Jennings stepped into the doorway to announce dinner just then, and Kate saw the glimmer of amusement in the butler's eyes and knew that he had overheard the exchange that had just taken place.

His lips twitching, Jennings intoned, "Dinner is served, Countess."

With a suppressed sigh of relief, Kate held out her hand for Blysdale's arm and together they led the way into the dining room. Kate had no great hopes for a calm dinner. They had just been treated to an example of Chalfont Blysdale's famous ill temper, and, mercifully, everyone had survived it intact. That was no guarantee that the storm was over, however.

Seated at the head of the dinner table, a thoroughly chastened Josh tried to make up for his obvious *gaucherie*. His cheeks slightly pink, he asked his sister solicitously, "What did you do today, Kate?"

Kate stared at him in astonishment. Never before had Josh taken an interest in anything she did. No matter how hard she worked to restore Cliffside to productivity, he'd remained oblivious to her efforts. She regarded him with a sense of amazement and wondered if her mouth was hanging open. Blysdale must really have struck a nerve. Hmmm. And here she hadn't thought her oldest brother had one.

Finally, words came to her. "Why, I spent the morning overseeing the men digging the drainage trenches for that north pasture that I told you might be used for hay if we could get it dry enough."

"Oh?"

Strike while the iron is hot, Kate told herself. Maybe, just maybe, Josh would learn something about his farms. "Yes," she began eagerly, "cows and sheep kept churning the trenches there into useless mud puddles, so I decided to keep them off the pasture and try to grow a crop there instead."

"Sounds like a good idea," Josh said vaguely.

"Thank you." Kate's tone was dry, her enthusiasm fading. Obviously, her brother couldn't care less about what she did with his property, so long as he didn't have to do it.

Blysdale said, "You are most fortunate in having such a well-informed and able sister, Clifton."

"Eh? Oh, yes. Kate's a wonder. Did the same thing for Rushmore at his place too, don't you know."

Blysdale's eyes were stormy as his gaze locked with Kate's.

Kate mentally threw up her hands. She feared her dinner table was rapidly disintegrating into a battlefield.

"No," Blysdale said quietly, a muscle jumping in his jaw, "I hadn't known that any other . . . man had"—he hesitated an instant too long before saying from between clenched teeth—"benefited . . . from your sister's expertise in estate management."

The depth of his anger surprised Blysdale. He realized that he could cheerfully wring Josh Clifton's neck. His temper had flared at learning that the able Lady Kate had been victimized by yet another man who should, instead, have cherished her, and he was having trouble getting it back under his habitual icy control.

Suffering fools gladly had always been beyond him, and both her dead husband and her damned dolt of a brother were fools not to know what a treasure she was. Kate was a woman made for loving, not a blasted workhorse!

He let his gaze run over the creamy flesh of her shoulders and the wealth of silken hair that hung to her hips, barely constrained by its fragile prison of gold netting and pearls. What the hell was the matter with the men in her life? The woman was breathtaking. Couldn't they see? Didn't they care?

Kate regarded Blysdale steadily, holding her breath. Were they going to be treated to another bout of his renowned bad temper? She had the strange feeling that this one, too, might be in her behalf, but she couldn't be certain.

His eyes burned at her like signal fires, but Kate couldn't read them. From the depth of his scowl, she couldn't decide whether Blysdale was defending her or disapproving of her.

Fortunately Josh, determined to reclaim the goodwill he thought he'd lost, distracted the sardonic Blysdale just then. With purposeful good cheer, he occupied his former Colonel's attention for the rest of the dinner hour. At its end, Kate was easily able to escape as the cigars and port were brought in for the men.

She hurried to find Jennings and asked him, "Would you please send word to the stables that I need my mare?"

Jennings looked, for an instant, as if he were going to protest her riding out alone so late.

Kate put a hand on his sleeve and said, "Please, Jennings."

Knowing it was useless to attempt to dissuade her, the

old retainer said simply, "Will that be all, my lady? No groom to accompany you?"

"Yes, thank you. Only my mount. I'll ride alone." Kate regarded him steadily for a moment longer, willing him to understand that she must go, and must go alone. She saw the worry in his eyes, saw that he could hardly hold back from voicing his objections—and that he was a little hurt that she refused to confide in him. Then she was gone, running up the great stairs.

She hated it that she'd hurt her old friend, but there was no way she was going to be guilty of involving Jennings in any illegal activity. Not even obliquely. Certainly highway robbery was illegal, but, oh, how she wished she *could* confide in him. Keeping him in the dark was so difficult for her, knowing how worried he was about her.

Rushing into her dressing room, she rang for Dresden. There would be no getting out of this gown without assistance.

Dresden bustled in with a smile, and Kate was careful to return it. "I shall want a riding habit, Dresden."

"A riding habit! But Lady Kate—"

Kate went on as if Dresden hadn't spoken. "Dinner was heavy, and I'm in need of some exercise after merely sitting on my horse all day supervising the men."

Dresden looked as if she wanted to protest more fully Kate's leaving the castle at such a late hour, but she held her tongue.

"I shan't ride for long, Dresden. I know that would worry you." She saw the relief in the older woman's eyes, and that distressed her, too. Her voice was warmer as she assured her, "I'll be fine. Truly."

"I'll try not to worry then, my lady."

As Kate watched in the mirror, Dresden placed her hat on her head to hold her heavy hair against the rigors of riding. Then she handed her employer her gloves and riding crop. Her lips tightened for an instant, as if she, like Jennings, struggled to hold back words, then she blurted, "Be careful, my lady."

The comment stopped Kate in her tracks. She turned and looked back at her abigail. Dresden really *was* so dear to her. Impulsively, she reached out and gave her a quick hug.

It wasn't until she was running down the back servants' stairs that she wondered what Dresden knew that had prompted her last remark.

Kate arrived at the inn a few minutes before the appointed time. Making certain no one was in the area, she ghosted into the enclosed backyard of the inn and put her horse out of sight in the lean-to there. Just as stealthily, she opened the door to the basement of the inn and entered. Once inside, Kate breathed a sigh of relief.

The candles on the table that Linden had brought down to the basement for her use were already lighted, and the whole place was swept clean. Kate smiled at his consideration. As if she weren't already immeasurably grateful that he was helping her by meeting her clandestinely here. She could hardly confer with him in his public room at any time, nor, indeed, could she even appear in the village in daylight without attracting notice. Everyone in the area took an avid interest in the comings and goings of the family from the manor.

As she sat down at the table, Kate glanced at the far wall of the cellar. Proof of Seth Linden's high regard for and trust in her was there. Brandy kegs and racks of expensive wines clearly proclaimed his involvement with the sometimes ruthless men know as the "gentlemen." If they should learn of and object to her coming here to his cellar, it could harm Linden's trade with them, and therefore his business. The fact that her own brother frequently went to sea with the smugglers wouldn't sway them one bit.

Linden came down the stairs carefully balancing a tray. "Your ladyship," he greeted∙her as he placed the tray on the table. The wonderful fragrance of brewing tea wafted from the teapot.

"You have news?" Kate asked him.

"Aye. Not as much as I wish I had, but news. It's about

those two ex-soldiers who've been snooping around. I've
made sure that I served those two men who came with Lord
Blysdale myself, every chance I've had. Between serving
'em dinner and getting them their drinks, I've learned they're
looking really hard into the shipping"—he raised his eyebrows comically at her—"such as it is, hereabouts."

He glanced pointedly at his wine racks, then shook his
head in bewilderment. "They've asked some mighty pecu-
liar questions, though." Linden was clearly stumped.

Kate's heart tightened. "Then you think that they *are* spying on the smuggling that's going on here?" *Oh, dear God,
why did Josh have to chase after adventure by smuggling!*

Linden scratched his head. "That's the problem, Kate. I
get the feeling that it's not really the brandy and such that
interests them. There's something else, but blast me, I just
can't figure out what. They were pretty careful of what they
said when they thought there was a chance that I might be
listening.

"When they thought I wasn't because I was whistling
through my teeth while I polished glasses at the bar, they
talked about reporting straight to Lord Blysdale tomorrow
evening before supper, though. They're waiting for some information they're gonna get from London. And I have to tell
ya that I think that's when the cat will come out of the bag."

"Where are they going to report to him? Do you know?"

Seth Linden stirred uneasily in his chair. "Aye, and it's
going to be up to you to overhear 'em, Lady Kate."

"Up to me?" She shot him a startled glance.

"Aye. I can't, because the meeting's set to take place at
Cliffside at the old castle tower."

"Ah. That makes sense. The tower is about the only place
I can think of that they might meet secretly. But how will
we learn what they have to say?"

"Kate, be sensible. You'll just have to spy on Lord Blysdale."

Kate rode home in an upset at the thought of spying. Things
didn't get any better for her when she arrived back at Cliff-

side Manor, either. She hadn't even crossed the threshold before Jennings handed her a sealed note from Seth's older brother, who had an inn closer to London where the road to the sea turned off the turnpike. He was the one who gathered most of the information on coach movements in her direction. In addition to gathering and passing on that information, he was the man who, by virtue of having fathered a large family of them, was in charge of the boys who ran the messages to Kate.

Standing there in the open doorway, she broke the seal and read the brief note. *A coach is headed your way. This one with two men in it. Be very careful.*

Kate could feel her shoulders start to sag. Refusing to let them, she lifted her chin, thanked Jennings, and hurried up to her rooms.

As she sped down the hall, she wished with all her heart that this coach would be the last she would have to stop. That this coach would be the one to hold the proof she sought. That she could intercept a shipment of stolen jewels and force the man carrying them to identify the real thief. Then they could clear her brother Hal's name and have this whole unlovely business over with.

She felt as if she were, like Atlas, balancing the weight of the world. Keeping the frequency of her night forays from Hal—and keeping him from dashing out, broken leg and all, to spare her having to perpetrate the holdups—was getting more and more difficult. Because of that, she was glad that Jennings had given her the message at the door. That had saved her at least one quarrel with her favorite brother.

Her problem with Hal not wanting her to go at all, and the additional one of keeping her comings and goings hidden from everyone else in the manor had been trouble enough. Now, with the newly added burden of protecting Josh and his stupid smuggling activities from Blysdale and his men, Kate felt she was getting too close to the end of her rope.

Struggling out of her riding habit and into the male attire hidden in the back of her clothes press took an effort that surprised Kate. It also told her she was overtired. As she changed, she prayed for the strength to accomplish her goals.

When she opened the castle wall at the bottom of the secret stairway, she stood there in the darkness for a while, just wishing that this could all be over. Wishing she could rest. Then she squared her shoulders and headed for the stables.

It was late enough that all the grooms would be in their beds. She knew she'd be unobserved. The barn smelled of hay and horses and well-kept leather. The only sounds were the soft, even breathing of drowsing horses, an occasional deep, contented sigh, or the sharper breath of a horse blowing dust from its nostrils.

Kate led Star from his stall and carefully blacked out the white marking on his forehead. Then she tacked up and mounted her stallion. Walking him from the barn out into the moonlight, she halted him for a moment and sat still, just admiring the scene before her. The night was so beautiful, so peaceful and calm, with the deep, sweet blue of the moonlit sky and the silvered earth dreaming beneath it.

Suddenly, Kate felt as if she were completely at odds with the peacefulness around her. She felt as if she were going to burst apart at the first loud noise.

If she couldn't have respite from her self-appointed burdens, then she had to have a momentary change. Turning Star, she sought out the winding path that led down to the beach. If she hurried, she could afford to give herself this small pleasure. She could get to the high road that led down to Clifton-on-Tides by riding along the beach, but it was a longer way than riding through the woods. Right now, though, Kate desperately needed to feel the sea wind in her hair.

There was no escaping the fact that she had to go to the high road. She had to find the proof that would free Hal from suspicion, and her only hope was that she might intercept the jewels on that road.

Since her most serious purpose in life had become that

of freeing her beloved brother Hal, she couldn't afford to pass up a chance that she might intercept the jewels. She had no intention of doing so.

There was no question in Kate's mind that she must go there . . . but Kate had already begun to hate that road.

Chapter Nine

Chalfont Blysdale, muffled in a dark cloak, sat at the mid-point of the trail he'd decided the highwayman would have to take to get to the high road if he was, as Blysdale suspected, coming from Cliffside. His own investigations of his friends' disappearances having come to a temporary standstill, Bly was determined to discover the youthful highwayman's identity.

Already he was certain the culprit made a habit of "borrowing" Lady Katherine's big black stallion, and that certainly meant he was a member of her household. From what Bly had observed of the great horse, Star wasn't the kind of animal that made friends with just anybody.

Of course the lad would have to have blacked out the white star on the stallion's forehead, but that was a simple matter. He'd often darkened white markings himself, in his line of work for the Crown.

He'd already decided that the man he sought wasn't one of the grooms. The smooth skin around the highwayman's eyes had bespoken not only youth, but also a life spent mainly indoors. So he'd opted for one of the indoor staff, probably a footman. He hadn't discovered which of the footmen it could be, as none of them he'd seen had green eyes, but then, there were so blasted many of them! Cliffside had an army of servants, and he knew damn well he hadn't seen every one of them.

At any rate, if the highwayman rode tonight, he'd soon know who he was, and with that nagging little question out of his mind, the way would be even clearer to concentrate fully on the disappearance of his friends.

On his way back to Cliffside from his meeting in town with his men, he'd heard that there was a coach headed this way. He'd learned of it gladly, as he was spoiling for trouble. The promised report from London hadn't come and irritation at this lack of information from his men had put Blysdale in a mood as dark as his clothing.

Frustration was again the cause of his bad temper. He hated having to wait longer. His gut was in a knot. He had the urgent feeling that time was running out for his missing friends.

Nothing. Jacobs and Dawson had had nothing to report that had any bearing on the disappearance of Mathers and Smythe. They were good men, his best men. If there had been information available, they'd have gotten it. Whoever was behind all this was clever . . . and damned careful.

Jacobs and Dawson were as frustrated as their Colonel.

Bly's teeth grated together. Dammit! Englishmen didn't simply drop off the face of the earth. Not in England, anyway. Somewhere, someone knew just what had happened to his two friends and, by God, he was going to find the men responsible for their disappearance.

When he did, he'd torture the truth from them if he had to. He could do it. The ancient skill was no longer foreign to him. He'd had the dubious pleasure of learning more than a little about torture when he'd been a captive of the French. In a good cause—and there was no better cause to Blysdale than recovering his friends—he'd not hesitate to use his painfully acquired knowledge. "Let none of life's lessons go to waste," he muttered. And then he smiled.

The smile was savage.

His favorite horse shifted restlessly under him. Lucifer was as tired of waiting as·his rider was becoming. "All right, old boy," Blysdale murmured, "we'll call it a day." He started toward Cliffside, mildly disappointed. It looked as if his prey wasn't going to . . .

"Stand and deliver!" The cry was borne to him on the night wind from far away. Aha! His young highwayman was at it again!

The savage smile became a reckless grin. "Let's see if we can get there in time to catch the lad, Lucifer." He touched his spur lightly to his horse's side, and was off.

Kate had the travelers, two well-dressed men, standing outside the coach, and was searching it with one hand while keeping her eyes, and her pistol, on her victims. She found nothing. Nothing obvious, nor any secret compartments— and Kate, having gone to the foremost carriage makers in London to learn of all the ways secret compartments could be built into coaches, would have found it had there been one.

Disappointment weighed heavily on her as she exited the coach. Was she never going to find the proof she needed to clear Hal's name? Stepping down, she ordered in her gruffest voice, "Remove your coats, please, gentlemen."

She'd ride away with the men's garments and search them in a safer place. Their coats would be the first things she'd ever stolen, but she saw that these two were not men she could count on to stand quietly while she rifled their pockets.

The two men exchanged glances. Slowly they struggled out of their fashionably tight jackets. Then, suddenly, the man nearest Kate lashed out with his coat, entangling her hand that held the gun. The second man leapt forward and pinned her arms to her sides.

"Now then! Let's see who you are!" The first man reached for her mask.

Raw fear flashed through Kate like lightning! She tried to yank her arms free, but the man holding them was too strong for her. In a flash her mind filled with an awful vision of her body, weighted with iron chains, twisting in the wind as it hung from a gibbet. Her heart quailed. Nevertheless, she lifted her chin and held her head high.

Tears she refused to let come threatened. Who would take care of her brothers now? Who would raise Jamie?

"Stand and deliver!" The two men spun around at this new threat. A man muffled in a dark cloak sat astride a tall black horse just beyond the dim circle of light cast by the side carriage lamp. Brass fittings gleamed from the pistol in his fist.

"What the hell?" one of the men exclaimed. His companion caught him by the arm to keep him from advancing on this second menace. With the other hand he kept his grip on Kate.

"Hands up, both of you!"

The men from the coach obeyed, cursing, and Kate was free. Free! She acted swiftly. Moving stealthily back away from the scene, she scrambled up on Star. Her legs were weak with a combination of fear and relief but she made it into the saddle. She turned him quietly. Instantly, they galloped away.

When the sound of her horse's hooves had faded, the man who had interrupted her capture pulled his cloak down from where it had hidden his face and demanded, "What the devil are you two doing here?"

Kate fled through the woods as if all the fiends of hell were in pursuit. Star caught her sense of urgency and stretched full out. Trees were indistinct shapes that whipped past, their huge trunks no more than a blur, their branches bludgeons that missed her only because Star swerved to save her.

Hanged! Dear God! She would have been hanged if that highwayman hadn't come along. She would have been identified! Her family would have been shamed. Shamed for centuries!

Her mind gibbered thanks to a Merciful God for bring-

ing the highwayman just then. Just when she needed him
more than she had ever needed another human being in her
entire life. Her head spinning with relief, her heart full of
gratitude, and her face streaked with tears, she spoke aloud
toward the heavens, "Thank you. Oh, thank you!"

Then she pulled her mighty stallion to a halt and dismounted. Clinging weakly to his muscular neck, Lady
Katherine Elizabeth Clifton Halsted, Countess of Rushmore, bent over and lost her supper.

"Blysdale!" Kate's victims were stunned.

"The same," the man on the horse acknowledged dryly.

"Dammit, Bly. When did you take up robbing innocent
travelers?"

"I haven't, Stone," Blysdale told his dark-haired giant
of a friend, "but I couldn't let you harm the lad."

"Why the devil not, Bly?" The blond man was trucu-
lent as he pulled his coat back on. "He's a blasted highway robber. Holds up innocent travelers, like Stone said."

"There is very little about either one of you that would
qualify you for the description 'innocent,' MacLain."

Stone was impatient for an answer. "I say, Bly. Why
didn't you let us turn that young blighter in to the author-
ities?"

"I owe him."

"How?"

"He saved my life."

"He did?" MacLain was astonished. "That stripling?
How?"

"I was dying of boredom on the last leg of my journey
here, and he held up my coach. He saved me from dying
of *ennui.*"

Stone snorted while MacLain gaped.

Stone whispered, "It means boredom, dolt," and ducked
a punch from MacLain.

"Come on," Blysdale invited. "There's an excellent inn
nearby. I'll buy you supper and you can tell me why you're
here."

• • •

Back at the Cliffside stables, Kate shook uncontrollably as she removed the blacking from Star's forehead. It had been such a near thing. Her voice quivered as she told the great horse, "Oh, Star. I was so afraid. I was so afraid. All my thoughts were in chaos. What would my family do without me? And how could they bear the shame my being hanged would have brought down on them?"

Star nickered softly and pushed at her with his velvet muzzle. She hugged his neck. "I even w-worried about how *you* would g-get home. *If* you would get home." She leaned her head against his. "I was frantic, so frantic, at the thought of losing you. I . . ."

She stopped talking and shivered harder as she recalled the events just past. Finally, she put the soft cloth she'd used on Star's forehead in her pocket to hide it from prying eyes and went out into the night to the house.

At the inn, in the smoke-filled public room, Blysdale watched as his guests sprawled back in their chairs and lit the clay pipes the innkeeper brought them. Soon their smoke joined the cloud hanging just below the ceiling of the white-walled room.

"Good tobacco," Stone said. "Why don't you blow a cloud with us, Bly?"

"I never form habits that might someday dictate to me."

MacLain rubbed his lean middle with one hand while he removed the pipe from his mouth with the other. "Good food, too. Thanks, Bly."

"You're welcome." He leaned back in his own chair and let his gaze weigh them. "And you may be in my way. Why are you here?"

His friends both sat forward as one man, glaring. Stone growled, "Blast you, Blysdale, you don't own all England. MacLain and I can go wherever we care to!"

"Perhaps." Blysdale stared at him until he looked away. Stone cursed under his breath.

MacLain's jaw tightened. "By Jove, you're a high-handed bastard, Blysdale."

"There's a great deal at stake."

"What?" Stone demanded eagerly. "Have you a lead on what happened to Mathers and poor old Smythe?"

Narrow-eyed, Bly shot him a furious look. "Keep your voice down."

"Sorry."

"But have you?" MacLain was eager, too.

"Yes. But after I tell you, I want you to go to Taskford and wait there until I have need of you. Is that agreed?"

They fought it an instant, but under his cold-eyed regard finally capitulated. "Agreed," they answered in unison.

"Too many strangers might alert the man I'm after, so I thank you."

Stone grumbled, "Couldn't explain that before you glared us down, though, could you?"

Blysdale acknowledged his remark with, "No. That's not my way," and leaned toward them. He already knew there was no one within hearing distance. He'd stationed his own two men at the only table that was even close. Nevertheless, his voice was scarcely above a whisper when he told them about the slavers and what he'd been trying to discover.

Stone and MacLain hung on his every word.

The next day just before noon, a note arrived at the castle. Jennings presented it to Kate at the table.

She stared at the folded piece of foolscap for a long time before she opened it with trembling fingers, praying it wasn't news of another coach heading their way. She still wasn't over the fright she'd gotten. Maybe she never would be. The nagging fear that she might not ever get over it sickened her. For if there were a coach on the way down from London, she would have to go, regardless of her fear. She had no choice.

With a sigh of relief, she read: *B's men will be there*

sometime late this afternoon. Be ready to spy on him. S.
She frowned. There was that awful word, *spy,* again.

Spy! There were few things considered more despicable than spying. Why, even the brave, selfless men who'd saved countless British soldiers' lives by spying on the French during the Peninsular War were looked down on! Dreadfully looked down on. And now here was Seth Linden, her friend practically since birth, telling her *she* had to spy against Chalfont Blysdale. And, as if simply spying on any man wasn't bad enough in itself, this one was her houseguest on top of it! The whole idea was repulsive to her.

Gordon Mallory breezed in just as Kate pocketed the note. His entrance gave her the perfect excuse to leave the room by the opposite door. How she wished he would stay out of Cliffside. Resentment of his Josh-granted freedom to enter her home without being announced sped her steps.

"I say, Katherine," he called to her retreating form. "Where the devil are you off to?"

"To any place where men remember not to use such improper language around ladies!"

When Kate was gone, Mallory smiled a cold smile. One more slight delivered by the beautiful Kate. One more insult to make her pay for. Getting even was going to be very satisfying.

Upstairs in her dressing room, Kate kicked at the pile of dresses heaped at her feet on the pale-toned Oriental carpet. "Spy on Lord Blysdale!"

She'd come up to her rooms to obey Seth's note and get ready, but nothing she owned had been ordered from the *modiste* with the express intention of being worn to spy on anyone! Kate had already pulled half of the gowns from one of her wardrobes without finding anything even remotely suitable. That and seeing Gordon Mallory had her out of sorts and grumbling, "Spying is going to feel like a dreadful thing to do."

Though she might think the selfless men who'd saved

countless British soldiers' lives by spying on the French should be treated like heroes, everybody else seemed to scorn them. Try as she might when she was living in London to point out the wisdom of knowing the enemy's intention in advance, she'd never convinced anyone that their English spies were unsung heroes. Sometimes she wondered if the majority of her class ever used their heads for anything more than keeping their ears apart.

Scowling, she went to a second armoire and pulled out more dresses. "And what the devil do you wear to spy on someone?" Soon she had another pile of jewel colors and fabulous fabrics at her feet. Dresden was going to have a fit at the mess she'd made!

Frustrated, she brought out yet another dress, a deep green gown of softest wool. The garment was a rather full skirted gown, but at least it would be *quiet*.

The silks and satins at her feet whispered and hissed like snakes when she stirred them. And the taffetas! Lord, she might just as well have a herald to announce her approach if she decided to go about her onerous task in one of them. They would obviously never do if she were expected to creep about eavesdropping on the sardonic—and unfortunately, extremely alert—Lord Blysdale.

Right now she was wearing a simple muslin day gown, and thought it quite comfortable, and though she had never before thought of her apparel in just that light, it was *quiet enough,* as well. She sighed. The problem with her muslins, though, was that they were all too light in color. One could hardly lurk in dark corners in a gown as bright as sunshine.

If only she'd liked some of the darker fabrics many of her friends wore, she'd have been all set. She didn't, however, like the rich paisleys and dark calicos that were in fashion. And the plaids! If they weren't someone's clan tartan, she abhorred them. So none of those choices were even available for this adventure. No, she'd wear the dark green wool gown, and just pray the day didn't become too warm for its long sleeves and high neck.

"At least, it covers a lot of you in a suitably dark shade," she told herself as she held the dress against her and studied the effect in the pier mirror. "And thank the dear Lord," she offered wholeheartedly, "that it buttons down the front!"

Hearing the sound of her shoulder seam splitting as she pulled off the blue-sprigged muslin Dresden had helped her into earlier, she muttered, "Damn." She knew very well that ladies didn't use such language, but cursing made her feel less vulnerable, somehow. And, anyway, wasn't she pretending to be a male when she held up coaches? It was a weak excuse, but it was the only one she had. And she needed excuses—for a new vulnerability had entered her life with her almost-capture last night. She shuddered to remember.

"Thanking your Maker in one breath and cursing in the next. What are you becoming, Katherine?" She was in a tangle, all right. A terrible tangle!

That thought brought quick tears. Kate dashed them away with the back of her hand. No matter. She must be brave and firm. So much depended on her. Indeed, it *all* depended on her.

Everything in life seemed to have depended on her from the day she'd left the loving protection of her doting parents to become the Countess of Rushmore. On the day they'd returned from their honeymoon, Kate had had the management of her young husband's estates handed to her. And a few days later, the responsibility for his querulous parents had been thrust on her, as well.

Widowed, and with her own parents dead in a carriage accident, she'd returned home and found she had to work to try to save her own family—their estates, reputations, and possibly even lives. In seeking respite, she'd stepped from the frying pan into the fire. It looked very much as if instead of a sanctuary, Kate had found a workhouse.

Sometimes she wished . . .

She threw up her head and firmed her jaw. Wishing was for those who could afford the luxury.

Watching her own stormy expression in the pier glass, Kate quietly donned the dark green wool gown. As she shoved each tiny, wool-covered button through its button-hole, she felt as if she were latching herself into a prison.

To be free to perform her onerous mission, Kate sent word that she had a headache and would take her noon meal on a tray in her rooms. Her brothers immediately opted for going to the tavern to eat.

For one breathless moment, Kate was afraid that Blysdale would go, too. Then she would have to get word to Linden that the innkeeper would have to spy on him. There was no way she could be inconspicuous sneaking around at the inn—even in a dark green dress!

Blysdale told Jennings that he would take a tray in the library, however, and Kate breathed a sigh of relief.

She felt an odd little twist in her heart when Jennings told her he'd invited her youngest brother, Jamie, to join him.

When they were both safely ensconced there and being attended by Jennings, Kate was free to go watch for the arrival of Blysdale's informants.

The men she watched for came, finally in the late afternoon. Two soldier-straight men, they'd ridden up from the east side of what was left of the castle, rather than arriving by way of the long front drive to the manor. There was no doubt in Kate's mind that these were the men Linden had told her were working for Blysdale. They had the same military grimness about them.

They avoided the manor house completely, and went instead to the old castle mound with its still-standing square Norman tower that looked out toward the sea. In her youth, Kate had used that tower to escape her brothers when she wanted to be left alone to read.

There was a fairly comfortable room in the bottom of the tower, with a table and several old chairs. Jennings had had the furniture brought when he found out that Kate used the Norman keep as a refuge from her teasing brothers.

Saving the upper tower for warm sunny days, Kate had always had a fire in the lower room's cavernous fireplace on cold or windy days so she could read in a comfort that would have been impossible in the tall, wind-whipped upper tower. It was to this favorite room of her childhood that she saw the men heading.

With a feeling part of annoyance, part of admiration, Kate realized that Blysdale must have spied it out earlier and told his men how to get to it. Clever of him. Once there, they'd be safe from observation, as no one could approach without being seen.

Kate made up her mind in a flash. Blysdale was still in the library—no doubt with Jamie asking him question after question about the army. Perhaps his men weren't so cautious as he. Perhaps they would simply sit and wait for him, not feeling any need to keep watch. If so, Kate would have no problem.

Once Lord Blysdale arrived at their meeting, however, she was certain that not even a mouse would be able to cross the expanse of grass between the manor house and the ancient Norman tower unobserved. If she were to reach a safe place to spy on Blysdale and his men, then she must chance dashing over to the tower now, before the formidable Blysdale arrived.

Gathering her skirts, she ran for as long as she had the cover of the hedges that still grew on the tower mound. When she came to the end of them, she let her skirts fall again and walked calmly over the last open space. This was her home, after all. Who could possibly object if she decided to walk across to the old tower to watch the sea by twilight?

That would be her explanation if she found she needed one.

Kate reached her goal unobserved, sighed a quiet sigh of relief, and stood listening at the entrance to the tower. The two men were in the room at its base, just as she'd expected. She could hear them moving about. Creeping to the doorway, she carefully peeked in and saw they were both busy at the fireplace, their backs to her.

Darting across the open doorway, Kate took up a position behind the heavy door. The stone steps leading up the tower were just opposite her position. She would hide up there around the first turning, then come down to eavesdrop at the door when Blysdale arrived.

If they didn't close the door, she could stay hidden behind it. It seemed a good plan. Thus assured of safe hiding places, Kate settled down to wait for Lord Blysdale to join his men.

Chapter Ten

In the library, Blysdale had finished his luncheon and was trying to deflect Jamie's questions.

"But you *do* you like my sister, don't you?" Jamie was insistent.

A picture flashed through Blysdale's mind. He saw Kate in his bed, her long, creamy limbs tangled in his sheets, his sun-browned hands tangled in her magnificent hair. For an instant he could smell the scent of her—roses and jasmine and the sweet warmth of woman. The vision surprised him. He wasn't prone to such things.

He looked down at Jamie. Suddenly he was uncomfortable. It was a novel experience. He knew what kind of "liking" the boy had in mind, and hated to disappoint him. "Yes," he said finally, "I like Lady Katherine well enough."

"Oh." Jamie was clearly disappointed in spite of Blysdale's effort. He took a deep breath and said, "My French tutor says that *je t'aime assez bien* is just about like not caring for somebody at all. *Assez bien* means 'well enough' in French, you know."

"Yes, I know." Blysdale spoke French as well as he spoke

English. His mother had been a French noblewoman, after all.

He finished his port rather more quickly than was his habit. Knowing his men were probably here at Cliffside by now was making him impatient. He needed to go to meet them.

He also needed to leave this eager little boy who longed so desperately for more of a family than his inattentive brothers represented. Needed to get away before he had to admit that he was not fit to be part of the sort of family the boy longed for.

Blysdale would rather be facing French cannon than the wistfulness in Jamie's eyes.

Striding across the castle lawn to the old Norman tower, with Griswold in his wake, Blysdale breathed deep of the salty sea air. "Here's hoping the men have discovered something that will put us on the trail of Mathers and Smythe's abductors, Gris. God knows I'm haunted by the feeling that time is growing short."

"Aye. That's because yon twits in London took so long to inform you of what's going on hereabouts."

"It took the London group a while to find the truth. And it cost them two of their men to unearth it, as well, remember. They did their best."

Bly was certain that Mathers and Smythe had been abducted, because he didn't feel that clawing emptiness that tore at his gut whenever he thought of Ashley Stoddard. Ashley had been the first of the Lucky Seven to die—foully murdered by a man who simply coveted his horse.

Ashley Stoddard's death had left such an empty space in Blysdale that he was certain he'd always be aware of the death of a close friend. Lacking that desolate feeling about Mathers and Smythe from the first news of their disappearance, he'd been quick to set an investigation in motion. Now, as more time passed, he was terribly anxious to discover their whereabouts. He sensed that the danger that threatened them was worsening, and deep in his heart, he knew they needed him desperately. He could only pray he wouldn't be too late.

Blysdale took the crumbling steps to the keep in two bounds. Griswold stamped up them behind his employer.

Kate heard their footsteps and drew even farther back into her dark corner behind the door. When they hesitated before entering the tower room, she put her hand over her mouth to keep even her breath from giving away her presence.

"What's wrong, sir?"

"Nothing, Gris." Blysdale chuckled. "Nothing at all."

After a moment, Blysdale went on into the room. Griswold followed, shaking his head, and Kate could breathe again.

"Good evening, men," she heard Blysdale say.

"Good evening, sir." So they *were* military. They addressed Blysdale as an army officer, not as a nobleman. Obviously, Lord Blysdale had won a respect from these two men that transcended matters of mere birth. Kate was impressed.

"What have you learned?"

One of the men answered, "There are definitely clandestine sailings, just as you suspected. The last one was two weeks ago."

Kate stifled a sigh of relief. They didn't know that Josh had gone out with the smugglers just the other night. These men might not pose the threat she feared, after all. They didn't seem to be very observant.

Blysdale spoke for some time in a voice too low for her to make out what he said. Just when she was ready to explode with frustration, his voice rose and he told his men, "Well done. Keep a sharp eye on the port and on that ship in particular. If you see her provisioning . . ."

Provisioning? Was the man dotty? Nobody needed provisions for a jaunt across to France.

". . . or getting ready to sail, contact me immediately. Especially if you see"—he hesitated, then said—"passengers being brought aboard."

"Yessir!"

Kate heard chairs scrape back and pressed farther into her corner. They were getting ready to leave.

Then she jumped when she heard a fist slam down on the table inside the room. "Men!" she heard Blysdale say, "This smuggling has to be stopped!"

Oh, glory. Blysdale *had* come here to spy on the "gentlemen," and her own brother Josh was one of them—even if it was just sporadically! Fear for Josh rose in her. How could she stop him before he got caught? How could she stop Blysdale from catching him?

Even in her distress she watched carefully as the two men left. They were grinning. That was odd. Did they so relish the chase? That made them all the more dangerous. And here she had thought them less of a threat only five minutes ago.

She shook her head at her own foolishness, then flinched at the sound her hair made, swinging against her shoulders. She must guard against the smallest sound, for Blysdale was coming now.

He stopped and stood quietly just on the other side of her door. Kate held her breath.

Griswold's gruff, "What is it, my lord?"

"Go on, Gris. I'll be along presently."

"Whatever you say, sir." The older man's tone betrayed his bewilderment, but he left.

Kate heard his footsteps fade as the valet left the tower. A long minute fraught with tense silence dragged past.

"Breathe, Kate. I know you're there."

Panic filled her. Her first instinct was to run. Then she was incredulous. How could he possibly know she was there? He couldn't. She hadn't made a sound. That reasoning made her scornful. He was bluffing. Guessing. Hoping to get her to betray herself.

And why should he assume that if there were someone spying on him it would have to be her? That thought made her angry.

When he pulled the door back to reveal her, then smirked and, lifting an eyebrow, inquired mockingly, "Yes, Kate?" it made her angrier. He was always so cool, so able, so controlled, so self-contained. He made everybody else look like bumbling ninnies!

Kate didn't know about the rest of the world, but *she* was heartily sick of this perfect example of *sangfroid*. Furious, she attacked. "How dare you come here and abuse the hospitality of my home to act as a spy for the revenue service!" It wasn't a question, it was an accusation she flung at him.

She wasn't ready for the fury she saw in his face. Before she could stop herself, she fled it, running partway up the stairs of the old tower.

He caught her in two bounds, seizing her arm and wrenching her around to face him on the narrow stairway. "Madam," he snarled at her, "I am no cursed revenue officer, and I lower myself to spy for no man!"

He grabbed her shoulders as if he wanted to shake her. His much-vaunted self-control was shattered by her accusation.

Kate raised her hand to strike him for so ungallantly pointing out the fact that she *had* lowered herself to spy. He'd just caught her spying on him!

Their bodies brushed in the narrow confines of the stairwell, and instant attraction flared between them.

Kate took one startled breath. Her wide-eyed gaze locked with his startled one.

Then Blysdale snatched her against his battle-hardened body and kissed her, hard.

Rockets and the sound of great, golden bells went off in Kate's head. She melted against his lithe form. *Just for this one kiss,* she told herself when she heard the bells, *just this one.* She returned the kiss with uninhibited passion.

But Blysdale was clearly the enemy, and Lady Katherine Clifton Halsted did *not* kiss her enemies, bells or no bells! With a superhuman effort, she took her hands from where she'd entwined them in his thick, dark hair and moved them to his chest. Sighing regretfully into their final heated kiss, she shoved him away with all her might.

Blysdale, already off balance from their kiss, reeled back

a step. His head met the granite wall behind him with a sharp crack.

Free of his masterful embrace, Kate ran up the rest of the stairs and grabbed the ancient, nail-studded door at the top.

Blysdale charged up the stairs at her, the sweet taste of her sigh in his mouth, a pain in his head, and fury in his heart.

Kate strove to slam the door in his face. The task was beyond her.

But not beyond Blysdale. Grasping the edge of the door, he bellowed, "You want the blasted door shut, do you?" He slammed the ancient door so hard it rattled in its frame. "There! It's shut, dammit!"

Kate watched him with huge eyes, backing away.

Blysdale followed, his head lowered, his eyes flaming at her from under his dark brows.

Kate realized as she fetched up hard against the wall, that Blysdale's *sang* was no longer *froid*. She stretched imploring hands toward him and tried hard for a cool tone as she told him, "We really shouldn't be doing this, you know, Colonel."

Blysdale stopped as if she'd shot him. The fire slowly died from his eyes. He straightened and drew a long shuddering breath. "You are quite right, of course, Countess. One doesn't make passionate love to one's hostess." He bowed gracefully. "My apologies."

That was it? He could actually regain control of himself so quickly? So easily? Kate was dumbfounded. Of all the unflattering . . . She stood staring at him in astonishment.

Blysdale laughed.

Kate saw that he had beautiful teeth. She realized then that she'd never seen them before. His tight, infrequent smiles had never revealed them. Beautiful teeth or not, Kate didn't think the situation called for laughter.

"What is it?, Kate?"

"I . . . I . . ." She had absolutely no intention of sharing her thoughts with him. She hadn't gathered enough of them back from wherever they'd scattered with his kiss.

He smiled a slow smile. His voice lowered and became silk. "Yes, Kate?"

The wretch knew exactly what she'd been thinking! Knew how she'd been effected by his kiss. Knew she was surprised at his easy surrender to her plea to stop. Even knew, perhaps, that she was just the tiniest bit disappointed. Had been, she amended hastily. That she *had been* the tiniest bit disappointed.

Well, she wasn't now! Not now that he'd laughed at her. Now she was in command of herself again and she was out for blood. Throwing her head back, she looked down her nose at him. "I do not recall giving you permission to call me by my first name, your lordship," she told him. Frost edged her every word.

"Do you not, Kate?" He began moving toward her again. "Shall I help you remember?"

She waited for him to stop at a comfortable distance. At the prescribed distance. She expected him to stay at arm's length, but he didn't. His eyes were warming, too.

He was close. Too close. She could no longer manage to look down on him. She'd have backed up in order to try to do so, but she was already pressed against rough stones, and still he took another step.

Kate knew she'd soon again feel the strength of his body against her own. In expectation, her knees seemed to be losing their ability to hold her weight. She tried to move away sideways, before it was too late, but he reached out and grasped her arm, holding her lightly, but nevertheless holding her in place.

"Do you not remember, Kate?" he repeated, goaded into bullying her by her hypocrisy. She knew as well as he did that something had passed between them when they met. Something that he was as determined to deny as he was to force her to admit.

Kate saw that determination in his face, and became wary of it. His voice became as soft as aged velvet. His bright blue eyes seemed to go smoky as he told her, "I remember, Kate. I remember it well." His voice deepened. "Very, very well." He nuzzled her hair and inhaled as if he'd waited too long to discover the scent of it. "It was in the great hall. The day I arrived."

Somehow he'd changed his grip on her arm and now kissed each finger of the hand that he held instead. "You stood there, gilded with sunlight, and we looked deep into each other's eyes and yours told me as clearly as if you had spoken the words aloud that I could call you anything I wanted to call you. Anything." He gave her her Christian name. "Katherine." He bent his head to whisper against her lips and murmured her nickname. "Kate." His lips touched the shell of her ear as he leaned farther forward to kiss behind her ear and breathed, "Anything at all. Even . . ."

Katherine was having trouble trying to breathe. She needed to take a deep breath, but her body refused her command. Her startled gaze lifted to his eyes as he finished kissing behind her ear. She saw their heavy lids hood them as he placed a kiss in the palm of her hand and whispered, ". . . the best name of all, Kate. . . . Mine."

Sanity clamored somewhere in the far reaches of her mind. If she didn't do something soon to break the spell this austere man was weaving around her, she knew she'd be lost. Already she could feel every bone in her body melting, already feel strands of the invisible web he wove binding her to him.

"Liar," she managed to gasp. "I never . . ."

His lips touched the corner of her mouth.

Kate's senses went spinning. With a mighty effort, she grabbed what she could of them and set them straight. Her voice was husky as she choked out, "Colonel Blysdale."

He stopped kissing her throat and looked at her, "Yes, Kate?"

"We really must stop this." She struggled to sound firm. Clearing her throat she told him, "We are in a compromising position here, and I clearly remember you stating just yesterday that the stars would fall from the heavens before you'd wed."

She shoved against his well-muscled chest and squirmed to get free. It was pointless. He held her easily. She tried again, "I'd hate for us to be forced to marry if one of my brothers should catch us like this." She pushed his wonderful warm hand from just beneath her breast and held his mouth from hers by placing trembling fingers against his chin.

Blysdale groaned and slammed his hands onto the wall at either side of her. "You're right, of course, dammit. I'd be forced to do the proper thing, and you'd be tied for the rest of your life to a battle-scarred cynic."

Kate didn't think that would be an exactly horrible fate, but she'd die before she told him so.

Blysdale dropped his arms, and Kate was free to move. She didn't want to move—except straight back into his arms, but her pride forbade that. He'd let her out of them too easily, and hell was going to freeze over before she forgave him for it!

So she went straight to the door and tried to open it. She couldn't manage to release the old, rusted latch. She'd never had it oiled because she'd never wanted to close the door until she'd had the ignoble desire to slam it in Lord Blysdale's face.

Blysdale was there beside her. "Here. Permit me." He seized the handle and pulled. Then he pulled harder. Giving the door a substantial yank with no visible result, he turned to Kate and raised an eyebrow.

"Oh, dear," she said. "It really is stuck, isn't it?"

"I would say so."

"You shouldn't have slammed it." One look at his wry expression and she amended, "*We* shouldn't have slammed it."

By Jove! His eyebrows shot skyward. A female who shared the blame instead of shifting it to somebody else! He had to say, "You are a most unusual woman, Lady Katherine."

Ah. So, now that they were in a compromising position, I'm suddenly Lady Katherine, am I? What happened to Kate? What happened to "mine"? Maybe it was going to take more than hell freezing over for her to forgive him!

That line of thought was depressing. She shied away from it. "Am I?" she asked coolly.

"Indeed you are. You're willing to share the blame for the door's being stuck. Most women of my acquaintance are constantly striving to shift blame for any negative situation away from themselves."

"I fear that it was my own desire to shut the door quickly that led to your doing so."

"Among other things." His eyes warmed with remembrance. He smiled softly.

Kate turned away toward the window. She didn't think she could weather another of his kisses. Not and keep her head. Looking out the window seemed her safest course of action. "I don't see anyone," she reported, "but perhaps if we called out, someone might hear and come liberate us."

"Very well." Blysdale didn't think there was much chance of raising a rescue in that fashion. All the windows in the sprawling manor nearby had been closed against the coming night, and the stables and everything else that might have had men outside working were on the other side of it.

He was right.

They shouted until they wore out the effort, then looked at each other. Kate said, "It's hopeless, isn't it?"

"I'm afraid so. There's no one within earshot."

"What shall we do?" Tears of frustration misted Kate's eyes. Suppose a coach came and she wasn't there to stop and search it and it was the very one with the proof she needed to save Hal? She was so upset by that thought she feared she would cry.

"When we are missed," Blysdale, moved by her tears, said as gently as if he spoke to a child, "they'll mount a search, and when they come over this way, we can call down to them to come unlock the door."

"It isn't locked."

"Ah, but it may as well be. And that is not the only lie we will tell."

"Lie?" Kate didn't like the idea of lying. It was bad enough that she had holding up coaches to answer for.

"Yes," Blysdale assured her. "We will say that you brought me up here to see the magnificent view of the Channel and the surrounding country, and that the wind slammed the door shut."

Kate smiled. Then she gave a gurgle of laughter. "Yes. I can see that that is a much better story to tell them than the truth."

Blysdale's expression became instantly grave. "And just what is the truth, Lady Katherine?"

Chapter Eleven

"The truth?" Kate looked at him squarely, her eyes narrowed. Resolutely, she ignored the truth *he* was getting at. She was more interested in having Blysdale tell her what he was doing at Cliffside than she was in discussing the fact that she had decided that it was necessary to spy on him in order to ascertain his purpose.

She decided that attack was the best policy. "I think you must be the one to tell the truth, your lordship. After all, you're the one who is here visiting a man you cannot admire, and indeed don't even seem to like, because *you* have need of being here." She put up a hand to still his protest, noting with satisfaction the way his cheeks flamed.

Odd, though. Surely she couldn't have embarrassed him. She pushed that idea aside and went on. "And you're the one who has two men staying at the inn who ask questions everywhere and sneak here to this old ruin to report the answers to you."

"My lady is extremely well informed." Blysdale's expression was guarded. Behind a cool facade he wrestled with the slur on his honor. It was perfectly true that he was accepting the hospitality of a man he did not particularly like, but he didn't appreciate hearing it from that man's sister.

"This is not London, Lord Blysdale. Here one can scarcely breathe without people commenting on it."

It was Blysdale's turn to move away toward the tower window. After a long moment, he turned back to face Kate. His expression was grave, his eyes bleak. "Very well, Lady Katherine. All that you say is true. Since, in reality, it is *your* hospitality that I'm trespassing on, I'll share my concerns with you. And may God forgive me."

His eyes narrowed and he seemed to be weighing her in some fashion. "I hesitate to speak, Lady Katherine, for I truly believe that women should be protected from the uglier things in life." He silenced her objection with a gesture. "My efforts to discover what happened to a pair of my good friends has uncovered facts that are really not fit for a lady's ears."

Kate regarded him steadily. Unconsciously, she lifted her chin. "Go on."

"Very well." He paused a moment, then said, "My two very good friends, the Duke of Smythington and Viscount Kantwell, disappeared while traveling in this neighborhood. Extensive inquiries made by men I hired in Bow Street failed to turn up any hint of their whereabouts. Further probing among the residents of the underground in the stews of London indicated that possibly they fell victim to a vicious band of men who are engaged in the . . . the sale of human beings."

Kate gasped. "But that's slavery!"

Blysdale nodded. "Yes. It is." He went on slowly, waiting for her to throw up her hands and cry "Enough," as all the other ladies of his acquaintance would do. When she didn't, he went on. "Careful investigation by my men—the two who were just here—has revealed little more than that the slavers operate their very lucrative business out of your charming seaport."

"But English noblemen? *Sell* English noblemen? Surely no one would dare!"

"I don't imagine that Mathers and Smythe were *planned*

captures. It's my guess that they were more targets of op-portunity."

"By 'targets of opportunity' do you mean that they may have blundered into something and been taken prisoner to keep them from talking about—or for that matter to keep them from attempting to stop—this terrible practice?"

"Exactly."

"How horrible." She crossed her arms over her chest and rubbed her hands up and down her arms.

Instantly, Blysdale was all concern. "Are you cold?"

Kate was getting chilly. In spite of the fact that the days were getting longer and warmer, with the night, tempera-tures still dropped sharply. Even now the tower was cooling in the evening breeze.

Blysdale stripped off his coat and draped it around her. It was still warm with the heat of his body, still smelled of his masculine scent. Kate shivered in feminine reaction to being enfolded in his garment.

"Blast. You *are* cold." He looked around them. "I've got to get you down from this damned tower."

"As you said, they will miss us and come searching." She looked out at the darkening sky. "When we don't show up to dress for dinner, someone will sound the alarm. Either my Dresden or your Griswold."

As she finished speaking, the wind shifted to blow di-rectly into the window of the tower room. Within seconds, it had strengthened and was whirling dust up from the an-cient stone floor.

Blysdale led Kate over to the window and drew her down to sit beside him on the floor beneath it. "At least here the wind will pass above us."

Kate smiled at him and curled her feet under her for warmth. She was grateful now that the dress she'd criticized earlier did have a full skirt as she tucked it in around her legs and feet. Even with that precaution, the centuries-old cold in the stone floor struck through her wool dress. She looked over her shoulder at Blysdale.

He sat with his back against the wall and his arm resting on the knee of one draw-up leg. The fine lawn of his shirt fluttered when the turbulent air struck it, and she knew he had to be cold.

Nothing about him betrayed any discomfort, however. He looked perfectly relaxed. His head was tilted back to rest against the unyielding wall behind them, and the expression on his face was calm. Obviously, he intended to tell her no more about the terrible thing that had happened to his friends—and surely to others, as well.

Kate hunched down into his coat and drew her knees up to her chest. She was determined to learn more about the horror he'd just spoken to her of, cold or no cold. Suppose her brother Josh should run into such men while he was out playing smuggler with Gordon Mallory? If the band Blysdale was hunting would steal a duke, what would stop them from snatching up Josh, a mere marquess?

Then a flash of sheer terror shot through her as another thought struck her. For that matter, what would stop such men from taking beautiful little Jamie when he wandered the woods and hills on his pony?

Her heart turned to a block of ice as she thought of that. Jamie. Sweet, innocent Jamie in the hands of slavers. God alone knew what his fate would be. And God alone knew how she'd be able to bear such a catastrophe.

"Lord Blysdale."

"Yes?" He turned to look at her, and Kate was again conscious of the strength in his face.

"I know you're reluctant to discuss this, but I must ask you to tell me more about this band of slavers."

"There isn't a great deal more to tell. They prey on the innocent and the lonely—those who have no one to care about them or to ask what became of them if they should disappear. They bring them here to this area, my informants tell me, and ship them off to princes and pashas in the Middle East."

Kate was silent for a long minute. "Do you have any idea where they keep these poor people while they are waiting for the ship?"

"No, I haven't been able to find that out." His face became grim. "But I shall."

Kate recognized his statement as a solemn vow. She had no doubt that he'd fulfil it. She shuddered.

Blysdale moved closer, reached out, and pulled her against his side. After a moment's resistance, Kate leaned into him. After another moment, she got as close to his side as she could snuggle, relishing the warmth he offered.

"Thank you," she said matter-of-factly.

Blysdale had to chuckle.

She felt the rumble of it under her cheek where she had pressed it against his very hard-muscled—and wonderfully warm—chest. "Why are you laughing?"

"I'm enjoying you, Lady Kate. Your matter-of-fact acceptance of the heat my body offers amuses me. You've treated it as if I had merely put another log on the drawing room fire."

It was Kate's turn to laugh. "I see." She tried to look up at him, but, being unwilling to take her cheek from his chest, could only see the underside of his chin. It was a very strong chin. From where she cuddled, she could detect a faint cleft. "Obviously I failed to be properly missish about your embrace, my lord. Frankly, though, I thought it no more than a gentleman's effort to keep a lady warm. As you said, like putting another log on the fire."

Blysdale laughed long at that. "God, Kate. You're a treasure. You're as bold and capable as any camp follower. I congratulate you!"

She drew back then. Heat forgotten, she reared away from him and stared at him, incredulous. "Camp follower!" Outrage filled her voice to the point that it bounced off the far wall.

"Now, Kate." His words might sound placating, but the slash of a grin he wore was anything but.

She'd been right. His teeth were beautiful. Why in the world didn't the confounded man smile more? When he did, he was twice as handsome and looked ten years younger besides. Someone ought to tell him so. Her mind was busy with another matter at the moment, however. "How dare you compare me to a—a—" She sputtered to a stop.

His laughter faded, and his eyes became serious. "Ah, Kate." He touched her face, holding her chin briefly with his long fingers, letting his gaze rove over her features. Then he let go, as if leaving her completely free to weigh his next words. "The bravest and most resourceful women I've ever known have been those who followed the army. They nursed the men as often as they saw to their baser masculine needs. They kept the cook fires and laundries going, sometimes under the harshest of conditions. Sometimes they cooked and served their men's meals with bullets flying over their heads. They might have flinched, but they didn't ever falter. And never did they complain of the many and sometimes awesome hardships.

"Coarse and vulgar they might be, but they really are remarkable women, Kate. I've done you no disrespect by comparing you to them."

Kate felt oddly humbled. Blysdale's honest praise of a segment of humanity that she'd been raised never even to admit knowing about, much less to think about, had touched and, yes, shamed her. After a little while, she was able to say, very softly, "Thank you."

Blysdale experienced a tightening around his heart. To deny it, he tightened his arm around Kate. Like a proud father when his child had learned a difficult truth, he told himself. The faint warmth of her slender body seemed to burn a path down his side. The feelings it engendered were far from what a proper father should feel.

"I can help." Kate spoke firmly, her voice raised to be heard over the wind whistling around them.

Blysdale thought he must have misunderstood. She couldn't have meant to aid him in the manner his male mind eagerly leapt at. He asked rather weakly, "Help?" He'd never been bewildered before. He didn't like the sensation.

"Yes. Help. I know every nook and cranny of this area. Every cave by the sea. And I know when it is safe, and when it's not, to enter every one of them. Don't you think a cave is the natural choice of a place to hide people you don't want found?"

Hope flared in his eyes.

Kate went on, "And, of course, I know every barn and abandoned building of every sort, as well—though I imagine your men have scoured all of them."

Blysdale scooped her up and sat her in his lap. Startled, Kate started to protest. Then she decided with her usual practicality that they would both be warmer this way and kept still.

After all, she had on a wool dress, long sleeved and high necked, with Blysdale's jacket over it, and *she* was cold in the wind that whipped through the tower. Blysdale had on a fine lawn shirt. Propriety could go hang. She decided to stay where he had so highhandedly put her.

Drawing from the wealth of wisdom about the male animal that she'd gained as a married woman, she promised herself that she would, however, sit very still.

"There!" Blysdale stated in perfect satisfaction. "Now I can see your face."

Indeed he could. Their noses were almost touching. Kate saw that he had white flecks in his deep blue eyes. Then she saw them change and go smoky, and her own widened.

Blysdale saw her eyes get big and her lips soften and a desire to kiss the woman he held tore through him like a storm surge. He curbed it sharply. Hadn't he recognized that he was totally unfit for marriage just this afternoon in his conversation with her youngest brother? Lady Katherine was not fodder for his cannon. She wasn't the stuff of which mistresses were made, and a mistress was all he, Beelzebub Blysdale, deserved. With a sigh that shook them both, he acknowledged that and bowed to it. As he'd once told this enchanting woman, the stars would fall from the sky before he would decide to marry.

"Are you cold?" It was her turn to ask him the question.

"No, my lady. I'm not cold."

"Of course you are!" In the interest of keeping him warm,

she put her left arm around his shoulders, turned to face him, and drew his coat across them both with her right hand.

Blysdale smiled. "Are you worried about keeping me warm, Lady Katherine? If so, I assure you that your mere presence, ah ... where you are ... is doing an excellent job of raising my temperature."

Kate marshaled her forces to scold. Seated as she was, she was well aware of the effect her body's proximity and the little half-turn she'd just made toward him was having on his. She wasn't a green girl. She'd been married to a lusty man for three years, after all.

So why pretend frosty offense? She had every confidence that this strange, unbending man would offer her no disrespect, would never do her harm. Why set up paltry verbal defenses against the possibility, then?

So instead, Kate looked into his laughing eyes and tried not to smile. "Here." She rose quickly from his lap and tucked his coat around him in the same manner she tucked Jamie into bed every night.

Thoughts of Jamie had brought thoughts of Hal and tore away her peace. Hal! Her mind should be on clearing Hal, not on the intriguing Lord Blysdale. Here she was locked in the tower like some princess in a fairy tale hidden cozily away with her very own dark knight, when she should be home where she belonged so that she could receive word of a coach coming—if word were sent her.

All the happiness Kate had felt only a moment ago as she'd tucked his coat around Blysdale drained away. In its place, she felt only guilt at her lapse from duty and an urgency in her spirit that drove her to the window. There she stood peering out into the dark, craning out the window to look toward the village.

Kate had two vital needs now. One was to see if there was any kind of a signal telling her that a coach was on its way—the second was to give her heartbeat a chance to slow.

Blysdale leapt up and put his jacket back around her. What the devil was she so anxious to see? In the dark? Looking in a direction from which no help could be expected to come?

He kept his hands on her shoulders to hold the coat around her in the wind that rushed out of the night. He could feel the tension in her, as, taut as a bowstring, she stared off toward the village of Lesser-Clifton.

"What are you looking for, Kate?"

"Nothing!" she answered too hastily.

"Ah. And what will you do if you find this 'nothing' you're looking for so hard?"

She twisted around to look at him. Ignoring his question, she burst out, "I must go! I must get out of here." Kate could feel the desperation rising in her. It was as strong as an actual physical force. She went to the tower room door and yanked at the latch.

It held firm, despite the enthusiastic kick she gave the bottom of the door.

When she finally gave up and turned back, her dark knight, Blysdale, was gone.

Chapter Twelve

"Nooooo!" Kate gave a wild, despairing cry and threw herself across the tower room to the window. Thrusting her upper body out of it, she looked frantically for the man who had been here with her only a moment ago. "Blysdale!" she shrieked at the top of her lungs, sheer terror in her cry.

"Yes, Kate?" He was just below her, calmly clinging to the rough stone of the tower's outer wall.

"Oh! Oh, how you frightened me!" Her heart was in her throat. She sagged weakly against the side of the window opening.

Clinging comfortably to the stone wall, Blysdale reminded her, "You mentioned that you had to get out of the tower, Kate. Since you suddenly seemed impatient with the idea of awaiting rescue, I'm merely going to attempt to reach and open the door from the other side."

A lull in the wind made it seem as if even the night were holding its breath with Kate. Concern for his safety seared through her.

"You must come back up! What if you should fall?" Far, far below Blysdale, Kate could see the waves dashing against the stones at the foot of the cliff on which the tall tower stood. Her knees almost gave way. "Please! Come back!" She stretched out and down to try to grasp his wrist.

"Silly wench! Have a care! You'll fall out of there if you aren't careful!"

Kate was too terrified that he might lose his grip to be offended by his name calling. She could see that the tower stones were damp with sea spray whipped upward from the Channel by the wind, and that wind was getting stronger. Blysdale's shirt luffed and strained in it like a sail.

Suddenly, Kate's hair was blown across her face, blinding her. When she cleared it away with eager, trembling fingers, it blew back again from the other side and clung to her face like some malevolent, live thing, denying her sight. Thrusting her hands into it hard, she shoved it back and away from her eyes.

No longer blinded, she looked for Blysdale. He was nowhere to be seen. The place on the irregular wall of the ancient tower where he had clung was empty. Kate sobbed, "Oh, no. Oh, dear God, no!"

He was gone! While she'd fought to clear the hair from over her eyes, he'd fallen down into the raging sea. The blood drained from her head. Her ears rang. It was all her fault!

Kate's knees gave way and she sank to the cold stone of the tower room. She huddled under the window in a tight ball of utter misery. Pressing against the cold hard stone of the wall with her face buried in her hands, Kate sobbed and sobbed. She had caused his death. If she hadn't leaned out the window to look toward the village . . . if she hadn't been so concerned that she might miss a coach . . .

Oh, why hadn't she just been patient? Just waited for someone to come looking for them? If only she had listened to Blys . . .

"Kate. Kate!" Someone had lifted her to her feet and was gently prying her hands away from her face. Someone who spoke in a soothing, deep voice. She looked up at the intruder with eyes aswim with tears and a heart fearful to believe them. It was Blysdale!

"Oh, thank God! You're alive! You're all right." She touched his face, traced it with her fingers, smoothed her fingertips across his cheeks, his lips. Then she held his face with both hands and kissed him hard and long, she was so relieved.

An instant later she thrust him away and exploded at him, "How *dare* you frighten me like that! I thought you were dead! I thought my selfish concern with my own business had caused you to attempt to climb down the tower." She knew her eyes were as wild as the words she couldn't stop from pouring out, but she didn't care. He was alive!

He was fine!

She was hysterical.

"I thought you'd been killed! That it was my fault. I thought that you'd fallen and been dashed to pieces on the rocks down there in those terrible, terrible waves. I thought I'd killed you!" She began to sob again, great gulping sobs.

Blysdale reached out, took her in his arms, and held her close. "Ah, Kate." His voice was gentle, his breath warm in her ear. "Dear Kate. No one has ever cried for me before."

He smoothed her wind-tangled hair back and kissed her on the forehead. "It's all right, Kate. I'm safe. I'm here."

Kate sniffled. Her sobs had ceased. Blysdale's hands were making warm, calming circles on her back. She stiffened slightly. Sniffed. "I'm here," she heard him repeat.

"Yes! You are." She shoved away from him so hard he staggered back a step. "I've been hysterical—hysterical!— at the thought that I'd sent you to a watery grave, and here you stand as cool as . . . as a cucumber!" Her brows snapped down. "How did you do it?" she demanded.

"Kate. What the devil ails you? Your moods swing like a weathercock." He was staring at her as if she'd taken leave of her senses. "I climbed down to the window just under ours, swung myself in, and dropped onto the stairs there. Then I came up and opened the door."

"Then I came up and opened the door," Kate mimicked. Then she shouted full in his face, "Why didn't you *tell* me that was what you were going to do?"

"Because," Blysdale shouted back, "I had no idea you were too stupid to realize it for yourself!"

Kate's mouth dropped open. She was totally outraged. No one had ever shouted at her in her entire adult life! And to call her stupid! If she'd had her pistols, she'd have shot him!

"Katherine? Lord Blysdale?" This voice was calm.

Both their heads spun to face the doorway. Hal stood just inside the door with a lighted lantern in his hand and Jamie beside him.

"What in the world are the two of you doing up here?" Hal's bewildered gaze went from one to the other. "If you don't come down and dress soon, we'll all have a very late dinner."

"Griswold," Blysdale told his valet as he dressed for dinner, "that woman is going to drive me crazy!"

"Aye?" Gris smoothed the black superfine of Lord Blysdale's evening jacket over his broad shoulders.

"Yes!" Blysdale looked into the pier mirror and told his friend quietly, "I need a stickpin." Then, again a little stridently, "Yes. She kissed me, Gris. Grabbed me like a recruit might grab a doxy and kissed me. Kissed me as hard, too, dammit. It was no gentle ladylike buss, I can tell you."

"Did she, now?"

"Damned right she did."

"Then what did she do?" Griswold kept his head bent over the jewelry case so that his employer and good friend couldn't see the laughter in his eyes. He'd never seen his officer rattled before. He was enjoying every second.

Blysdale snatched the black pearl stickpin from his batman's hand. "Then she shoved me away as if *I'd* been the one to cross the line." He grumbled as he placed the pearl precisely in the center of the knot in his cravat, "Shoved me so damned hard I actually fell back a step."

"She didn't!" Griswold was openly grinning now, waiting for Blysdale to look at him. "Not exactly dainty, our Lady Katherine."

Blysdale spun round, scowling. When he saw the grin on

Griswold's face, his own was a study. Finally, he threw his head back and laughed long and hard. When he stopped, he shook his head, smiled, shook it again, and ordered, "Open the door, damn you, Adam Griswold. I don't intend to be late for dinner."

In her own bedchamber, Kate was warm at last. Warm from the bath her dear and attentive Dresden had had ready for her when she came in from the tower. "Thank you, Dresden. That was just what I needed." She sat still while the abigail combed the tangles from her hair. "It was cold in the tower after the sun went down."

"I'm glad you had on that wool dress, my lady. You'd have been frozen through if you'd gone up there in the muslin we put you in this morning."

Kate didn't want to go into why she'd changed her clothing, so she rushed to say, "It was so foolish to be caught in the tower by that door having slammed in the wind. I should have told a footman that I was going to the tower to show Lord Blysdale the view. Then all this fuss could have been avoided."

Good Lord! Just listen to me! She was mouthing the lies Lord Blysdale had suggested while they were prisoners.

How could that man so throw her out of kilter? She was a sensible, practical woman. She was no giddy girl to be put off stride by the attentions of a single man. As Lionel's wife, she'd managed whole ballrooms full of men. Yes, and as Josh's hostess here at Cliffside, as well. What in the name of all that she held dear was happening to her?

She hadn't been her calm, quiet self since the Earl of Blythingdale had arrived. The man was a positive menace to her peace of mind. If he wasn't fascinating her, he was aggravating her. With him around, something was always throwing her off balance.

Why she was even imagining that Dresden and Jennings had entered a pact to spy on her! Her nerves must be getting unsteady, indeed, if she thought her two most trusted retainers were trying to spy out her secret! She certainly didn't need a fascination for the acerbic Lord Blysdale further complicating things.

Even now, regarding her reflection, she saw that her cheeks were flushed. She put her hands up to them. They were hot to the touch. Blast that Blysdale. How could he make her blush merely because she was thinking about him?

Suddenly, she was impatient to get downstairs and get dinner over with. Then she could return here, put it all out of her mind, and go to sleep. Since it looked as if she were going to begin having reactions like those of some young ninnyhammer, she'd prefer to have them in the confined privacy of her own bed.

"Just twist my hair up any way you can, Dresden. We'll get the rest of the tangles out of it tomorrow."

"Lady Katherine!" Dresden looked as if she might swoon. "You must look your best tonight. In addition to our usual group of gentlemen, that handsome rascal Gordon Mallory has come and is staying to dinner."

Now it was Kate's turn to look as if she might swoon.

Chapter Thirteen

Knowing that she was going to find Gordon Mallory awaiting her in the drawing room, Kate went down to dinner feeling as cheerfully confident as if she were going to be burned
at the stake.

She was fairly certain she wasn't going to enjoy the
evening ahead of her. Loathsome Gordon Mallory was going
to be at her table tonight, and with Blysdale there looking
on, she'd have no choice but to be nice to him. The prospect
was enough to ruin her appetite, and she *had* been famished.

She glanced in the mirror at the top of the stairs. The
woman who looked back at her as she hesitated in front of
the mirror was perfectly dressed in an expensive dinner gown
of taffeta that changed subtly from blue to green and back
again with her every rustling movement. From the toes of
her matching taffeta slippers to the top of her jewel-bedecked
hair, she was exquisite. Except that, while above the styl-
ishly low-cut square neckline the woman's face that stared
back at her might be calm, the expression in her eyes
was . . . harried.

"Fair enough," Kate muttered. She *felt* harried. She knew
she was about to be caught in a clash of wills between two

powerful men, one honorable and the other—the other was Gordon Mallory. Unfortunately there wasn't anything she could do about it.

Without a doubt, Gordon Mallory would already have made it clear that he thought he owned her. And who would assure Blysdale that it wasn't so?

Like some featherless peacock, Gordon Mallory would never be able to resist strutting in front of a strange man, and for him, being able to show himself in company with the Cliftons and hint that there was to be an alliance with Kate was something to strut about.

Dinner was going to be a miserable affair at best. Oh, she could pretend that she didn't know anything upsetting was going on, act as if she were unaware of any tension, but it would be a sham. With the attraction for Chalfont Blysdale that she couldn't seem to rid herself of pulling her one way, and the aggravation Mallory always caused in her, Kate knew she was in for a difficult evening.

On top of it all, she didn't know how Blysdale would react. They had just been so open and honest with each other in the tower. Had established some sort of dizzying relationship that lifted her heart. And they had kissed! Dear Heaven, if Gordon Mallory was insinuating that he was Kate's future intended, Blysdale would have every right to feel that she had betrayed him. Which she most certainly had not!

As if it weren't enough that she was unable to convince Mallory that she was never going to engage herself to the obnoxious beast, she now had to fight the sinking feeling that her feelings for Blysdale were more intense than she wanted them to be.

Would he now reproach her as he remembered the ardor with which she had returned his first kiss? Or the feeling she'd put into the second one when she kissed him after she found him alive and safe back with her in the tower?

She sighed heavily. No matter how much she might want to, she could hardly explain to Blysdale how matters stood between the obnoxious Mallory and her.

In the first place, nothing would be said in front of her, Gordon would be careful to see to that, and she'd look a perfect fool to assume it had been said at all. Blysdale would think her as conceited as she knew Mallory was! And in the second place, one simply didn't offer explanations that would—as if it were possible to do so with a man like Mallory—humiliate a guest at one's table. But with a house full of guests, when would she see Blysdale alone? Why did Chalfont Blysdale have to choose now to enter her life? She didn't have the time for a Grand Passion! Oh, well. By the time Mallory was finished, there would be nothing left of passion of any kind between Blysdale and her, anyway.

Blast social conventions! Too often they hampered more than they helped. That was certainly so in this case.

And blast Gordon Mallory! The man was a low-born braggart. He'd act like a dog with a prized bone. Unfortunately, Kate knew, she was that bone.

As she neared the drawing room, Kate's sense of humor took over. The image of being fought over by two snarling dogs that her last thought had conjured up brought a smile. Clinging to this wry bit of humor like a lifeline, Lady Katherine, Countess of Rushmore, went on into the arena.

Waiting in the drawing room, Blysdale was fighting to keep his rage under control. Josh had just said, "And may I present Mr. Gordon Mallory, my very good friend and my sister's soon-to-be fiancé?"

The mild introduction had hit Blysdale with the fury of a lightning bolt. For an instant he was stunned. Then his mind exploded with wrath.

Damn her! Kate had conveniently neglected to tell him that little fact! He felt as if he'd been dealt a death blow.

She had wept for him, by all that was holy! The perfidious wretch had actually cried when she'd thought he'd fallen to his death from the tower, and her frantic kiss had been balm to his long-wounded spirit. For the first time in his life his heart had been touched by a woman. And had opened to her. And all the time she'd been promised to another man, blast her. To this man. To this tall, handsome Irishman with a confident smile on his face and his hand outstretched in greeting.

Only a lifetime of practice kept Blysdale's true feelings from showing in his face. On the outside he smiled his usual tight, perfunctory smile as he took the offered hand. On the inside, he was cursing his hostess and the capricious fate that had brought him to her.

"How do you do, Mr. Mallory." His voice was cool, his manner haughty. "Please accept my congratulations on your coming betrothal. Lady Katherine is a most extraordinary woman."

Mallory's eyes lit with interest. Clearly, he recognized Blysdale as a man to be reckoned with ... and perhaps as something more? Perhaps as a rival for the fair Kate? His smile became a grin.

Blysdale saw it and correctly interpreted it as a challenge. Had it been over something else—something that didn't threaten to tear the very heart from his body—Blysdale would have accepted Mallory's challenge with the quirk of an eyebrow. This, however, was about Kate, who had penetrated his every defense and taken up residence in his every thought, and he could permit himself no such latitude. He kept his expression bland, his eyes noncommittal. Mallory's obvious disappointment gave him some little satisfaction, at any rate.

By the time Kate came to stand in the drawing room doorway, there was chill in the air she could feel.

When the perfunctory greetings were over, Blysdale ghosted to her side. "I was not aware you were betrothed, Lady Katherine," he told her in a cold, intentionally bored drawl. "I have just been introduced to your fiancé."

Kate's good intentions went flying. Hostess or no hostess, she wasn't going to stand still for this!

Her mouth was already open to hotly straighten him out, when her heart gave a leap and fell to the soles of her feet. If she'd learned as much about Blysdale as she thought she had, to explain that Gordon was a menace who pestered her beyond bearing might be to sign Gordon Mallory's death warrant. Or at least be the cause of major discomfort coming his way.

Thanks to Josh's constant barrage of fearsome tales about his former commanding officer, she knew of Blysdale's rather horrid reputation of having several times come to the rescue of damsels in distress with . . . excessive vigor. Josh had even intimated that once Blysdale had emasculated a rapist named Treckler.

While Kate might devoutly wish an even worse fate on Mallory when she was angry, she wouldn't put him at such risk when she was not. Nor Blysdale, either, for that matter. Gordon Mallory had a well-earned reputation for possessing a great deal of skill as a brawler.

No, even if etiquette would allow it, discretion forbade explanation.

With her anger cooled more by willpower than by inclination, Kate let herself really look at Blysdale. Her heart actually missed a beat when she did. One look at him, at the way he stood there, straight as a rapier, his face carefully controlled—and Kate knew that behind his cool facade he was hurt. His eyes were smoky with emotion—wounded.

Kate's heart twisted. She knew he'd been hurt only because the enigmatic, unbendable Blysdale had let his defenses down with her . . . and gained this seeming betrayal as his reward.

He was angry, too, but Kate could accept that, she understood it. While they'd been locked in the tower she'd certainly given him every reason to think he was the only man in her life. It brought Kate her own pain, yes, and anger, too, to realize that the attraction she'd shown Blysdale she felt for him had been used, even if unwittingly, to do this to him.

If only there had been time to see him before she came downstairs! But what could she have told him? That there was going to be a blowhard at the table who pretended to have a claim on her that was utter nonsense?

And wouldn't that have been lovely? Blysdale would either have laughed her to scorn, or he'd have believed her

and begun a war of cutting repartee at the dinner table designed to irritate Mallory into apoplexy . . . or a duel.

But all that was irrelevant. She hadn't even known that
Mallory was going to be in the house, much less invited to
dine, until just before she'd left her room. She'd been as
caught off guard as Blysdale, a victim of circumstance.

Kate bit back a sigh. A pain grew in her that must match
that felt by her saturnine dark knight. It left her feeling hollow inside. There was nothing Kate could do for either of
them at the moment, however. She was bound by those
damned social conventions again.

So, moving with her usual serenity into the center of the
gathered group, Kate accepted a wineglass of her favorite
sherry from Jennings and smiled around at them all. Thank-
fully, not one of the men there could tell that her heart was
aching.

Jamie, however, seemed to sense something. He just knew
that there was something wrong with Kate. He was so proud
to be allowed to eat with the adults, now that Kate was in
charge here at Cliffside, that he didn't want to do anything
to upset anybody. So he just went up to his sister when no
one was looking at him, and slipped his arm around her
waist.

Kate had to fight back tears as she gave him a quick hug
in return.

Somehow, Kate was managing to get through dinner. Much
was as usual. Josh ate too much, Hal ate too little. But as
to the rest, conversation at the table was stilted, to say the
least.

Blysdale fingered his dinner knife and stared too hard at
Gordon Mallory every now and then. When Mallory said,
"Kate, my love, when are you going to tell me when you
will marry me?" Blysdale's hand tightened on the knife.

Kate said firmly, "This is hardly a subject for the dinner
table, Mr. Mallory." She stirred food around her plate without eating a bite and wondered if Blysdale were wishing he
could cut Gordon Mallory's throat.

At that moment, she wondered if she could help him do it!

Jamie watched and saw it all, but couldn't figure it out. He sighed.

"Are you all right, dear?" Kate asked him.

"Yes, Kate. I was just finding life a little puzzling."

"We all do, lad," Blysdale spoke to the boy, but his gaze sought and held Kate's, still accusing. "We all do."

Kate bit her lower lip and met his gaze steadily. How she wished he could see what was in her mind. In her heart.

Blysdale couldn't see into a woman's heart, of course. He saw best what another man presented to him, and that was a picture of a woman who'd returned his kisses with passionate abandon, and a man telling all those at her dinner table that he had a claim on her affections. Blysdale was, before anything else, a man and, being a man, wounded pride blinded him to everything else.

When it came time to leave the gentlemen to their port and cigars, Kate couldn't escape fast enough.

Upstairs in her rooms, Kate finally fought down the tendency to weep. She wiped her eyes, blew her nose, and accepted a bad situation with a pledge to straighten things out as soon as the opportunity presented itself. She had barely caught her breath when there was a soft knock on her door. She called, "Enter!" and Jennings brought a note to her.

"Are you all right, Lady Katherine?"

"I'm fine." From somewhere she dredged up a smile. "Thank you."

Jennings recognized his dismissal. Reluctantly he opened the door, turned to look piercingly at her one last time, and finally left.

Kate waited until the door had closed behind him to open the note. It was what she'd come to dread. Seth had written to tell her that a coach had come down from London and was heading her way.

She closed her eyes for a moment, wishing with all her heart that she didn't have to go. Then she squared her shoul-

ders and rang for Dresden. She'd need her abigail's help to
get out of her dinner gown.

Kate approached the road the expected coach would have to
take to reach the sea, positioned Star in the roadway, and
told him, "Steady, my love." Then she drew her pistol and
pulled her mask up into place.

The pounding of hoofbeats and the jangling of harness
filled the air. The faint gleam of carriage lanterns pierced
the night, and Kate shouted, "Stand and deliver!" But her
voice wasn't as firm as it had been before. Before she'd been
caught and held and nearly unmasked and identified. Nor
was her hand as steady.

The occupants of this coach were not so formidable as
those two men had been, however. They were a man and
wife, respectable citizens, who were only too eager to obey
her order to come out of the carriage.

They stood uneasily outside, the wife clinging to her husband's arm and watching Kate fearfully. "Don't do anything,
John Coachman!" she quavered. "He'll kill us for sure."

"Now, Matilda," her husband soothed, "surely not, since
we are being cooperative." In spite of this brave assurance,
his eyes held the glassy look of fear as he stared down the
barrel of Kate's pistol. Deep inside, Kate felt an unpleasant
emotion uncoiling like a snake. She was ashamed to frighten
these innocent people so.

Resolutely she ignored her conscience. Hal's welfare had
to come before her feelings. So nevertheless, she searched
the interior of the coach with her usual efficiency, denying
to herself that her hands shook as she did. She found nothing. She opened the woman's jewel case. A quick look
showed her no piece of jewelry that would have excited the
greed of the jewel thief she sought. She closed it gently, not
even disappointed. She'd known she'd find nothing.

Her spirits sank. Was she never to find a trace of the jewels that were being stolen in London and transported to the
Continent from this area? Was she never to find anything to
clear her brother Hal's name?

She stepped close to her victims. The woman shuddered and hid her face against her husband's shoulder. She clung to him and sobbed. Kate deliberately roughened her voice as she commanded, "Turn out your pockets." She ordered him to do it as a matter of course, knowing there would be nothing on the man to help her, either.

When he complied, she fought down a sigh and gestured for them to get back into the coach. They had barely complied, the woman weeping openly, when Kate shouted at the top of her lungs, "Yah! Get up!" and discharged her pistol.

The horses lunged forward into their traces. The coach jerked into motion. From his box the coachman plied his whip, and in a thunder of hoofbeats, they were gone. Soon only a cloud of dust remained to attest to their having been there.

Bone weary, disappointed beyond belief . . . and thoroughly ashamed of herself, Kate turned Star and headed for home.

Chapter Fourteen

Kate slept heavily and awakened in the morning feeling un-refreshed. She asked the maid who came to stir up her fire against the lingering morning chill to bring her hot choco-late. Something sweet, Kate had learned, often gave her a boost to start the day, to get up and get busy.

When the chocolate came, she held the cup and sat think-ing, sighing between sips. Terrible burdens crowded her mind. Deception, troubles, lies. She hated them all, yet she had willingly made them a part of her life.

She gave an unladylike snort and threw back the covers. "Part of your life," she grumbled. "Ha! You've made them the entire fabric of your existence, Katherine Elizabeth."

And? she asked herself with disgust.

"All right!" she admitted. "And heartbreak." She picked up her wrapper from the foot of her bed and drew it on. "I've added a little heartbreak lately, too."

Stalking across to the window, the lace-trimmed hem of her gossamer negligee trailing across the lush Oriental car-pet, she looked up at the sky far above the Channel. As a child, she'd believed that that must be where God lived. She still turned her eyes skyward whenever she needed comfort.

There was a sharp rap on her hall door, and Dresden bustled in. "And what will you wear today, my lady? What are your plans?"

Kate sighed as she turned away from the window. "Any day gown will do nicely, Dresden. I plan to spend the morning in the study going over accounts."

"I know I'm not supposed to say so . . ."

"Go on, Dresden." What could one more problem matter? Kate waited to hear it.

"Well . . ." The abigail hesitated, then blurted, "Your brother should do that job."

Kate smiled. Dresden was always her champion. Kate certainly wasn't going to spoil it, even by defending her indefensible brother. "I only wish that he would. I admit I find the ledgers so tedious I can hardly bear it."

As she hurried off to get her employer's dress, Dresden muttered, "But you do bear it. Just like you bear everything else around here." Out loud she called back, "I'll try to find something you won't mind getting ink on."

Though Kate pretended not to hear what her abigail had muttered, it did feel terribly nice to have someone notice and sympathize. Whether it was the comment Dresden made, or the hot chocolate she'd drunk, Kate didn't know, but she knew she'd found the energy to go down to breakfast and the study with a lighter step than she'd had when she'd first gotten up.

Bypassing the breakfast room, she went straight to the study. The last thing she wanted to do was to bump into Lord Blysdale or Gordon Mallory. Or, Heaven forbid, the two of them together!

Blysdale was an invited guest—even if he had invited himself—so, though it set Kate's teeth on edge to admit it, he had every right to be there in the breakfast room. To her, Gordon was a pest who simply showed up whenever he pleased and always overstayed his welcome. Never knowing when he was going to run tame about the manor, she wasn't willing to chance a meeting. Especially with her feelings for Blysdale urging her to eliminate Mallory.

When the footman on duty there opened the study door for her, Kate ordered, "Would you send Jennings to me, please." Then, going to her desk, she sat, sighed, and resolutely pulled the topmost of a stack of ledgers to her and opened it. Before she got the first line read, Jennings entered the room.

"You sent for me, Lady Katherine?"

"Yes, Jennings. I'd like a tray in here, please. My usual breakfast."

Jennings cocked his head and Kate felt like a child again, once more being asked to explain her actions to the concerned butler. She chuckled and humored him. "I have a lot of work to do on the estate accounts. I'll get more done if I don't get stuck entertaining guests."

Jennings bowed himself out. Not before Kate saw the twinkle in his eyes, however. Kate muttered, "I'm glad somebody finds amusement in my predicament," and started to work on the books.

The door opened quietly. "Talking to yourself, Kate?"

"Gordon!" He'd startled her. For a big man he moved very quietly. "So you're here at Cliffside . . . again," she said without enthusiasm. Wishing he'd go away, she suggested, "Have you had breakfast?"

"I was lingering over it, hoping to have you join me, when I saw the footman come in to get Jennings." He closed the door and leaned back against it. "Thinking you'd probably sent for him, I followed him here."

Kate frowned. "I have a lot of work to catch up on, Gordon. I ordered a tray to save time." She pretended to find something to do in the open ledger, hoping he would have the good grace to take the hint, go away, and leave her to her work.

"Ah. So that's it."

She raised her gaze to meet his. "What else could it be?"

"I thought for a moment that it might be a desire to avoid seeing me—or Lord Blysdale? Or perhaps the opposite. Perhaps a desire to be *with* him?" He watched her narrowly.

"Lord Blysdale, Jennings tells me, is an early riser who

is generally gone out riding before I ever come down." Kate's voice had an edge. "You, as you very well know, I *never* want to see."

"That's an odd way to feel about the man you're going to marry."

She bit back the answer that she wouldn't marry him if he were the proverbial last man on earth. If she could, Kate wanted to keep Mallory from spreading ugly rumors about Hal and the jewel thefts until she could clear her brother's name, and she knew he'd spread them if she offended him more than she usually did. Dear Gordon was nothing if not spiteful.

If local society shut Hal out, he would be inconsolable. So instead of informing Mallory of the slimness of his chances of arriving at the altar with her in tow, she said, "I am but recently widowed, Gordon. To contemplate a marriage to anyone now would dreadfully upset the Rushmores."

"Do they still hope you might be breeding?"

"That's indelicate of you, Gordon!"

"Oh, come, Kate. Even those silly old fools know you'd be showing signs long before now if you were pregnant by their sainted son. It's been eight months. Waiting the full year proscribed by the laws of title inheritance is nothing short of ludicrous."

White with outrage at his coarseness, Kate rose from her chair. "The Rushmores are still grieving for Lionel, still upset that their line ends with him. They are not 'silly old fools.' They are loving parents who have lost a son. Their only son."

Mallory made a dismissive gesture. "Enough about the Rushmores."

"Then let's consider *my* feelings. Perhaps I need time to grieve, too," she challenged him.

He was across the room and had grabbed and snatched Kate out from behind the desk before she had an inkling of his intentions. "It's you I want to talk about, not your grief nor your former in-laws. I want you, Kate, and I've waited long enough!" With that he crushed his mouth down on hers.

Kate knew the folly of fighting a force superior to her own, so she simply stood unresponsive in his embrace. The fact that he awoke no response to his passion made no difference to Gordon Mallory. He kissed her long and hard, while Kate clenched her teeth and wished she had her pistol.

When his hand closed on her breast, she raked it with her fingernails as hard as she could. At the same time she gave a mighty shove to be free.

Mallory let her go and stepped back, staring at his hand. "Damn you, Kate! Look what you've done. You've drawn blood!"

"Good! I wish you'd bleed to death!"

He drew his arm back to deal her a backhanded blow.

"Mr. Mallory!" The shout rang out from the doorway. Jennings stood there with a tray he'd almost dropped, an expression of shock and outrage on his face.

"Jennings!" Kate couldn't remember when she'd been so glad to see anyone. Except, of course, for the highwayman who had interrupted her capture the other night. "Please put my tray here." She pointed to and retreated behind the desk.

There she quickly opened and reached into the center drawer. When her hand reappeared, she held an old dirk— a family heirloom they now used only to open letters. The fulminating look she gave Gordon Mallory left no doubt in his mind that she intended to use it on him if he attempted to grab her again.

"Yes, your ladyship." The old butler's voice quivered with suppressed anger. He took an incredibly long time placing a linen runner on the tooled leather top of the desk, setting her silver in place, putting down her plate, and finally lifting its silver dome from her breakfast. "I trust this choice is to your liking, Lady Katherine."

Jennings was standing closer to her than he had ever come since she was a child, and Kate could have hugged him. He was doing his best to protect her from a man twice his size and half his age. Her heart filled to bursting with affection for and pride in him.

"It's just fine, Jennings. Exactly what I myself would have chosen. Thank you." She hoped her words weren't falling over each other, she was so eager to get the faithful old man out of the study before he got hurt. Having just seen this new and wonderful facet of her persecutor's character, she now had to be certain to keep her servants safe from his temper. Dear Lord! Just what she needed, another duty.

Kate could see that Jennings sensed her urgency and understood its cause. Stubbornly he refused to leave his mistress, fussily pouring her tea and adding the cream and sugar Kate was used to taking for herself. Then, suddenly, he seemed struck by a thought, bowed to Kate, and tight-lipped, hurried from the room.

"Officious lout, isn't he?" Mallory was smiling again.

"*I* call that 'officious lout' a faithful servant, thank you! And while we are about it, I call him a wonderful old gentleman. A *gentleman*." She glared at Mallory, cold fury in her eyes. "Since *gentleman* is a term I can't conceivably use to describe you, however, I'd like you to leave my house."

He lounged with one hip on the side of the desk opposite her, picked up a quill, and brushed it back and forth over his chin. "Well," he drawled, his eyes insolent, "when you get right down to it, Kate, it's not precisely your house, is it? Josh is Marquess and master here. Not you."

Kate could feel her teeth grind together. He was right, of course. As long as Josh wanted him around, there was nothing she could do about it.

The tense atmosphere in the room underwent a rapid change a moment later as Hal's quiet voice said, "I think, Mallory, that if Kate wants you to go, the least you can do is vacate her immediate vicinity, don't you?"

Kate looked up to see her brother in the study doorway with Jennings and two footmen just behind him. She was hard put to hide how greatly relieved she was.

Mallory grinned widely. Above the grin, his eyes glittered with malice, "Ah. Little brother and his minions to the rescue. I bow to a superior force." He turned to Kate and leveled a finger at her. "I shall see you later, Katherine." It was clearly more threat than promise.

Katherine lifted her chin and glared down her nose at him. The instant he was gone, trailed by a watchful Jennings and the two burly footmen, Hal opened his arms and Kate fled into them.

By time for lunch, the restlessness and impatience building in Kate was more than she could control. She was past ready to put the ledgers away and do something that would take her out of the house, away from duty, and out into the bright and lightly breezy day.

Convincing Hal that the scene he'd witnessed between Mallory and her had been nothing more than their usual quarrel had taken all her skill and concentration. Ever since, she'd caught herself looking out the window again and again, until she knew she was not going to get anything else done. The urge to get outside for some exercise and air finally overwhelmed her. She shoved the ledgers back into the stack at the edge of the desk and walked briskly out of the study.

"Jennings, please have Star saddled and brought around."

"Yes, your ladyship." His eyes assessed her, reassuring himself that she was none the worse for the scene in the study.

"And, Jennings?" Kate waited until he looked straight at her. "Thank you, Jennings."

She knew he understood she was referring to his having brought Hal to her rescue. Giving him her very best smile, she watched him color, saw the pride in his eyes. Then he bowed. "It was my pleasure, Lady Katherine."

As soon as he'd gone to instruct one of the footmen to alert the grooms, Kate ran upstairs and along the hall to her suite. She had to fight the urge to unbutton her gown as she went, she wanted so badly to be out in the sunlight. It was as if the spring day had cast a spell on her that she was completely unable to resist—a spell that offered escape and sent her rushing to get out into the day.

• • •

Star thundered up the last hill on the estate and slowed to a walk at Kate's signal. Today the great black stallion was her rescuer, her magic carpet, her liberator. All her crushing burdens and awesome responsibilities were left miles behind.

She felt like a bird loosed from its cage, finding pleasure in her freedom. She laughed aloud at the sheer joy of being out of the manor, away from her brothers, and of momentarily putting aside the sense of duty she felt toward all three of them. Today, this afternoon, she was going to refuse to be practical Kate. For these few hours she was going to relax.

Before her was the downward sweep of the land to the cliffs of the sea and, beyond, the tiny seaport village of Clifton-on-Tides. The Channel was calm today, with long, rolling swells and only small whitecaps at widely spaced intervals. It was deep blue under the clear blue sky, and Kate had never seen the village that nestled there beside it look more peaceful.

Now, having learned from Lord Blysdale what took place there, she wondered how that could be. Surely the village folk were unaware of the nefarious trade Blysdale claimed emanated from its shores. Was it the unconscious desire to repudiate that claim that had drawn her here?

Usually Kate rode inland, where there were trails to meander along, wildlife to see and woods to explore. Where there were fences and hedges that she and Star could fly over together. Where she could talk to her horse without the wind snatching her words away, as it did here on this bluff overlooking the sea—or chance anyone overhearing such foolishness. Star was her sometimes confidant, after all.

She smiled at that and had leaned forward to stroke his satin neck, when suddenly the great horse whinnied a greeting that shook her in the saddle. Startled, she looked up to see a single horseman approaching.

In effect, the rider had her cornered. The sea was on her right, the steep hill before her, and he came from the only direction by which she could easily retreat. She gathered her reins. This was too deserted a place to encounter Gordon

Mallory. The man had too uncertain a temper now that Blysdale had come on the scene.

Then Kate saw that the horse was a tall, well-conformed
black, not the liver-chestnut behemoth that Mallory custom-
arily rode. And this man wasn't heavily built or a bruising
rider. He was slender and rode so well he seemed to be part
of his mount.

An instant later, her heart gave a leap and Kate recognized Blysdale. Strange, but even though she knew that his
temper where she was concerned was even worse than Gordon's "uncertain" one just now, she didn't fear meeting *him.*
So instead of touching Star with her spur, she hid the smile
that rose to her lips and waited for him to approach.

"Countess." He didn't smile as he touched the brim of
his hat to her.

"Lord Blysdale." She could see that he was more angry
with her now than hurt, contrary to the way he'd felt the
previous evening. It made her feel a great deal better. With
a radiant smile she told him, "How nice to see you."

Blysdale merely lifted an eyebrow.

"And where have you been that I see a cobweb on the
shoulder of your jacket, my lord?"

The expression on his face was as startled as if she'd told
him there was an arrow in his back. Blysdale looked over
his own shoulder to locate this reported gossamer offense to
his valet. "Ah." He frowned as if he'd never even had lint
on one of his jackets, much less blood and gunpowder. "So
there is. I imagine I acquired it when I was searching the
cellar of that house over the second hill west of us."

"Oh. That's the Brumidges' country house. They're away
just now."

"How long have they been gone?"

"Since last spring. Almost a year now. Mrs. Brumidge
suffers with rheumatism, and the family is presently resid-
ing in Bath in hopes that the waters will help her." She tilted
her head and watched him. "You're lucky you didn't run
into their watchman."

"Ummm."

Kate laughed. He sounded such a grump. It seemed that the beauty of the day had not affected Lord Blysdale. That was understandable. The matter of his friends' disappearance must weigh heavily on him. Evidently he wasn't capable of putting aside his responsibilities for a while as she had. She was callous to have thought he might.

After a moment she became serious and offered, "Look, Lord Blysdale, I have given the men on Cliffside their orders for the spring planting, and I've caught up on my book work." She smiled winningly. "Why don't I go about the countryside with you? I truly fear you will get yourself shot if you don't have . . . a local . . . to vouch for you when you're caught trespassing."

She hoped her hesitation before and after the word *local* would serve to remind him that he had used that word in his letter when inviting himself to Cliffside. Then he could hardly refuse her assistance. And he just *might* smile.

Blysdale sat staring at her for a full moment. Laughter lit her face and made her incredible green eyes shine like the emeralds they resembled. Was that mischief he saw in them?

She was so damned beautiful. She could stop a man's heart when she looked at him that way. Even his.

"Well?" Kate demanded. "Will you accept my help or not?"

Blysdale bowed from his saddle. "Lady Katherine, I will humbly accept whatever you might wish to offer me."

Lady Kate looked as if she weren't quite certain how to take that, though he was willing to bet that there wasn't much doubt in her mind that it had been a *double entendre*. The day was splendid, however—full of sunshine and bird-song, and if he chose to solace himself for her betrayal last night with a little sarcasm at her expense, he felt she had no right to mind.

"Come," she was saying, "we'll ride down to the sea. I shall want other clothes when I take you to explore the caves, but I can show you where they are, at any rate." She touched her blunted left spur lightly to her horse's side and, snorting once, the stallion tossed his head and tore off, eager to show Blysdale's mount his heels.

Blysdale was beside her in a flash, and they galloped head-long down the hill neck and neck, with Kate's windblown hair and her soft, delighted laughter floating behind them. He almost grabbed her bridle when she headed for the rock-strewn stream at the foot of the hill, but saw she didn't need him to save her from a fall. She was more than a competent rider; she was magnificent.

Blysdale smiled. For today he'd call a truce. When hostilities reopened, he'd make her pay for the Irishman, but for now they'd just enjoy this perfect day.

They sailed over the tumbling water side by side, drew rein, and walked their horses sedately into the seaside village.

"Is there an inn?" Blysdale asked her. "I could do with a pint of ale. Trespassing is dusty work."

"There's a tavern down by the dock, but you won't find Clifton-on-Tides's tavern as clean as Seth Linden's inn at Lesser–Clifton, nor the ale as good, either."

"You sound disapproving, Kate, as if this one of your villages is inferior to the other. And tell me, how does a lady know which of two ales is best?"

Kate grinned at him. "Even ladies get thirsty, Lord Blysdale. Ratafia and orgeat are neither one thirst quenching, you know."

"Thank God, I don't know from personal experience." It was Bly's turn to grin. "Too sweet by half, I should imagine."

"You're absolutely right," Kate answered, distracted by a man she saw.

She'd seen someone she recognized. Blysdale would bet on it. Could it be a man she knew to be in Gordon Mallory's employ? Someone who'd tell him they'd been seen together?

"What is it, Kate?" His glance followed the direction of her own, to where a man slipped around the corner of a building. Obviously, Blysdale sensed, something about him troubled her.

"I'm not sure," Kate answered him, her gaze locked on that corner of the building around which the man had disappeared. "I think, however, that we will not go to the caves just now."

Blysdale regarded her steadily. "Very well." He knew positively then that she had seen someone she didn't trust. That interested him. Did she suspect the person of being involved with the slavers?

That idea sent a fresh burst of anger through him. Could it be that this woman who so fascinated him had knowledge of the dastards who'd stolen his friends? No! He refused to believe that. That was just his surly nature trying to poison his opinions.

Surly or not, he wasn't so poor a judge of the fair sex as to have misread her to that extent. Especially after he'd forgotten himself so far as to call her his and to kiss her.

No, Kate Halsted was an honorable woman. He'd no doubt of that, though he'd certainly tried hard enough to work one up after that handsome lout in her drawing room had all but informed him she was his betrothed, damn his eyes!

Something was amiss there, though, he felt certain. He'd lived this long because he was never wrong about people. He wasn't going to start denying his instincts now just because he'd sustained a near-fatal wound to his foolish heart.

Someday, he knew, Kate would explain what hold that braggart had over her and allow him to run Mallory through. The mere thought of that event brightened his spirits considerably. A good fight was something he understood only too well, and the rather large Irishman looked as if he would prove a formidable opponent.

Blysdale smiled, looking forward to that time. He felt like a knight errant awaiting the bestowal of a commission to discharge for his lady fair. Devoutly he hoped the day that Kate would finally decide to confide in him would come soon. Until it did come, however, he settled down to enjoy this day.

Blysdale had never been alone with his Kate, except for their memorable hours in the tower, and he vowed that he wasn't going to waste this time wishing it away. "Since we're not going to the caves, Lady Katherine, shall I take you to the tavern instead?"

Kate seemed to know he was half joking. She obviously delighted in telling him, "Yes."

Chapter Fifteen

As they'd arranged over their tankards of ale in the dingy tavern the previous afternoon, Kate met Blysdale in the stables the next morning just before dawn. She wore a crisp white blouse tucked into a full, dark wool skirt from decades ago and a full-skirted man's coat that had belonged to her great-grandfather, the capacious pockets of which were bulging.

Seeing Blysdale stare at her outfit, she smiled. If Blysdale was surprised to see her so unfashionably dressed now, she wondered how he'd react when he saw her in the caves.

"Good morning, Lord Blysdale. I trust you took my advice and wore old clothes."

He didn't tell her it was the color of his coat that made him ready to ruin it, he just smiled and looked her over from head to toe. Bly thought Kate looked like a charming ragamuffin in her odd, ill-fitted clothing. She was certainly a far cry from the stylish lady in the red, military-styled habit that he'd taken to the tavern the afternoon before. He chuckled. "I'm afraid I don't have any clothes as old as those you're wearing."

Kate grinned. "How remiss of me." She turned and smiled

in a more ladylike fashion as she accepted Star's reins from the groom who held the horses. "If I'd thought of it, I'd certainly have offered you a crack at the trunks in the attic, too."

Bly tossed her into her saddle as if she weighed nothing and swung easily into his own. "Thank you all the same, but I've already availed myself of this excellent opportunity to get rid of one of my tailor's grosser mistakes."

Kate's gaze swept him. He looked fine to her, every inch the fashionable gentleman, in a dark brown coat and doeskin riding britches. She couldn't tell by his appearance what it was about his outfit that displeased him. "Is it a case of coat by Hoby, boots by Weston?"

A crack of laughter escaped him. "Indeed, I believe you have the right of it." They gave the horses their heads and walked away from the stable to get the kinks out of their mounts' muscles before asking for a faster pace. Blysdale was still smiling at her suggestion that the realm's finest bootmaker had made his coat, and the best tailor in England his boots. Later, if the occasion arose, he'd tell her that the reason he didn't like the coat was simply that he never wore brown.

Kate looked over at him and decided that the usually sardonic man was really quite handsome when he relaxed and smiled. She wished they could continue their companionable foolishness for the rest of the ride to Clifton-on-Tides. She already knew him well enough, however, to know that he'd return to thinking of the hunt for his missing friends shortly. But, oh, it had been absolutely splendid to hear him laugh. She smiled secretly. Even if he did sound as if he didn't really know how.

Someday, when all this was over, she vowed she was going to teach the saturnine Lord Blysdale really, freely, to laugh.

Side by side through the mists of morning they rode across the estate. When they came to the hill on which they'd met the day before, they cantered down it this time, waded the stream instead of jumping it, and walked once more into the village.

The fog from the Channel that still clung to the ancient buildings and swirled like drifting smoke through the village streets partially hid them, and their quieter approach enabled them to pass through Clifton-on Tides without being noticed. It was a simple thing, then, to hurry around the first head-land before the tiny seaport awakened, and the overhanging bulk of the cliffs there hid them from prying eyes.

"I think we made it through the village without being seen." Kate smiled over her shoulder at Blysdale.

Blysdale looked back, every sense alert. After a moment, he answered with assurance, "Yes. There's no one follow-ing us."

Kate shrugged off the faint annoyance his so positive as-sertion caused her and said, "The first cave's just up ahead."

They rode over sand still shining from the ebbing tide. Kate led the way and watched carefully for the occasional patch of quicksand sometimes created by currents of water that ran under loose sand. At intervals along the way, they splashed through pools that glimmered in the faint light an-nouncing the dawn.

As they rode the tide-washed sands, dark cliffs towered above them, their sheer bulk dwarfing the puny pair of rid-ers at their base. The sea dampness made the sand almost firm under their horses' hooves then slowly dissolved the hoofprints away as if they had never been made. As a child, Kate had considered seeing her footprints slowly disappear magic—beach magic done by a caring father God to amuse his younger children. Now something was wrong with that image. Now, the sands seemed sinister.

Kate gave a little shiver. This beach had never given her such a feeling when she was a child. Then, it had been a wonderful place for children to play, seeming to welcome the picnics and bonfires of driftwood and the youthful shell seekers who lit them.

Now it was as if the place had undergone some dreadful change and become hostile since her youth. She could al-most imagine, as she looked back at the disappearing hoof-prints, that it conspired to erase any proof of their existence.

Kate glanced at Blysdale and saw that he was tautly alert. His narrow-eyed gaze took in their surroundings and left her with the impression that he missed nothing. Somehow, Kate wasn't comforted, though.

The mouth of the first cave was a large, dark break in the foot of the cliff. Wide and low, it seemed to swallow the feeble light of early dawn. The horses pricked their ears forward and lifted their heads as they approached it. The boom of the surf echoed off the back wall of the cavern, and told them it was a dangerous place.

Urging a reluctant Star on with her voice, Kate rode him into the cave. The stallion's iron-shod hooves slipped as he scrambled over the sea-wet rocks, and he whickered nervously. Passing from the day's half-light into the cave's deep gloom disquieted the stallion. Star's ears flicked back and forth.

Kate could see that he didn't like this place that smelled so strongly of damp and seaweed. "It's all right, boy." She slid from his back and stood caressing him until he relaxed. "Stay here and wait for me," she told him quietly.

Blysdale looked at her a little skeptically. His own mount, a seasoned veteran of battles in which cannon had always played a prominent part, was sidling around to look back out of the cave at the sea booming on the rocks a hundred yards away.

Blysdale decided to make certain he wouldn't have to walk back to Cliffside Manor. Quickly, he slipped a pair of well-padded hobbles out of his saddlebags and expertly fastened them around the pasterns of his horse's front legs.

Kate turned to her own mount and pulled a small lantern from one of her large saddlebags. Handing it to Blysdale, she reached into the capacious pockets of her ancient coat and brought out the candle for it and a flint and steel to light it with. When he'd lit the candle and affixed it to the candle holder in the lantern, Kate accepted it from him and put the flint and steel back into her pocket.

"You're an amazing woman, Lady Katherine," he told her with a grin.

"Thank you." She proceeded to amaze him by reaching matter-of-factly to the fastening of her skirt, undoing it, and letting the garment fall to the cave floor at her feet.

She stood tall and slender in dark men's britches and her riding boots for an instant, pretending not to see Blysdale's faint expression of shock. Then she bent and scooped up her skirt and placed it carefully behind Star's saddle.

Blysdale watched, holding the lantern, until she'd finished arranging her skirt. "As I said, amazing. Who but you would find a use for a woman's discarded skirt? Only you'd have made it a quarter blanket." He let his admiration show. That was better than letting her suspect the effect seeing her long, smooth, slender legs were having on him. Far better. "Well done, Lady Katherine. That'll protect his loins against any chill that might come to him here in this drafty cave."

"Too bad *you* didn't wear a skirt."

"Somehow, I don't think so."

They laughed together then, and Kate's heart lifted. He'd forgiven her. At least for today. It was, she well knew, more than he thought she deserved.

Kate turned and led the way into the darkness at the back of the cave, guided by the light of the lantern Blysdale held aloft and her childhood memory of the cavern. "This one is rather shallow," she told her companion. "Some of them go back hundreds of feet. The cave next to this goes back farther than I've ever dared to venture."

They walked along the sea-swept floor of the cave with relative ease and completed their inspection of it in less than ten minutes. Blysdale was looking hard for anything that might indicate men had been held captive here, but there was nothing.

Kate could feel his disappointment.

As they made their way back to the mouth of the cavern, he asked, "Does the sea enter all the caves, filling them completely?"

"The next one, the one I haven't gone all the way back into, is dry when you get into it a bit. The floor slopes upward sharply at first, then more gradually, but still upward beyond the reach of the tide. My brothers would never let me go very far in it as there are many tunnels and side chambers. They were certain I'd get lost." She smiled at him. "Frankly, the wind howls through them and makes such mournful sounds that I never tried to get them to change their minds." She enjoyed the way she could be honest with this man, freely admitting a young child's temerity.

"You can wait for me at the mouth, then." He saw her resistance to the idea of being left behind, and smiled one of his rare smiles. "I'll need you there to call me back to safety in case *I* get lost." He moved closer, suddenly wanting to touch her, wanting to reestablish the rapport they'd had before the other night and Gordon Mallory.

Kate didn't know why her knees started to melt, but when he took hold of her shoulders and said in a husky voice, "You want to keep me safe, don't you, Kate?" they almost gave way under her. She twisted free, said grumpily, "Of course, I do," and headed for the horses.

She wasn't ready for another scene like the one in the tower. Lord Blysdale seemed to be better able to handle them than she was.

Blysdale watched her go with a twisted grin. He'd routed her without wanting to. Reaching Lady Kate again was going to be a challenge.

Watching her, he frowned suddenly. An instant later he gave a slight start. There was something about her as she moved away from him that had touched a faint chord in his memory. He frowned harder, trying to pin the fleeting memory, but Kate derailed his thoughts with a gruff, "Come on."

They rode to the mouth of the second cave, and discovered the way further into it was blocked. A fall of rock had occurred at some time, and the wall it formed effectively cut off their progress.

"How odd." Kate was puzzled. "In my whole life I've never seen anything like this." She slid down off Star and walked forward. She stood peering into the gloom for a moment, then came back to get the lantern Blysdale had carried over, its candle still burning, from the first cave. With it, she went to inspect the rock slide.

Blysdale followed her, murmuring, "What is it that makes you so intrepid, my splendid Kate?"

Ignoring that question, she told him, "There's no way around this. Nor over it either."

"No, there certainly doesn't seem to be," Blysdale agreed. Then he turned and walked straight out of the cave, to a point some distance from it. There he turned around and stared up at the top of the cliffs for a long moment.

When he returned to the cave it was to find Kate slithering down from the top of the rock slide, the lantern clutched in her hand and held rigidly away from her body to keep its glass safe. When she reached the floor of the cave, Blysdale was there to steady her.

She took his arm with her free hand and used it to hold her balance while she lifted her left leg and bent backward to look at the shining leather of her riding boot. "Drat! I think I've scratched it."

"Here." Blysdale turned her from him. "Let me see." He inspected the back of her boot, carefully checking its fine, supple leather for any sign of damage. He could understand her concern. The boots were of especially fine workmanship and perfectly fitted Kate's slender calves. Her boots had undoubtedly been made by a master craftsm . . .

Then it hit him. The boots! That was what had been nagging at the back of his mind—Kate's boots! They were just like the boots of the youthful highwayman who'd held up his coach. Now, more pieces of the puzzle crowded in. The highwayman's grace of movement. His height and his slender stature—they were Kate's. The smooth, well-cared for skin around his eyes—green eyes, he was certain of it now, of course, because they'd been Kate's eyes. Kate's lovely green eyes!

The highwayman hadn't been a young man, as he'd thought. No young footman from Cliffside had "borrowed" Kate's stallion. There'd been no young footman—the highwayman had been Kate!

An agonized cry escaped him. "Ah, blast it, Kate!"

He bit off the rest of the accusation that rose to his lips. Swallowed the scold with which he wanted to lash her for daring to undertake such a dangerous pastime, and thanked his lucky stars he'd discovered what she was up to in time to stop her before she got seriously hurt.

He blanched to think what his two friends, Stone and MacLain, might have inadvertently done to her that night he'd interrupted their capture of the young highwayman she pretended to be. They'd been a little careful because they thought her a youth—what if they'd handled her as if she were a man? What the devil was she thinking to take such chances? How dare she!

"Is it torn?" she asked about her boot. "Is that why you sound so upset? You mustn't be. These are my very favorite boots, but I *can* get others."

Boots! The blithering wench thought he was mourning a pair of boots! What a featherbrain! Yes, she could get another pair of boots. Hell, he'd buy her dozens of pairs just like these. But where would *he* get another Kate when she lay in her blood on the highway, shot down like a dog by some man whose coach she'd stopped?

His raging fear for her gave birth to anger as he swore he'd see to it she never played highwayman again. "No, your blasted boot isn't torn!" he snapped at her. "It's only scratched." He yanked her around and dragged her toward the horses. "Now let's get the blazes out of here!"

Kate yanked back. She didn't care to be manhandled, even by Blysdale. "I can walk, thank you. My leg isn't broken. Only my boot is scratched." What in Heaven's name ailed him? He was the most mercurial man she'd ever met. One moment he was a pleasant companion, amiably exploring caves with her, the next he was an angry curmudgeon she'd have to be insane to want to spend the rest of her life with!

Blysdale realized he was giving too much away. Why the deuce he seemed to lose his very nature whenever he was in this woman's company he couldn't fathom. He could understand, however, that he must get a grip on himself. Taking a deep breath, he fought for calm.

"Sorry, Kate. I didn't mean to drag you along like that, but come, let's go. I don't want us to be seen here."

That was true. The hairs on the back of Blysdale's neck were prickling. In spite of the rest of his intelligence having gone begging when he'd realized Kate was the highwayman, his survival instincts were still in perfect working order, and they were warning him that danger was approaching. "Quickly, Kate, tell me. Is there another way off this beach, or must we go back through Clifton-on-Tides?"

"No. There is another way. We can go the long way around, but it will take hours longer."

"Put your skirt on and let's get out of here." He pulled her skirt from Star's hindquarters. Star snorted and danced away. Blysdale glanced uneasily back toward the headland that hid the little seaport and held her skirt out to Kate.

She sensed the urgency in him and bit back the remark she'd been about to make. Dropping the skirt over her head, she fastened the waistband hastily. She'd hardly gotten it done before Blysdale grabbed her and tossed her up onto her stallion. Leaping to the back of his own mount, he seized her bridle and galloped off.

Kate's head snapped back as Star lunged forward, and her temper snapped with it. She was ready to let fly at her escort when she heard a shout behind her. Glancing back, she saw three men running in their direction. One of them was shaking his fist.

Only Blysdale's quick action had saved them from being identified—or, worse yet, apprehended.

Chapter Sixteen

They tore along the beach like a pair of madmen, the horses laboring in the wet sand, great globs of it flying up behind them. Still running full out, they rounded the next headland. Only then did Blysdale slacken their pace.

"There's a path to the top of the cliffs." Blysdale raised his voice to be heard over the crash of the surf and the heavy breathing of their mounts. "Do we take it?"

"No," Kate called back to him. "There's a better one farther on."

"How far?"

"Not very. Stay on the beach, but keep close to the base of the cliff. The land curves out a bit here and we could be seen by the men behind us!"

They both looked back. The three men were out of their line of sight so they were currently unobserved, but they needed to reach and get around the next promontory. Only then could they consider themselves safe from their pursuers' eyes.

Due to the curve of the cliffs, the headland that had been hiding them would not do so in a few more yards. Time was running out.

"Sorry, boys." Blysdale spurred his horse to greater effort, dragging Star relentlessly along.

"Stop!" Kate cried. "You'll kill the horses!"

Better the horses than you, my love, he thought as he spurred on. Then he was cursing himself for not having brought a pistol. It would have been a simple thing to have strapped on his sleeve gun this morning, but he'd left it off ever since he'd been here in this quiet section of the country. He hadn't even worn his knife. Now if anyone were to seriously threaten Kate, he'd only his Far Eastern skills to protect her. And they would be useless if their assailants had firearms.

The horses were blown by the time they reached the next headland. Their lathered sides were heaving. Still he forced them on until they'd rounded it.

The instant they had, he drew rein, vaulted off, and pulled Kate from her saddle. While she railed at him, he loosened the saddle girths of both mounts and began walking them slowly.

"How could you! You could have injured them," Kate accused. Turning to her stallion she ran along beside him. "Star. Are you all right?"

"For God's sake, Kate! Do you really expect the beast to answer you?" He knew as well as she did that the huge horse could find some way to indicate his feelings, because his own mounts could. He was being eaten alive with anxiety for her safety, though, and wanted to lash out at anything, even at her, to ease it.

Still, some part of his mind was astounded at his behavior. What the blazes was the matter with him? Never had he been so disturbed when he most needed to be cool! If this had ever happened to him on the battlefield, he'd have been dead long ago. His brow furrowed in a scowl to end all scowls as he strived to pull himself together.

Star chose that moment to indicate his feelings about being abused. He reached for Blysdale with strong yellow teeth. Blysdale hardly looked as he slapped the horse away.

"Star!" Kate was shocked.

So was Star. He reared up away from Blysdale's blow with his nose stinging, tore the reins from the man's hands, and spun around to plop his head against Kate.

"Oh, Star, did he hurt you?"

"Ha!" Blysdale snarled at her. "No little slap is going to bother a stallion. Yours is just spoiled and wants his pampering."

"Pampering! First you try to run him into the ground, then you hit him, and then you accuse me of pampering him when he comes to me for reassurance. How can you?"

Blysdale sighed heavily and let it go. "Just keep him walking if you don't want his legs wrecked."

Kate knew he was right, of course. After such an effort, if the horses weren't kept moving their legs would stock up. They had to keep their mounts moving in order to keep the blood from settling in the delicate veins of their lower legs or the horses would never be quite as sound again.

They trudged on, the sand scratching the fine leather of their boots. Little by little their tempers cooled.

"You raised him from a foal?" Blysdale's voice was kind now. He was fairly certain they were too far ahead of their pursuers for Kate to be in any danger and was beginning to relax again.

After a sullen moment, Kate responded, "Yes." Then, admitting that Blysdale may have had to do what he'd done to keep them from being identified by the men she was almost sure were Mallory's, she said a little less churlishly, "He's the son of my favorite first mare."

"Then he must mean a great deal to you."

"Yes, a very great deal. He's my"—she hesitated, knowing she was about to sound totally ridiculous—"my friend." She ran a loving hand down Star's sweat-roughened neck.

Blysdale didn't laugh. He just walked on. Kate noticed that when his mount reached out and touched his muzzle to the man's sleeve, Blysdale stroked it. Maybe that was why he hadn't laughed. Maybe he understood.

Kate slogged on after him. She felt much more in charity with him, somehow. Obviously, he was a man who understood having a rapport with his horse. Kate smiled. That was something else they had in common. Something almost as important as a love of reading.

Overhead, the sun was burning away the fog, and the day was brightening. Here at the base of the cliffs, the sand had had a little time to dry out a bit, and it was deeper, harder going. Glancing to her right, Kate saw that the tide was turning. Even so, they still had time to reach the wider, safer path that led to the top of the cliffs.

As if he'd read her mind, Blysdale asked, "How far is it to the path you want to take to the top?"

"Very close now. Just around the next promontory." She brought Star up even with Blysdale's gelding and walked beside him, the two of them between their horses. "What shall I call you?" She was a little breathless from the heavy going.

He looked at her and grinned. "What do you want to call me?"

Kate laughed, reading his thoughts. "No. You're safe. I'm over the desire to call you something unrepeatable in polite company. The horses don't seem to be harmed, and I'm sure you abused them as you did only to keep us safe from prying eyes."

"Or worse." His voice rumbled as he said it.

"Worse?"

"Yes. Suppose those men thought we were too close to something they didn't want discovered."

"Oh." Kate's eyes grew round. "I hadn't thought of that. Yes. They could have been smugglers. But we didn't find a cave in which contraband could have been hidden, so what were they worried about?"

"What indeed." His voice was deathly quiet.

Kate stopped walking. Horror dawned in her eyes. "You think they were connected with the slavers." It was a statement, an accusation.

"Perhaps. With you along, I wasn't willing to take any chances in order to find out."

"You'd have taken a chance if you'd been alone?"

He grinned down at her. "No. I'd have gotten out of there a whole lot faster if I hadn't had to drag you."

Kate's mouth fell open. For an instant, her eyes were almost as wide again, then she laughed and said amiably, "Liar."

They continued walking, Kate, tall as she was, having to take three steps to Blysdale's two long strides. After a while, Kate asked again, "What shall I call you?"

Darling would be nice, Bly thought, and was startled. *Now where the devil did that come from?* He worked to sound calm as he said, "Oh, I don't know. Have you tired of 'Lord Blysdale'?"

"Long ago. Besides, you are constantly calling me 'Kate'—why should I be formal?"

"Hmmmm." He appeared to give the matter thought. "I suppose then that 'your lordship' won't do either?"

She slapped him with the buckle end of her reins, careful not to jab Star's mouth with the bit as she used it. "Wretch. Give me a name. Surely you have one. Everybody does."

"True." He looked beyond her to see if they were being followed. He was glad to see that they weren't. "My Christian name is Chalfont."

"Chalfont." Kate said it thoughtfully.

"More 'shall' and less 'chal,' please. It's French, you see. Think of the 'ch' in *château* and you'll have it."

"Is that all? I mean is that your only given name?"

"I see you don't like Chalfont any better than I do. Unfortunately, I was given only the one name, my French family's surname, so you'll have to make do with it."

Only one first name. Everybody in the nobility had more than one Christian name! Kate had cousins who dragged half a dozen Christian names through life. Blysdale's parents had named him with as much thought as one would use to name a *dog.* Fierce resentment on his behalf rose in Kate.

Bly was saying, "Or call me simply Bly, as my friends do."

They were being a little idiotic, he thought, but there wasn't anything important to do as they rested the horses in preparation for the climb up the cliff face, and he was finding it rather nice. She was good company, his Kate. All the women he'd known before her—except for the camp followers, of course—would have been complaining and demanding to be put back on their horses long before now. But his Kate was . . . He stopped so suddenly that the horses shied. *His Kate! Now where the blazes did that come from?*

"What is it?" Kate was all concern. "Is something wrong?" She tried to look everywhere at once.

"No." He started walking again. "Nothing's wrong." *Nothing I can tell you, Katherine Halsted. I'm just suffering some sort of fanciful delusion. I'll get over it,* he thought grimly.

Kate pointed. "There's the path up."

"We'll walk up and save the horses. That way they'll be ready to ride when we get to the top."

"Of course."

She hadn't minded being told she'd have to toil up the steep path, either, he noted. Kate was indeed the extraordinary woman he'd told her blasted Irishman she was.

He stood just looking down at her. If he . . . but there was no need to consider, even for an instant, that he might inflict himself on any woman as a husband, much less Kate. He knew too well that at heart he was a savage man—not one who could ever be domesticated.

"I shall call you Bly, then," Kate said quietly, holding out her hand to shake his as if they were men meeting for the first time. "And I shall hope that you will count me among your friends."

Their ride back to Cliffside was long and uneventful, and Chalfont Blysdale was quiet all the way.

Chapter Seventeen

It was dusk by the time Kate and Blysdale rode their weary horses up to Cliffside Manor. Jennings flung wide the huge double doors and astonished Blysdale by exclaiming, "Where have you been, Lady Katherine? We've all been worried." in exactly the same tone of voice he'd used to scold her years ago when she'd stayed away from the house too long.

She smiled at him fondly. "Lord Blysdale and I took the long way back from Clifton-on-Tides. I had forgotten just how very much longer it was. I'm sorry I worried you."

Blysdale was staring. He wasn't used to servants speaking so forthrightly. He wasn't used to servants who *cared.* When the butler said, "Well, you'd best hurry to dress," as if he were instructing a child, and added, "Cook will be upset if her roast should get overdone waiting for you," it was more than he could take. Never had there been such warmth in his home, and seeing it was tearing at something in his vitals. Bowing to Kate, he murmured, "If your ladyship will excuse me?" and bolted.

When Blysdale reached his bedchamber, Griswold had his employer's clothes laid out and waiting for him to change into after his bath. As Blysdale strode into the room, Griswold grabbed up toweling and padded his hands. Then he lifted the huge copper canister full of steaming water from where he'd stood it just inside the fireplace to keep warm and added it to the water that had become lukewarm in the ornate bathtub standing close to the hearth.

"You'll be late for dinner if you don't shake a leg, sir." Smug didn't begin to describe the look on his face.

Bly gave him his due. "Well done, Gris. But how the devil did you know when I'd be here?"

Griswold smiled at that and then frowned. "Now that's an odd thing, sir." He helped Blysdale out of his riding coat, then bent to pull off his boots, scowling at all the tiny scratches walking in the sand had made in them.

"What's an odd thing?" Bly stood in his stocking feet, tearing away at his sadly crushed cravat.

"The way people's movements are known here in the manor." He reached for the shirt Blysdale shrugged out of and folded it loosely while he ran a professional gaze over his master's well-muscled torso. That was a habit he found impossible to break after all the army years. All those years he'd spent checking for wounds after battles that had left his Colonel too exhausted to feel any but near-mortal ones had firmly ingrained the habit.

At least nowadays there weren't ever any wounds, and Griswold never failed to thank God. Griswold considered that absence of wounds recompense enough for the shade of boredom life had taken on since army days.

Blysdale settled in the tub and began scrubbing away the day's ride. He hated being dirty, a condition he'd frequently had to endure while serving on the Peninsula. "How do you suppose that's accomplished, Griswold? How *do* they know where people are?"

"Well, sir, seems, near as I can tell, that they have a system—a network, like—of young lads that pass the word somehow about anybody they see coming this way." He shook his head. "Can't figure why. Maybe it's a point of pride."

Bly grinned. "A very sage deduction. Keep your eyes peeled. Something of interest to us might turn up."

"Won't be easy. Haven't seen any arrows flying."

"Arrows?" Bly was puzzled.

Griswold chuckled. "Don't you remember in those old tales of Robin Hood how they shot arrows from one man to the next to warn Robin that intruders were on their way into Sherwood Forest?"

"Hmmmm." Bly was keeping his mouth firmly shut. With his valet pouring water over his head to rinse the soap out of his hair, it seemed prudent, and that was just as well. He wasn't quite ready to share his discovery that Lady Katherine was the highwayman.

"Anyhow," Gris promised, "I'll soon get to the bottom of it." He wrapped his Colonel in a drying sheet as he stepped out of the tub. "Maybe I'll find a clue in that boy that brought the note to Lady Katherine shortly before the two of you got in."

Bly spun around, demanding, "What boy?"

"The same one that's come twice before. Comes around suppertime. Always has a note for her ladyship. Sometimes he takes back an answer. He's waiting for one now, unless I miss my guess."

"And you say this lad has come here this evening?" Blysdale's usually quiet mind was spinning.

"Yes, sir. He's still waiting for Lady Katherine to answer the note, and I have our John Coachman in the kitchen keeping an eye on the lad."

"Quickly, Gris." Bly threw off the bath sheet. "Get me together. I have to get downstairs to see what's going on. Hurry!"

"Do hurry, Dresden." Kate tried hard not to sound impatient. "I want to get downstairs."

"Well, your ladyship, it's hard to dress your hair when it's still so wet from your bath, but I'll try to rush some sort of style into it. At least we got all the sand out." She looked hard at her employer's reflection, meeting the mirrored gaze. "There was sand in your hair, you know. Were you riding on the beach?"

"Yes. I was. Lord Blysdale wanted to see ... the sea," Kate finished lamely. Great Scot. Did she think she couldn't even be honest with her own, dear Dresden? What was her life coming to? She couldn't help it, though. She didn't want it known that Bly and she had been visiting the caves. Even trusted Dresden could let a word drop in front of the wrong person, and that could be dangerous.

She shifted impatiently.

Dresden correctly interpreted Kate's squirm. "I *am* hurrying, Lady Katherine."

That was certainly a familiar way of scolding. Kate sat statue-still as a result.

"Thank you, Dresden. I know you're doing your best."

Encouraged by her employer's courtesy, the abigail ventured, "You'll have need of the hare's foot for your nose, my lady." She couldn't hold back her reproof. "You've gotten it quite sunburned."

"No. No powder." Kate knew she mustn't have anything that marked her as distinctly female on her face tonight. She couldn't afford it. The note the boy'd brought from Linden had told her there was a coach heading this way from the general direction of London. If it turned toward the sea, she must be on the highway to intercept it. And highwaymen did not wear powder, no matter how sunburned their noses were.

She shivered slightly at the thought of having to go hold up another coach. She was weary and her courage seemed to be at low ebb. It had been since her near capture.

"Are you cold, your ladyship? Shall I get you a shawl?"

"That would be nice, Dresden. I'm a little tired, and I think I do feel a bit chilly this evening as a result." But it wasn't a chill from the temperature. Kate felt as if a rabbit had run over her grave.

She stared at her face in the mirror. She looked so tense. Was she having some sort of premonition?

God forbid.

And God grant that this one would be the coach in which she would find the proof to free Hal from suspicion, for truly, she didn't care to play the highwayman much longer. Somehow she felt certain she was running out of luck.

She couldn't think of that just now, though. She had a dinner to get through.

Looking back at the mirror, Kate gave her reflection an anxious perusal. Indeed, her face did show signs of a day in the sun. Well, that was to be expected. She'd planned to spend an early morning in the caves on the other side of Clifton-on-Tides, not spend the entire day riding across sunny fields. Drat Blysdale and his desire to escape being observed returning to Cliffside. Not that she meant that. He'd been right to be cautious, she knew.

Besides, on the brighter side, she had to admit that she'd enjoyed riding beside him all day. She'd admired the way he'd automatically husbanded their horses' strength and picked the easiest paths for them. Enjoyed the places he'd chosen to rest their mounts, as he always seemed to find one with a lovely view.

She'd loved the companionable silence in which they'd ridden, too. The absence of the idle chatter and the fawning compliments that ruined most rides she'd taken with members of the opposite sex had been wonderful.

She smiled at her reflection and acknowledged that most of all she'd liked the way he'd expected her to be able to keep up with him. He'd looked her over carefully a time or two, and nodded as if satisfied with what he saw. Not once had he offered to slacken the pace or add more halts than were needed for resting the horses in order to coddle her. That had filled her with a pride-filled sense of gratification.

Suddenly Kate laughed.

"Oh!" Dresden was startled. "What is it, Lady Katherine?"

"Nothing, Dresden. I just had . . . an . . . odd thought." And she certainly had, for she'd just realized that today Lord Blysdale had once again found her every bit as durable, *and therefore as admirable,* as his much-praised camp followers!

• • •

At dinner, Blysdale watched Lady Katherine Elizabeth with the same careful attention he'd have given a top French spy. It wasn't an unpleasant task. She was a beautiful woman. He wondered why he hadn't seen that when they first met.

Too tall and too dark a blond to be a "Diamond of the First Water," she was nevertheless completely satisfactory to him. She fit in his arms very well and matched his own lean body hip to hip and thigh to thigh in a manner he found most pleasing.

Tonight she was particularly beautiful in a low-cut gown of blue and green that showed off her perfect figure and brought out the green of her eyes. Or was it the hint of sunburn across her cheeks that gave her green eyes an extra sparkle with its rosy contrast? That thought pleased him best because she'd gotten that sunburn while she rode beside him most of the afternoon. He'd discovered that he liked having her beside him.

Kate turned to tell Jennings something, and the bodice of her gown pulled tight across her breasts with the movement, causing the soft flesh above the décolletage to swell. Blysdale felt his body harden in response.

Kate had that effect on him more often than he cared to admit. He'd had it when she'd dropped her skirt around her booted feet early this morning, revealing her long, slender legs tightly clad in the boy's britches she wore to climb through the caves. She had lovely legs. Long and smooth. He'd had to fight the desire to run his hands down them, then very slowly up again to . . .

Blast! He was as randy as a new recruit on his first visit to a brothel. What the devil was the matter with him? Kate was a woman to marry, and all the world knew that he was a man allergic to the idea.

They'd made their way through the dinner courses to the dessert by the time he admitted that he would have to get himself back under control—strive to banish visions of all that heavy deep golden hair spread out on his pillow . . . spread out on the sandy floor of a sea-washed cave, or on the deep green grass of one of the meadows over which they'd ridden today! Anywhere. Anywhere at all as long as he could be there with her, spent and burying his face in the wealth of her hair.

Blysdale shifted uncomfortably. Desire for his hostess burned through him like flame.

For a moment, he thought of easing his physical problem by sending for his mistress. Maria and the interesting games she knew no longer seemed to interest him, though. Perhaps it was time he let her go. She was a beautiful woman. She'd have no trouble finding another protector, and he'd be generous, as always.

"I say, Colonel. What did you think of it?"

Blysdale had no idea what topic was under discussion. Far less what he, personally, thought of it. Obviously, the distraction his longing for Kate provided was making him remiss as a dinner companion.

With an effort he tore his mind away from the tantalizing images it formed of himself making love to Lady Katherine sufficiently to contribute to the conversation.

It was by no means as interesting.

Kate was. He could see tension rising in her as dinner progressed. By the time the port and cigars were brought out for the men, Blysdale could see that she was as taut as a bowstring. At dinner's end, when Kate excused herself and left the room, she sped like an arrow shot from one, as well.

What had sent her away so quickly? And why was she so tense? Had the boy brought word of a coach she felt she had to stop and search? God forbid!

Stretching luxuriously now they were only men, Bly gave a great yawn. "Gentlemen, I fear I had too much fresh air this afternoon." He rose and lifted a languid hand in farewell. "Good night."

He sauntered as far as the door, exited, then increased his pace. Taking the stairs three at a time, he gained the upper floor. He was running lightly down the hall to the door of Katherine's suite an instant later. Slipping into an alcove opposite it, he concealed himself behind the large urn from the

Ming dynasty that stood on a tall pedestal there and waited. When Kate emerged, he would follow her.

Half an hour later Kate had still not left her rooms. Surely by now she'd had time to change out of her dinner gown and into her boy's britches? Blysdale could wait no longer. Anxiety rose in him. Kate must come to no harm!

Quitting his hiding place, he ran full tilt for the stairs. He didn't know how, but he was certain Kate had another way out of her rooms. He could feel that she was gone. He was out the front door before the footman on duty there could get out of his chair. "Your lordship! Shall I get you a horse? Let me send for a groom!"

Outside on the vast gravel carriage sweep there was no horse waiting that Bly could steal for his purpose. Cursing, he ran for the stables.

Nothing would help calm him but catching Kate and ridding himself of the terrible premonition that drove him. "A horse!" he demanded. "Your fastest horse!"

"The fastest horse is the master's Dragonslayer, your lordship," one of the grooms told him. Blysdale followed the man as he ran to a stall apart from the others where a huge chestnut stood pawing and tossing his head.

The horse had caught their excitement and was raring to go. "Good boy!" Blysdale told him. "We may need that enthusiasm before this night is over."

Suddenly Griswold appeared at his side with Blysdale's own saddle over his arm. He was breathing hard. "I waited for you to come out of the dining room with the other gents, Colonel. When you didn't, I looked for you all over." He took several needed breaths, almost panting. "Wanted to tell you that boy that brings the notes to Lady Katherine stirred something up, but couldn't find you." He gulped air. "Finally saw you tearing off in this direction." He stopped talking and concentrated fully on catching his breath.

Blysdale snatched the saddle from him and tried hard not to slap it on the strange horse's back. Lowering it gently, he slid it back to smooth the hairs under it and drew up the girth. It fitted well enough. Bly had had it stuffed so it could fit a number of horses, not a single, specific one, as custom dictated. The cavalryman in him knew the folly of trying to carry a separate saddle for each charger in his string.

The groom handed him the horse's bridle, and Blysdale slipped it on the big gelding. Turning to his friend, he clapped him on the shoulder and said, "Good man, Gris." He gave him the explanation he owed him. "I left the dining room early to see what Lady Kate was up to."

He was in the saddle and had reined the big horse around to face the stable door before he'd finished speaking. "Wait here for me!" he ordered as he galloped away.

Chapter Eighteen

Blysdale told the big horse under him, "Fly, damn you, fly! We have to get to Kate before . . . " Before what? What was he so fearful of? What had his guts in a knot and his heart in his mouth? "Oh, God, Kate." His very soul twisted in an agony of apprehension. "Be safe."

He spurred viciously, and the chestnut increased his speed. Trees flew by. Huge gouts of turf were thrown up as the horse dug his hooves more fiercely into it to propel himself and his demon rider onward.

Suddenly a cry came out of the night. "Stand and deliver," was borne faintly to Blysdale on the night wind. He leaned lower and asked his mount for greater speed. It wasn't possible. The big horse was already giving all that he had.

Blysdale moaned in frustration and rode as he'd never ridden in all his days, husbanding the strength of the horse under him. Finally, what seemed an aeon later, he glimpsed light through the trees. Carriage lamps! He was almost there!

An instant later, he could see Kate's slender figure entering the coach. She had her pistol trained on its sole occupant. Good girl. She searched the coach with her free hand, never taking her eyes off the man.

Bly pulled his mount down to a walk. To burst in on Kate might break her concentration, cause her to do something careless. The wind was in his face. He knew the sound of Dragonslayer's hooves had not carried to her up there on the highway.

He was still too far away to be any help to her. Again he cursed himself for not bringing a pistol. There'd been no time!

Kate exited the coach and gestured the owner back into it. Bly could tell by the set of her shoulders that she had not found whatever it was that she'd been searching for. But she wasn't watching the man in the coach! "Look out!" he shouted, spurring forward.

It was too late. Before Kate could turn back to the coach, its occupant had snatched a pistol from somewhere and discharged it straight at Kate's back.

Everything happened at once. Kate threw up her hands, sending her pistol spinning up high over her head. She staggered one step. Then she began to fall.

Star reared and charged the coach, teeth bared, shrieking his fury. The coach horses bolted, slamming their owner back against his seat before he could reload.

Bly rammed his mount forward and leapt from the saddle. Snatching Kate to him with one arm, he plucked her pistol from the air with his other hand and fired it at the man in the careening coach. The man's sharp cry brought him no satisfaction. All he could see, all he could think about was Kate. Kate, who lay limp in his arms, her eyes closed, their long lashes resting on her rapidly paling cheeks.

"Aaaaah! Nooooo! No, God!" Blysdale howled like a wounded dog as the universe spun around him and the stars fell from the sky, rocketing to earth through his grief-shattered mind.

Blysdale had no idea how he got back to Cliffside Manor. He only knew that Griswold met him before he got to the house and tried to take Kate from him and was rewarded for the attempt with a vicious snarl. He knew that he took the back servants' stairs up to her rooms. And he knew that once there, Griswold had forcefully pried Kate from his arms.

Blysdale stood in the middle of Kate's bedchamber with his head lowered as if he were going to charge someone and strove to pull himself together. While he did, Griswold began to ease Kate out of her boy's coat. It was Kate's sharp cry of pain that brought Bly back to himself.

"How bad is it, Gris?"

"She was lucky. The ball tore along her shoulder blade instead of piercing it. Must have been a light caliber, or maybe the powder was old. Otherwise, it would have penetrated the bone and she'd be dead."

Bly swayed like a swooning girl at the strength of the relief that hit him.

"Are you all right, sir?" Griswold was astounded. Nothing shook Beelzebub Blysdale.

"I'm fine." He met his batman's searching gaze with his heart in his eyes. "She means the world to me, Gris." He looked away for a moment, then looked back. "Make her well."

"I'll do my best, sir," Gris answered softly.

Bly held Kate against him, bare to the waist, as gently as if he cradled a newborn. Griswold cleaned and bound her wound, passing the bandages around her three times to be certain the dressing wouldn't work loose if she fretted.

Suffering the tortures of the damned, Bly held her as tenderly as a mother holds her sick child, and just as fervently prayed that she'd get well. When her bandage was secured in place, the men pulled her night rail gently over her head and down around her before divesting her of her boots and britches.

Again Bly lifted her—flinching when she moaned at the pressure this put on her wound—while Griswold turned the covers down. Together, they tucked her into bed.

Griswold told Bly, "We need a doctor, sir."

"No! Would you see her hanged? She was holding up a coach when she was shot!"

Griswold's eyes were as large as saucers. "Now, then.

That's a habit you'd not told me she had, sir." When the shock wore off, Griswold was stiff with reproach.

Bly brushed it off with an impatient wave of his hand. "I wasn't certain that my coach hadn't been the only one. And it was her secret, Gris, not mine."

Some of the stiffness went out of his old friend.

"If the man who shot her reports the holdup, the doctor will have been alerted to look out for gunshot wounds. We dare not chance it."

Gris turned a troubled face toward the bed. Kate lay there as still as death.

Bly ran a hand through his hair, his face grim. Never in all his days had he felt so helpless.

With a raised eyebrow, Griswold watched him rake his fingers through his hair. He'd never seen his employer distracted enough to employ that gesture. He frowned. "I'll do my best, sir," Griswold promised Bly again. " 'Tisn't a grievous wound. We just have to hope she won't take a fever." He touched his employer's shoulder. "I'll go get something for fever, just in case." The door closed softly behind him, and Bly was alone with Kate.

She moaned, stirred, and cried out with the pain that movement caused her back. She was instantly conscious.

Bly, well used to wounds and the effects they had, waited for her to see him. She looked dazedly around her bedchamber for an instant, then her gaze cleared, focused, and settled on him. "Lord Blysdale," she gasped, "where is Star?"

"Kate, Star is fine, safe in his stall."

"How . . . how did I get here?"

"I believe I carried you here in my arms."

"Did you use the secret passage?"

"No," he replied, realizing that that must have been how she got out of her rooms without him seeing her. "We were evidently lucky not to have been seen on the back stairs."

"I must tell you how to use the secret stairway." Frowning slightly, she explained the workings of the secret passage, adding, "The fleur-de-lis you press to open it is between the first and second brocaded panel in my dressing room.

The second panel is the secret door to the stairway," she concluded.

"Good. Now we will be able to move about more freely."

She smiled slightly at that, even though her brow was furrowed with pain. Then she asked, confused, "Didn't you just say you *believe* you brought me here?"

"Yes." Bly flushed slightly. "I seem to have gone a little berserk when you were shot. Beyond shooting the black-guard back, I don't seem to have any memory of the event from the time you fell."

"Oh. I hope you didn't hurt him badly."

"Didn't hurt him!" Bly was incensed. "I hope I killed the bastard!"

She started to chuckle, thought better of it, and smiled a tight little smile instead. "That's hardly fair, Bly. I did hold . . . him up, you know." She was uncomfortably aware now that she couldn't take big breaths to support her speech.

Bly opened his mouth to deny hotly the man's right to live after shooting Kate. Then he closed it. "Very well." He shrugged elaborately. "I suppose we travelers have the right to respond irritably when you highwaymen accost us."

Kate laughed. Her laugh was cut off by a grimace of pain. "Oh, don't make me laugh. It hurts."

He was instantly contrite. "Sorry."

"No, you're not. You were trying to make me laugh. Sadist."

"Actually, a smile was the most I hoped for. The joke was in rather poor taste, after all."

"Speaking of hurt, how badly am I?" Her steady gaze demanded the truth.

"You were lucky." He made his gaze as rock-steady as hers, hiding his anxiety. "The ball didn't put a hole in you as it might have if you'd been turned squarely to the pistol. It scored a long gash across your shoulder blade, instead. Won't kill you, but probably hurts like the devil."

"Hmmm."

He looked into her pain-filled eyes. "When we dress it again, you'll have to be on your stomach. You can lie that way if it's more comfortable. Either Griswold or I can help you turn."

Kate pressed her hands into the mattress to test her ability to turn without help from either of the men. "Oh!"

"Yes." Bly smiled a crooked smile. "I wouldn't try that again."

"Never fear," Kate gasped.

Behind a carefully bland face, Blysdale felt as if his heart were being torn from his body. Dearest God! He'd gladly suffer again every pain of every wound he'd ever had if he could just take the pain of Kate's from her now. Never in his life had he felt so helpless. To distract her, he said, "We must plan."

She frowned, her eyes narrowing. "What do you mean?" Her expression was guarded. Obviously she was thinking about the coaches she'd stopped.

It wasn't what he'd meant, but as long as she was thinking in that direction, he'd take advantage of it. "Ah. Now you're going to explain to me why you're holding up coaches heading for Clifton-on-Tides."

She looked at him a long moment. Pressing her lips firmly closed, she held them there by the simple expedient of clamping her teeth down on them.

"Kate." It was half command, half cajole.

She was too weak to stand against it. Tears streamed from her eyes, as she realized that now she would fail in her mission. On a sob she said, "It's for Hal. I'm looking for proof of his innocence. He's been accused of being the thief that's taking everybody's jewels."

"The thief they call the Mayfair Bandit?"

She nodded.

"And that's why you've taken up highway robbery?"

Kate didn't like the edge his voice had taken on. She rushed to explain. Concern for the pain she'd experience was insignificant beside her concern over Lord Blysdale's attitude. "It's not as bad as you think. I had men investigate the robberies in London. Bow Street runners. They located an informant who told them the jewels were leaving England out of Clifton-on-Tides."

"If the informant told them that much, why didn't he tell them the identity of the thief?"

"He couldn't." Kate didn't really want to tell him the rest, but she had the awful feeling she was going to.

"Why not?" Blysdale's face was a study in suspicion.

"Because he, uh, bled to death." She cringed away from the bright blaze of fury in Bly's eyes. "He'd been stabbed, you see," she finished lamely.

"Stabbed to death," he said reasonably, his tone denying what she could see in his eyes. Then he exploded. "God and all His holy angels! Stabbed to death!" He spun away from her, taking two quick strides then spinning back. His hand was in his hair again. This time it looked as if he might yank out a fistful. "Good God, woman. Are you telling me you're trying to stop the coach of a man who might murder you?"

"Please don't shout. You can probably be heard all over the house."

He glared into her petulant face. "Dammit, Kate, you drive a man to shouting. And don't be stupid. The walls are too thick here in this part of the manor for anyone to hear my shouting. They're castle walls, for God's sake!"

"Yes," she admitted, "that's true."

His manner softened. "Kate. Don't you realize that you're dealing with a murderer as well as a thief?"

The petulance gave way to fresh tears. "Oh, Bly. I can't help that. The only clue I have is that the jewels come here from London. I have to clear Hal. I just have to!"

Griswold came into the room, bearing more medications. "What was all the shouting about? I could hear you all the way down the hall in your bedchamber, Colonel."

Kate threw Bly a smug look, while she surreptitiously wiped away her tears.

While she did, Bly told Griswold about the secret passage from Kate's dressing room, then ordered, "If the boy you've observed bringing messages to her ladyship turns up again, I want you to bring him to me."

"Suppose he has other ideas?"

"Gag him. You'll have to blindfold him anyway to get him through the secret passage. Lady Kate will hardly want that given away."

"Aye. The lad should enjoy all that. And I suppose sending one of the grooms or a footman to fetch you to the stables would be too simple."

"Out of the question. I'm not leaving her, Gris."

"Very well." Griswold turned away, muttering, "I suppose we can buy the boy's silence before he goes to the magistrate to tell him we abducted him."

"Don't be such an old woman, Gris."

"Old woman, is it? You'd best keep in mind that this ain't the Peninsula, Colonel. This is England."

"Yes." Bly's expression turned deadly. "This is England. Where peers of the realm can be abducted." His nostrils flared. "I hardly think questioning a single boy will trouble me."

Griswold was chastened. "Very well, Colonel. If the boy sets foot on Cliffside, you shall have him."

"Good."

Griswold left and Bly crossed the room back to Kate.

She looked up at him. "Thank you for all you have done."

He shrugged it off. "It's lucky for you that I'd decided to ride this evening."

"Why did you?"

"Because I care very much about a certain young highwayman's safety, and I felt it might be threatened this evening."

Kate's eyes widened. But she made no comment.

Blysdale decided to let her off the hook for the time being. She was never going to play highwayman again while he drew breath, but he didn't have to tell her that right now. So instead he smiled a very small smile and asked, "How do you feel?"

"Merely tired." She held his gaze with her own. "You were speaking to Griswold of your missing friends."

"Yes."

"Do the plans we must make have to do with them?"

"No. Those plans don't concern you now, Kate." *Now or ever. You shan't rush into every available danger, my love.*

"I shall be fine soon."

"If there's no fever."

"What a cautious man you are."

"Say, rather, experienced."

She tried a smile. "Well, certainly you are more conversant with gunshot wounds than I, but you must admit that I have more experience at holding up coaches."

It was his turn to try to smile. "Yes, I concede that you have." *So far. If that boy comes, I'll be standing my horse in the middle of the blasted high road from tonight on.*

"If not plans to rescue your friends, then what plans should we be making?"

Her eyes were bright with interest. And perhaps with something else. He laid his hand on her forehead. There was no elevation in her temperature. Thank God.

"Plans that explain your altered condition, Lady Kate."

"My altered condition?" She raised her eyebrows. "What on earth are you talking about?"

"The scar you'll have on your back."

"Oh. Yes, I suppose that would come into question with summer ball gowns."

"Undoubtedly." The thought of her lovely back having been marred saddened him. She was so beautiful, his Kate. Imperfection should have been forbidden to touch her.

"So what do you suggest?"

"Later, when your wound has healed to look like a scratch, we'll arrange a riding accident, tear your habit across the shoulders, and tell everyone that a tree branch gouged you and that is how you got the unfortunate scar on your back."

He watched her expression carefully. In spite of her scorn at the idea that she might have been stupid enough to ride that close to a low-hanging tree branch, she seemed still attentive. "That will take care of later," he continued. "But for now, we have other problems."

Kate contented herself with a questioning glance. She was so weary, and she had too many bedclothes piled on her. It was getting hot in the room.

"For instance, how will we explain your absence from the dinner table? How shall we keep your abigail from learning—and reporting to your brother—that you are wounded?"

"Oh. Yes." Kate was troubled. "Those *are* problems."

"Yes. I think I have solutions to them, but I want your opinion. I propose that we tell everyone that you have contracted some fever. One to which your youngest brother, Jamie, was also exposed. You'll say you don't want to risk anyone else catching whatever you've got, so you want only Jamie to bring your meals. You'll also want him to stay here with you."

"Why that?"

Bly spoke slowly and patiently. "His presence will furnish you with the chaperon you will need in case the visits that Griswold and I will make in order to take care of your wound should ever be noticed. We will, of course, use the secret stairway, but one can never tell. This blasted place seems to have eyes and ears."

"Hmmmm. But having Jamie cooped up here is going to be difficult for him. He's an active little boy."

"He'll just have to be *inactive* for a while."

Kate's brows snapped down. "Has anyone ever told you that you are exceedingly high-handed, Lord Blysdale?"

"Frequently."

Kate murmured, "Obviously it doesn't bother you."

"Obviously it does not." He smiled at her. "Save your strength, Kate. Don't waste it getting into a pelter. With your little brother in residence here in your room, your reputation will be somewhat safe."

He watched her closely to see if she understood what he was saying. "Griswold and I will use the secret stairs. We will be with you almost constantly. Therefore, so must your brother be. Your reputation has to be preserved."

He saw that she was in agreement, however reluctantly.

"I shall explain to Jamie," he went on. "He's a bright, good lad and I'm certain he would never give us away. Then we'll tell—"

Bly never got to finish his sentence. There was a light tap on the door of the suite, and immediately Dresden bustled in.

Swallowing a curse, Bly leapt out of sight behind the heavy draperies at the nearest window. The draperies had barely stopped swaying before Dresden entered the bedchamber.

"Oh, your ladyship, I came the minute I heard that you'd come up to your room. That inconsiderate Jennings didn't even mention it!" Dresden shook her head in disgust. "And just look. You've gotten yourself into bed with no help at all."

Pain or no pain, Kate had to smile. She'd had plenty of help, if Dresden only knew. "I'm fine, thank you, Dresden. Just tired and sleepy. Too long a ride, today, I suppose. And you mustn't scold Jennings, he didn't see me come in."

"That does make me feel better. Will you be wanting anything, my lady?"

"No, thank you."

"Very well then, I'll just go back downstairs. Ring for me if you need me."

"I shall. Thank you, Dresden."

The abigail recognized her dismissal. She turned and curtsied from the doorway. "Good night, your ladyship."

"Good night, Dresden." Kate's head fell back against her pillows. The brief exchange had taken all her strength. How odd.

"That's normal." Stepping out of his hiding place, Bly kept his voice soft in case the abigail was nearby.

"What's normal?"

"Being exhausted after being wounded. I've often thought it's from the shock of it. One's body seems to be outraged." He considered, watching her again. "It's worse if there's a lot of blood loss."

Kate wrinkled her nose.

Blysdale smiled. "No. You didn't lose a lot of blood."

"You're reading my mind again."

"Probably."

They were quiet. He pulled a chair over and sat beside her bed. When she reached out to him, he took her hand gently in his, without speaking.

Kate closed her eyes and rested, holding his hand. Somehow she knew she could draw strength from his calm presence.

Bly caressed the back of her hand with his thumb in a slow, soothing rhythm. Listening carefully, he heard the rhythm of her breathing slow to that of his caress. He'd used the trick before—to ease the passing of a dying drummer boy.

His mind shied from that train of thought, but plunged into another he'd been avoiding. Vividly he saw the scene on the highway again. With piercing agony, he recalled how he'd felt when he saw the shot strike her. Remembered how the very stars had seemed to fall from the sky when he'd thought she might have been killed. Thought that there might be no more Kate to ride beside him ever again. And he longed to have Kate ride beside him.

For the first time in his life he wanted a woman to share it. This woman. But he knew he could never ask her to. He was Blysdale. The soldier known as Beelzebub Blysdale, a man without any of the gentle virtues a woman needed to complete her life with a man.

Even now, when his heart was torn by her pain and his mind blighted at the very thought of losing her, he couldn't give her the caring words a woman must expect—must need.

Earlier, he'd held himself in derision to hear his practical words about chaperons and secret stairways. Coolheaded. His words cool, yes, and his actions. Those that she had observed, at least. They were cool to the point of coldness.

He grinned a crooked grin to remember the actions she hadn't seen. Like the snarl he'd aimed at Gris when his friend had attempted to take her from his arms. And there had been a few other heated moments when he'd thought Gris might be hurting Kate as he dressed her wound.

Recalling how intrepid he'd thought Kate was to act the highwayman and how fearless he'd thought her brought a smile. Still, he hadn't told her how brave, how incredibly brave he thought her. He hadn't complimented her in any way.

Then, because he needed her so much to fill the void his love for her had carved into his life . . . because he wanted it so desperately that he couldn't help it, he wondered if maybe, just maybe, this incredibly brave young woman— because she was so brave, could ever . . .

Enough! He'd seen a sufficient number of hopelessly lost causes during his army life to recognize this as one. And surely he'd had his fill of forlorn hopes. He shook his head and shook himself mentally. Enough.

Going to the table Griswold had cleared and set up as a station for taking care of Kate, he stirred one of the medications into a glass. Bringing it back to the bed, he handed it to her. "Here, drink this." He supported her head with one hand while he held the glass to her lips with the other.

Kate drank obediently, then coughed, grimaced, and demanded, "What *was* that?"

"Something to help you sleep. We'll talk tomorrow." He put her head back down on the pillow. As her eyes closed, he longed to kiss each lid, but he refused to let himself. Instead, he gently smoothed her hair over the linen under her head. He delighted in touching each silken strand.

He grinned lopsidedly as a thought hit him. At last, he was getting his wish—but certainly not in the way he'd hoped to. He *was* getting to see Kate's hair spread over a pillow, all right.

In addition to all the other drawbacks he was experiencing, the pillow just wasn't his own.

Chapter Nineteen

"We'll talk tomorrow. . . ." As from far away, Kate could hear his deep voice soothing her, comforting her. "We'll talk tomorrow. . . ." Blysdale's words had been running through Kate's mind all night. The laudanum he had given her had caused her to sleep deeply. She'd barely moved. Now the drug was wearing off, and she wanted to shift her position.

Her whole body was numb from lying on her back all night. So she did shift—or began to—and a cry of pain, her own cry, woke her completely.

She lay gasping, her eyes closed tight against the pain. When the pain lessened, she opened her eyes and found Blysdale leaning over her.

"Bad?"

"Ummmm."

"Just relax and give yourself over to the pain." The tears in Kate's emerald eyes hurt him like a knife wound.

Kate closed her eyes and tried to do as he said. A few minutes later, she looked at him in amazement; some of the deep lines drawn around her mouth by her pain were gone. "It works," she whispered. "Not completely, but enough."

"An old soldier's trick." He smiled at her, took out his handkerchief, and gently wiped the tears from her cheeks.

"Why in the world is anyone a soldier when he constantly risks feeling like this?"

"Ah. That's a very simple question, Kate." He picked up a glass of water and mixed in a little wine.

"Pray answer it then and . . ." She eyed the glass he held and hated the certain knowledge that he was going to lift her head to help her drink from it. Thirsty as she was, she wasn't looking forward to that. "And . . . tell me the simple answer."

"We *simply* don't believe we will ever be wounded."

"Oh, come now." She shot a glance at the glass and then returned her gaze to him. "How often have *you* been wounded?"

"Eleven times," he told her lightly. "With varying degrees of severity, of course."

"Eleven times!"

His grin was crooked. "It was a very long war."

"And you never learned? You never decided that soldiering was a dangerous profession? One in which you could get hurt like this?"

"Well, yes. We learned." He slipped his hand under her neck. Into the beautiful silk of her hair. Into the warmth of her lovely nape.

"The first wound was a surprise." He was deliberately trying to amuse her. "And the second a decided shock. Rather an insult to our immortality. But we did learn."

He watched the apprehension dawn in her eyes, and knew she dreaded having him lift her head and stretch the ball-torn muscles in her back. "But you see," he murmured as he inched her head up from the pillow, "by then it was too late."

"Too late?" She asked the question on the indrawn breath she intended to hold to get through this.

"Yes. By then there were other matters involved."

The look she shot him this time was a little panicked. "What other matters?"

"Duty, for one. Stubborn pride for another." He began

raising her head higher. "And honor, of course." He saw her bite her lip against the pain he was causing her and tried harder to distract her. "And fallen comrades. Men whom we admired—and loved like brothers. Men whom we had watched die."

She was completely distracted by his words now and he lifted her the last few inches and pressed the brimming glass to her lips.

Kate drank greedily. She didn't even mind that some of the water ran over the rim of the glass and down her chin and cheek. She was only grateful that Bly had guessed—no, had known—how thirsty she would be and had filled the glass to its fullest for her.

"Thank you," she gasped. "Thank you for the water, too."

Bly lowered her as quickly as he could, ending the tension on her wound. "You're as brave as many a soldier, Kate."

She gave him a watery smile. "I wish I could believe that. I fear I'm being a crybaby."

"Don't. You're not."

"Bly?" She tried the short form of his surname and found it fit. It fit the sardonic man she watched, and it fit comfortably in her mind, on her tongue.

"Yes?"

"I'm so tired of lying on my back."

"It's helped your wound." He saw that at this point she not only didn't care, she wasn't sure she believed him. "It will be painful for you to have me move you to your side. That's what you want to do, isn't it?"

"Yes, please."

He reached for her then, enfolding her gently in his arms. Then he waited. Her arms started to come round his neck, but pain stopped her, and she gasped as he lifted her from the place she lay and put her back down on her side. When he drew back from the bed, he watched helplessly as she accustomed herself to the pain of having been moved.

No word of complaint escaped her. Finally, she opened her eyes and said, "Thank you."

And he wanted to weep.

Just then, "Kate?" The new voice was tentative.

Kate turned her head a little and saw Jamie standing just behind Blysdale. "Jamie!"

"Yes, Kate. Colonel Blysdale has explained to me what happened."

"Oh?" Kate's glance shot to Bly, questioning.

"Yes. Lord Blysdale said that a man in a coach shot you, and that you don't want anyone to know because it would upset them all."

"Yes, that's true." Kate waited to hear what else was coming. Surely Blysdale hadn't told the boy that she robbed coaches! She locked glances with him.

He raised one eyebrow and smiled a twisted smile.

It was clear she wasn't going to learn anything there. She looked again at Jamie. "What else did the Colonel tell you?"

"That we are going to say you have a fever." His earnest gaze never left her face. "And that I have been exposed to the same fever, and nobody else is to come near you."

"That's right, Jamie, and that will keep everybody from worrying. Will you mind?"

"I don't mind fetching things and bringing you meals and all, but it's going to be awfully hard to be here always to be your chaperon, you know."

"But it seems that I'll be needing one, dear. And you're the only one who can do it."

Jamie sighed and squared his shoulders. "I know. Colonel Blysdale explained to me that his batman has to take care of your wound, and that he himself was going to be nursing you and that it would be highly improper to have them do either of those things without a member of the family present." He cocked his head to one side. "He says it's just like having the doctor come. You have to have somebody there to say that everything went as it should."

Kate smiled. Bless Bly. He'd gotten the idea across without scandalizing her youngest brother.

Suddenly, she wondered how they were going to dress her wound without scandalizing *her*. She'd been unconscious when they had dressed it last night, but she knew from her bandages that she had been bare from the waist up when they were applied.

She wondered if she had survived being shot only to die of embarrassment!

A quick look at Blysdale showed her he was perfectly aware of her thoughts. Again. Was he amused at the turn they had taken? She couldn't be certain. One thing she wasn't mistaken about, however. Old soldiers didn't make very sympathetic bedside companions!

Blysdale could see the little frown of annoyance on his Kate's face. Was she thinking he lacked proper sympathy for her condition? God. If she only knew how eaten out with worry he was over her. If she could even begin to guess how anxious he was that she might get the fever that so often struck down those he'd seen wounded during the Peninsular campaigns.

His stomach was in such a tight knot with anxiety over her that he could only hope she'd continue to think him heartlessly unconcerned. A positive attitude on her part would go a long way toward her healing.

"Will it take you very long to heal up, Kate?" Her brother wanted to know.

"I have no idea, Jamie. I've never been shot before, you know."

"Well," he decided philosophically, "I suppose I shall be able to bear it. Colonel Blysdale has promised to teach me how to play chess." He started to turn away, then faced her again. "And Kate?"

"Yes, love?"

"No amount of anybody being here is going to stop us all from worrying about you."

Blysdale turned the boy away before he could see his sister's quick tears.

That night the fever struck. Kate thrashed and moaned, tossing her head back and forth on her pillow as her skin grew hotter and hotter to Bly's touch.

Blysdale's jaw was clenched so tightly that a muscle jumped along the edge of it. His eyes were slate blue with misery. He demanded cloths and a bowl of water from Griswold. Then he placed cool cloths on Kate's forehead, one after another. Despair threatened to overwhelm him when he saw how quickly they warmed there.

Griswold ran through all the usual remedies for lowering fevers. He even brought up a spirit lamp over which he brewed herbs he hoped might help. When none of his concoctions did, he told Blysdale, "There's nothing for it, sir. We'll have to bathe her to cool her down. We can't let her stay this hot, much less let her get any warmer."

Bly didn't know just how that was going to be possible with Jamie sleeping on a cot in the adjacent dressing room. Jamie was taking his role as family representative very seriously. How he would react to them stripping his sister to bathe her fever down was not something Bly was easy about.

Bly was perfectly capable of binding and gagging the boy and throwing him in the back of a wardrobe to keep him quiet if that was needed to help Kate. The secret stairway opened into the dressing room, and Gris would have to go down it to reach the well. While he debated what course to take, Griswold smiled and said, "Never fear, Colonel, the boy is sleeping well. He'll not awaken for anything less than a cannon shot."

"Good!"

As if to prove the truth of what he'd said, the batman went out the secret passage to get a bucket of cold well water without making the slightest effort to be quiet. While Bly held his breath, Jamie simply turned over to face away from the light coming from Kate's bedchamber and continued to snore softly.

Bly went to Kate's bed and drew the pale, silver-green damask bed curtains around it. For a full minute he stood inside them just looking down at her. His heart clenched every time she moaned or turned restlessly.

Staring at her and twisting his hands wasn't going to help a damned thing! Discarding his coat, vest, and cravat, he prepared to get down to business. Bending over her, he began to unbutton the line of tiny buttons that ran down the front of her nightgown.

Her hot, silky smooth skin was rosy with fever and dry as autumn leaves to his touch. As gently as he could, he slipped the night rail over her head and off. She lay before him in nothing but the bandages Griswold had used to dress her wound last night. Bandages that were stark and glaring white against her heat-flushed skin.

Even in his agony of mind he noticed that she was wonderfully made, his Kate. Her legs were even smoother than they'd appeared when she'd been dressed in her men's riding britches. Her feet were narrow, the bones fine. For a moment, he just stood and marveled at the perfection of her body, and at something more. Where did such a slender body store so much courage?

He wanted to touch her. To kiss every inch of her, to feel that smooth skin under his lips. To taste it with the tip of his tongue. But he wouldn't, of course.

Only if Kate were conscious and fully aware of his actions could he permit himself to caress her. And he wouldn't then, either. Because she was never going to be his.

His Kate was not for him. She was all that was fine. Loving and caring and kind. With his loveless childhood and violent past, he could never live up to her. His Kate deserved more. She'd earned it by her self-sacrificing love for her family—by her care of the tenants on her family's land and her careful stewardship of her brother's heritage. She was magnificent, his Kate. She deserved the best.

He laughed a bitter laugh at that. He *was* the best. The absolute best at so many things. Riding, shooting, fencing—they called them the manly arts, and at them he excelled. But not at the things that he knew kept women happy for a lifetime. Except for lovemaking, he excelled in none of those.

The man he wanted for Kate would be the gentle, loving sort of chap who would notice her moods and compliment her perfume and her gowns. He'd remember to compliment her looks, too, and never forget gifts for her on the anniversaries of the special days they'd share in making their life together. And Bly would be glad for them.

If he didn't tear the man's throat out in a fit of jealousy. Somehow . . .

"Well, are you going to take this blasted bucket or not!" Griswold was standing outside the bed curtains holding a heavy bucket of cold water.

Bly startled out of his musings and wondered how long he'd kept Gris standing there. Parting the bed curtains, he took the bucket with a gruff "Thanks."

"Here. I brought this from my knapsack." He handed Bly a rough groundsheet. "At least it's waterproof. It'll save you soaking her bed."

"Aye. Give me a sheet to put over it, though, please. I'll not have her skin touch this rough surface."

"Here you be," Griswold thrust a clean sheet smelling faintly of lavender through the curtains to Bly, keeping his face carefully averted. His voice held a hint of surprise. Never once had he heard his Colonel ask him for anything with a "please" tacked onto it.

Orders were Blysdale's way, not requests. Griswold knew he must truly be upset over the state of the young lady they tended. Or could he be . . . ?

No. Griswold shook his head at that thought. Love 'em and leave 'em, and pay generously for the privilege. That was Blysdale. And Lady Katherine wasn't one of those fillies. He was just being an old fool, getting himself all excited over nothing. He knew better than to think that he, or anyone else for that matter, would live long enough to see Beelzebub Blysdale leg-shackled! Marriage was not for Chalfont Blysdale.

Inside the privacy of the tent formed by the pale green bed hangings, Bly rolled up his sleeves and dipped the first cloth into the bucket. Wringing it out, he began the task of attempting to cool the fever out of the lovely body lying helpless in front of him.

She'd begun to moan and to mutter, caught in the claws of the fever. Then she called out "Hal!" and tossed fitfully.

She cried out again, "Hal, I'm so sorry. I tried. Really I did."
Tears trickled down her cheeks. "I tried so hard. Even when
I was afraid."

Bly twisted the next cloth so hard the fabric gave way.
He wished it were her brother's neck. Either of her older
brothers! Hal for getting into trouble and running away without proving his own innocence or shooting the damned bastard who'd falsely accused him . . . and Josh! That scapegrace
had piled his endless responsibilities on his sister's shoulders—these very shoulders he was running the cooling cloth
over.

They were so slender, so seemingly fragile.

He had to concentrate on wringing out the next cloth a
little more gently. Thoughts of Josh Clifton, the careless, callous head of Kate's family, gave unneeded additional strength
to his hands and he didn't want all of the cloths destroyed
past usefulness.

"I know you didn't do . . . it, Hal. I know you didn't steal
those jewels. I just haven't found the right coach yet. I will,
though. I will."

She twisted quickly, and Bly had to grab her to keep her
from plunging off the bed.

"I will. I'll get the proof. I'll . . ."

"No, Kate." Bly told her in a low, firm voice. "You'll
stop no more coaches. You're through risking your life for
your brother."

She lay absolutely motionless. Had his words penetrated
to her fevered mind? Bly fervently hoped so, because he
meant every syllable of them. If he had to shoot the handsome second son of the house in order to stop his gallant
sister from playing highwayman, then he would.

What was one more life on *his* hands? Hadn't he lost
count of the men he'd killed over the years?

True, most of them had been killed in the heat of battle,
where he and other Englishmen had killed for their country,
but several had been killed merely to preserve his life until
he could get back to England and the War Office with the
information he had gained from the dead man's papers.

These last were the deaths that made him a pariah in his own eyes—those killings done in cold blood to escape captors before they discovered his identity or retrieved the secrets he'd stolen from them. The hardness that had come alive in soul then had fused with the bleak memories of his loveless childhood and created the harsh man he was now.

Beelzebub Blysdale. He'd not been surprised when Griswold revealed that sobriquet to him. He found it apt.

"Oh! I'm so hot." Kate thrust her fingers through her hair and tried to drag it away from her. "Ah!" The pain in her back stopped her. Her eyes flew open. "Hot. I'm so hot." Her gaze rested on him, focused, and registered what he was doing. "Oh, Bly. That's you." She turned her head back and forth on her pillow. "I thought it was my old nurse . . . trying to make me feel better."

"I am trying to make you feel better, Kate." His voice was calm, his body tight with his effort to keep the concern out of it.

"I think . . . that . . ." Her voice trailed away, and the fever stole whatever she'd been about to say. Twisting in an effort to find a cooler spot, a more comfortable position, she drifted away again.

"What is it that you think, my bonny Kate?" Bly wanted to hold her there. Wanted her to speak. Wanted her to beat this heated monster that held her in its claws. But there was no response.

The night wore on. Every muscle in Bly's body ached from his labors. His shoulders felt as if he'd been swinging his saber against a whole battalion of French hussars for the length of an entire day.

Griswold spoke from outside the damask refuge created by the bed hangings. "Will you be wanting me to relieve you, Colonel? You've been at it all night."

"No!" Blysdale was shocked at the murderous rage that rose in him at the mere thought of another man touching his Kate, running his hands over her body, over her silken skin. Seeing her lying there unclothed.

"Is she better, sir?"

"I don't know." His voice was full of despair. "Gris, I don't know."

"Och, now. You're weary, Colonel. Gather your wits. Is she tossing and turning as much? I can tell you she's not moaning or crying out as she did the earlier part of the night."

Blysdale pulled himself together. He stopped hating himself for touching her with his unworthy, battle-bloodied hands and really looked at Kate. And she was resting more quietly. The frown of pain that had marred her forehead most of the night had faded to a faint line between her winged brows. She was responding. She *was* better.

He bent closer and tested her temperature with his lips against her forehead—his hands had long since lost all ability to feel. She was cooler. Praise Almighty God!

Then, as he watched, tiny beads of perspiration formed on Kate's upper lip. He went dizzy with relief. Thank God, the fever had broken!

Almost immediately, Kate's bandages were saturated with perspiration. Her lovely golden hair was becoming dark with it around her face.

"Gris! The fever has broken."

"Thank God!"

"Yes." Blysdale's mind was suddenly overwhelmed—crowded with the faces of the scores of men whose fevers had never broken. Men who had died tossing and crying out for their wives or mothers. For families they would never see again. And he made it a prayer of thanksgiving, "Thank God." He closed his eyes, and murmured again, "Thank you, God."

Out in the vast bedchamber, Griswold promised, "I'll have the fire built up in a minute, Colonel!"

And Bly knew the second part of the ordeal was about to begin.

Chapter Twenty

Blysdale gathered Kate, wrapped in a mass of dry bed-clothes, into his arms and held her against his chest. He stood still for a long moment, relishing the weight of her in his arms, the feel of her against him. Then, his cheek pressed tenderly against her hair, he walked carefully to the fireplace, cherishing his precious burden.

Griswold, his concern plain on his seamed face, moved aside from putting logs on the already blazing fire, and Bly knelt down on the hearth without relinquishing his burden. Kate clung tightly to his neck with arms that spasmed with each chill that shook her frame.

Griswold had made a pallet from several blankets to cushion the stone hearth, and wet down their edge nearest the flames to prevent them from combusting with the heat. Bly positioned Kate on it and removed the linens in which he'd cocooned her so they, and consequently Kate, would be safe from the fire. He placed her as close as he dared, as he wanted her to absorb as much of the fire's warmth as he could get for her.

"Oh, B-B-Bly." She tried to smile, but the chill that took

her made it a pitiful effort. "I w-w-was so hot. N-now, I'm s-s-s-so cold!"

"It's nothing I haven't seen before," he told her calmly—and cursed himself for his seeming lack of sympathy.

"W-well, it's n-new to me!" She tried to scowl at him.

"At least now you are coherent."

"Y-y-yes-s-s."

"That's a great step forward from what you were with the fever." The deep concern in his eyes denied the seeming indifference in his tone. "You were out of your head then."

"Out of m-my h-h-head?" Her teeth chattered constantly, making speech difficult for her. She tossed her head, obviously impatient with her weakness. "C-can't you get me w-w-warmer, Bly?"

He laughed without mirth. His eyes were wicked. "The way I generally warm a woman would hardly do in your present condition, Lady Katherine."

Kate struck out at him feebly. "Th-this is no t-time to be b-bawdy, Blysdale. I'm s-s-shaking to p-pieces here."

Jamie came out of the dressing room, his hair sleep-tousled, his gaze directed to the empty bed. "Oh. Has Kate's fever broken?"

Griswold blocked the boy's view of the fireplace as he answered him, giving Bly time to cover Kate again. "Aye, laddie. The fever's gone, but now she has the chills to get through." He sought a way to get rid of the boy. "Go and change your clothes. Your sleeping in those you have on hasn't done a great deal for them, you know."

"I couldn't leave Kate last night!"

"Of course you couldn't. But you can now. For a little while, at least. And you can bring her some breakfast and a big pot of tea when you've finished breaking your own fast."

"Yes. Oh, yes, Mr. Griswold. That's a very good idea." Glad to have something useful to do for her, he sped to the door. He saw Blysdale looming over Kate and said, "Kate'll be all right with the Colonel looking after her until I return."

Blysdale called to him, "Remember, Jamie, we are *not* here. You are taking care of your sister all by yourself."

"Yes, sir." His eyes were wide at the very thought.

"And, if anybody asks, tell them she's resting quietly, and mustn't be disturbed."

"Y-yes, d-dear-est, p-p-p-please be c-careful not to g-give me away." Kate tried to reinforce Bly's warning.

Tears came to the boy's eyes. Ignoring his stricken sister, he cried, "But she isn't resting quietly, Colonel. She's shaking awfully."

"I know, Jamie, but I have her here near the fire now, and we hope she *will* be better by the time you come back. So it won't be too much of an untruth, will it?"

The boy was reassured. With a wide smile, Jamie promised, "I shall be back as soon as I can." He opened the door. Halfway through it he turned back and called, "And I'll bring you your breakfast, Kate!" and was gone.

The face Bly turned back to Katherine was grim. "Now," he told her, purpose in his voice, "let's see if we can get you warmer."

Kate started to protest when he began to strip her covering from her a second time, but stopped when she felt the heat thrown off by the flaming logs touch her bare skin. Being warm was more important to her now than being modest. Modesty had never kept anyone from shaking apart. "S-s-strange."

"What's strange, Kate?"

"I f-feel the heat, b-but it doesn't w-warm m-me."

Bly's chest constricted. Working like an automaton he stripped the last vestige of covering from her. She lay on the edge of the hearth naked before him. The firelight bathed her limbs in a rosy glow and shot highlights of gold through her hair. His male mind registered and admired her perfection, but his whole attention was focused on a way to stop the awful tremors that shook her.

When he touched her, he could feel on the backs of his hands the heat that generated the glow that gilded her limbs.

It heated his hands, but it merely bathed the surface of her skin; it failed to warm her. She was cold under his touch.

His face grim, he began massaging her, rubbing and slapping vigorously to encourage her blood to circulate, to bring warmth back into her body. So near the roaring fire, he was burning up. Still Kate shook as if she would fly into fragments.

"Oh, s-stop, Bly. Th-that h-hurts."

He was sure it did. The friction of his rough cavalryman's hands on her delicate skin must be akin to torture. The sharp, quick blows had to be stinging her, at the very least.

He didn't care. He couldn't let himself care. He'd seen too many men shake until the light left their eyes and they'd been closed in final sleep.

That wasn't going to happen to his Kate. Not if he had to rub the skin from her fair body to bring life back into it!

Finally, after what seemed to Bly like hours, the wracking waves of shivering that contorted her became less frequent and finally, finally the tortuous tension in her slacked off.

When she began to relax, Bly gathered her again in the blankets and linens in which he'd carried her here to the hearth.

"Bly." Her voice was weak, barely a whisper. "Thank you." Her heavy lids closed for a moment, then she raised them again with an obvious effort. Looking up into his face, she smiled a tremulous smile, reached an unsteady hand out of the nest of blankets Blysdale had made for her, and flicked a drop of sweat from his chin.

She smiled wider when he looked startled.

He had indeed worked himself into a lather trying to restore warmth to her body in a room that to him was hotter than a Spanish summer, but he hadn't expected her to tease him about it.

After he carried her across the room and laid her on the bed, Kate grasped his arm weakly. "Lord Blysdale," she said faintly, "this has been . . . a *most* improper morning." Then, still smiling, she fell into an exhausted sleep.

And Colonel Chalfont Lord Blysdale, battle-hardened soldier and master spy, lowered his head to hide the tears of relief that sprang to his eyes.

Jamie kicked at the door until Bly leapt up from the chair beside the sleeping Kate's bed and opened it. He found the child standing there with a tray as wide as the boy was tall. It was laden with every manner of food from the abundant breakfast buffet downstairs. About to slide off the tray's edge was a gigantic pot of steaming tea. As it slipped, Bly caught it deftly by the pouring handle and took the tray from Jamie with his other hand.

"Oh, sir. How can you do that? I could hardly carry that tray with two hands. Jennings even had to bring it all the way up the stairs before I could take it from him."

Griswold came forward to take the tray in his turn and told Jamie, "The Colonel's hands and wrists are strong from his saber-swinging days, lad."

"Oh." Jamie's eyes went wide with adulation. "Someday will you show *me* how to swing a saber? When I grow up, I want to be a cavalryman, just like you."

Bly looked down into the eager face. And suddenly he remembered how he and the cousins with whom he had spent his eleventh summer had passed glorious days endlessly playing at war. It had been the only happy time of his youth, and the memory was poignant.

His mother had forbidden him to go again.

Jamie, Bly realized, had no one with whom he could play, either, but for very different reasons. The village was too far away for him to go there regularly enough to make friends, and no one his age lived nearby.

So Bly found himself saying, "Of course I will, Jamie."

There was a surprised grunt from Griswold, and Bly shot a glance at his batman. With a weary grin he added, "And you and Gris and I will try a few charges on horseback, as well."

Griswold shot him a nasty look that softened when he heard Jamie's hopeful, "Oh, could we? Could I? When can we . . . ?"

"Someday soon, we'll hope." Bly placed his hand on Jamie's shoulder as a pledge. "First we must get your sister well." He looked over at the four-poster in which Kate lay sleeping peacefully at last. "When she wakes up, do you suppose you could get her to eat some breakfast?" He looked down at his sweat-drenched shirt. "I really need to bathe and change."

"Oh, yes. I'm sure I can. I helped feed the orphan calf we had in the barn last month. Kate can't be any harder to feed than that."

Bly's eyes widened at this comparison between a calf and his lovely Kate. He had to work hard at it, but he managed to keep himself from making a comment.

Griswold was having a coughing fit.

Bly glared at him to be careful not to wake Kate.

Then, suddenly, there didn't seem to be anything more for him to do. He realized that he was weary, and sweaty, and very, very relieved. And . . . empty.

Quietly he ordered, "Show me the secret way out, Gris. I need to go swim in the lake."

When Kate opened her eyes the next morning, a clean-shaven, perfectly dressed Lord Blysdale sat beside the bed watching her. Her first reaction was one of pleasure at seeing him, and she smiled.

Immediately, memories came crashing in from the day before. This man had had his hands all over her body! She could feel a blush rise from the feet he'd so vigorously massaged to the shoulder he'd bandaged with bandages that had, by necessity, wrapped around her *bare* breasts. The blush had no trouble continuing to the roots of her hair.

"Ah," Blysdale's face was without expression. "I see you remember the delightful day we spent together lying before the fire."

"Wretch!" Blushes fled. The man was outrageous.

"Wretch? My dear, you wound me."

Kate saw the mischief in his eyes. She thanked her stars that she was a widow, and well used to being touched by a man. If she'd still been a maiden, she'd never have survived the shock of Blysdale's care. But she had, and thanks to him and the way he'd tirelessly worked over her chill-racked nude body, she was alive and getting well. Somehow, this didn't seem the place for outraged modesty.

Pulling the bedclothes up to her chin, she pretended to glare at him. "I'm the one wounded, Lord Blysdale."

"Superficially. The fever was the only real threat to your well-being."

Her hand rose to her neck. Her fingers touched the collar of a nightgown. "I have on a night rail," she said with some surprise. "I thought I was . . . uh, unclothed when you returned me to my bed."

"You were." Bly's voice was matter-of-fact. "I thought you might be more comfortable with something on."

"You . . . " She began again, "You . . . "

"Yes, Lady Katherine, *I*."

"You put this night rail on me." Her eyes were clouding.

He leaned toward her, his expression that of a man who feared he'd made a wrong choice. "Would you rather I'd let Griswold do it?"

She blushed again at that, but managed, "Of course not."

"Then would you rather I'd left you . . . as God made you?"

"I hardly think we are any longer at the point in our association that you have to avoid the word *naked*, Lord Blysdale." There was heat in her voice.

Bly knew that some of it came from embarrassment, and decided to help her over it. "Quite. But ladies occasionally prefer to entertain me wearing something."

Kate's eyebrow lifted at the word *occasionally*. "So you put me into my nightgown."

He bowed slightly from his chair. "It was my pleasure, I assure you." The corners of his mouth twitched.

First Kate's mouth dropped opened, then her eyes flashed.

Then she saw the absurdity in the situation and burst into laughter. "Bly, you are the most ridiculous man! How can you sit there and . . . and tease me so. Don't you know that if I had anything nearby I'd throw it at you?"

"It's a danger I hadn't considered."

"As if you'd care. You'd duck it. Or catch it!" She looked at him assessingly. "I wonder if you'd throw it back."

"Not at you, Kate." One corner of his mouth lifted. "I never throw things at ladies."

"I do believe you're going to smile."

"I do, from time to time."

"But never very often." She began to try to sit up.

Bly got up immediately and helped her. Then he stuffed pillows behind her to keep her sitting up, deliberately not looking at her as she handled her pain.

"There," she said as she settled back, "that's better."

"You look better, Kate. Almost as if your wound weren't troubling you. Why?"

She looked wary. "I just think it's more polite to sit when your guests are seated, I suppose."

"I'm certainly glad to hear that, Kate."

She narrowed her eyes. "Oh?" It was said very cautiously, as if she knew she was opening herself up for some attack.

"I'm just glad to learn it's only that you'd prefer not to entertain a gentleman lying down, Kate"—his voice lost its note of sly insinuation and hardened—"and *not* that you are hoping to get out of that bed and back to the high toby."

"The high toby?" She looked as if she didn't know what he meant.

"You know perfectly well that I'm referring to the game— the very dangerous game—of robbing coaches that you've already admitted to me that you've been engaged in."

She answered him hotly, "I have not been robbing coaches, Lord Blysdale!"

He regarded her steadily.

She dropped her gaze momentarily, then was glaring at him. "I do not *rob* coaches." Her lips tightened and she looked sulky for an instant. Then she assured him in a grudging tone, "I have never *taken* anything." She shrugged lightly, winced a bit, and informed him primly, "I merely search coaches for—"

"Yes. As you told me. For jewels that will prove your brother Hal innocent of the charge that jackass Baron Runcason made? Why bother? Hal could have laughed him down. No one would have sided with the baron if he had. Only Hal's flight from London society gave credence to Runcason's voiced suspicions."

"Hal—" Kate was ready to defend her brother.

"Hal was a fool," Bly interrupted harshly. "Everyone knows the blighted baron has it in for your family. Even I know it, and I'm famous for not giving a damn what goes on in London society."

Kate let her head fall back against the pillows Bly had placed behind her, defeated. "Yes," she said in a tight little voice. "You're right." She sighed. Tears spilled, and she wiped them away with the back of her hand. "But Hal hated the suspicion with which he was greeted at every turn. And he could hardly fight a duel with a broken leg!"

Bly was instantly contrite. Blast *him* for a fool! He leaned forward and gathered her into his arms. Pulling her gently from her bed, he sat down again with her in his lap. "There, there. Don't cry, my love. It'll all come right."

"Oh, how *can* it, Bly? Everything is in such a mess."

"You're tired. You've had a terrible shock, and you're not yet recovered from your wound. . . . "

"Yes. That's the point. How shall I take care of everything when I am stuck here recuperating?"

"First of all, you no longer have to. While you were asleep, I informed your brother Joshua that your fever was probably brought on by too many responsibilities." He gave her a moment to absorb that, then added, "I then strongly recommended that *he* take up his own. Though he's not at all certain he will do as well as you have done, he has promised me that he will try."

She squirmed restlessly in his lap, trying to look straight at him. "Josh doesn't keep promises if he doesn't want to."

Kate kept her voice steady even as she blushed to realize the effect her thoughtless movement had had on the man
attempting to comfort her. First the tower, now here. You'd
think she'd learn!

Blysdale took a deep, steadying breath and tried to ignore the quick urgency he was experiencing. "Josh *will* keep
his promise to me." He shifted Kate's body slightly, as his
own needed more space suddenly. His level voice revealed
nothing of the desire that was boiling through his blood.
"People do not break their promises to me."

"And if he does?" She challenged him pettishly, as a child
might. Embarrassment was part of her distracted state, but
the growing excitement of her own body's response to Bly's
arousal accounted for most of it. She was dizzy with wanting him. Oh, why couldn't he see?

"If Josh does break his promise," Bly answered her
huskily, seeing the passion in her eyes, the glow of it on her
cheeks, "then we shall just have to hope that Hal is ready
to become the Seventh Marquess of Cliffside."

He stood then, catching her to him with an arm about her
waist that was like a steel band—holding her tight against
his lithe frame, holding her up, holding her prisoner to his
desire.

He watched her as his lips approached hers, watched her
eyes cloud and close, as, capturing her sigh, he took her
mouth.

Kate's arms, pain or no pain, went up to encircle Bly's
neck. Never in all the years of her marriage had she been
kissed like this, never so masterfully. Suddenly she understood the stories she'd heard of women who gave up everything for love. If they had been kissed like this, had their
very souls drawn from their bodies at some magnificent man's
command—then it was no wonder that they'd counted the
world well lost.

Kate understood, because right now, *she* was counting the
world well lost. Right now she wanted nothing but to belong to this man forever. She knew that, from this moment

on, anything Chalfont Blysdale wanted from her she would gladly give him.

She arched her body to be closer to him, feeling with an electric awareness the strength in him, the passion in him and wanting . . . wanting him.

Bly kissed her throat, tasting the sweet firm flesh there with his open mouth. He moved lower and kissed the swell of her breast. His mind was spinning, as hunger for Kate drove him.

Some distant part of his mind taunted him. Where was the proud Lord Blysdale who was noted for his slow, deliberate lovemaking? Gone! That man had soared into oblivion the night the stars fell and he'd thought he'd lost this woman in his arms, his Kate, forever. In his place was a humble man who dared hope he might be allowed some happiness. Who hoped that the conniving fates that had made his life a bleak ruin would forget to look his way just this once—and permit him to forget what sort of man they had made him.

"Kate." His voice was husky with passion. "Kate, I—"

The door to the suite burst open and Jamie ran in. "I'm sorry I took so long, Kate. I have your breakfast. I just have to get a place ready to put the tray down." He pushed things aside on a table by the windows. "You're out of bed! That's wonderful. Do you want to eat over here?"

Blysdale lifted Kate easily and slid her back into the bed. Rearranging the pillows behind her, he cleared his throat and told her brother, "She'd better have her breakfast here, lad. She really isn't up to getting out of bed yet."

Kate saw how Bly's eyes burned at her, full of promise, full of love. She couldn't resist. Intentionally letting him see her longing for him, she said in a seductive voice, "The way I feel right now, I wish I could spend the rest of my life in bed."

Blysdale was stopped dead. Her words held him as effectively as chains. Her look set his heart racing.

Blysdale didn't have any idea how her husband had behaved, but if her little brother hadn't been present, Kate

Halsted would have begun learning how dangerous it was to tease a real man. If Jamie hadn't been there, he'd grant her wish in a heartbeat.

"Are you all right, Kate?" Jamie asked, coming over to them. Concern was in his eyes and in his young voice. "Are you? You sound to me like you're getting a bad cold."

Chapter Twenty-one

That afternoon——as soon as Blysdale returned from wherever he'd fled to keep Jamie from hearing his laughter as he strode away down the hall—he took Kate out onto her balcony.

"There." He smiled down at her. "Isn't it better to be outside?"

"Yes." She looked out at the Channel sparkling in the sunlight and took a deep breath of the fresh, salt-flavored air. "Yes, it is. It's awful to be cooped up inside when the day is fine, isn't it?"

"I always thought so. Griswold tells me that I once ordered the surgeons-in-charge to knock out a wall if, when the weather was fine, they wouldn't carry us wounded out of whatever dank building it was they were using as hospital."

Kate's eyes grew soft. After a long moment of quiet regard, she asked, "And did they?"

He laughed. "No. They told me I was in no condition to be carried anywhere and to shut up." He smiled as if sharing a joke. "I got absolutely no respect. Neither rank nor station impressed those surgeons." He chuckled. "Finally, I got Griswold to sneak me off to the woods. At least I could breathe there."

Kate voice was as soft as her eyes, "And is that how Griswold got to be so good with wounds? By taking care of yours?"

Suddenly Bly looked embarrassed. He'd given too much away. Kate had that effect on him. It was too late to back down, though. "Well, it was a long war, and rather a bloody one." He was speaking cautiously now, not wanting to shock her—or to raise sympathy for himself in her. Chalfont Blysdale didn't need anyone's sympathy. He never had. He terminated the subject with a brusque, "Griswold saw his share of wounds."

He turned away from her then, and leaned on the low stone wall of the balcony. For a long time there was silence between them as he watched the gulls wheeling over the water.

Kate sat and watched him. Watched the tension their conversation had bred in him slowly drain away. Watched as he seemed to come to some decision and waited calmly until he turned back to her.

"Kate?"

"Yes?"

It was his turn to study her. "How serious is this friendship you have with Mallory?"

She caught her breath. This was nothing she'd expected.

His eyes bored into hers. He would demand an answer. What could she say?

Nothing but the truth would do, she realized. There must never be anything but the truth between them. Not anymore. She sat thinking. Even the truth had to be carefully presented to Bly. First she wanted guarantees. "I want to tell you the truth, Bly. First, however, I must have your word that you will honor my wishes in this matter."

He stiffened, and Kate suspected that he thought she was going to ask him to understand and honor her love for Gordon Mallory. If she'd been dealing with any but the dangerous man before her, she'd have laughed.

"I want you to give me your word that you will not harm Gordon Mallory as a result of what I'm about to tell you."

His bright blue eyes darkened.

"What is it you're going to tell me?"

"Bly. Promise!" She sounded as if she were speaking to Jamie.

His expression became thunderous. That muscle along its edge jumped in his jaw. With obvious difficulty he grated out, "I promise."

"Very well." She patted the foot of the chaise longue he'd had Griswold drag out onto the balcony for her. "Come sit here."

He stayed where he was a moment longer, his expression stubborn now.

"Oh, for heaven's sake, Bly. Come here."

He pushed away from the place he'd been leaning and came to her. His gaze locked on her face, he finally sat.

"You don't make anything easy, do you?" she asked.

He smiled then, a tight, twisted smile. "I suppose I don't," he admitted reluctantly. The smile grew imperceptibly. "It doesn't seem to be in my nature."

She sat looking at him, thinking how much she loved him and wondering how best to begin. With Chalfont Blysdale, one organized one's thoughts. Otherwise reactions could become dire.

Finally, she was ready. "When we were children, Gordon Mallory was always envious of us. His family had money— his grandfather was a very successful merchant—but they had no rank. There were no titles in his family." She made a little face. "And absolutely no breeding."

Bly's eyebrows shot skyward.

Kate went on. "He always hung around with Josh. Neither Hal nor I had any use for him, really, and we hated the way he would manipulate Josh."

Blysdale was beginning to look puzzled.

"To make a long story short, Gordon thought that if he could marry me, he would have it all. His father's money, and my rank and good name. I refused him, of course, and ended it by marrying Lionel."

"Who the hell's Lionel?"

"Lionel was my husband, the Earl of Rushmore, and well you know it. Be quiet."

Bly looked mutinous.

Kate cocked her head and lifted an eyebrow. "Do you want me to go on or not?"

He frowned and closed his lips with obvious firmness.

"Very well. When I came home after Lionel died, Gordon began to beg me to marry him again. It didn't matter to him that I was still in mourning, it doesn't matter that I reject him again and again. He simply refuses to take no for an answer."

Blysdale was still silent, but he was having trouble with it.

"He still refuses to understand that no power on earth would make me marry him. He still pesters and bullies me about it. And . . ."

"And what? What is it you don't want to tell me, Kate?"

"There's nothing I don't want to tell you, Bly. Really there isn't. It's just . . ."

"Just what!" Bly raked a hand through his hair. "Why is it you can't confide in me, Kate?"

"Because it isn't my secret, Bly."

"Whose is it, and what is it?"

Kate hesitated only an instant. "It's Josh's, and the secret is that he goes out on smuggling runs with Gordon."

"That's it? That's all?"

"Well, you have to admit that if you were a revenue officer, it would be quite enough." There was a twinkle in her eyes. She thought to remind him of their first misunderstanding there on the steps of the old Norman tower . . . and of their first kiss.

But Blysdale's eyes went dark and stormy—slate blue like a sea under heavy dark clouds. He was holding words back with a visible effort. So Gordon Mallory was into smuggling, was he? His thoughts raced. Then why not something bigger? Much bigger. Why not the smuggling of good English souls to the hell of slavery in the Middle East?

"What is it?" Kate was alarmed.

Bly slipped an arm around her and kissed her absently on the forehead. "Your brother is a dolt. He could ruin himself and disgrace your whole family if he were caught smuggling. But that's easy enough to put period to, and I shall, if I have to wring his fool neck. It's Mallory that I'm thinking about. And not just his pursuit of you, for I'll stop that as well."

"Then what is it? What . . . ?"

Blysdale rose, looking as if he might erupt. He took two brisk turns around the terrace and returned to Kate. "I'm not ready to tell you now, Kate. Later, when I've thought it through."

She looked at him a long moment, impatient to know. Impatient to share his thoughts.

"Kate." He looked down at where she reclined, and the expression in his eyes changed. The stormy blue disappeared, and a look that stopped her breath came into them. "Will you just get well, my love, and let me do the rest for now? Haven't you carried the burdens long enough?"

"Oh, Bly. I'm so used to it that it's become a hard habit to break."

"Even if I promise to keep you informed of developments? That way you won't die of curiosity—which fate is"—his tone became dry—"I feel sure, the one you're dreading."

"Wretch!" He knew her too well.

"Yes, my love?"

"Sit," Kate commanded.

After the slightest of hesitations, he reseated himself. But not on the foot of her *chaise longue*. This time he sat facing her so close their lips would touch if either of them leaned forward just a little. His hip was against hers. He was leaning on the hand he'd placed on the other side of her, and he was watching her like a hawk watching its prey.

Kate's voice was considerably weaker than it had been

when she'd ordered him to reseat himself. "I still will have to hold up every coach coming to Clifton-on-Tides until I get the right one, you know."

Bly leaned forward those few separating inches. His mouth claimed hers gently. It was a comforting kiss, without the demanding heat of the kisses he'd given her this morning. Even so, it completely disoriented Kate.

Blysdale sat back again, waiting for her to continue.

"Where was I?" Her eyes were dazed.

"You were robbing coaches that came conveniently near your home."

"Oh, yes. So I was." She looked at him and shook her head. "Well, that's about all, really. That's the only responsibility I feel I must keep for myself. And, to return to the point this conversation was centered on, I am certainly not betrothed to Gordon Mallory."

"Devil take Gordon Mallory."

He kissed her then, with all the hunger and heat that had been in his kisses that morning. And Kate kissed him back as if she had waited all her life for a man like him.

"Kate," he breathed as he ran his mouth over her cheek to the place under her ear that he kissed next. "My sweet Kate."

"Oh, Bly." She melted in his arms as he nibbled his way down her neck to kiss where her shoulder joined it. Kate kissed him just where his hair met his collar, and felt his quickly indrawn breath cross the skin on her breast. "Bly?" Suddenly she had a question.

He lifted his head and regarded her a little impatiently. "Yes, Kate?"

"Do all your friends call you 'Bly'?"

"Those few men I call my friends do, yes." He was looking at her quizzically.

"Then . . . "

"Then what, Kate?" He tilted her chin up and kissed her just under it.

"Then what shall I call you?"

" 'Bly' won't do?"

"Surely you have a first name." She put her hand on his that was inching up to her right breast.

"Of course I have. You already know it." He was breathing a little harder than he had been. "It's Chalfont. I told you at the caves."

"Yes, you did, but I so hoped you had another. Perhaps a softer one that you were ashamed to tell me."

He lifted his head long enough to give her an insulted look and returned his attention to her throat.

Kate sighed. "Shall I call you Chalfont?"

He picked up his head again to glare at her. "At your peril."

"You don't like your name?" Kate's own breath was coming a little faster now, as warm ripples of pure desire pulsed through her.

"No."

"Why not? Where did you get it?"

"My maternal grandfather was the Duc de Chalfont. A fearful tyrant, he died a few years before the French would, no doubt, have cheerfully beheaded him. My mother married a man she didn't love to escape him. Now may we stop prattling about my name and get on with it?"

Kate sensed the desolation his life with such people must have been, and her heart filled to overflowing with love for him. With the desire to make it all up to him.

"Kate?" He shook her lightly and inched his hand farther toward her breast.

Kate laughed low in her throat and let go of it. With this amazing man, she had absolutely no objection to "getting on with it." When his hand closed over her breast, and his thumb caressed its aching point, she murmured, "Oh, my darling," and waited for his kiss.

"There," he said against her lips.

"There?" she asked, confused, only wanting his lips on hers again.

"There is the name you shall call me." He kissed the corner of her mouth and nipped her lower lip gently. "Darling. From now on, to you, I am 'Darling.'"

Bly had stretched out to lie beside her on the *chaise longue,* and Kate eased down until she was almost lying under him, the better to see his face, his beautiful blue eyes. Eyes that were as blue and bright as a summer sky again, passion lighting their depths. When her face was even with his, she told him, "Very well, *Darling,* that shall be your name."

"Kate." He loomed over her, his weight on his elbows so that he could look down into her face. "I will never be able to tell you how much I hated to think of you as betrothed to any other man."

She smoothed his hair back from his forehead and kissed him there. "I'm so glad."

"I wanted to kill him." He narrowed his eyes. "For just one insane moment there in the drawing room I wanted to kill you both."

She chuckled.

Bly retaliated by touching her other breast, and she moaned softly instead.

"I thought you never wanted to marry, Lord Blysdale." She pulled his hand away and asked, "Didn't you tell me the stars would fall from the sky before you wed?" She ran a finger down his lips to keep him from answering immediately. "So what difference would a betrothal make?"

He growled low in his throat, and Kate knew any discussion of a betrothal to Gordon Mallory was over. When he spoke, it was to say, "I was intrigued by a woman who could do all the things you can do."

"Ah. You were charmed by my ability to drain pastures and to store grain?" Her eyes teased him.

"Fool." He kissed her fingers, then enfolded them in his large, long-fingered hand. "I'd never met a lady with the courage to spy on me and my men before. A woman who could ride beside me all day." He opened his hand and recaptured hers that lay in it. "And not complain at the pace."

He opened her hand and placed a kiss in the palm. When she sighed, he flicked her palm with his tongue and kissed it again. "And who could be a quiet companion."

Kate opened her mouth to inform him that she was not *ever* a prattling peagoose. Bly took advantage and fitted his mouth over hers, plundering it with his tongue.

Kate surrendered. Clinging to his shoulders, she gave herself over to his mastery, to the depth of his kisses and the caress of his hands. Her senses rioted.

Bly pulled away to tell her, "Never had I thought to find a woman I could spend the rest of my life with, Kate. Never before you."

"And the stars?" she managed to gasp.

"The stars tumbled from the sky when I saw you shot, Kate. My whole universe crumbled."

"Oh, my dear." Tears sparked in her eyes, tears of sympathy, tears of joy.

Bly leaned to kiss her again. This time it was a tender kiss. It held all the sweetness he had never had in his life, all the tenderness he had never experienced, and all the longing that burst through him at the thought of sharing such things with her. It was a kiss that promised he would cherish her always.

Bly lifted his head to look her straight in the eyes. "I love you, Kate, I want you for my own. Marry me, Kate."

"Oh, my Darling, I w . . . "

"Kate!" Jamie's voice rose over the sounds of the surf on the rocks below the balcony. "Kate, where are you?"

Bly rose in one fluid movement and replaced the light cover Kate had had over her before he'd displaced it in his passion. "Here, Jamie," he called. "Your sister's out here on the balcony getting some fresh air."

To Kate, he said softly, "Do you think you would mind dreadfully if I just tossed him over into the sea?"

And then Jamie ran out on the balcony and plopped down next to his sister to show her the baby rabbit he had found.

When Kate looked up from the tiny ball of fur, Blysdale was gone.

Chapter Twenty-two

That evening when Blysdale came to Kate, he was clad all in black, as he so frequently was, but instead of his usual snowy shirt and cravat, they were black as well. Even though he seemed more sinister than she'd ever seen him, just the sight of him sent her heart soaring and made her whole body tingle.

But something was wrong.

He didn't come into her outstretched arms.

What had happened? Looking at him more alertly, she registered the awful grimness in his face. His lips were a tight line, hard, unyielding. There was none of the softness there with which he'd kissed her only a few hours ago.

The lover she'd held close in her arms was gone.

Feeling as if her heart were caught in a cold fist, Kate searched frantically for an explanation. Her gaze ran over his lithe frame and found it. In his black-gloved right hand he held a blaze of jewelry—flashes of multicolored lightning that spilled through his fingers.

The coach! Kate's heart leapt. Bly had taken her place and had robbed a coach. The *right* coach! While she'd lain helpless in her bed, the coach she had been waiting for had come. Yes, and would have gone, as well, leaving her none the wiser. Except that Bly had been there. He had stopped it.

Her wonderful Bly. Without caring about the dangers, the terrible ramifications if he'd been caught, he'd taken on her guise of highwayman and had saved the day . . . and her brother as well. And he'd done it for her! Kate's joy threatened to overwhelm her. She looked from the jewels to his face, her face glowing with it.

But there was no answering joy in Blysdale's visage. Approaching the bed where Kate lay, he dropped the jewels into her lap. "There," he said harshly. "There's the proof you needed."

Kate's smile died. She frowned at him. What was the matter? His whole presence was as dark as the clothes he wore. What had happened to the man she loved?

"Bly?" Then, "Darling," she corrected herself, "what is it? What's wrong?"

He closed his eyes and swayed.

"Bly!" She threw back the covers to go to him. Unheeded, bright gems scattered off her lap and onto her bedclothes. "Oh, my Darling! Are you hurt?"

"No! Don't get out of that bed!" It was almost a shout. His gaze locked on her bare, narrow feet, her long, lovely legs, uncovered to the place her nightgown clung high on her thighs. Desire rushed through him—soul-shattering desire for a woman he could never have.

Still, he couldn't look away as she obediently slipped back under the covers. In his mind, he could hear his own voice ranting, *Don't! Don't come near me with your body all warm from the bed I'd hoped to share and so beautiful it breaks my heart. For God's sake, don't come near me, for I'd not be able to keep my filthy hands off you, and I'm not fit for you to touch, my Kate, my love.*

Coolly he told her, "I've learned the identity of the jewel thief for you." *And to do it I have behaved unspeakably. I've done to another human being the painful, degrading things that were done to me when I was a prisoner of the French.*

*Done things I swore I'd never do. Inflicted pain no man
should have to suffer. And I've done it for you, Kate, all for
you. Done it to force the name you need from the lips of the
thief's courier. For you. Because there is nothing I wouldn't
do for you, Kate. Nothing.*

No hint of his agony showed in his voice as he told her,
"His courier was in the coach I stopped an hour ago." His
voice held grim satisfaction as he informed her, "This time
the Mayfair Bandit's henchman didn't get to bleed to death
before he could speak."

Kate didn't know what to do. His attitude bewildered her.
She wanted him to take her in his arms. Yearned to hold
him in hers. She wanted to kiss away the terrible strain she
saw on his face, and thank him for saving her brother. To
share this moment of triumph, his and hers, with him.

But he was behaving so oddly. She didn't know what
to do.

By some deep, feminine instinct she knew that something
horrible had happened to him, to this wonderful man she
loved with all her heart. . . . And whatever it was, it had happened because of her.

"Bly," it was a cry from the heart. "Tell me what's wrong!"

Blysdale stood staring at her without answering. How
could he tell this bright, shining woman what a black-hearted
monster he had made of himself in her service?

Striving for some point of contact, any point of contact,
Kate touched the ropes of pearls and necklaces of diamonds,
emeralds, and rubies that had, just a moment ago, been in
his gloved hand. Holding on to them as if by doing so she
would somehow reach him, she wracked her mind for something, anything, with which she might bring him back to reality. Bring him back to her!

In desperation, Kate asked the first thing that entered her
mind, "What else happened, Bly? Please tell me. What happened to you?"

"Nothing." He told her in a dead voice. "Nothing happened to me."

With a flash of intuition, Kate said, "Then tell me what happened to the courier."

Blysdale looked at her with startled eyes, eyes that had recently seen hell. He'd no idea how she had guessed that, but he told her, "I tortured the name you needed out of him, Kate."

"Tortured?" She hated the way her voice sounded. Thready, horrified. This was Bly, and nothing he could do could horrify her. She took a deep breath, steadied her voice. "Come here, Bly." She patted the bed beside her. "Come here and sit by me, Darling."

He looked at her a long moment before moving closer, but he didn't sit. Could she really want him anywhere near her after he'd just told her what he'd done?

"Bly." Her gaze captured and held his. "Do you think I could love you more than life this afternoon and cease to love you now because night has fallen?"

He stared at her, saying nothing.

"Or do you think that I could love you right on up to the time you performed some act that might not please me and stop?"

He was frowning, but he was listening.

Then Kate's intuition flared like a torch, illuminating *his* thoughts for her. "Oh, dearest God. That's what *she* did, isn't it?"

"What who did?" There was a wariness in his eyes that bordered on fear.

The sight of it in this, of all men, tore Kate apart. She leapt up and flung her arms around him. "That's what your mother did!" Kate spoke with absolute assurance. "She loved you when you were good, and withdrew her love whenever you did something that displeased her." She reared her head back to look full in his face. "That's it, isn't it? That's the truth. And that's why you think I have stopped loving you— because you did something of which you're ashamed."

He was looking at her as if she were a sorceress.

She grabbed his shoulders and shook him. "That's it, isn't

it? And that's why you can't bear to trust any woman with
your heart!"

Proud Chalfont Blysdale dropped his head. For his life
he couldn't meet her eyes.

Kate reached up and took his chin gently in her hands.
She raised his face. "It's not that way with me, my Darling.
I love you with all my heart, and I always will. Nothing you
could ever do could change that. Never. Ever. You are my
own true love, my dear dark knight. And I am yours forever
and completely."

She watched as hope dawned faintly in his eyes. Saw the
fear there, too, and knew he was afraid to believe she loved
him, incapable of believing himself worth loving. Her breath
caught on a sob, and she pulled his head down and kissed
first one of his beautiful blue eyes and then the other. Then
she slowly and surely fitted her lips to his and kissed him
long and lingeringly, with all the sweetness of her love for
him.

When she spoke again it was in a breathless whisper.
"Now come to bed, my beloved, where you belong."

With a groan that loosed a lifetime's pent-up agony,
Blysdale scooped her up and fell with her onto her bed,
showering her with kisses.

There, among a king's ransom in jewels and with a passion that outshone them every one, he made his Kate truly
his own, and in doing so, he accepted from her the healing
for his damaged soul that no one else could give him.

Chapter Twenty-three

Griswold was waiting to accompany his Colonel on the next round of his search when Lord Blysdale rode into the dew-drenched stable yard and handed his lathered horse to a waiting groom. "Walk him well," Bly ordered. He didn't bother to apologize for bringing the horse back to the barn in that condition. The stable hands had seen him return all the others he'd ridden properly cooled out.

Mounting his second horse of that morning, Bly waited for Griswold to get into the saddle then rode out of the stable yard. Long years of training kept him from leaving the area at the gallop as he wanted to, but it was with scant patience that he walked, then trotted, the first few hundred yards to loosen both horses' muscles.

"What had Jacobs and Dawson to report?"

Griswold rode forward to be at his side. "Nothing. They drew a blank in the area you had them search."

"Ranging farther afield would be a waste of time. The answer has to be nearby. If they're holding as many people as I suspect they are, they'd be foolish to keep them very far from the port."

"That makes sense," Griswold agreed. "It would be taking a foolish chance to move any large number of people very far to get them to that ship. They might be discovered."

"Yes. Exactly." Bly turned his horse toward the Channel. Gris followed.

"They have to be holding them in the caves," Bly was thinking out loud for Gris's benefit. "It's the only answer. These men aren't the sort who take chances. We'd have had them by now if they were."

Gris grunted his agreement with that. Then he asked, "Why are you so certain we'll find the answers in those caves, though?"

"Because they have to be there. The captives have got to be near the port, and there must be enough of them to make up a shipment if the ship is getting ready to set sail.

"The ship moored in Clifton-on-Tides is provisioning, which means they're ready to sail, and nothing of a commercial nature has been loaded. Their only purpose, as far as I can determine, is to go sell captives into slavery in the East."

"That makes sense."

"After this morning's sweep of the area I'm so positive that they're underground that I'd stake my life on it."

"Very likely that's exactly what you *are* doing, Bly." Griswold's expression was grim. "Whoever's behind this is ruthless. Slavers are the scum of the earth."

Bly almost told his batman, *And Mathers and Smythe are my friends. They're the best friends I have left except for you and Taskford.* He didn't, of course. He just turned a face full of purpose to Griswold and told him, "I don't intend to lose anyone else I care for, Gris."

Recognizing the depth of feeling in his Colonel's voice, Griswold wisely held his peace.

They rode on in silence.

Back at the castle, Kate awakened. Bly had awakened her before dawn and told her that he was going to search out the place the slavers held their captives. Kate had clung to him and kissed him desperately, urging him to keep safe—wishing he would stay.

Bly had laughed and accused her of attempting to bewitch him from his duty, kissed her, hard, one last time, and told her to go back to sleep. And Kate had slept late, exhausted by a night of lovemaking beyond her wildest dreams.

She stretched now, smiling. Had any woman ever been so much in love?

Dresden interrupted her euphoric remembrances by coming in with the footmen carrying the copper bathtub and the huge canisters of hot water for her bath. Despite the fact that Dresden looked a little disapproving when she said, "Lord Blysdale informed me that you would like a bath, your ladyship," everything went well, and soon Kate was bathed, perfumed, and dressed.

Dresden had just put the finishing touches on Kate's hair and was winding up for a lecture when suddenly there was a knock at her door and it burst open as her youngest brother rushed in.

"Look, Kate!" Jamie held his bunny out to her. "His eyes are open now. I do believe he's going to be all right, don't you?"

Kate smiled as she answered. "Yes. I do think so, dear. You and Cato rescued him from Cook's cat just in time." Kate had heard the tale of the rescue from Dresden as she'd bathed.

"Cato's a good old hound. He didn't even chase the cat." Jamie scowled. "What makes cats do such awful things, Kate?"

"Hunting is their nature, Jamie. It's the way God made them."

"Well, I hate it."

"Would you rather be overrun with mice and rats?"

The boy make a face. "Ugh. No."

"Well, without cats we certainly would be." She ran the tip of her index finger along the tiny rabbit's head in an effort to pet him. He kicked out with his hind legs. "Did you know that cats are given the credit for stopping the Black Plague?"

"What? Jamie looked as if that was just too much to believe, even from Kate. "Is that true, Kate?"

"Yes. When the cats decimated the rat population, the plague went away."

Jamie frowned. What does 'decimated' mean, Kate?"

She told him, "To decimate means to drastically reduce."

Oh." He was awed by the thought. After a moment, he said, "Well, I guess I shan't be as bad as most boys about cats, then."

"I'm glad to hear it." Kate reached out toward him. Jamie scooted closer and leaned against her side.

"Hmmm," she told him as she hugged him hard, "I like this."

He snuggled against her. "I do, too. You always smell so good, Kate."

She laughed. "Thank you. You smell good, too."

"I do?" He wanted to be told how.

"Yes." Kate sniffed him dramatically. "You smell like sunshine and hay and fresh air."

He burst into a peal of laughter. "Well, I'm just glad that I didn't play with Cato today. If I'd wrestled with him, you wouldn't be telling me I smelled nice, I'll wager."

"True." She held him tight. After a second or two, she said, "I shall miss it when you get a little bigger and won't let me hug you anymore."

"Don't be silly, Kate. I shall always want to cuddle."

Kate smiled, wishing that were so. Tactfully, she changed the subject. "Would you like to go riding later?"

"Oh, yes!"

"Then we shall. I'll have the horses brought round right after luncheon."

Jamie looked out the window toward the Channel. "I hope the weather holds."

Kate looked out. There were dark clouds far away, but they didn't seem to have much movement in them. There was a good chance they could have their ride. English weather was nothing if not changeable. By the time they finished eating, it would probably be clear.

Blysdale and Griswold had tied their horses under the brow of the hill on which they sprawled. Slightly below them lay the sea cliffs that Kate had shown Bly. They were alternately sun-dappled and shaded as the clouds scudded over them from the Channel.

"Looks like weather coming in from the Continent, sir."

Bly grunted agreement.

"Do you think there'll be much to see if the weather turns foul?"

"Hard to say. Depends on how badly the slavers want to hide what they're up to."

"What makes you think that your friends are here, Bly? How could they be? There's naught here but a hill."

"The other day on the beach, Lady Katherine tried to show me a cave that she said had many branches and tunnels. The mouth of it had been blocked, however, so she couldn't."

"And?"

"I think it's been blocked on purpose. The fall of rock was too regular, and the tunnel too completely blocked for it to have been a normal rock slide. If my guess is right, the captives are being held in the tunnels of that cave until they can be sent to the Middle East and sold."

"Aye. 'Tis certain we've all scoured the countryside, and none of us have found the first sign of any other place they could be hidden."

"I'm convinced they're here, and that the entrance to their prison is concealed somewhere on that hill."

Griswold pulled a spyglass from his belt and began searching the area before them without another word.

Kate and Jamie cantered over the brow of a hill and stopped just on the other side, down out of the wind.

"It looks as if the weather is taking a turn for the worse, Jamie. I think we'd better go home before we get wet."

Jamie threw a glance at the lowering sky and sighed. "Yes, Kate, I suppose we must. But can we do this again soon? I've had *such* a good time."

Kate looked at him and suddenly realized that this brief time with her was probably the only companionship the boy got. Josh overlooked him completely, and Hal had been away, as she had. Sadly, there were no boys his age anywhere around Cliffside Manor. Jamie must be lonely. "Jamie?"

"Yes, Kate?" He had to raise his voice to be heard over the rising wind.

"I wonder if you would like to ride with me sometime when I'm going around to check on things here on Cliffside?" Saying that, she realized that she would, in spite of Blysdale's firm assurances that her brother was going to take up his responsibilities, be checking on Josh. How she wished that weren't the case, but she didn't trust him to see to things. Not yet, anyway.

She continued to Jamie, "It wouldn't be a whole lot of fun, I know, but," she added for kindness, "it would be very nice for me to have your company."

"I should like that very much, Kate. Thank you!"

From the eagerness shining on his face, Kate wondered if anyone had taken *any* time with the boy in her absence. She vowed she'd be sure to do so from now on.

"Come on." Kate turned her mount toward home. "We'd best head back if we don't want a good soaking!" With her riding whip, she pointed to the Channel where there was a line of rain dimpling the water as it marched steadily toward them. "Look."

They cantered away side by side. The horses moved easily and were well matched as to pace. Kate had chosen them carefully when she'd sent word to the stables earlier, and they stayed together with no effort.

As they rounded a copse of young trees, both horses slammed to a halt. Jamie was almost thrown out of the saddle by his mount's violent stop. Kate reached out to steady her brother.

There in front of them, blocking their path, was a line of

three horsemen. Two were brutish-appearing men mounted on shaggy, ill-bred animals. Both men looked as if they'd never been on a horse before in their lives.

The man in the center was Gordon Mallory!

Blysdale saw Kate and Jamie tear over the brow of a distant hill and head for home. Obviously they were trying to outrun the squall coming in from the Channel.

"Nice riders," Gris commented.

"Yes." Bly followed them with his gaze.

Kate and Jamie disappeared into the next little valley, and, smiling, Bly watched for them to come back into view as they surmounted the next hill. Longing to see her made him feel she was taking longer than necessary to negotiate the next rise. Love was making him anxious about her. Because he could no longer imagine a world worth having without her, the ever-present fear that something might happen to his Kate twisted in him.

When another minute had passed without sight of her, Blysdale cursed, lunged to his feet, and ran for his horse. Throwing himself into the saddle, he shot off toward the valley into which his Kate had disappeared.

Griswold wasted only one startled instant staring at the retreating figure of his friend before running for his own horse and leaping into the saddle to follow.

Chapter Twenty-four

Kate glared at the three men blocking her way and demanded, "How dare you deliberately close the way to us, Gordon? Move aside! Can't you see we wish to get by?"

The taller of Gordon Mallory's two companions leered, gaptoothed, "And what makes ye think we'll *let* ye go by, my pretty sweetling?"

Shocked and angered that such a shabby man would speak to a lady like that, Jamie cried in his best grown-up voice, "Move aside. My sister wishes to pass!"

"Blimy! Looka here, looka here," the same man said. "The boy's a right tasty morsel, too. He'll fetch a good pri—"

"Shut up!" Mallory snapped the sharp command and the man fell silent.

Suddenly, it was so quiet here among the trees in the little valley that the creak of saddle leather could be heard. And in that silence, the words Mallory had tried to keep Kate from hearing sank into her mind with all their dreadful connotations. These horrid men had just considered her brother as a marketable item, she'd no doubt of it!

Slavers. These were the men that Blysdale suspected of having taken his friends, and they were not chance-met by

Mallory, either. These men were obviously under the leadership of her detested neighbor. The certainty of his evil exploded into her mind and made her blood run cold.

Fearful of the threat these awful men posed to her beloved Jamie, Kate could even hear the frantic beating of her own heart, hear her own shortened breathing.

What no one heard, however, was the stealthy approach of the man who stood quietly to one side of them, each of his rock-steady hands filled with an already cocked pistol.

His voice was as soft as the rising wind, but full of deliberate menace. "I believe I heard the lady say that she wished to pass."

All three men started. Their heads whipped around to face his way. No one moved.

Even so, Kate closed her eyes in relief for an instant. Bly was here, all would be well. When she opened them, relief fled.

One of the brutes was flinging a knife at Bly!

Kate tried to shriek a warning. The cry died in her throat, seized there by an awful fear. She could only gasp, "Bly!", her heart in the single word, her eyes full of her love for him.

Time slowed to an eternity. Instantaneous actions slowed to take minutes. Kate could see the man on Gordon Mallory's other side pulling a pistol from his belt.

Kate whirled her horse around to put her own body between the armed man and Jamie. She knew by some deep instinct that she mustn't interfere with Blysdale, knew without reason that he'd no need of her feeble assistance. Her heart in her throat, she couldn't take her eyes off him.

Bly seemed merely to sway a few inches to one side, and the knife hissed past his throat. Without so much as a change of expression he shot the second man from the saddle before the thug could bring his pistol to bear.

Gordon Mallory looked down at his fallen henchman for a moment, then up at Kate. "Well, Kate," he told her coolly, "it looks as if Lord Blysdale has cleared the way for you to pass." Carefully avoiding looking toward Blysdale, Mallory spun his horse and galloped away. It wasn't until he was well out of the range of Blysdale's pistol that his back relaxed.

The panicked man who'd flung the knife at Blysdale looked from Mallory to Blysdale, yanked his horse around, and tore off after his employer like a faithful dog.

Now true relief flooded through Kate, and her strength seemed to leave her. She wanted nothing more than to fall from her saddle into Bly's arms and cry her heart out. This day, coming as it did on top of just barely being allowed out of bed, and having—so delightfully—been allowed very little sleep last night, had been too much for her. Just right now, she couldn't cope alone anymore. More than she needed her next breath Kate needed Bly's arms around her.

And then they were. Pulling her from her saddle, he embraced her fiercely, holding her as if he'd never let her go. Suddenly Kate lost the desire to cry.

"Are you all right?" His voice was rough with anxiety for her.

"Am *I* all right?" Kate snatched her cheek from his chest to stare at him, incredulous. "Am *I* all right? Bly, I wasn't the one they were hurling knives at!" She slid her arms around him and held him ever closer. "You were the one in danger."

Bly actually snorted.

Kate leaned back in his arms again and looked up at him. Her curiosity was sharply piqued. There had been a world of comment in that curt sound, but she couldn't have interpreted its meaning if her life had depended on it.

"Well?" Bly's question held a hint of impatience.

"Why in the world did you make that . . . odd sound?"

He told her as if he were telling an annoying child, "Because it seemed so ludicrous to me that you would be concerned for my safety against such a small force of inept villains when I was the one with my fists full of pistols, that's all."

"Bly, there were three of them, and you had only two shots."

"My dear, though I love you all the more for your concern for me, I'd like to remind you that there were three of them only briefly."

"Yes, and then you had only one shot left against two of them."

"Ah, my ever practical Kate. What you don't know is that I have another gun up my sleeve."

"How . . . ?"

"There's no time to explain the mechanics of an arm holster to you now, Kate." He kissed her briefly but thoroughly and returned her to her saddle. "Later. Now put your loving mind at ease and get home before this rain drenches you." He turned to Jamie and said as if they had just casually run across each other, "Good day, Jamie."

"Good day, your lordship." Jamie's voice was faint, but he sat up very straight and said in a stronger voice, "Never fear, sir, I shall see Kate home safely."

"Good lad!"

Kate smiled at her youngest brother. She was so terribly proud of Jamie and the brave way he had conducted himself through all of this, she wanted him to know it. When she turned back toward her beloved, he was gone.

After an instant of stunned disbelief, she shook off the luxury of helplessness she had allowed herself and gathered her reins. As she did, the first of the rain reached them.

"Come! Let's hurry, Jamie," she called to the boy. He was staring at the dead man on the ground at their horses' feet. Seeing his morbid interest, she rode to close beside him and said gently, "We'll send someone back to take care of this man Lord Blysdale has shot. Come away, dear."

Her words were the last spoken before the first blast of the storm reached them. "Yes, Kate," Jamie answered, and the words were snatched away by the wind.

Kate saw rather than heard him, and together they turned toward Cliffside and galloped off, seeking to outdistance the rain. Kate's thoughts were as chaotic as the clouds bearing down on them. As they rode, the shock of the encounter with Mallory and his thugs faded and after another moment, the horror of the ugly little man's death rose in her.

Bly had killed the man as simply as one would swat a fly! She could hardly comprehend it even now. How could she equate this cold warrior with the gentle, loving man she had taken to her bed last night? He had told her he was a harsh man, and she hadn't wanted to believe that. But now, the truth, in the person of the man he'd shot, had lain at her feet.

Bly had shot that man through the heart and killed him. In front of Jamie. And her. Even now, she was having trouble believing it. Trouble, too, with the remembered warnings he had given her about himself. Suddenly, they were all too real.

Surely, he could have simply wounded the man. Shot him in the shoulder or the arm if he'd feared he might miss the hand that held the pistol. But Bly had shot the man down like a dog.

Kate had seen death before—everyone had by the time they reached her age—so death was no stranger. She had always seen it as a *fait accompli,* however. Someone—a friend or a relative—died of an illness, gradually, and you saw death coming as you visited them. Or you attended a funeral and viewed with sorrow the forever-stilled body of a neighbor.

Never before had Kate seen sudden, violent death. Never seen someone she knew . . . someone she loved . . . coolly and mercilessly deal out death to another living being.

She wasn't sure she could handle that thought. Could she accept the fact that the very hand that had caressed her body so lovingly last night had been the hand that held a gun and pulled the trigger to end the life of another human being just a little while ago?

Suddenly, Kate could hardly breathe.

"Kate! Kate, what is it?"

She pulled up in the shelter of a grove of wind-twisted oaks and turned toward her brother.

"Kate. What's wrong? You look wild."

Did she? Oh, dear Lord, she supposed she did. "I . . . I am upset that you saw that man killed, Jamie."

Jamie's expression became scornful. In an instant, it was as if he were grown. "Man? Surely you jest, Kate. That wasn't a man. That was a foul piece of human scum." Jamie's eyes held a wisdom Kate deplored as he reminded her, "And he'd have shot Lord Blysdale dead if Bly hadn't finished him first. Would you rather *that* had happened?"

The horses stirred restlessly as the storm grew in intensity around them. "No. No, of course not," Kate cried from her heart.

"Then don't be missish. Lord Blysdale rescued us from those awful men, never doubt it." He scowled fiercely. "And they all three *needed* killing, if you ask me!"

"Jamie!"

His horse spun around once under him and bogged its head down trying to grab the bit. Jamie's grown-up scorn dissolved into the concerned expression of a very young boy again. "Please, can we go now, Kate? I don't think my Jupiter is going to stand still much longer."

"Yes. Yes, of course." Still distracted by the state of her mind, Kate sent her mount toward home. The animal shot forward, as anxious as its rider to escape the worsening storm.

As she rode, Kate realized she was deeply grateful for Jamie's good sense. By the time they reached the stables at Cliffside, his bracing words had set matters straight in her mind.

Bly told Griswold, "It's Mallory. Damn him to hell!" He was white-faced with fury while they re-tethered their horses under the brow of the hill. As they walked back the short distance to the top of the rise from which they'd been searching the cliff top, Bly told his friend, "Mallory's working with the slavers, if, indeed, he's not their leader."

Just then, as the two reached the crest of the rise, the storm broke over them. The wind tore Griswold's response away.

Behind them down the hill, their horses neighed and pulled

at their reins as heavy raindrops drummed down on them like fists.

"This is going to be bad! Better head for Cliffside, Colonel!" Griswold shouted to be heard.

Blysdale hesitated for an instant, looking back at the area he'd planned to search. Then another thought struck him. "Blast me for a fool, Gris! Let's go!" He ran for the horses. Gris followed hard on his heels.

Now Bly's belated thoughts drove him, and he cursed himself as he ran for his horse. What if Mallory turned back and sought out Kate? Why hadn't he thought of that possibility? Was he so besotted with Kate that he wasn't able to think clearly any longer? Heaven forbid. Kate or no Kate, he still had to find and rescue Mathers and Smythe. But the only thoughts that filled his mind at the moment were of Kate. His Kate. Always Kate. And right now, she might be in danger.

As if to punctuate that thought, lightning sizzled a glaring path through the sky over their heads and split an oak not far from them. Thunder drowned out the terrified whinnies of their horses as Bly approached them.

Griswold's mount broke free and would have plunged away but Blysdale grabbed his reins as the frantic breast ran past them. Giving that horse to Gris, Bly vaulted into his own saddle, ripped free the reins, and they were away.

Lightning struck the very tree to which the animals had been tied and split it to the ground. Flames flared and were drowned by the fury of the storm.

Even a rider of Blysdale's caliber had all he could do to control his terrified mount. His horse was determined to go straight home to the barn and the safety he knew was there. Bly was equally determined to ride a line that would intercept Mallory if Mallory turned from his original direction in an effort to catch Kate.

Bly's mount fought him with bucks and snatches at the bit in his mouth, but in the end Bly won and rode hard for the crest of the next hill. Topping it, Blysdale sighted his quarry. In spite of the driving rain, he could see Gordon

Mallory and his remaining cur galloping toward Mallory's own estate.

Satisfied that Kate was safe from Mallory, Bly turned back toward Cliffside and let his mount have his head. With a final kick, the horse settled down and dropped into a flat-out run. Griswold's mount followed, ears flat and eyes rolling. Side by side the men rode, bent low over their rain-lashed mounts.

The horses, maddened by the lightning, terrified by the thunder of the storm breaking right over them, were no longer under control. The whites of their eyes showed in the dimness of a day gone dark. Bly and Gris were mere passengers as, leaping ditches and hedges, the horses clawed their way across the cliff-side hills, desperate to reach the safety of their stalls.

Without slowing they rushed into the barn, driven by the pelting rain. Whinnying to their stablemates, they skidded to a halt in the dry dirt of the barn aisle and stood nervously champing their bits, the riders on their backs unheeded.

"Your lordship!" The head groom came running. "You should have gone on up to the manor. One of the grooms would have brought the horses down here and saved you such a wetting."

"We've been wetter, laddie," Gris stepped down and informed him wryly, "but not much." He shook himself like a dog and water flew.

Bly vaulted off and they gave the steaming horses to the man. Bly demanded, "Did Lady Katherine and the boy arrive safely?"

"Yes, your lordship." The head groom smiled. "They came in just before the heavy rain started. They're both safe and snug up at the manor." He looked at the dripping nobleman in front of him and added with a wide grin, "And they were only a little damp, sir."

Bly relaxed visibly. Kate was safe.

He and Griswold strolled together to stand at the barn entrance and watch the weather. Illuminating wide stretches of dull gray sky, the lightning flashes were more distant now.

The wind was calming down to no more than a breeze. They waited for the rain to stop as the storm moved away.

"What now, Colonel?" Gris kept his voice low, accustomed to keeping Blysdale's business private.

"Now we get into some dry clothes and plan our next move."

Chapter Twenty-five

As dark and forceful as the storm they'd just experienced, Bly's bitterness bore down on him as he and Griswold walked the long lane from the stable area up to the manor.

Kate. His beloved Kate. She'd seen him shoot a man dead. Seen the man drop out of his saddle without a sound, dead before he hit the ground, and Bly had seen the horror on her face, and had watched her identify him for just what he was. Now he had to accept the fact that she knew that all he'd told her about himself was true. He was a harsh man, a warrior spirit who'd been a soldier too long.

It hadn't been cold-blooded murder. He'd shot in self-defense and it should have been obvious. In other circumstances, he could have just winged the scum and left him alive. In fact, he would have preferred to have left him alive to reveal the location of the entrance into the caves if he'd had a choice. But he'd shot the miscreant dead because he'd had no way of knowing the man's intentions.

Common sense might dictate that Blysdale was the man's target, but what if he hadn't been? Suppose the man had harbored some warped idea of shooting at Kate? Or at Jamie?

Though there'd been only a slim chance of that, it had been a chance Bly couldn't take.

So now Kate knew what sort of a man he truly was. Knew him to be a man who could kill without regret. Without hesitation.

He smiled a lopsided smile at that. If, in his past, he *had* ever hesitated, he would have been dead long before Lady Katherine Elizabeth had had a chance to meet him.

Griswold glanced at his friend, saw Bly's grim smile, and knew his Colonel was having black thoughts. "What is it, sir? What's the matter?"

Bly merely shook his head, and they walked on through the light rain, the gravel of the long drive crunching under their boots. Bly's musings remained as dark as the clouds scudding away inland. His heart, if he considered he had one, might be breaking, but he forced himself to ignore it.

There was no way he could avoid the most painful truth, though. That was that he knew how Kate felt about him— about his ability to kill in a split second. Her horrified face had told him.

Resignedly, he admitted that her feelings should have come as no surprise. Kate was a gently bred female, so how could she be anything but horrified to learn that the man she'd thought she'd been in love with could do such a thing?

Bly's heart was heavy with the realization that, though he'd given his heart irrevocably to the wonderful woman who had healed its ancient wounds, Kate would now have nothing but regrets for the night she'd spent in his arms.

Blysdale took the last steps to the manor door two at a time. He was eager to get his bath and get into dry clothes. At least he could get the dirt of the day's ride off. Unfortunately, he knew of nothing that could bathe away the memory of the horror in Kate's eyes.

Knowing that he had nothing left now but his avowed resolve to rescue Mathers and Smythe, he acknowledged that it was better to work to discover the fate of his two good friends than to sit and mourn a love that was lost to him forever.

• • •

An hour later, clad in dry clothes and a forbidding expression, Bly mounted the horse he'd sent for and rode to the cliff-side hilltop he'd occupied earlier with Griswold. The day had cleared and warmed slightly and there were only light wisps of clouds scudding across the bright blue of the sky. Nevertheless, Blysdale wore his heavy campaign cloak. He wanted it to lie on the damp of the recently rain-soaked ground.

The cloak swung and floated from his shoulders as he rode. Dark blue, from his days in the army, it was one of few departures from his habitual black garb. From frequent experience, he knew that he could lie under a bush, cover himself with the cloak, some dirt, and a handful of leaves, and be almost invisible. That was his intention today—to be an invisible presence on the hill until he learned the location of the entrance to the prison cave that he knew had to be there under it.

Tethering his horse deep in a grove of trees, he pulled his pistol from his saddle holster and walked stealthily to the place he'd chosen. Settling down to wait, Bly placed his pistol close at hand, pulled out his spyglass, and began rubbing on it the soap that would keep its brass from sending off reflections that would give his position away.

Jamie ran to find his sister. "Where is Kate, Jennings?"

"Lady Katherine is in the study, Master Jamie."

Blond curls bobbing, the boy ran to the study. With the sky clear again, he was hoping he could get her to go for another ride. If they hurried, he thought they just might catch a glimpse of the man Colonel Blysdale shot before the men sent to "clean up the little mess" got everything tidy.

Breathless from his long run, Jamie begged, "Kate, can we go riding again?" His eager face shone at her. "The storm's gone. The sun's shining."

"Oh, Jamie." Kate was genuinely sorry, knowing how starved he was for attention. "I can't right now." She gestured at the papers spread out on her desk. She wanted the books to be in perfect order for Josh—because it was beginning to look as if he *did* intend to do as he'd promised Bly. "I have several matters I must see to here. Why don't we go tomorrow? I'll be free then."

Still preoccupied with the task she'd set herself, Kate smiled to herself as she marveled at the truth of that. She really would be free to ride with Jamie. Though she could scarcely believe it, Josh actually was taking over the management of his own estate. Evidently the age of miracles had not passed!

She knew that Bly was the miracle-maker in this particular case, and fell to musing about him. What an awesomely commanding man he was, to so rule the lives of those around him. That he ruled her brother through the respect that Josh had for him, she didn't doubt for a moment. Josh hadn't enough sense to be fearful of Lord Blysdale.

After today, she had no trouble imagining that many men were, however. She gave a little shiver as she remembered how he had saved Jamie and her from Mallory and his two thugs. Though the memory was horrid, still her pride in her lover's ability to protect her was something she couldn't deny. He was truly her own dark knight—a fearful adversary.

"All right, Kate," Jamie called as he left the room. "I'll ride with you tomorrow."

Kate, lost in thoughts of Blysdale, barely heard him leave. Fearful. That was an awful word. To be full of fear was a terrible prospect for anyone. She was glad Josh wasn't fearful. He was her brother, after all, and the head of her house. It would have been a blow to the family's pride if he'd been afraid of Blysdale. That Josh acted out of respect for his Colonel was acceptable, however, and it brought her a little glow of sisterly pride.

Fearsome did, however, certainly describe Chalfont Lord Blysdale. She'd already noticed that his mere presence caused men to conduct themselves with more than their customary caution. For an instant, she relived the scene on the windswept path through the hills. With a little thrill she recalled how Bly had just swayed slightly to avoid the knife flying toward his throat from the first of Mallory's henchmen. Then, without even blinking at that attempt to kill him, Blysdale had coolly dispatched the second man who was trying to kill him before the man could shoot.

Kate repressed a little shudder as she recalled the calm deliberation with which Bly had shot the man who was pulling out a pistol to kill him with. Bly made it seem all so . . . casual.

A faint ripple went through Kate. Her upbringing told her she should think the feeling was revulsion. But it wasn't. Again it was very like . . . pride.

She could feel the blush that rose to her cheeks. Was it from shame at her heartlessness? Or was it confusion? She knew, whatever else she felt, that mixed with it there was pride that the man she loved had come to her rescue, and that he was strong enough and capable enough to do so without forfeiting his own life in the process.

Was he ruthless? Perhaps. Even certainly. But what would have happened to her and to Jamie if he had not been? The men who'd stopped them had indicated that they were not going to let her pass. They were dreadful, unsavory characters—brutes seemingly without any finer feelings.

Her skin crawled to think that those coarse creatures were part of the slavers Blysdale was seeking. Those thugs could be the very men who had captured his friends! Somehow, seeing them in the flesh had made the whole thing seem even more horrible.

Gordon Mallory had been there, too, and he'd done nothing to curb the tongues or the actions of the two ill-kempt men who'd had no intention of letting her pass. Gordon hadn't even reacted to the situation until the man had started to say that Jamie would fetch a good price. Price! Oh, dear God, the whole idea was so awful.

With a sinking heart she put the last of her resistance to the idea of a lifelong neighbor being a villain aside. Those men *were* slavers and Gordon Mallory *was* a part of it!

With that admission came fear, and Kate gasped as she

realized that Mallory and his men constituted a very real threat to her youngest brother. Because today, Jamie had become a prize they coveted.

Kate's head came up and she dropped the bills she had in her hand. Where was Jamie now? He'd left after promising her he'd ride with her tomorrow. Surely he was safe somewhere in the house. Playing with his tin soldiers or reading one of his books, probably. Jamie had long ago learned to amuse himself.

Suppose, though, he'd gone out? Maybe even decided to ride without her? It would never occur to him that the dreadful episode that had happened after lunch might spell future danger. He might even, with a boy's fascination for the morbid, have gone back to watch the two footmen who'd been sent to take the thug's body to the magistrate. If so, he might be riding alone!

Fear for her brother hit her. Anxiety overwhelmed her. She rushed out of the study and down the hall. Jennings would know where Jamie was. "Jennings!" she called, and broke into a run.

Footmen stared as she rushed past them. Up ahead of her near the great hall, one tore off running to find the butler. An instant later he returned and pointed at her as she rushed toward him. Jennings hurried into view. "Lady Katherine! Whatever is it? What's the matter?"

Kate slid to a halt on the well-polished floor and clutched Jennings's arms. "Jamie! Jennings, where's my brother? Where is he?"

"Now, now." Behind his reassuring smile, Jennings looked concerned for her. "No need to get upset, my lady. Master Jamie went out riding is all. He promised not to go off Cliffside. He also promised to be home before dark, and the day is fine."

Kate heard him and blanched. She saw that Jennings thought she was overwrought and was trying to calm her, but Jennings didn't know what had happened, because Blysdale wanted to keep it a secret until they could trap the slavers!

Kate knew, though, and Kate couldn't be calmed. A terrible foreboding had seized her. Jamie was in danger! She knew it! She must get to him!

Wild-eyed, she cried, "Tell Lord Blysdale I've gone to look for my brother!" She grabbed a riding crop off the hall table and ran out the front door to the horses kept there at the ready. Flinging herself into the saddle of the nearest, Kate kicked the animal into a gallop while the groom stationed there gaped after her.

Jennings stood in the doorway, looking after Lady Katherine, too. She rode astride on a man's saddle with her skirts blowing up and her lovely long legs exposed for all to see. He knew that something had to be dreadfully wrong. "Laraby!" he shouted.

"Yes, sir?" The footman was at his elbow, his eyes as big as saucers, his shocked gaze fastened on the fast-disappearing figure of his slender mistress.

"Go find Lord Blysdale. Hurry!"

"Yes, sir!"

Kate pushed the big gelding mercilessly. Great clumps of rain-soaked turf tore loose and flew into the air with every strike of his hooves, while she bent low over his neck and urged him on with her voice as well as her heels.

They charged around a bend in the path and Kate threw herself back in the saddle and hauled in her reins to avoid a collision. Ahead of her, blocking the path, were four horsemen strung out across the path.

Kate had eyes for only one of them. The one who had her youngest brother, Jamie, trussed up like a Christmas turkey, lying across his saddle bow. Gordon Mallory.

Mallory, a welcoming smile on his handsome face, sat waiting for her. "And here you are, Kate, just as I expected. It's so gratifying to know I was right. I felt perfectly certain, you see, that I'd get *you* if I took Jamie."

"Couldn't find him nowhere, Mister Jennings, sir," Laraby reported.

"Then find his man." Jennings was deeply worried. "Find Mister Griswold."

"Ah, that's easy, Mr. Jennings. Mister Griswold's in the stable, sir."

"Go!"

"Yessir!" The footman left at a dead run.

Five minutes later, Griswold strode breathlessly into the great hall. "You sent for me? What's amiss, Jennings?"

"It's Lady Katherine, Mr. Griswold. She tore out of here not a half hour ago saying, 'Tell Lord Blysdale I've gone to find my brother.' Concerned about young master Jamie, she was. And I have to admit I'm concerned about *her*. I've never seen her behave so wild-like. Never."

"And where is the boy?"

"He left to go riding about twenty minutes before she did, but at the rate she was going I've no doubt she's caught up with him by now."

"Good, then they'll be easier for me to find if they're together." Gris spun on his heel and headed for the last of the horses habitually kept by the front door for the messengers and errand-running staff. As he mounted, the groom asked him anxiously, "Shall I go get other horses, sir? There are none left now for the business of the house."

"Suit yourself, son." Griswold kicked his mount into a gallop. "Or ask Jennings!" he shouted back in an effort to help the bewildered groom. Then he concentrated on getting the most out of the horse under him as he headed out across the hills toward the cliffs overlooking the Channel.

He had to find Blysdale and he'd bet his life that that was where his Colonel would be. He had to find Blysdale because, unlike the uninformed Jennings, Griswold knew about the slavers in the area.

Out on the windswept hill overlooking the cliff tops, Blysdale lay under the low-growing branches of a scrub oak. His dark cloak was wrapped around his reclining figure from head to toe, making him almost invisible there in the lengthening afternoon shadows.

There had been nothing to observe all afternoon, but now a movement far off to one side of his line of vision caught his attention. Turning from the hill he'd been watching, he tried to focus his glass on the galloping horse and rider. Before he could identify them, they disappeared. Uneasiness rippled through him and brought him to his feet. He moved forward to crouch beside a boulder, from where he'd be certain to see the horse and rider when they reappeared. Long moments passed before they did.

Kate looked at Gordon Mallory with all the loathing she felt for him. "Give me my brother, you beast. How dare you treat him like this?"

"Ah, Kate." Gordon Mallory smiled benignly at her. "I find no difficulty in treating him in this fashion. In fact, if you prove disobliging, I'm sure I can find it in myself to treat him far worse."

"Ye don't want to mark 'im, Mallory. Prince Aswab likes 'is boys without no blemishes."

Gordon ignored the man. He was intent on discovering Kate's reaction to the man's words.

Kate was all but overcome by her reaction to his words. She had no difficulty grasping their meaning. Bile rose in her throat. This prince of whom they spoke had to be a pervert who preyed on boy children. Even protected as she had been most of her life she had at least heard rumors that such monsters existed. Now she had proof!

Oh, dear God! Not Jamie! How could she save him?

They were moving even as she frantically searched for a means of rescuing her brother. At Gordon's curt order, one of his animals-in-human-clothing had grabbed the bridle of her horse and was beginning to lead it away. Kate, infuriated, struck him with her riding crop.

The man grabbed her wrist and twisted. Kate's cry of pain was lost in the howl of outrage that came from Gordon. He thrust his mount between Kate's and the man's and tore his hand from her bridle. "If you touch her again, I'll kill you!"

The man scowled at Mallory, but backed away.

Kate snarled at Mallory, "Don't you dare touch me, either," with such ferocity that he stared. He dropped the hand that was reaching for her bridle.

Then he threw back his head and laughed. "Oh, I intend to do more than just touch you, Kate. Much more. And when I am through, you'll beg me to marry you."

"I'll see you dead first!" The blazing promise in Kate's eyes as she looked at him caused Mallory to turn his own away.

"Let's get out of here," he ordered his men.

Kate, with her face set and her eyes full of hatred, followed after the man who held her little brother, tied hand and foot and gagged with a filthy rag, across his saddle.

Instead of the lone horseman he expected, Blysdale saw a group of riders come up over the hill. They were riding close together through the mist that rose around them in the cooler evening air, and it was difficult to make them out. The wind off the sea carried no sound of voices to him, but as he watched, he saw the gesture with which the leader ordered two of the men to dismount. When they had, they went to a low heap of boulders and pulled brush away from a well-hidden opening.

Blysdale was elated. It was the entrance he'd been seeking! Thank God! The riddle of the prisoners' whereabouts was solved, he knew it. He hoped, too, that the mystery of Mathers and Smythe's disappearance was soon going to be solved also. What a boon to be able to free his old friends!

He turned back to run for his horse. It was time to call in reinforcements. Sliding down the hill to the grove of trees in which he'd tied his mount, he freed it and leapt into the saddle. Turning it toward Cliffside, he sent it into a headlong run.

In the cave under the cliff-side hill, Mallory tossed Jamie to one of his men and grabbed Kate by the arm. "Hold the boy safely," he ordered. They had traversed a long, almost straight

tunnel in from the hidden entrance, and were standing in a
large cave full of rough furnishings. Kate could see that the
"room" was designed to be used by the large group of men
Mallory must have under his dishonorable command. Just
now there were only five men present, but the number of
cloaks hung on hooks along one wall told her there were
many more somewhere.

She tried to pull her arm free, but Mallory's grip never
slackened. "Ah, no, Kate." He leered down at her. "I have
plans for you." He shook her arm lightly, rocking her play-
fully. "And they include holding you even tighter, my love."

Kate struck him hard with her free hand, leaving a bright
red handprint on her handsome captor's cheek. "Free us this
instant, you cur!"

"Now, Kate. Is that any way to speak to your future husband?" The smile he gave her held no warmth. Above it, his
eyes promised retribution for the slap she'd just dealt him.

"You'll never be my husband, Gordon Mallory!"

"Oh, I think perhaps you'll change your mind about that,
my proud Kate." He caressed the arm he held with his thumb.

"Never!" Kate tried again to pull free. "I'd die first."

"Ah. But you are not the one in danger of dying, are you,
Kate?" He nodded to the man who held Kate's brother, and
the man drew a wicked knife and held it carefully against
Jamie's throat.

Kate's knees almost dropped her. "No! Don't. Don't hurt
him. Don't . . . "

Ignoring the knife that his captor held loosely under his
chin, Jamie was busy trying to rub the gag from his mouth
against his shoulder.

Mallory said, "That depends on you, Kate. Just
how . . . shall we say . . . *obliging* are you willing to be to
keep your little brother alive?"

She understood him perfectly. He wanted to bed her in
exchange for Jamie's safety. Loathing filled her and spilled
out of her eyes at him.

"I'd marry you, Kate . . . after a night or two." His smile
was wolfish. "If you begged me to prettily enough."

Jamie finally had the gag out now. "Don't do anything
he wants, Kate. Don't! He's scum. And he won't hurt me!"
The boy twisted around to look at the man who held his
arms. "You heard these pigs. They don't want to even mark
me because of some old prince somewhere. I mean money
in their pocket. They won't let him harm me. They won't."

"Shut that brat up!" Mallory looked ready to do murder.

The man holding Jamie put a hand across the boy's mouth.
But he did it gently, and Mallory didn't miss the message
that gentleness sent.

He shifted his grip on Kate to hold her around the waist,
her back pressed hard against his body. "Two guards outside. Two in the passageway." He took refuge from his doubts
about his men in issuing them orders. "The rest of you start
getting the prisoners chained together for the walk to the
ship. Load them heavily. I want every one of them to carry
three times the usual weight. If we run into the coast guard,
we'll need them to sink quickly." With that, he half-carried
a struggling Kate into a side cave fitted with a heavy door
and slammed it shut behind them.

His men, left out in the roughly furnished room, smiled
knowingly at each other.

Jamie looked from one to another for an instant, then
kicked the man who was holding him in the shins.

Chapter Twenty-six

Exultation coursing through him at the discovery of the entrance to the caves, Blysdale rode, hell for leather, back toward the manor. Now that he knew where to search for Mathers and Smythe, it was time to send for Taskford, Stone, and MacLain. Hardened soldiers, they would be of inestimable value. Certainly, they were as concerned with recovering Mathers and Smythe as he was, and God knew he had urgent need of them, as the cave was well guarded. His friends were able men-at-arms, and they'd make up a band that would be more than a match for the small army of thugs amassed by Gordon Mallory.

Blysdale knew he had to have his friends come to back him up. If he should be killed in his attack on the cave, then they must free the prisoners.

Charging up the next hill, Bly met Griswold as he rode up from the other side. Both horses skittered to a halt.

Gris asked, "Where are you going?"

"To summon reinforcements. I've seen the entrance into the caves." He turned his horse toward the manor again.

"Colonel!"

Bly's attention was caught by his friend's troubled ex-

pression more than by his words, and he paused. "What's
afoot, Gris? What's wrong?"

"I'm not sure anything is wrong, sir, but Lady Kate's
gone running off looking for young Jamie and gotten Jennings all in an uproar. He says he's never seen her so wild.
He sent me for you."

Bly went still as death. "He's known her all her life, Gris.
If he's worried, then so are we. Which way did she go?"

"I'm following her tracks. She came this way."

Bly looked down at the rain-softened ground. He read
what he saw there in a glance. "One horse moving like the
devil was after it," he read. "That's not good. Kate's not one
to abuse her mount. She must be frantic about something."

"Aye."

Bly turned his horse and sent it down the trail Kate had
left. As he rode, he called over his shoulder to Griswold,
"Women have strange connections to those they love, Gris."

"Aye, sir." Griswold caught up to him. "Intuition, too."

"True. She must feel Jamie to be in some danger."

Both men rode faster, their attention on the widely spaced
hoofprints made by Kate's mount. Griswold said, "Judging
by the lengths of these strides, your Lady Kate is flat-out
flying, sir."

"Aye, and nothing but fear for her brother would drive
her this hard."

Griswold decided that it would be better if he didn't agree
with his Colonel's statement out loud.

Both men were grimly silent as, anxious-eyed, they urged
their horses on.

In the cave-room into which Mallory had dragged Kate, he
yanked her to him. His arms were like bands of steel and
he held her close, thigh to thigh and chest to breast. Grasping her chin, he tried to force a kiss on her.

Kate managed to free one arm. With a superhuman effort, she lightly placed her fingers over his lips and drawled,
"Really, Gordon. You're acting like an untried schoolboy."

Startled, he looked at her sharply. Drawing his head back,

he stared down at her face, his own full of suspicion. "What are you up to, Kate?" His death grip on her slackened only a little.

Kate made no move to escape his embrace. "Up to?" Her voice was calm, her manner relaxed.

It was fortunate Mallory couldn't guess the amount of effort it was costing her to seem casual. Kate was desperately stalling for time, hoping against hope that Blysdale had received her message from Jennings and knew that she had gone to look for Jamie.

Jennings would have told him how desperate she had seemed. And Blysdale would come for her. She had only to postpone the rape that was clearly Mallory's intent until Bly arrived.

Removing his hand from her hip, Kate walked slowly out of Mallory's slackened embrace and pretended to inspect the room. The furnishings were rich and out of the ordinary. Under other circumstances, and in another place, she wouldn't have had to pretend an interest.

All the while Mallory watched her suspiciously. His shoulders were hunched forward, his head thrust at her. With his fingers curved like talons, he looked like a bird of prey ready to strike.

Kate was shaking inside, dreading the physical attack she wasn't sure she could avoid, but she preserved a casual mien as she sauntered about the huge room. Stopping to study each article of its furnishings that seemed worthy of note as she went, she was careful to throw glances of approval for his selections Mallory's way.

Rich tapestries had been hung to cover the rough stone of every wall of the cave. Their vibrant colors lifted the mood of the place from dank cave to attractive hideaway.

The furniture in this strange room was fabulously expensive. French, and gilded, with all its upholstery done in satin that gleamed in the light from a multitude of silver candelabras.

There was only one incongruous note, an ornately carved

sword rack hung over a chest that stood against one wall. Several expensive rapiers were crossed at their points in it.

Kate turned and lifted her eyebrow. "This seems a bit . . . out of place."

"I'm afraid I'm really quite proud of my fencing skills, Kate. I couldn't resist including them."

She nodded acceptance of his comment as if it were a matter of little interest to her, but her blood chilled to hear that he had enough skill to be so proud of it. She wanted him to have no such advantage when Bly came for her.

"I must compliment you. This chamber is lovely, Gordon. You must mean to be comfortable in the time you spend here." She was relieved to see him begin to relax. Most of the fire left his eyes.

Pleased with her open admiration of his handiwork, he said, "Actually there was none of this luxury here before yesterday. Until then, I made do with some boards over a pair of kegs for my desk, and a crate to sit on. It was enough. I could easily do the business I needed to do here with that." His smile became catlike, and his eyes warmed again. "Then, after I saw you wrench your horse around to protect your little brother when the shooting started this morning, I realized that I might have a way to bring you to your senses where I am concerned."

Kate had to work to keep out of her face the anger and scorn she felt at the way he had chosen of threatening Jamie to "bring her to her senses." Shaking inside with anger, she turned to pretend to admire one of the tapestries. "This is French, of course?"

"Of course. The French have always been superior when it comes to needlework." He smiled again. "Are you trying to avoid the subject you know is at hand, Kate?"

"No," she lied. "I am actually impressed with what you have done here." That would have been true under other circumstances.

"Come, Kate. Let's be honest with one another. You're not stupid. You know that I'm involved in something illicit, even if you haven't guessed what it is. I shall tell you soon.

It will be my pleasure to tell you all that I've accomplished to regain my fortune since the death of my wastrel father. And of course, I will be able to do so with impunity, as a wife cannot testify against her husband, you know."

"Regain your fortune?" Her surprise showed in her voice. "I had no idea you had lost your grandfather's money."

"Not I, Kate. My father. The stupid fool turned gambler in his old age and lost it all. However, he has paid the price, and I have recouped the fortune."

"Paid the price?" Kate wished she hadn't said that the instant the words were out of her mouth. In her effort to cause delay, she'd been careless.

"Yes, Kate. Paid the price. I killed him most painfully to repay him for his foolish gambling." Mallory smiled. "He died a much wiser man."

Kate had to work hard to hide the horror she felt. Under any other circumstances she wouldn't have been able to, but now, her very life was at stake and, more importantly, Jamie's as well. Was Mallory mad? No, she decided, not mad, just truly evil. "Gordon, I'm certain you shouldn't be telling me these things."

"As I told you, you can say nothing. A wife cannot testify against her husband."

Kate decided that to answer him in any way other than the refusal she had always given him would make Mallory suspicious, so she said, "You mistake matters if you think I will ever consent to be your wife, Gordon."

"Oh, you will, Kate. One way or another, you will."

She lifted her chin and looked at him with all the scorn she had always felt for him.

"Ah. You never change, do you, my dear?" He smiled a smile that chilled her. "I suppose I should be disappointed if you did. Paying back all the slights you've done me all our lives wouldn't be as satisfying if you changed, Kate."

Kate couldn't hide the shiver his words caused.

"At any rate, I finally came to the conclusion just the other day that if you were ever going to change your mind about becoming Mrs. Gordon Mallory, I would have to devise methods to help you do it. The first I struck upon is the most pleasant. But if it doesn't do the trick, I have another."

He turned around in a circle, indicating all the treasures in the room. "First there is all this, Kate. It is all for you. After all, I could hardly enjoy exploring your charms in this room's former setting. The idea of taking you on a rough board desk had no appeal, I can assure you. So I had all these things brought in to make our first night together comfortable."

"Never!"

"Oh, yes, Kate. Tonight. Once I struck on the idea of capturing Jamie as a means of bringing you to heel, I knew my difficulties were over."

Kate turned away so that Gordon couldn't see her distress. It was a mistake. She found herself facing the bed, a massive affair with heavy damask hangings in wonderful colors that matched those of the tapestries on the walls, bright, jewel-like colors that belied the darkness of Mallory's intent. With an effort, she kept herself from turning away from it too quickly.

Her stomach knotted with fear. Gordon Mallory was bigger than any man she knew. Stronger. She'd have no chance against him once he got her into that bed! Her back still turned to him, Kate pretended to look it over as she searched the room with her gaze, hoping to find a weapon to use against him.

All the while she did, she was frantically praying that Blysdale would come before it was too late. Before she was crushed under the weight of Mallory's body, powerless to keep him from his foul deed. *Oh, dear Heaven, please!* she prayed desperately.

She began reminding God, as she had as a child at prayer, of anything she thought might help Him who needed no earthly assistance. She reminded Him that Bly had been in the army most of his life, and that surely he'd be able to follow the hoofprints of her horse from Cliffside and that . . .

"Are you afraid, Kate?"

"What?" She pretended scorn. "Afraid? Of course not."

"Ah."

"Why should I be afraid of you, Gordon? I've known you all my life. I just don't relish the idea of being raped by you."

"It doesn't have to be rape, Kate." He was practically purring at her. Crossing the little space between them, he reached for her.

Repulsed, she moved to trail her fingers over the polished surface of the desk that stood against one wall. Hiding her revulsion, she said calmly, "Then things will have to change, won't they?"

He looked puzzled. "Change?"

"Yes. For instance, I'm thirsty, and you haven't even offered me a glass of water, much less wine."

Her words stopped him, then galvanized him. "You'd like wine? A very good idea. Wine has always made lovemaking more pleasant." He hurried across the room to the door. "Your brother and I brought some excellent champagne back from our last smuggling run to France." He laughed. "I'm sure he won't mind me sharing it with his sister."

Smiling at her over his shoulder, he opened the door and told the man on guard outside it, "Bring two bottles of champagne from the south cave."

"Yes, Mr. Mallory."

The man moved off to do as he was told, and Mallory began to close the door. Before he shut it all the way Kate heard the sound of a whip cracking and an anguished cry.

The blood drained from Kate's face. All pretense fell away. "You beast! You're a slaver! You loathsome animal, how could you?"

"Ah. So the mask is off now, is it, Kate?" He moved purposefully toward her. "So much the better. Playing the gentleman with you would not have been half so enjoyable. I like my women with a little fight in them. It makes the ultimate conquest more interesting. So fight me, Kate. Forget that you are *Lady* Katherine for once!" With that, he reached out and snatched her to him.

Chapter Twenty-seven

Faster and faster, Gris and Bly followed the tracks of Kate's horse to the point where the animal had skidded to a stop to avoid a mass of other horses whose prints in the churned muddy ground told the story. There'd been a number of horses waiting there for some time, and when they'd left, Kate's mount must have been among them, as there were no tracks of a single horse from that point on. The implications were clear.

Bly's voice was almost unrecognizable as he ground out, "Mallory has Kate!"

From that instant on, Griswold was unable to keep up with him. When Bly arrived at the hill nearest the entrance to the caves, he vaulted from his horse and turned it loose. He'd no need of the reverberations its galloping hooves might send through the ground down to the cave giving his presence away!

Griswold caught up with his Colonel and snatched up Blysdale's reins to keep his mount with them. "Wait. You can't go in there alone! You'll be badly outnumbered."

Unheeding, Bly headed for the lower hill. The hill with

the entrance to the caves. The caves where Kate was. Where
Mallory had Kate.

Gris put his mount and Bly's horse across his Colonel's
path. "Stop, sir. This is suicide!"

Bly strode around Gris and the horses.

Cursing fluently, Gris again interposed himself and the
two horses between Bly and his objective. "Bly! Think, man!"

Bly went on, his strides lengthening with his determination to reach Kate.

"Dammit!" Again Gris rode his horse across Bly's path
to stop him. Seeing Bly's eyes, he leaned down from his
saddle and shouted full in his face, "You'll be *useless*!"

Useless! The word stopped Bly cold. Useless. Unable to
help Kate. The fury that had driven him began to cool and
solidify into something more intelligent . . . and even more
deadly.

He shook himself like a man shaking free of a night-
mare. "Gris." He looked at his friend as if seeing him for
the first time. "You're right, of course." It was hard to make
himself admit it, but Gris was right. If he stormed the cave
entrance in his present mood he'd only get himself killed.
That wouldn't help the situation a whole helluva lot.

He made himself take a deep breath.

Gris saw sanity return. He dismounted. "That's better, sir."

"Thanks to you."

"You did look as if you needed a little help stopping, if
I do say so myself."

Bly grinned a cold, lopsided grin. "Plans, Gris."

"Yessir!" Out of old habit he snapped to attention, awaiting his orders.

"You ride for Jacobs and Dawson. The innkeeper, Linden,
too. Jacobs says he's a good man. Then ride for Taskford
Manor. Stone and MacLain are there, waiting. Commandeer
Lady Katherine's brothers last. They're closest, I know, but
Hal is incapacitated with that broken leg, and we don't want
that headlong fool, Josh Clifton, rushing in, alerting them and
getting himself shot before we're up to strength."

"Aye, Colonel." Gris saluted and swung up onto his horse.

"And see that they all come well-armed."

Gris scowled. "As if I'd forget that! But you've forgotten that you're unarmed."

"I never forget anything, Gris, as you well know. Pistols aren't indicated here, yet. I'll sneak in and see what I can do to clear the way and whittle down the odds."

"Aye." *And to keep Lady Kate from harm—whatever the cost to yourself.* "Just keep telling yourself, sir, that most of all, your lady wants you alive."

Bly took another deep breath and tried to impress that idea on his mind. He nodded curt agreement and ordered, "Go. Take both horses. You've a lot of riding to do."

"Yessir." Griswold hauled both beasts around and sped away.

Behind him, Bly uttered the word he'd been holding back. "Hurry!"

And galloping down over the hill, Griswold whispered the words that, like his friend, he'd kept himself from saying to his face, "Be careful. For God's sake, sir, be careful!"

Blysdale, his coat closed at his throat to hide the white of his cravat, moved silently through the lengthening shadows toward the entrance to the caves. Circling around behind the two huge boulders he knew concealed it, he approached with caution. He knew there would be guards, but how many? Slipping into a deep crevasse in the boulder nearest the water, he waited and listened, impatience to reach Kate gnawing at him.

"When do we sail?" a man's voice asked.

"Turn o' the tide," another answered.

"And when might that be? Not all o' us is sailors, y' know."

"Tide should turn around midnight."

"Crikey. I hopes we can get 'em all on the ship by then."

"Aye. The ones getting over the fever don't move so smart, 's true."

"At least they move. More'n you can say for them what we lost to it."

They laughed then, and Bly was able to determine that there were only two of them. No problem. Silencing two men simultaneously was a simple matter.

He stepped out of his hiding place and moved to where the guards could see him. By the time they did, it was too late. He killed the nearest with a sharp blow to his throat, and the other died with the hilt of Bly's knife protruding from his. Neither man made a sound.

Blysdale might have allowed both to live if they hadn't laughed about the death of their captives. As it was, he felt he'd done humanity a service.

Bly retrieved his knife and cleaned the blood from it on the shirt of the man he'd killed with it. His face expressionless, he opened the heavy entrance door a crack and stood listening a moment before slipping through.

Immediately, a man from down the long tunnel in front of Bly called to a comrade, "Danny! D'you just feel a draft?"

"Nah. You're just getting the wind up. That's the draft you feel." The second man convulsed over his joke.

The sound of his laughter covered the gasp of his companion breathing his last. By the time Danny had finished enjoying his own joke about his companion's supposed cowardice, Bly had his head in a hammerlock. One quick twist and the man's neck snapped.

Beelzebub Blysdale was in excellent form.

The entrance and the tunnel down into the caves cleared of guards, Bly stood in the shadows at its lower end and surveyed the room there. Four men occupied it. One was asleep in a chair propped against the wall. Another was engrossed in paring his nails with his knife. The other two had a frayed and dingy pack of cards spread out on a rough table between them and were playing some game by the light of a smoking tallow candle.

Four enemies dead and no alarm given. So far, the score was good, but these four might present a problem. Blysdale blended with the shadows as he considered it.

• • •

Griswold stopped to rest his lathered horse and ran an expert eye over the one he'd been trailing behind him. The second horse might have covered the same distance, but without the weight of a man on its back, it was in much better shape.

After impatiently allowing ten minutes rest time, Gris tied the first horse to a tree a little way back off the road, marked the spot, and swung into the saddle of the second horse. He was again on the way to Taskford Manor for the reinforcements Colonel Blysdale needed to rescue his Lady Kate.

At Taskford Manor, Harry Wainwright, Earl of Taskford, stood at his ease under the mammoth oaks that shaded this side of a huge pasture. With no small pride, he was showing Stone and MacLain his latest crop of Thoroughbreds.

Stone leaned his arms on the high top rail of the pasture fence and remarked, "By Jove, Harry, these *are* prime goers. I haven't seen their like anywhere in England. What a lucky dog you are to have our famous Regina Landry to head up your breeding program."

Careful not to phrase his next comment so that disrespect could come to his beloved Regina, and magnanimously overlooking Stone's "our" in reference to *his* wife, Taskford said, "I'll have you clods know that *I* did the planning for this crop of foals. Regina was so busy with the twins that she was willing to let me decide which mares to breed to Talisman and which to Golden Sovereign."

MacLain looked for an instant as if he'd make some comment about Regina breeding, too, just as Taskford had thought he would. When he saw his friend watching him with such a close eye, he changed his mind. "Great horses, Harry. You've every right to be damned proud of 'em. The twins, too."

Harry shook his head. It was obvious that he felt there was nothing he could call MacLain to task for, but that he knew from the juxtaposition of his friend's thoughts that MacLain had regretfully swallowed a ribald joke of some kind.

Suddenly, there was a sound of galloping hooves and a mounted footman arrived from the house, his white wig slightly askew. "Your lordship! My lady says that you must come at once!"

Taskford didn't waste time questioning the man. Regina was increasing. Had something gone wrong? God forbid!

The twins! Was one of them injured?

Or could something have happened to the other children, Thomas or Philydia?

He groaned aloud. Being a family man was more trying than waging a war! Spurred by anxiety, he hurled himself onto his horse and tore off in the direction of the manor.

Stone and MacLain jumped into their own saddles and followed in his dust. The startled footman trailed them at a more leisurely pace now his duty was done.

At the house, Harry found his wife, Regina, in earnest conversation on the doorstep. It took him a second to recognize the man she was talking to. It was Blysdale's batman, Griswold! Flinging himself off his mount, he called, "What's afoot?" He took the steps two at a time and slipped his arm around Regina. "Are you all right, darling?"

"I'm fine, but there's trouble at Cliffside, Harry. You'll need weapons, and Mr. Griswold can explain as you ride. You must hurry, dearest." She gave him a little push toward the interior even as her hands clung to his. Her anxiety for his safety was plain to see.

MacLain stepped close to reassure her. "Don't fret, Regina. Harry will be fine. We'll look after him."

Regina's eyes misted. She was pregnant again and her emotions ran close to the surface. "Thank you. You and Stone are our dear friends."

Taskford exploded from the house just then, swept her into his arms, and kissed her long and hard. He released her so suddenly that she staggered, then he charged down to the horses. The footman who followed behind him was loaded down with all manner of weapons.

The butler steadied Regina even as he shot a thoroughly disapproving look at her husband. Wentworth had come from

Regina's home, Charnwood. As far as he was concerned, Regina came first in all things.

Regina patted the butler's arm and smiled at the eagerness and enthusiasm with which her husband and his army friends chose weapons to use in their rescue of her friend, Lady Katherine, and hopefully their two missing friends as well. "Taskford!" she called.

Harry turned in the saddle to look at her and the world disappeared. Their gazes locked, and love flowed between them like river current.

"Be careful, my love," she called. "Come back to me."

He nodded, his eyes giving her his promise before he turned back to storing the weapons he'd selected about his person and on his saddle. Then, distracted by the mission ahead, he touched spurs to his horse and was gone, pounding down the long gravel drive beside Griswold with his two friends in close pursuit.

Regina shook her head. Even in so grave a matter, they were like boys getting another chance to play a dangerous game that they had truly been missing.

Regina sighed, exchanged a resigned smile with her butler, and went back into the house to await word of the outcome of their perilous adventure . . . and to pray.

Chapter Twenty-eight

Clumps of mud flew from under pounding hooves and spat-
tered the mounted men as they charged over rain-soaked turf
and through the standing water left by the earlier rain. They'd
obtained fresh horses at the last inn and had no need to spare
their mounts as they raced to the cliff top that held the entrance
to the prison cave. As Gris led the way to the now familiar hill,
Taskford and he rode shoulder to shoulder.

By the time they arrived, dusk had softened the contours
of the land and mist had all but erased from sight the low
boulders strewn across its surface. Gris only hoped he could
guess between which of them the entrance to the caves was
hidden. Bly had sent him off with only a gesture to indicate
the direction of the entrance.

Taskford dismounted, drew out his spyglass, and studied
the terrain before him. Stone and MacLain flanked him and
sat their horses while they watched the hilltops around them,
Stone looking south and MacLain north.

After only a moment, MacLain reported, "A single horseman coming up fast, Harry."

Taskford handed his glass to Griswold. "You'd know him
quicker than I."

"Yessir." Griswold trained the glass on the approaching horseman. "It's Linden, the innkeeper from Lesser-Clifton, Major," he reverted naturally to the use of Taskford's army rank. "He's the friend of Lady Katherine's who's been helping her by giving her the information she needed to hold up coaches." He turned with a grin to enjoy Taskford's incredulous "What!"

"Aye, Major. Lady Katherine has been trying to catch a shipment of the jewels copped by the Mayfair Bandit. She needed them—and the man running them—so she could clear her brother Hal of the accusation that he was the Bandit."

"My God." Taskford shook his head, accepting it. "That sounds uncomfortably like something my own Regina might try. Did Lady Kate get him?"

Gris looked uncomfortable. "More or less."

"More or less?"

"Well, Major, actually . . . Lady Katherine got herself shot." Taskford's alarm was palpable.

Gris hastened on, "Then the Colonel took over and held up the coach that had the Mayfair Bandit's courier in it."

"I assume, since you aren't upset, that Lady Kate was not seriously wounded?"

"True, sir. Though 'tis a shame she was hit at all, she only got a bad graze across her back."

"But the Colonel turned to highway robbery in her stead, is that correct?" Taskford asked in a dry voice. His concern for his wife's friend Katherine satisfied, he was totally calm again.

"Aye. That's correct, sir."

Taskford's handsome face broke into a grin as he realized what Blysdale must feel for Kate. "So that's the way the wind blows, is it?"

"Aye, sir." Griswold grinned back at him. "A regular gale."

"Well. It's about time old Bly got smitten."

"Aye, sir." Griswold agreed with enthusiasm. "That it is!"

"Now we just have to get them safely out of that cave so I can see this with my own eyes!"

Linden rode up to them then, and further conversation on that subject had to wait. Taskford was glad that Stone and

MacLain had been out of earshot. The fact that Blysdale had fallen at last was too good to waste on a windy hill. The indomitable Blysdale's fall called for many a toast, with brandy following each one of them, at a comfortable fireside!

First the business of the moment, though, and the exciting expectation of at last finding Mathers and Smythe. He stuck out his right hand in greeting to Linden. "Taskford," he introduced himself to the innkeeper. "You're Linden?"

"Yes, your lordship. Is there any word on Lady Katherine or little Jamie?"

"We've only just arrived, but in a few minutes we expect to join the party down there. Blysdale went down into the caves over an hour ago, determined to keep an eye on Lady Katherine."

"God grant that that's sufficient to save Lady Kate, and that he's all right," Linden murmured.

Griswold, unwilling to consider that anything might have happened to Blysdale in the considerable time he'd been gone, told Linden, "Believe me, Mr. Linden. Lord Blysdale will be sufficient, one way or the other." Then he asked, "Did you stop off to tell them at Cliffside what was going on, as I asked you to?"

"Yes." Linden frowned. "But I still don't understand why you didn't go get them first. They were closest."

"Well," Griswold spoke consideringly, "Mister Hal is pretty helpless with that broken leg, you know."

"Yes, and he'll hate that like fury when he loses out on the action."

"True. That particular Clifton is a splendid young man." Gris looked a little uncomfortable. "But it was the Colonel's specific request that we hold off on the Marquess, you see."

"Yes," Linden heaved a great sigh. "I do see. Hal is my friend, and there's not a finer man anywhere—but Josh is an addlepate. Despite his reputation for being a good man in the *front* of a cavalry charge, I'd not want him *behind* me with a loaded pistol in a fight, either. Especially one that has Kate's safety at stake."

"You've said it," Gris admitted.

Taskford took over and explained their presence to Linden. "We're here to back up the Colonel in the rescue of Lady Kate and the recovery of two of our friends. God grant they're among the prisoners this Mallory's holding. The bastards out-number us, so there'll be no frontal attack—no cavalry charge." He grinned at the innkeeper, thinking of Linden's comment about Josh and cavalry·charges. Then he became grave, and the light of battle kindled in his eyes. "So here's the plan, men." Taskford gestured them to surround him and laid out his strategy for each of them to arrive at the cave entrance un-detected.

Moments later, they'd tethered their horses, split up, and were ghosting across the mist-shrouded hillside to their sev-eral positions. Each man's route had been chosen to give the men the best chance to converge unseen on their target—the prison cave.

Down inside the caves, in the sumptuously furnished room to which Gordon Mallory had dragged her, Kate was sip-ping champagne and trying desperately to think of a way of escaping. She'd been unable to find a weapon anywhere that she could reach. The rapiers on the wall were out of the question—she'd never make it to them, even if she'd known what to do with one when she obtained it. The champagne bottle sitting near her wasn't heavy enough to use as a blud-geon, even if she could snatch it up before Mallory realized her intent.

The candelabras were heavy enough to smash him into un-consciousness, but they were so ornate and many-branched that they would undoubtedly prove too unwieldy. And again, there was the problem of getting hold of one before Mallory caught her. Kate didn't want to be caught by Gordon Mallory.

She knew with a chilling certainty that once Mallory laid his hands on her again, he'd not let her go until he'd forced his will on her.

Because she had no other weapon, Kate turned on her charm.

• • •

Blysdale saw his chance to take out a few more enemies when one of Mallory's men left the room he was watching so intently. From somewhere deeper in the cave, there was the sharp crack of a whip and an anguished cry. The stocky slaver who'd been trimming his fingernails put down his knife and shoved himself out of his chair with a curse. "Damn that O'Grady! Ain't life bad enough for them poor sods without he lays that whip on 'em?" The man couldn't know it, but by his bellowing for O'Grady to "Lay off 'em, ya dog!" as he walked down toward the lower cave, he'd earned his chance to live.

The man who'd been dozing startled, then rasped out, "Shut your clapper, Bowers. Who cares whether they feels the whip 'ere or in Araby, I'm trying ta sleep!"

Bly whispered so softly it was no more than a breath of air, "Then let me help you." He reached out and clamped his hand on the back of the man's neck, and the man slept on—for eternity.

Then, silent as a shadow, Bly glided across to the two remaining men. They were as unconcerned with the plight of the prisoners and as untouched by their pain as the sleeping man had been, and Bly acted accordingly. Simultaneous blows to the backs of their necks made it impossible for them to interfere with his rescue of Lady Kate. Or, for that matter, to interfere in anything else. Ever.

A minute later the man who'd gone to stop O'Grady wielding his whip returned. He never knew what hit him, but because of his compassion for the prisoners, Blysdale had decided to let him live. Maybe he'd be able to try to figure out why he alone had been spared, but his captor doubted it. Swiftly Bly trussed him up and gagged him.

Now, only O'Grady and whatever other guards were below remained. Bly moved the bodies out of the line of sight of anyone entering the room from below or from the tunnel that led in from the hilltop. Then he stood listening for a moment as he decided his next move. He wasn't even breathing hard.

Bly heard men coming back up from the lower regions of the cave complex. Looking around for someplace to hide, he spotted a shadowed recess four feet deep with a heavy wooden

door at the back of it. He slipped into the nook an instant before three men came up out of the lower cave. He pressed his
back hard against the door.

"We've got 'em fixed up good," the first man to enter the
room said. "Lots of heavy chains on 'em, like the boss said."

"Yeah," the man just behind him agreed. "We put so much
chain on 'em, they'll sink like rocks if we have to toss 'em
over the side."

A third man growled, "Well, let's hope there ain't no revenue officers sailing 'round out there tonight."

Bly's perusal of the men showed him that the middle one
had two pistols stuck in his belt. The others each had one. Four
shots. The chances were good that at least one of them might
put him out of commission, and Bly had no intention of being
rendered unable to find Kate. He'd wait. Soon they'd relax and
get careless.

As he threw himself down into a chair, the first man said,
"I don' know about the two of you, but I don' need to lose
my share o' the sale because we had to dump our cargo. With
the twenty of us to split the half the boss leaves us, it's little
enough as it is."

Twenty! Bly wondered where the others were. He watched
as these three settled themselves. These three and nine others
would be a job of work. Possibly one that he couldn't get done
alone. He hoped Griswold had gotten the reinforcements he'd
sent him for, or things just might get difficult!

On the other side of the thick wooden door, only a few yards
from Blysdale, Kate smiled coolly at her host. "When did you
start this venture into slave trading, Gordon? I'd have thought
you too fastidious for such a sordid occupation, personally."

"Would you really, Katherine? From your treatment of me,
I'd always thought that you considered nothing beneath me."

That was rather too near the truth to leave Kate entirely
comfortable. Her honesty got the better of her common sense.
"Yes." She lifted her chin and told him, "People simply don't
believe, you see, that they have monsters among their acquaintance."

Mallory burst out laughing. "Ah, Kate, you do intend to keep things interesting for me. When you asked for wine, I was afraid you intended to surrender peacefully to keep from getting hurt." The falsely jovial expression on his face changed to one of malice. "But no, not Lady Katherine of Cliffside Manor. Always the superior, judgmental one. Always the one to deal out slights and snubs to the Mallory lad, weren't you, Kate? Well, now the tables are turned, and I'm in the superior position! And now, Kate, finally the battle lines are drawn. I rejoice to see them. God knows I've waited long enough for this! Just keep in mind that I intend to be the victor."

Kate ran. Pretense would gain her nothing now. She reached the door and drew back the heavy bolt, but as her fingers clasped the latch to lift it, Mallory caught up to her, twisted his fingers in her hair, and yanked her away from the door.

Kate cried out with the pain of it, and turned to face him, her fingers ready to claw his eyes out.

Mallory pulled her to him, pinning her arms to her sides with one of his. He shoved her hard against the wall so that she couldn't draw up her knee to thrust it into his groin, and chuckled to have foiled her attempt.

His mouth closed over hers, hot and wet. As it did, he used his free hand to force Kate's mouth open with unbearable pressure on her cheeks. His tongue entered her mouth the instant he was successful.

Kate bit it. She regretted infinitely that the strength of her bite was lessened by the grip he had on her jaw. She wished she could have bitten it in two!

Mallory pulled his head away to promise quietly, "If you bite my tongue again, Kate, I'll have Jamie's cut out."

Kate spat in his face without thinking.

The expression in his eyes became one of barely suppressed excitement as Mallory wiped the spittle away.

When he invaded her mouth again and his hand grabbed her breast, tears of awful frustration streamed down Kate's cheeks, for with that single threat, Mallory had reminded her that only her surrender would keep her little brother safe.

Chapter Twenty-nine

Outside, pressed against the door in the recess formed by the thickness of the stone wall of the cave, Bly heard Kate's cry. His blood drained from his face. Dear God! Kate! So this was where Mallory had brought her!

Bly's first impulse was to slam open the door and rush through it to Kate, but good sense prevailed. If he crashed his frantic body against the door and it was locked, he'd only warn Mallory.

Taking a deep breath, he commanded himself to calm down. He could very well put period to any rescue attempt on his part by running full tilt into a pistol trained on the door he entered.

Long experience told him that, impatient or not, the first thing he had to do was to find out what kind of a force he was immediately up against, consider his options, and, in this case, learn how he could best help Kate. "Reconnoiter, you fool," he murmured to himself, and grasped the latch of the heavy wooden door. With the greatest stealth he tried it. It lifted! The door was not bolted, thank God!

Lifting the heavy wrought-iron latch with the utmost care, he began opening the door by inches.

• • •

Outside, above the ground mist, the night was clear and the stars were beginning to appear. Taskford met the others as they arrived at the entrance to the caves and pointed at the two dead men Bly had left in his wake. "No signs of a fight. Obviously Blysdale has been here," he said in a low voice. "He's inside, so go carefully."

Stone and MacLain nodded. They understood him perfectly. Neither one of them had a desire to end up dead because they'd blundered into Blysdale in the dark.

Taskford turned to the innkeeper. "Mr. Linden."

"Yes, sir?"

"Would you be so kind as to wait out here to direct the rest of the reinforcements when they arrive? Jacobs and Dawson have been staying at your inn, so you will know them, and Mr. Griswold assures me they are on their way. When they arrive, tell them to follow us with caution. That we don't know yet what we will find down there."

"Yes, sir!"

Griswold added, "Tell them that this is the place for which they have been searching."

"I will, sir." Linden was eager to help in any way he could. After seeing the two dead sentries, however, he was more than glad to be able to stay aboveground. He'd no desire to meet a man in the dark who could kill as efficiently as Lord Blysdale. Especially since he had no idea whether or not Lord Blysdale would remember him well enough to recognize that they were on the same side in this.

"Stone, MacLain, come with me," Taskford ordered as he gestured for Griswold to open the way.

Stone grinned. "I thought you'd never ask."

Quietly, Griswold lifted the wooden hatch that covered the tunnel entrance and, with Taskford leading the way, they slipped inside. Harry stopped as soon as he'd made room for the other three, and they stood, motionless, waiting for their eyes to become accustomed to the gloom of the tunnel.

Two silent shapes on the tunnel floor attested to the fact that Bly had accounted for another pair of Mallory's band.

The glow at the end of the tunnel gave them enough light to avoid the bodies as they crept down toward the room there. When they'd almost reached it, they discovered three more men who'd recently been sent to meet their Maker, while a fourth lay with his ankles and wrists bound together with his own belt and a gag stuffed in his mouth.

"This one must somehow have failed to offend our Bly," Stone murmured as he stepped over the unconscious man.

Instantly a rough voice from the room in front of them demanded, "Did you men just hear something?"

In the alcove with the door at the back, Blysdale didn't wait to see if the man was referring to his movements. He opened the door to Mallory's den, slipped in, and bolted it firmly behind him. The three men outside were going to stay outside, now, and he was free to deal with the piece of human debris that had *his* Kate pushed against the wall not far from where he stood just inside the door.

White rage roared over him. He took in Kate's resistance and her attacker's abuse through a red haze. How dare the bastard! It took all the strength of will at his command not to tear the man away from her, all his control to say quietly, "I do hope that I'm interrupting," as he sped to the wall where he saw a display of swords.

He had to hand it to the Irishman. He was as cool as Bly himself. "Well, actually, you are," Mallory said. "However, I can easily have you removed." He edged toward the door, his fingers reaching to pull back the bolt Bly had shot home.

Kate slid along the wall to put distance between herself and Mallory.

Bly wrenched down and threw one of the swords like a throwing knife. It quivered and sang as it stuck in the door beside the bolt. "Your weapon, Mallory. Don't make me put the next one in your back to keep you from inviting your men to join us."

"So it's to be swords, is it?" Mallory said as he pulled the rapier out of the door. "I've always preferred bare knuckles myself, and it would have given me great pleasure to pound that so aristocratic face of yours to pieces."

Bly bowed. "Perhaps another time." He smiled a lopsided smile. "If there should be another time." Without taking his eyes off Mallory he said quietly, "Get out of the way, Kate."

Kate looked from one man to the other and made her decision. Without hesitation, she jumped up to kneel in the middle of the bed.

Griswold, Taskford, and his friends heard the song of swords crossing at the same time that Mallory's three henchmen did. When the thugs leapt to the doorway carved into the living rock of the cave, Taskford, Stone, and MacLain were right there behind them.

Inside, Blysdale and Mallory fought, Blysdale coldly and implacably, Mallory with skill and passion.

"I'll kill you, Blysdale!"

"You're certainly welcome to try," Bly told him.

The almost disinterested reply sent Mallory into a flurry of deadly activity. All his strength, weight, and ferocious anger went into a fusillade of blows.

Bly was hard put to parry the thrusts, but still he said coolly, "You're good, Mallory. Perhaps I won't be bored after all."

Mallory gave a whoop of anger and began beating at Blysdale with his sword like a rank amateur.

Bly deflected every inexpert blow and smiled.

On her knees on the bed, Kate watched with round eyes and an awful fear in her heart. Mallory was so much bigger than Bly! His reach was longer, and the weight he could and did put behind each thrust so much greater.

She couldn't stop her anxiety from filling her mind, clouding her ability to think clearly. Bly! Her beloved dark knight was in danger! As he had bragged to her, Mallory was obviously an expert, and every advantage was his— even knowing where the furniture was placed, she realized as Bly, retreating ably before an aggressive series of blows from Mallory, backed into the desk and was trapped there against it.

Mallory grinned and increased the fury of his attack.

Bly smiled his twisted smile, locked his blade with his opponent's, and caused Mallory's rapier to slide down the blade of his own to be caught and held there on the desk's shining surface. Grinding down on Mallory's blade, Bly pivoted on the ornate basket of his own sword and vaulted over the heavy piece of furniture.

As he did, his back was toward his opponent for an instant. With a cry of rage, Mallory ripped his blade free.

Kate shrieked.

Mallory lunged and, in a coward's strike, ran his blade through Bly.

"Bly!" Kate's agonized cry rang through the cavern as Blysdale staggered and almost fell. Shaking his head, he turned with difficulty to meet his enemy. Kate fought her own tangled skirts to get down from the softness of the bed and run to Bly.

Outside the door, Taskford heard the cry. "That's Kate!"

Stone and MacLain left off playing with the men they were fighting and charged the door, leaving their opponents unconscious behind them. Taskford dispatched his and joined them. Griswold yanked at the door handle.

"Damn thing's bolted!" Stone howled in frustration when he saw it didn't budge.

"Break it down!" MacLain threw himself against it.

Watching him bounce off the sturdy door, Taskford shouted, "Kate! Can you get to the bolt?"

Inside, Kate cared nothing for the bolted door or for rescue. Her entire being was centered on Bly as he sagged, bleeding, against a part of the wall just out of reach of Mallory's rapier.

Bly, white-faced with anger and the pain of his wound, gasped, "That was . . . no gentleman's thrust, Mallory."

"Ah, but then, I am no gentleman, as Kate would be happy to tell you."

His eyes blazing at his foe, Bly said in a carefully bored

voice, "What a pity she didn't tell me sooner." He paused significantly, then finished. "But then, Kate has never been one to state the obvious."

Mallory drew his lips back and bared his teeth in a snarl. "Damn you! That remark will cost you your life, my fine Lord Blysdale!"

Kate, ignoring the dictate of her heart that told her to run to Bly, ran instead to unbolt the door. As she fought the heavy bolt back, she watched the men over her shoulder. Her heart stopped as she saw Mallory make his move, while the man she loved seemed to stand helpless.

Mallory slammed his free hand down on the desk's top and vaulted over it at Blysdale who stood defenseless, his rapier point down at his side.

Kate screamed, "Nooooo!"

Mallory grinned as he soared over the desk, his sword at the ready and aimed at Bly's throat.

The grin faded as, quicker than the eye could follow, Bly flicked up his point and held it firm as it skewered Mallory through the chest.

The bolt drawn, Kate did something she'd never done in her life. With a soft sigh, Kate fainted.

Taskford and Griswold were the first to try to get through the door. They saw Bly, bleeding profusely from his left shoulder, bending over his fallen enemy.

In order to get to him, they had to move Kate to open the door far enough to get through it. Taskford scooped Kate up in his arms and followed Griswold, who had passed him to run to his Colonel.

"Dead," Bly cursed himself. "Blast it, I didn't mean to kill the bastard!"

"From the looks of you, it seems to have been a good idea!" Gris tacked the last word on—"Sir."

Bly grabbed his batman's arm for support and demanded, "Kate! Is Kate all right?" Bly's gaze was locked on the still form Taskford carried.

Harry looked down at his burden and smiled. "She's fine, Bly. Women do this sometimes when the people they love get pinked." He turned to Gris. "Better stop that bleeding, Gris. He's beginning to look like a stuck pig."

"Getting to it, Lord Taskford, getting to it." Griswold tore bandages from Blysdale's ruined shirt, made a pad, and bound it tightly to the wound. "Best sit, sir, before you fall down."

Bly sank into a chair, cursing softly as Griswold applied pressure to the wound in his shoulder in an effort to slow the bleeding. A moment later he was demanding, "Kate! Kate, wake up!"

Kate moaned softly in response.

Stone spoke from the doorway. "Men running this way!"

Taskford dumped Kate, who was beginning to stir, as gently as he could on the bed and ran to the door. "Coming from down below." He assessed the situation quickly and added, "Definitely not our reinforcements." Drawing a pistol from his belt he stepped out to meet them.

Bly was right behind him, his bandage reddening as he moved to get there.

"Go take care of Kate, Bly. We'll look for Mathers and Smythe," Taskford told him. "You're in no shape for this."

Kate spoke from the doorway. "Then I'll help him. Those are *his* friends down there, too." Her voice was still a little faint, but the determination in her eyes was strong.

Bly slipped his good arm around her and kissed her on the forehead. "There's my Kate."

Then the men from the lower cave came into view. There were five of them. Taskford leveled his pistol at them and called out, "Surrender or die. It's over. Mallory's dead."

The men were undecided for an instant, then two of them put up their hands. Two others went for the pistols in their belts and died as Stone and MacLain calmly shot them down. The one who'd been undecided hastily raised his hands to join his fellows in surrender.

Bly motioned them forward with his weapon. "How many guards are still left below?"

"Four," the first of the men to surrender told him.

"Aye," the youngest of them said vehemently, "and they'll do for you when they've finished setting the charges to—"

"Shut up, you fool." The oldest of the men they held at gunpoint snarled at the youth who'd spoken.

Bly shouted, "Stone, guard 'em!" and headed for the lower cave in a stumbling run. Kate was after him in a flash.

"Kate! Dammit, come back here!" Taskford shouted, then he was running after her, cursing like the ex–cavalry officer he was. "I can't win this one," he muttered as he ran. "Either I get blown to perdition or I let Kate be. No matter which way it goes, Regina will never forgive me!"

"Keep your pistols on 'em, MacLain!" Stone shouted as he plunged down the tunnel after the others.

Halfway down the tunnel, they met Jamie coming up. "Powder kegs!" he shouted. "They're setting fuses to kegs of gunpowder to blow the cave up! They'll kill all those people!" Tears of horror and frustration ran down his cheeks. "What can I do?"

Kate ordered him as she ran, "Go up and tell them to find the keys to the chains! We must free the prisoners!" She didn't even know if there were keys to the prisoners' chains, but she did know that without a mission, Jamie would follow her down into the prison and die with her there if she couldn't stop the explosions.

Ahead of her, the wounded Blysdale had had to stop and lean against the wall for a minute while a bout of faintness passed, so Kate got down to the prisoners first. Men ran past her and up to air and freedom. Men who had cruelly denied those things to the captives below. Kate heard shots, but had no time to worry about them.

The stench that hit her as she reached the lower cavern almost stopped her in her tracks. All around her there were people chained to the walls like animals. Standing in their own filth, they cried out to her.

With so many voices, it was hard for Kate to make out what they were trying to tell her. Moving quickly to the nearest prisoner, she listened only to him.

"Gunpowder." He pointed with his heavily bearded chin. "Over there. Pull the fuses! Hurry!"

Kate spun away from him and ran through the gloom in

the direction he'd indicated. Guided by its sputtering sparks, she found the fuse in the first keg of gunpowder and yanked it free. Leaving it to burn on the rock floor, she looked for another powder keg. The man had said fus*es*. That meant that there was more than one threat. Peering though the dimness she finally located another. Its fuse was a great deal shorter than the one she'd just pulled.

As she started toward it, Bly caught up to her and grasped her arm. "Get out of here, Kate! I'll get that one! Get out where you're safe!"

Kate could tell by the slackness with which he held her arm that Bly was weakened by his wound. Certainly he'd never be quick enough to get to the other fuse in time! "Yes, Darling!" she told him sweetly, her gaze locked on the sputtering string many yards distant. Then she tore free and ran for the fuse.

This one she stamped out after she had torn it from the powder keg. She'd realized there might be gunpowder on the floor, and it would burn more quickly than any fuse and to much the same purpose. Thank God that hadn't occurred to her at the last keg. She'd have frightened herself to uselessness.

Obviously, her concern for her dearest dark knight was clouding her usually acute mind. She rushed back to where he was sitting on the first keg of gunpowder, his face so pale that it gleamed in the dim light.

She called to the man in chains, "Was that all? Only two?"

"Only two," came his reply.

Kate reached Bly. Her love was not a happy Lord Blysdale.

"Dammit, Kate!" Bly filled the air around him with relieved curses. "Why in hell didn't you run, blast you! What the devil were you thinking, anyway, you little fool? You could have gotten yourself killed!"

Kate placed gentle fingers across his lips, her eyes full of love. "Don't, dearest, you must save your strength." When he stilled, she removed her fingers and bent down and kissed him long and lingeringly.

"Ah, Kate." He dropped his head wearily against her. "I love you so much it frightens me."

From across the cave, the man who'd told Kate to pull the fuses from the gunpowder kegs cried, "Blysdale?" in an incredulous voice, then more strongly, "Blysdale, is that really you?"

"Mathers!" Bly leapt up and might have fallen flat on his face except that Kate had already grabbed him around the waist. With Kate helping him, Bly staggered only slightly as he hurried toward his friend.

Chapter Thirty

Gaunt and filthy, Mathers hung forward in his chains and grinned at Blysdale. "You look as bad as I do, Blysdale. Why don't you lie down before you fall down?"

"I'll lie down as soon as I finish my business here. I'm rescuing you, you ingrate."

Stone charged over with a lantern he'd found. "Mathers! Is that scarecrow really you?" The light of Stone's lantern revealed a tall man, his hair and beard long and matted, his once elegant clothes in tatters. One of his sleeves was caked with dried blood, but the sheer joy in his face at seeing his friends outshone the lantern.

Taskford arrived from above with a heavy bunch of keys and unlocked Mathers's manacles. "Here. Unchain the rest of these poor devils," he ordered, and gave Griswold the keys.

The minute Mathers was freed, he fell forward, his left arm dangling uselessly at an odd angle. "Sorry, old tops," he gasped as Taskford and Stone caught and held him up. "I guess I'm not quite ready for all this excitement." With that, his eyes rolled up in his head and he fainted dead away.

Stone scooped him up to carry him like a baby, as Blysdale told MacLain, "Find Smythe."

Taskford told Bly, "Let's get that wound seen to, Bly," and grasped Blysdale firmly by his sound arm. Seeing by the grim expression on Taskford's handsome face that he had little choice, Bly left the locating of their second missing friend to MacLain.

Kate walked beside him on his other side, and together they started up the long slope of the tunnel to the room above. The other prisoners followed slowly, wonderingly, as Griswold freed them.

Taskford, on the opposite side of Blysdale from Kate, kept a firm arm around his wounded friend. From time to time he looked at the bandage on Bly's shoulder, his expression grave. By the time they reached the sumptuous room to which Mallory had taken Kate, Bly was as pale as death.

"This is as far as you go, Bly. You're not moving from that bed over there until Griswold has seen to that wound and you've had a good night's rest."

Bly just closed his eyes as they helped him onto the bed. Deep lines around his mouth told them of his pain. "Ten minutes," he told them. "Then I'll be fine. Gris, find the brandy." He shot a glance at Kate. "There is brandy, is there not?"

Smiling at her beloved's snide remark, Kate told him boldly, "I should imagine so, though all I was offered was champagne."

Bly made that odd sound that so resembled a snort.

Kate was used to it now, however, and recognized it as Blysdale's expression of disdain. Determined not to be bested by her dark knight's implied criticism, she told him with false brightness, "But it was excellent champagne."

"Oh, God," he murmured, admitting she had won, and closed his eyes.

Griswold hid his grin as he said, "I have the brandy, sir. Would you like a sip or two before I pour the rest in that wound in your shoulder?"

"Blast you, Adam Griswold. You know damn well I would." Bly took the offered bottle.

"Hold hard, sir," Griswold warned when Bly returned the brandy bottle to him.

His lack of protest at the idea of having raw spirits poured into a fresh wound frightened Kate. She knew no one in his right mind would actually permit it if he weren't concerned about infection. Seeking reassurance, Kate looked over at her friend, Lord Taskford.

Harry's eyes spoke volumes to her from a face as concerned as her own. He tried to reassure her. "Bly has lost a lot of blood, Lady Katherine, but now that he's still, the bleeding will stop and he'll recover quickly, you'll see."

Kate smiled at him tremulously. When it came to Bly, she was never as courageous as she usually was. Loving him so much seemed to make her more vulnerable than she'd ever been in her life. "Thank you," she whispered.

Across the room, Stone had placed the unconscious Mathers carefully on the top of the large desk. MacLain put a pillow under his head, and then they stood just waiting for him to recover.

In the better light of this place, Kate recognized the two as the pair who had almost unmasked her. Her indrawn breath was sharp, then she relaxed as she realized that not only was there no way *they* could identify *her* but also that they were Bly's friends and therefore posed no threat to her.

As hard as it was for Kate to leave Bly, she knew she should be helping the stricken Mathers. Women naturally knew better how to deal with a swoon than men did, and she was convinced that that was all that was presently the matter with Mathers.

Kate wanted to get out of this terrible place and take them all to Cliffside as quickly as possible so she forced herself to walk away from Bly and Griswold. In addition to her own eagerness to go, she was concerned that all this might be having an adverse effect on Jamie. Moving quickly to Mathers's side, she poured him a goblet of wine and held it to his lips. As she did, Mathers's eyelids fluttered, and she told him, "Here, your lordship. Try to drink a little, it'll help you feel better."

As Mathers sipped the wine, outside the room, close to forty people, men and women, traipsed up the tunnel to the clear night outside. Scarcely able to believe that they were really on their way back to freedom, they moved with a pitiful wariness. They were emaciated and filthy, and they bore in their appearance mute testimony to the cruelty that had been Gordon Mallory.

Kate and Stone helped Mathers sit up. "I think we will all be happier if we get out of this awful place," Kate told Mathers, "so please tell me as soon as you feel you're up to leaving, won't you?"

She looked around her at the luxurious room Mallory had put together for her . . . seduction, then down at the tapestry that had been torn from the wall to cover the still body of her abductor. One long tremor shook her slender form, then Bly was there with his good arm embracing her, drawing her close.

"It's all right, Kate. It's over."

"I know, Darling." She buried her face in his throat, drawing strength from him.

"Are you all right?"

"Yes," she told him, "I just wish I were home. Are *you* all right?"

"Come." Bly took her out of the luxuriously appointed chamber, through the rough common room, and up through the tunnel to the open. Both of them grew more eager to be free of the horror behind them with every step.

When they reached the exit and walked out onto the cliff top, they halted in astonishment. Much to Kate's surprise, half the servants of Cliffside were there. Even Linden was there, helping a small army of footmen serve the former prisoners hot cider and scones, cheese, and cold sliced mutton.

Directing the entire operation was her handsome brother Hal, sitting in a pony cart with his leg done up in splints. Close beside him, a pair of beautiful Manton fowling pieces, rifles without peer, stood in the cart and proclaimed his willingness to act as defender as well as caterer.

Kate knew a moment's panic as she searched the crowd. "Where is Jamie?"

"There," Bly pointed out calmly, "over by the table with the cider on it."

Kate relaxed against him then, and was content just to watch the odd scene.

"Eat now," Kate heard Hal order brusquely, and knew her brother was carefully hiding his horror at the appearance of the liberated captives. "After you've eaten," he promised them, "and when you're ready, we shall take you to Cliffside Manor for baths and a rest before we help each and every one of you return home."

At Hal's words, most of the prisoners wept openly. Kindness broke them where cruelty had failed.

Only one had no reaction at all. A petite woman in a tattered ball gown simply stood with a strange, vacant expression on her face exactly where the person who'd been leading her had let go of her hand. Hal, seeing her condition, asked one of the footmen to bring her to sit with him in the pony cart. When she was safely seated, several of the women thanked him for this extra kindness, their eyes full of pity for the girl. "God bless you, sir," one of the women told Hal.

Josh, his horse protesting, arrived then with two large baskets of bread he was bringing from the manor. He found Hal at a loss from embarrassment, and offered jovially, "I say, Hal. What have you been frightening these good people with?"

That caused many of those within earshot to laugh, the laughter breaking them free of tears and the silence imposed by their captivity. Then, between voracious bites of the offered food, they poured out their stories.

It was a new, subdued Josh Clifton, Marquess of Cliffside, who found in their tales yet another incentive to manfully shoulder his responsibilities. Humbly, he realized that he had a lot to atone for. He was deeply ashamed to have offered his friendship to the fiend who had done this to good Englishmen and—women—and done it on his land and right under his nose. Just now, there was nothing he could do but try to be helpful, and he applied himself diligently to doing that.

When Kate and Bly had first come out of the tunnel, she'd been as astonished as the captives had been to see what her brother Hal had prepared. Now, she was more proud of him than she had ever been in her life. Her heart swelled to bursting. Then, when Josh came over to her, to ask if she was all right, the new expression of calm responsibility on his face told her that her cup was running over as far as the men in her family were concerned.

Bly stood quietly holding her hand and watched her absorb it all. As far as he was concerned, this longed-for comfort for Kate's sisterly heart was as late in coming as it was well-deserved.

Finally all of them began the trek to Cliffside Manor, the remaining slavers in chains. The pony cart with Hal and the silent young lady in it led a motley procession of carriages, traveling coaches, and farm wagons, and the mounted rescuers followed as a rear guard, adding to the ex-prisoners' sense of safety.

In the midst of the rear guard was Mathers, carefully but surreptitiously watched by Stone and MacLain as he sat Kate's horse, weak but proud. An alert Griswold rode close behind the three, while Taskford cantered back and forth along the odd procession, assessing the condition of the prisoners and watching for any who might need help.

Last of all came the wounded Blysdale, and his mount was carrying double. Kate pressed close in the circle of his good arm, striving to protect him from any discomfort the ride home might cause him. Her gaze was fastened on his eyes as if she could read in them everything he was thinking.

Bly smiled his crooked smile and asked, "Well, Kate?"

"I was wondering what you were thinking."

He waited a long moment before asking in turn, "About what, Kate?"

In other circumstances she would have informed him that

he knew very well about what, but this one was too near his heart. "About your friend whom we didn't find."

The horse's hooves beat out the rhythm of his walk for many yards before Bly, knowing he was about to open a vulnerable part of himself to possible ridicule, answered. "Kate, I wish with all my heart that he had been here. . . ."

When he didn't go on, Kate prodded, "But?"

Blysdale looked at her a long moment, studying her face in the moonlight before he shared what was in his heart. "Wherever he is, David is not dead."

"How do you know that, Darling?" Almost shyly, Kate used the name for him they had agreed she would call him. Certainly she asked the question gently, hoping against hope that his friend had survived the fever. Hoping with him, trusting his instincts.

"I don't feel that awful emptiness I feel when I lose those I care about."

She told him softly, as her heart swelled with the belief that he somehow knew the truth, "I'm glad, Bly. So very glad." She kissed his chin. It was all she could reach. Instantly she was crushed in an embrace that took the breath out of her.

Bly stifled the moan that threatened to come with the pain that shot through his shoulder as he roughly claimed her mouth. Kate believed him! His Kate trusted his odd, intangible certainty. She'd accepted the strange gift that haunted him.

Bly didn't care if his arm fell off.

Chapter Thirty-one

Before she'd gone up to let Dresden fuss over her, Kate had given her orders to Jennings. She had no idea how he was going to get enough warm water, clothing, and blankets down to the stables where the numerous prisoners were bathing and changing and bedding down, but she knew that he would somehow handle it all.

She certainly didn't expect, however, with so much to be accomplished, that all would be in readiness in the drawing room by the time she came down again, but it was. Smiling at Jennings, she let him know that as a butler he never ceased to amaze her.

By the time they'd all gathered in the drawing room it was warm with the fire that Jennings had sent a footman to build the minute he'd seen the too-thin man they'd brought home with them from the caves. In addition, there was a huge tray full of foods they could all manage without being at the dining room table, and tea and wine were waiting to be served.

Eager to hear Mathers tell them what he could, the rescue party had hurried to bathe the clammy feeling of the prison cave from their skin and change into fresh clothing.

They congregated quickly, every one of them having declined dinner, just as Jennings had anticipated they would.

Lord Blysdale was pale and wore a sling to support his arm in order to ease his wounded shoulder. Other than the pallor and faint lines beside his mouth, Kate's dark knight looked as haughty as he always did. Until he looked at her. Then his face changed and no one in the room was left with any doubt about his feelings for their hostess, Lady Katherine.

Kate was beautiful as she returned Bly's regard with her love for him shining in her eyes. She went to him as if there were no one else in the room. She knew better than to fuss over him, and once they were seated, she had to struggle against her inclination to place a pillow under his elbow to ease the strain on his sling.

Stone watched them settle side by side on a sofa, a half smile playing around his mouth. In his dark dinner dress, Kate thought her new acquaintance handsome and that, mercifully, he seemed to take up less space than he did in riding clothes.

When his smile faded, his face was marred by the slight frown it had worn since he and MacLain had failed to locate their second friend among the prisoners they'd freed. Frequently, he looked toward MacLain, who, even though he was immaculate, and certainly very properly attired, still managed to seem somehow disordered.

Of course, Kate realized, he was as anxious as the rest of them to learn from Mathers what had happened to their missing friend. With that single concern in the forefront of all their minds, every one of them focused their attention on the latest member of their group.

Even though Mathers looked actually quite handsome now he was clean, out of his rags, and properly dressed, he was far too thin, and the clothes he'd borrowed from her slender brother, Hal, hung on his gaunt frame. Mathers seemed unaware of the tension in the room. His clean-shaven face still drawn, he sat closest to the fire. He was deep in thought. The arm that had dangled so uselessly when they'd unchained him from the cave wall was heavily bandaged now and, like Bly's, rested in a sling.

Where Bly's sling consisted only of a dark ribbon, Kate noted Mathers's was a much bigger one, and was bandaged tightly to his chest so that the sling could not shift with his movements. Glancing at Griswold, she saw the worried look he wore whenever he looked at the emaciated Mathers. Obviously, the old soldier believed that Mathers would never regain the use of that arm. She prayed he was mistaken.

Griswold sat in a chair a little distance from the others, but, Kate saw, it was the chair standing outside the circle of friends that was nearest Mathers.

Kate waited until all of them were settled to explain why Hal and Josh were absent. "My brothers are still seeing to the needs of the other freed prisoners, gentlemen. So are most of Cliffside's staff." She smiled in the direction of her butler. "We have Jennings and a footman left to serve us, and Jennings purposes to do just that. Please, bear with us."

Jennings then moved from one to the other of them with a tray of sandwiches and biscuits, small plates, and napkins. He wore a tight little smile in answer to Blysdale's look of faint astonishment. Kate saw that it both amused and saddened him to realize that the man he was certain would be his future master had no idea that servants could care deeply for their employers. Knowing him as she did, she bet he was wondering if it were possible that Blysdale could be retrained.

The footman followed behind Jennings carrying goblets and teacups, wine, and the teapot. Tonight, with its overload of horror and excitement, no conventions were being observed.

When Jennings dismissed the footman and retired to the far side of the room, the issue burning in all their minds could no longer be ignored. The question hung in the air over Mathers like a heavy shadow.

Mathers took a deep breath and addressed it directly. "I don't know what happened to Smythe."

Absolute silence reigned in the drawing room as its occupants waited for more.

"He was the best of us." He paused, and his eyes misted. Then he shook his head and went on, "There was a fever. Many of us, including me, went down to it almost instantly." He looked around the room. "Half-starved, no one was resistant to it. Except Smythe, because, as you know, he was better padded than most of us."

The men smiled faintly to recall how they had always teased their missing friend about his appetite.

"Somehow," Mathers continued, "when the fever struck, Smythe—David—managed to talk the guards into freeing him to care for us. Told them he could help us." Mathers looked at Bly. "You remember how he was always concerned about all our welfare. Always wanting to doctor us."

Bly nodded and said toward Taskford, "I remember the time he was so quick to see if you'd been hurt by the glass from the shattered window at your card party, Taskford."

Taskford added, "I remember very well. He didn't stop to care that he could have been hit when he stood up to draw my drapes closed right after the shot shattered that window, either."

Mathers summed it up. "That was David. Always putting other people first. The most unassuming and unnoticed of our group, but possibly the bravest of all the 'Lucky Seven.'" He spoke the nickname for their group with scorn. Obviously, to him, "Lucky" didn't describe them anymore.

Stone and Bly exchanged a grim look. Kate saw they were ready to agree with their friend. One murdered in the Peninsular War, Mathers maimed, and one missing wasn't a good score.

Mathers went on, "This time, David convinced our jailers that he could save at least a few of us. Knowing that every death would mean that much less money in their pockets, they accepted his word that he wouldn't try to escape, and let him doctor us the best he could. And he did." Mathers sighed heavily. "And I think this time it cost him his life."

There was a soft murmur of dissent. A declaration of hope.

Blysdale seemed to turn in on himself.

Kate reached out and took his hand, and found it as cold as a stone. After a moment, he offered her a slight smile. It almost broke her heart.

She remembered how he had said that he could feel the loss of a good friend as if a hole had been torn in the very fabric of his being, how he'd reasserted it on their ride back to Cliffside. She wondered why he didn't share his opinion that Smythe was alive somewhere, but she saw that he had no intention of doing so, and that the reticence was painful to him. Had he shared something of the same sort at an earlier time and been doubted?

She wondered what she could do to help Bly through this awful time. She'd seen the cave where Smythe would have nursed those ill with the fever and understood how the others must feel. How could he have saved any of them under such dreadful conditions? How could he himself have survived? Common sense dictated against it, but Kate firmly believed Bly.

Mathers was saying, "I went down with the fever, after David . . ." He smiled a little and told Kate, "Smythe's name is David, and somehow I think of him that way now."

Kate smiled her understanding with tears in her eyes. How could you not call such a dear man by his Christian name?

Mathers finished the sentence he'd interrupted. " . . . After David had saved almost half of those who'd contracted the fever. By then, it was obvious that he was worn to the bone with his nursing. I remember thinking as my last coherent thought that he didn't stand a chance." The tears that had come to Mathers's eyes ran down his cheeks. He was not ashamed of them. Kate knew they were a memorial to his friend. "When I finally awoke, I'd survived, but all the children, most of the women . . . and David . . . were gone."

Kate and Bly walked in the garden, unable to sleep, unwilling to rest. Finally Kate broke the silence. "I'm so sorry."

Bly shook his head and walked on. After a while he said quietly, "Smythe is alive, Kate. I'd know it if he were gone."

Kate was surprised by his remark. Realizing he'd mis-understood, she looked at him steadily for a long moment, then told him, "*I believe you.* I meant that I'm sorry you couldn't tell the others."

"I'd feel a fool, and they'd never believe it. Men don't put stock in such premonitions, you know. I once told them that a group of our men who'd been sent to spy out the strength of the French troops in our area was only delayed. That they would return safely."

"And they didn't believe you."

"No."

"And the men got back safely."

"Of course."

Kate rose on her toes and kissed him tenderly from her heart with all her trust and belief in him. An instant later, she was crushed to him as Bly returned her kiss with a passion that burned along her every nerve.

The moon lit their way as they went back into the manor to Kate's bedchamber. There, in each other's arms, they forgot all the horrors.

Chapter Thirty-two

The next evening at dinner, it was as if everyone had decided to put all the tragedy behind them. The sadness that occasionally passed over one of their faces clearly proclaimed that it was a decision, not an inclination, but it allowed the overt atmosphere at the table to be fairly pleasant.

"You are especially beautiful tonight, Kate," Josh said from his place at the head of the table.

Kate was so startled that he'd noticed her after a lifetime of being ignored by him that she couldn't even answer him. Staring at him, she saw that he wasn't making some kind of joke, he was sincere. This new Josh was indeed full of surprises. She managed to say, "Thank you."

Bly laughed softly and took her hand. "It's not often that I see you at a loss, my Kate."

"Hmmmm." She ducked her head to hide her grin. "I was astounded."

Mathers told her, "If you think you can keep Bly from calling me out for it, I'd like to second your brother's observation, Lady Katherine."

"See there, Lady Katherine," Stone told her with a grin,

"if Taskford hadn't run off home to his Regina, he'd assure you that Mathers is well again."

"Oh? And how does one tell with such certainty?" Kate was ready to play this game.

"He's beginning to flirt. That's his one forte, or fault, whichever you may consider it. I leave it to you to choose."

Kate cocked her head to one side as if considering the choice. "Alas, I hesitate to judge. One comment is, after all, scarcely enough evidence."

"Be patient," MacLain told her. "As soon as he gets his strength back, Mathers will attempt to give our Blysdale a run for his money where you're concerned."

"At his peril," Bly said softly, but his eyes were smiling.

"Ah! Best go carefully, Mathers." Stone was grinning openly, and Kate knew he was greatly relieved to see Mathers's melancholy lifted.

They kept up their banter through the rest of the meal, reminding each other of past events they had shared in their army days, everything that was amusing in retrospect—but nothing that included their missing friend, David.

Kate sat silent and enjoyed watching them, seeing them together, realizing what good friends they were . . . and that the bonds of their friendship had been forged solidly in the crucible of war.

As Kate watched them, she realized that because she belonged to Bly, these were her friends, too. The warmth she felt at being surrounded by people she could trust, the relief that all the deceptions were over, flooded her. Now she could give over her every burden and just sit and enjoy watching these wonderful men.

Because Kate was able to efface herself, the men reminisced, and in reminiscing, healed themselves.

Finally Mathers realized they were leaving her out of the conversation and reminded the others. "We're neglecting our charming hostess, gentlemen."

Immediately Stone teased, "Very good point, Mathers, and we all must apologize for the talk of war." His smile grew. "That, however, gives us leave to approach another kind of battle. Tell us how you defeated the undefeated and impregnable Blysdale, Lady Katherine."

"Oh. Let me see." Kate frowned hard and thought for a moment. "I suppose you could say my conquest began when I slammed his head into the stone wall of a stairway and then, while he was still groggy from the blow, tricked him into locking us into the tower room at the top."

After an instant's surprise, the men laughed.

"Then," Kate, glad that Hal was in the stables seeing to the last of the released prisoners, continued blithely, "I carefully wormed from him the single condition under which he might consider marriage . . . it was a very difficult one to overcome, I do assure you . . . and one night I held up a traveling coach to fulfill it. That, combined, of course, with the discovery of the two of us alone in the tower room by my brothers, did the trick."

Even Blysdale was laughing now. Everything that Kate had said had a comically skewed bit of truth in it, but none of it revealed his true doubts or feelings, nor came anywhere close to why he loved her so madly . . . and he loved her all the more for that.

Mathers inquired with elaborate courtesy, "So you had to resort to highway robbery to bring him down, did you?"

"Yes." She sighed. "It was also how I met him, you know."

"Not really!" Stone cried, grinning.

"Oh yes, and I could see from the intense way he looked at me over my pistol that he was desperately interested in knowing me better."

"Aye." Bly pretended to scowl. "That I was!"

"My God!" Stone shot bolt upright in his chair and stared at Kate incredulously. "Don't tell me that was *you* who attempted to rob Mac and me!"

Kate cast her eyes down demurely and admitted, "Yes, I'm afraid that was I." She pretended to sigh. "One of my lesser successes, however."

Bly said calmly, "To clarify, I must insist that 'rob' doesn't really apply, gentlemen. Kate never *took* anything. She was merely trying to trap the Mayfair Bandit."

"I say," MacLain burst out, "*Mere's* not the word to use about that bounder. Trapping him is a job of work—especially for a female. The man's dangerous."

"Not anymore."

They all looked at Bly, instantly sobered. To a man they knew what Chalfont Blysdale meant when he said "Not anymore" in that tone of voice.

Mathers asked for them, "You caught him?"

"I killed him. The Mayfair Bandit was Gordon Mallory."

Everyone was silent. The tale had come full around, and they were solemn again.

"That man has a great deal to answer for," Mathers said.

"And I imagine he is already answering for his sins," Kate said with a shudder.

"Hear, hear," Stone lifted his wineglass and offered the cheer in a whisper.

The foolishness of the last few moments was over, the mood at the table serious again, and after a long, thought-filled pause, they fell to discussing news of London and the *ton,* so far as any of them bothered to know it. With Hal absent from their midst, their knowledge of the comings and goings of London society proved scant indeed, and after few minutes Kate excused herself and left the men to their cigars and port.

Blysdale found her in the garden among the roses. "Hallo, Kate. Are you warm enough?" He slipped his arm around her.

"I'm fine, but I've always been impressed by the way you warm me." She turned in his embrace and kissed the point of his chin.

He kissed the tip of her nose and demanded, "So I showed a desperate interest in you when we first met, did I?"

"Indeed you did. You stared at me so hard, I was afraid you would see right through my mask."

"I thought you were a youth just as you intended that I should, you know." He nuzzled her behind her ear, letting his warm breath feather the sensitive skin of her neck there.

"And did you guess I was not a youth the night you rescued me from Stone and MacLain? I wondered if my panic then had given away the fact that I was a female." She tipped her head and kissed the side of his mouth.

"No, not then." He left a tiny kiss in her ear.

Kate shivered and asked, "When, then?"

"When you thought you had torn your boot on the rock slide in the caves. I recognized them then and the way you moved and a dozen other things." He kissed her chin. "I was surprised you didn't remark my attitude when I cried out at my discovery."

She chuckled. "I thought you were upset that I'd marred my favorite pair of boots."

He pulled away from her and snorted.

"Bly! That is the most annoying sound!"

"It's the only one that expresses my sentiments at having been thought to be mourning a damn pair of boots!"

"Come back to me." Kate held out her arms.

Bly stood where he was, two feet from her.

"Shall we meet in the middle?" she asked him.

He smiled and took one step forward. She took the other in a rush.

"Kate."

"Yes?"

"It was a pleasure to see you so lively at the table. That is the sort of life I want for you, you know." He sighed. "And I'm so blasted *grim*."

Was he trying to renounce their love? Trying to leave her? If that were the case, how could she survive his rejection? How could she live without her dark knight now that he'd claimed her? Now that she'd lain in his arms?

Kate had to take a deep breath to steady herself as she put the fear that rose in her at that idea resolutely down and told him, "Well, that's just too bad, Lord Blysdale, for I want you, not pleasantries that mean nothing." Kate pressed closer, stretching up to put her arms around his neck.

He was thoughtful a moment, then his mood changed and Kate could breathe again. "So you defeated me by knocking my head against a wall and trapping me into being found alone with you in a deserted tower, did you?"

"Hmmmm." She tried to kiss him full on the lips, but he lifted his chin and prevented it.

"If I had only known you better then, we could have provided your brothers with a much more interesting discovery than two people about to freeze to death."

"Oh, yes. You really have proved much more interesting on several occasions since."

"Vixen."

Kate bit the lobe of his ear.

"So you *wormed* the fact that I would 'have to see the stars fall before I wed' out of me, did you? And here I'd thought I told you quite freely that the stars would fall from the sky before I married when you were trying so hard to find out if I had a wife."

"Pooh! I wasn't trying hard at all. At that point in time, I didn't *care* whether or not you had a wife!"

"Oh?"

"What do you mean, 'oh'?" His single word had held a wealth of scornful disbelief, and Kate was going to make him pay for it.

"I was under the impression that you had felt at least some of the same magical attraction that I'd felt the instant we met."

"Oh, no," Kate told him archly. "You must be mistaken."

"Brat. I know damned well I'm not mistaken."

"Really?"

"Yes, really. We must have gaped at each other for well over a full minute before Josh and Jennings got us moved on to the drawing room."

"Ah, well," she said airily. "If you say so. Perhaps that day at the drainage ditches I *was* curious as to whether or not you were married. I didn't want to be trifled with by a married man, you see."

"And what made you think I intended to 'trifle'?"

"Just a hunch." She plucked a rose and used it to trace his jawline, leaning back against his arm.